AMERICAN PHOENIX

SCOTT DANIEL

A Thomas Angell Publication

ISBN-13: 978-1-7352673-1-9
ISBN-10: 1-7352673-1-7

Cover design by: Sean Martorana
Printed in the United States of America

For Mom, who showed me the worlds beyond my own

For Dad, who taught me to love the Angels

We shall rise refreshed in the morning.

BENJAMIN FRANKLIN

Contents

The Course of Human Events

Prologue

Little Bird

Hellfire came to Washington on the wings of an angel, just before daybreak on a Tuesday.

It arrived from nowhere, a white-hot comet puncturing the star-spangled canopy of night. It hurtled across the Potomac at the speed of light and spiraled soundlessly through the hotel window, fluttering its jet black feathers as it flamed out on the thin red carpet...

...the creature whispered into the ether...soft and subtle as a silent echo...

((...get up, Benji...))

It's here...

I gripped the sheets tight, marinating in my own sweat as Colonel snored away in the other bed. I envied the old man and his quietude. Our visitor hadn't come for him...

((...get up, Benji...))

No...I'm hallucinating...

God knows how long I'd been awake. Reverie and reality blur together on nights like these. I close my eyes only to open them wide in a world next-door, crisp and clear as this one. Some might call it a lucid dream, but I'd never known a figment to break through the Looking Glass...

((...I said get up, Benji...))

I cursed as I threw off the comforter and slipped out of bed. I took one step and tripped, ramming my left knee into the ground. I bit down to stymie the rising howl of pain and crawled toward the smoldering carnage, where a dream came to die.

The bird was burrowed into the floor, charred black from beak to claws. I reached out to touch it. I had to be sure...

...it's real...

...a spirit made flesh, dead on arrival.

"So this is how it ends for you," I muttered.

The bird stared through me with its cold dead eye, iris widening as it drew me into its depths. A chill rode up my spine…

((…come and see, Benji…))

No. I'm not going back there.

((…he's right where you left him, Benji…))

I swallowed hard. There was no fighting it. I shut my eyes tight, surrendering to the void…and that cold, empty feeling…

…I can still feel it…

…

…the way the wind whips sharp through the National Mall…the green grass crumbles to gray ash in my hand…the sky shimmers blood red, a shade of crimson darker than black…

…a voice reverberates up Independence; it caroms around the hollow fiery shell of the Capitol, echoing back down Constitution and splitting me in two…a single word, from my own lips…

"John?"

…he was here…the boy was right here with all the rest…in the blink of an eye, he was gone…they were all gone…

"John?"

…another echo, then the cold dread of silence…the air is thick with fear, enveloping me with the suffocating knowledge that I am alone…

…I…alone…

…

…there had been millions here on this hot summer night in the District, living statues of alabaster and ivory…they reveled and danced in merriment and jubilee 'neath the rocket's red glare, each one greeting me as I passed…

"Good to see you, Benjamin…" (You too)

"How long has it been, Benjamin?" (Too long)

"You'll play again soon, Benjamin…" (God willing)

…I brushed past them anxiously…forgive me, I'd say…I'm in search of another…

…I scanned the horizon, through thick lines of elms and cherry blossoms and the dulcet scent of flowers…I listened intently through the ruckus of strings and horns and delightful chatter, homing in on that still…small…voice…

...that faint, evanescent whisper, rising to a shout...

...there he was...calling to me from the hillside, between the still waters of the Reflecting Pool and...

...that tree...that Great and Mighty Elm, bearing fruit of many colors...

"Come and see!" the boy cried, waving his arms with excitement. His freckled face creased as he smiled...

...I rushed through the throngs to embrace him, laughing and twirling him in my arms...I mussed up his brown hair and watched the world spin in his crystal blue eyes...

...John was his name, and he was mine...my flesh...my blood...

"Look!" he cried, leaping from my arms and kneeling before the Reflecting Pool, gazing deep into the water...there I saw it...

...a single Bluebird circling in the starry, spacious skies above the Washington Monument, carried on a song of the western wind...a beautiful anthem of brotherhood, resounding...

...from one sea...

...to another, the statues joining in the chorus as the Bluebird circled...

...and circled, spreading its wings like a lone eagle...

...as above lightning tolled...

...and so below thunder rolled...

...the Bluebird perched on the Elm, upon its strongest branch, and sang a new song...a song so soft and honey sweet that only I could hear...

((...chirp, chirp Benji...tweet, tweet...))

...those words...they hung in the air, the Bluebird measuring me in silence...the air grew thicker...my pulse grew quicker...my stomach turned sour...the Bluebird opened its beak...

...black smoke spilled forth, enveloping all but the midnight sky, peeling back to deep crimson...the Bluebird crescendoed from silence to a deafening whistle, and all around the statues cried out as they crumbled and fell...the Pool waters hissed and bubbled and boiled like thickest crude...

...the boy held steady, transfixed on the blackening Pool...

John! I cried voicelessly, Get away from there!

...then the world engulfed in violent flame...

...

...he's gone...

"John?"

...all is ashes, and I am alone...

...except for him...

...he rides in on a dark destrier, wearing a white hat and brandishing a scepter with the head of an axe...the Mall reverberates with the clips! and clops! of the horse's gallop, an ominous harbinger of iniquity...the warhorse slows to a halt, and the White Hat Man dismounts, striding forward with unbridled confidence...his face is veiled by shadow...on his lapel he dons the sharp star of Law and Order...

...he kneels before me stinking of oil and tar and lifts my chin with the scepter...he studies my countenance, grasping dust and ash in his hand and releasing it, over and over and over...a crooked half-smile creeps across his darkened visage...and those teeth...golden yellow as corn...

"Judgment is here," the White Hat Man growls...

...he seizes me by the scruff and ties me to his horse, dragging me uphill as he rides, dust and ash scraping my skin...I shake and rage and curse and spit into the ground...the White Hat Man throws me down at the foot of that Great and Mighty Elm, charred to cinder and naked to its roots...a single human form, tarred and feathered, dangles from its strongest branch...

...the Bluebird sings...

> *Here hangs John Brown*
> *A killer and a thief!*
> *His honey brought him lemons*
> *And she poured them in his grief!*

...the White Hat Man raises his scepter and turns back to the tree...five other men are there, veiled in shadows...the six of them raise their scepters, each with the head of an axe...the wind kicks, and all around me a shapeless chorus lifts its voice in song...the refrain echoes through the Mall as they whisper and shout again and again....

You came to set our house ablaze
  ((But you will not replace us!))
To teach our young your wicked ways
  ((But you will not replace us!))

...and so the White Hat Man crows...
"What say you, Brothers, of this Treason? What say you of John Brown?"
...the others point their scepters at me. "Guilty!"
...the White Hat Man smiles, that wretched golden smile...now he strikes the ground...
...the Earth cleaves...

...I fall down...

...and down...

...forever falling through this dark Abyss...

...above the Elm catches fire...engulfed in flame, the Bluebird takes flight...

...spiraling downward...

...closer and closer...

...blazing cardinal red...

...then angel white...

...then black as night, dead on the carpet.

I stumbled backward into the desk chair. I stared uneasily into the middle distance, fiddling with my wedding band. The clock blinked...*3:21*...*3:21*...*3:21*...illuminating the thick stack of roll sheets and ungraded essays and notes scribbled on hotel stationary.

This damned hotel. The Quicksilver at Pentagon City. Room 704. Same vision. Same hellscape. Every year, always before dawn, on the second Tuesday in March.

Never like this, though. Never did it cross over. Never did it demand a reckoning...

((...he's coming, Benji...))

I gripped my armrests tightly, resolutely. The winged devil stared back through me with that cold, dead eye, clutching something tight in its talons; something I hadn't seen. Painfully, I knelt again and slid the object from its claws...

...a single white feather. Unburnt.

The cold wind whistled through the window as lightning flickered behind the Capitol, rising in the distance beyond the Potomac. I ran my fingers down the length of the feather as the winged devil held me in its hollow gaze, pleading once more...

((...will you ride?...))

...defiantly, I answered aloud...

"No."

...as though I heard clearly...

"I won't play."

...as though I understood...

((...for want of a rider, then...))

The world fell silent, time marked only by the rise and fall of Colonel's breath. I wondered how the old man could sleep so, balanced on the cusp of two worlds. I wondered what I would tell him when he awoke to the inexplicable. Truth be told, I had no idea how our visitor tore through the veil between Here and There, or how it found me, Here and Now.

I only knew two things for certain.

Today, I would play a great and terrible game...

...and it would be the longest day of my life.

I

Lax Americana

One

Hard Beginnings

Neither horse nor rider had moved in a century; that morning I watched Grant and his valiant steed Cincinnati leap a thousand times into the rainy mist blanketing the Mall. Each time, the Union General brandished his saber and disappeared, then returned in a flash to his place on the concrete pedestal.

"Ben!"

Kathy Waylon stared daggers at me from under her cat-eye lenses. Behind her, twenty-two high school seniors huddled under umbrellas beneath the Ulysses S. Grant Memorial. Ms. Waylon cleared her throat.

"We have everyone," the mousy English teacher announced, motioning uphill toward the Capitol.

I eyed Grant again. Still. Silent.

Get some damn sleep, Upson.

I turned to my students:

"Alright, Warriors…"

"…come out to plaaaaay-ay!"

The class groaned. The golden-haired Reid Collins grinned behind a fresh black eye. I turned to the graying man in the West Point sweatshirt beside him:

"Colonel, stick to this clown like white on rice."

Colonel saluted and gave Reid a *"What's the matter with you?"* flick on the arm.

I pivoted to Ms. Waylon and the young man flanking her.

"Kathy, you have Mr. Atwater."

Tyson Atwater stared blankly from under his hoodie, a thicket of tape wrapped around the brown skin on his right hand, which he flexed intermittently.

I sighed. "Warriors, let's roll!"

I plodded up Capitol Hill, umbrella aloft. The class trailed behind me at a distance. I understood why; I was radioactive. Between yesterday's events – and that early morning visitor – I was of half a mind to fly us right back to Colorado to spend the rest of spring break at home.

And I desperately needed coffee.

No. Things are bitter enough as they are.

The Capitol loomed above, its gray-white dome blending seamlessly into the fog. Ahead, a young female staffer struggled uphill against the rain in a skirt suit and heels. *Poor thing.* No doubt she came here to serve in the Temple of the People, only to find it a den of thieves, all with knives drawn. *Especially now.* In the past few months, the battle between Congress and the White House had reached a fever pitch, recrimination following recrimination. It was exhausting. I often found myself daydreaming of a better time, when we all could return to some semblance of normalcy...

"Mr. Upson?"

I turned to see Daniel Bannister and Mackenzie Masuda jogging up, sopping wet and seeking shelter from the elements.

"Mom didn't pack you an umbrella, Daniel?" I asked.

Mac laughed. "Absent-minded professor left his in the hotel."

"Yeah," the lanky student body president admitted, shaking water from his hair. "And Mom won't share hers."

I turned and watched Daniel's mother Anna stare us down, slitting her throat with her finger.

"See, Mr. Upson? She's a *tyrant*."

I chortled, waving at the Capitol. "Catching a glimpse of your futures?"

"Actually, we had a question."

I shrugged. "Shoot."

"So," Daniel began, "I thought it was illegal for anything in D.C. to be taller than the Capitol...so why is the Washington Monument taller?"

I laughed. "Because there is no such law."

"Then why is nothing else taller?" inquired Mac, the state champion debater.

"Well, like most myths, this one shares roots with the truth: another law called the 'Height-of-Buildings Act.'"

"Original."

"Very. So back in the 1890s, Congress feared the skyscrapers in New York were unsafe and outlawed anything in D.C. over one hundred and ten feet. By then the Monument was already built."

Mac folded her arms and looked skyward. "That sucks. *She* should be taller."

"She?" Daniel asked.

"Her."

Mac pointed to the bronze woman shrouded in fog at the Capitol's apex. She donned a plumed helm encircled by stars; her sword and shield rested against her side as she gazed east toward the horizon.

"The Statue of Freedom?" I asked.

"She's a warrior," Mac asserted. "She looks *fierce*."

"She does."

"That's a badass helmet, too."

I chuckled. "Funny you say that. She was originally designed wearing a so-called 'Liberty cap,' kinda like the red floppy ones the Keebler elves wear…"

"Keebler elves aren't real," Daniel blurted. "We've had this conversation, Mr. U."

"Fudge Stripes don't make themselves, Daniel. Anyway, in Rome the cap symbolized one's release from slavery, and the Sons of Liberty adopted them as a symbol for the Revolution. But this statue was commissioned at the height of slavery right before the Civil War, and all this talk of 'emancipation' and 'freedom' didn't sit well with the man in charge of Capitol renovations. Any guesses who that was?"

They both shook their heads.

"Jefferson. Beauregard. Davis."

Daniel snapped up. "The Confederate president?"

"Yep. Davis said it was *'inappropriate to a people who were born free and would not be enslaved.'*"

Mac winced. "What about *his slaves?* He owned a plantation!"

"Also," Daniel weighed in, "he's ignoring the fact that we fought a Revolution against enslavement by the British!"

"Facts!" I laughed. "Facts don't make good stories, Daniel. That's all history is: one big story with limitless subplots. We write it and re-write it until we've traded the real story for a fairy tale that suits us, then we pass it down, generation after generation."

"Fake news," Mac said derisively.

"As they say: 'Print the legend.'"

"Print the legend?"

"It's from my dad's favorite Western. *The Man Who Shot Liberty Valance*. It's about a governor whose entire legacy was built on the lie that he killed an infamous outlaw threatening his town. Years later the governor admits to the press that he wasn't the shooter, but one reporter won't hear it. He tears up his notes saying, *'This is the West, sir. When the legend becomes fact, print the legend.'* He refused to hear the truth and, unfortunately, Americans today aren't much different."

Daniel stuffed his hands in his pockets. "So we just forget."

As we rounded the bend toward the Visitor's Center, I caught Freedom's penetrating gaze.

"Yeah," I said. "We just forget."

~

Stephanie's voice was pure melatonin; the red-jacketed docent pacing the floor of the Old Senate Chamber was as engaging as a slow cooker. I fought sleep by taking in the Capitol architecture. Two centuries old, it was still breathtaking. Each stone was neatly carved to the minutest detail, the work of master craftsmen.

We couldn't even build this today. I imagined centuries from now some alien civilization might chance upon it and think it a temple to our idols of stone.

Earlier I found myself admiring the graven image of the firstborn Son of Liberty, Samuel Adams, when a sturdy hand found my shoulder.

"I'll have a Winterfest!"

I smirked. Colonel recoiled.

"Sorry, Ben," he said sheepishly. "I forgot you were a tee-totaler."

I shrugged. "No worries, Sam. I owe you one for your help with that mess this morning."

"Hey," he laughed, "who among us hasn't had a flaming bird crash into their hotel room?"

"No shit."

"Any leads on that omen?" Colonel asked, half-serious.

I shook my head slowly.

"Probably heard me snoring and wanted to put us out of our misery."

"Seriously," I laughed. "You could knock out the sonar on a destroyer."

The Army vet roared. The popular substitute teacher was always good for a laugh. I'd never met anyone who inspired teenagers the way Lieutenant Colonel Sam Mariota did. Two days earlier, there hadn't been a dry eye at the Vietnam Memorial when he spoke of friends he lost to the jungle.

Behind Colonel, I spied Reid fiddling with the toggles on his windbreaker.

"How's babysitting?" I asked.

Colonel shrugged. "Fine. He's anxious to see the Andrew Jackson statue. Great great gramps served under Ol' Hickory, or so he tells me."

"You're a saint for putting up with him."

"Saint my ass!" Colonel patted his hip. "I'm just an elderly disabled vet on a fixed income."

Now I watched Colonel and Reid together as Russell Morrill posed Stephanie a riveting question.

"Have there been any Senate rumbles?" Russell breathed.

The class groaned; Stephanie reeled them in like a pro. "That's actually a good question. What's your name?"

"Big Russ," answered scrawny Chris Ewing, punching Russell on the arm.

"Well, Russ, there *was* a famous dust-up in 1856 over a very contentious issue. Anyone care to guess?"

The class inhaled collectively.

"Oh, come on guys, this is easy: *slavery!*"

All eyes darted to Tyson.

Stephanie sensed a shift in tension. "Soooo....anyway...Senator Charles Sumner of Massachusetts accused South Carolina's Andrew Butler of the 'rape of virgin territory' by pushing for slavery in the west. Enraged, Butler's cousin, Congressman Preston Brooks, *savagely* beat Sumner with his cane – "

Stephanie pointed.

" – on this very spot."

The gallery doors opened. Another docent entered, a woman in her seventies, frantically scanning the room. For a brief moment her glistening green eyes locked with mine. She lingered for a half-second, and then quietly slipped away.

Weird.

"Fortunately," Stephanie continued, "that probably won't happen again. I mean, underneath our differences, we're all Americans. We're not *still* fighting over slavery, right?"

A chill swept through the chamber. Tyson calmly stood up…

("…Tyson…" Ms. Waylon reached…)

…and walked out the gallery doors.

Stephanie clutched her neckerchief. "Did I say something wrong?"

I stood and shoved my chair under the desk. "No, Stephanie. This is an in-house issue. I'll deal with it. Continue without me. I'll catch up to you guys."

I stormed into the hall, furious…

…

…I looked both ways…

…

…*son-of-a-bitch, where is he?*

…

"Are you looking for a young man?"

I jumped. Behind me a thirty-something male staffer leaned casually against the wall. He held a tattered brown diary in his right hand.

"He came tearing through here a minute ago. He dropped this."

The staffer held out the diary and looked me square in the eye. His were a glistening green, just like the old woman's, and betrayed genuine kindness.

"Oh!" he pointed. "There he is!"

Down the hall, Tyson slunk against a column in the Small Senate Rotunda, playing with his phone.

"Looks like a little bird whispered something terrible in his ear."

The staffer laughed, then caught my glare and retreated into himself.

"I shouldn't have said that," he sighed. "I didn't mean to offend."

I looked the staffer up and down. His navy blue suit was neatly pressed, his dirty blond hair perfectly coifed and his shoes freshly shined. He had the air of an awkward Ivy League introvert with limited social graces. I sensed he thought I was angry at his dry jest.

"No worries," I said, searching for his name on his badge.

"You can call me Al," he offered, affably.

I smiled tightly, and then took off down the hall. When I looked back, Al was gone.

Weirder.

I approached Tyson and offered him the diary. He took it reluctantly and slid it into his hoodie pocket.

"I have nothing to say to you," he snipped.

"No," I replied, "but there *are* things you need to hear."

No response.

"Tyson, if you're not doing the tour, let me at least show you something else."

Tyson put away his phone, shrugging as if to say, *"Well?"*

"Follow me."

I led Tyson downstairs to the Cox Corridors, its tiled walls adorned with Allyn Cox's murals depicting iconic scenes of Americana. Between them lay inspiration…

"There," I pointed at a placard emblazoned with a quote. "Read that silently, then there are two more."

> *We defend and build a way of life, not for America alone, but for all mankind.*
> ~ Franklin Delano Roosevelt

"Now chew on this."

> *We must remember that any oppression, any hatred, any injustice is a wedge designed to attack our civilization.*
> ~ Franklin Delano Roosevelt

"Last one."

To venture into the wilderness, one must not see it as it is, but as it will be.
~ Carl Becker

Tyson finished, nodding slowly and pursing his lips. "Becker's in a wheelchair, too?"

I tilted my head. "Wheelchair?"

"FDR had polio. He was stuck in a wheelchair, you know?"

"I'm pretty sure I taught you that, Ty."

"Yeah. You did," Tyson laughed. "You're also a bullshitter who loves ra-ra speeches from guys in wheelchairs. Makes you feel good you're not in one, right?"

Tyson set his back against the nearest wall and slid down onto his bottom, wrapping his arms around his knees. I slid down next to him, exasperated.

"Tyson," I began, "I want to help you. I do. What you need to underst—"

"Why do you need me to love it?" he interrupted.

I winced. "Love what?"

Tyson waved his hand in the air. "All this. The mythology. I know you love it. Why is it so important to you that I do, too?"

I started to speak, then stopped. My stomach clenched, and my eyes searched the floor, as though wisdom could be found somewhere in the tile grout.

I exhaled sharply. "Because it's my duty."

Tyson scoffed. "Your duty."

"Ty...I teach this stuff...this 'mythology,' because I believe in it."

My eyes found the mural of George Washington laying the cornerstone of the Capitol.

"I believe in the promise of America," I continued. "Of what it could be. That's..."

I paused, catching my breath.

"…that's what my dad taught me. America began as an idea, when Thomas Jefferson declared that 'all men are created equal,' and then our Founding Fathers laid the first brick on that foundation, and we've been building and building on that brick-by-brick, stone-by-stone, ever upward as we work toward…well, a more perfect Union – *for everybody* – focusing on the positive and not what's past. My dad…"

I stopped to gather myself.

"These are the things my father taught me. So now…I feel it's my duty to pass them on to you."

Tyson stuffed his hands in his hoodie pocket.

"Yeah, well, the thing is, Mr. U," he bit off through clenched teeth, "you aren't *my* father, and I'm not your son."

I winced. "I know that, Tyson. I'm not trying to–"

"I don't need you," he shot, his emotions rising to the surface. *"And I don't need this."*

Tyson sniffed, his eyes climbing the walls.

"You're right about one thing, though. This place really *was* built stone-by-stone – but by *my* fathers, *not yours.*"

"Tyson…"

"And soon it'll be *nothing but ash.*"

I went cold and numb, and my voice quivered. *"What did you say?"*

Tyson's body shook. "You heard me. *Ashes.*"

I reached out and grabbed his shoulder. "Tyson, what are you telling me? *What do you plan on doing here?"*

Tyson narrowed his eyes, incredulous. *"What do I…?"*

Tyson fiercely wrenched himself free and stood over me, clenching his fists. In an instant, his rage turned to tears. He reached into his pocket, pulled out his diary and threw it *hard* against the wall.

"You've got some real *cajones,* Mr. U," he said. "First you teach me history, then you tell me to forget it."

My tongue caught in my throat. Tyson threw his hood over his head.

"But as for me and *my house,* we choose to remember."

Tyson took to the stairs, and he was gone.

I sat in stunned silence. A tourist poked his head around the corner at the commotion; I stood and ambled toward Tyson's diary. It had fallen open to a page with a single hand-written quote. I read it silently, then glanced up at the wall where the diary had hit. The quote on the wall mirrored the diary word-for-word:

> *Whenever a people or an institution forgets its hard beginnings, it is beginning to decay.*
> ~ Carl Sandburg

~

For the next ten minutes I meandered aimlessly through the Capitol Crypt. A nearby tour guide told a group of eighth graders that the remains of George Washington were buried there. I cringed at the egregious error. In spite of efforts to move him here, the Father of Our Country remained interred in his estate just across the Potomac at Mount Vernon, Virginia.

All the better. Leave the dead buried.

My phone rang. It was Ms. Waylon:

"Hey! Tyson just got back. Where are you? It's almost eleven."

"I'm uh…down in the Crypt. Just…thinking."

"Are you okay?"

"I'm fine, don't worry about me."

"I'm worried about you."

"Kathy—"

"What did you say to him? He's a mess."

"I'll explain later, I just—need time to think."

Ms. Waylon paused. *"…maybe listen instead of talking at him?"*

An uncomfortably long pause.

"You know he's not buried down there."

"Who?"

Ms. Waylon hesitated. *"…Washington."*

I hung up and cursed. Tyson's last words rang in my head:

((…as for me and my house, we choose to remember…))

17

I surveyed the mob of middle schoolers. My heart broke for them. They were coming of age in a house divided. *"The baneful effects of the spirit of party,"* as Washington called it. Dad always revered Washington, *"a cool voice of reason in rooms churning with fire,"* a man who saw value on both sides of a coin. I must have wandered to the Crypt to seek his guidance. *A fool's errand.* There were no ghosts in an empty tomb.

Bzzzzzzt. I checked my phone. It was a text from a blocked number:

The kid's right. You've forgotten more than you care to remember.

Wha – ? I typed out a reply:

who is this? how did you get this number?

The answer came as I hit send:

A little bird sang it to me...

I gripped the phone tight. *Al?*
Another quick reply:

Rotunda. NOW. You're almost out of time.

Hands shaking, I made my way to the stairs and ascended.

Two

Upon A Hill

Dim sunlight filtered into the Rotunda beneath the Capitol dome, casting shadows on the Revolutionary scenes encircling the round.

I scanned around from the center, searching the sea of faces…

Bzzzzzzt.

Shoe's untied.

It is. As I painfully bent my knee to re-lace it I tilted my head to the fresco above, where water colors danced on a celestial canvas.

The Apotheosis of George Washington.

A wave of unusual calm washed over me as I took in Constantino Brumidi's masterpiece. The Father of our Country looked divine, enthroned on a rainbow under a golden sky, flanked by one goddess holding an axe-headed *fasces* and another blaring a trumpet. Below them a woman in full battle regalia stood triumphant atop the personifications of Tyranny and Kingly Power. A bald eagle flew at her side, clutching a cache of arrows.

"Majestic, isn't he?"

The elderly docent from earlier approached, her eyes fixed on Washington. Her voice rang gentle yet potent, delicate yet strong.

"But also restless – like he wants to descend and remind us of truths long forgotten – or never told."

I stood. "Yeah, well, I'd stay up there if I were him."

"Oh? Why is that?"

"The weather, for one."

"Ah, but look." She pointed. "What does His Excellency sit upon?"

"A rainbow. See? Beautiful weather."

She giggled. "What precedes the rainbow if not the rain?"

Her shoulder-length silver-gray hair framed a remarkably youthful face, her years betrayed only by the creases at the corners of her eyes, shimmering pools of emerald green. I read her nametag:

PEARL

I shook my finger. "Clever, Pearl. I hadn't considered that."

"I'm not sure Brumidi did, either," she replied. "Who really knows an artist's vision? It would take a thousand lifetimes to unlock the secrets of this Capitol alone."

"You've uncovered many of those secrets over the years, no?"

She grinned. "How old do you think I am?"

I laughed. "No, no. You simply strike me as...observant?"

"Perhaps," she said, eyes shifting to and fro. "Though I'm more an observer of people, really. After all, three million visitors grace these halls each year."

I whistled. Pearl surveyed the mass of humanity around us.

"If you look closely, you can see their subtler contours, feel the burdens they carry on stooped shoulders, their hopes, their dreams – their *many* disappointments – as if you inhabit their very skin."

Her smile faded.

"Just as Mr. Atwater inhabits yours. Right, Mr. Upson?"

I pivoted, mouth agape. "Yeah. Ben Upson."

I shook her hand.

"History and civics, Milton Clark High School. Springland, Colorado."

"I'm Pearl, but you already know my name."

"And you mine. How?"

Pearl tilted her head. "Perhaps a little bird whispered it to me."

My heart raced.

"What happened between your two boys, if I might be so bold?"

I closed my eyes and exhaled. "It's a long story."

Pearl picked a thread from my sweatshirt.

"Go on, Ben Upson," she said. "Tell me your story."

~

It began the morning before at Mount Vernon, where George Washington's estate is preserved near to its original condition. Near the mansion, I came upon a circle of students surrounding two angry young men.

"...nobody's buying it!" Reid barked.

"What am I selling?" Tyson snapped back.

"Your race-baiting bullshit. We're sick of it."

"Truth hurts."

"Pfft, you can shove-"

"Hey!" I interrupted. "What the hell is going on?"

The petite Sara Finkelson piped up. "Tyson asked one of the workers why they don't call the Servants' Hall the 'Slaves' Hall.'"

"It's the *truth*," Tyson insisted.

"You were harassing him," Reid charged.

"Reid," I said, "dial it back by seven. Tyson, come take a walk."

Tyson's jaw dropped. "How am *I* in trouble?"

"Come take a walk."

We followed the forest trail hugging the Potomac River, a litany of flowers littering our path.

"Pick your battles," I said.

Tyson bit his lip. "You gonna pick my battles for me?"

"No. But not every hill is worth dying upon."

"I just asked a question. You think they paid these slaves to churn butter?"

"Washington called it the Servants' Hall, Ty. This place is about historical accuracy, not ...political correctness?"

Tyson nodded vigorously. "Right. So why don't they buy Negroes at auction and chain them in the 'Servants' Hall?' Make them wipe tables at the food court like, *'Yes, massuh! No, massuh!'* They can whistle *dem ol' timey Negro spirituals* and pray that the Good Lord'll take 'em home on a gold-plated chariot, *yessuh!"*

"Win a lot of friends this way?"

We passed George and Martha's conspicuous tombs to an artificial clearing. A circular stone stump jutted from the center. An epigraph was etched on its smooth-cut face:

IN MEMORY OF
THE AFRO AMERICANS
WHO SERVED AS SLAVES
AT MOUNT VERNON
THIS MONUMENT MARKING THEIR
BURIAL GROUND
DEDICATED
SEPTEMBER 21, 1983
MOUNT VERNON
LADIES' ASSOCIATION

I sighed. "Nobody disputes that Washington owned slaves, or that slavery is America's original sin. That doesn't make Americans racists today. Most are just decent people trying to get by."

"I get it," Tyson said. "Free speech has a decibel level. Be a good, quiet black boy, not a loud, angry black man."

He put his hand on his heart.

"Massuh, is you gon' show up an' save me from mah dumb brown self, jus' like ol' John Brown?"

I threw my hands up.

"Or *maybe* you want me to dance, just like ol' Jack Johnson. Gimme enough freedom to taste, but if I'm outta line, POP!" He punched his hand.

I covered my face.

"See no evil. But it's still happening." Tyson stormed off.

"There are two sides to every coin, Mr. Atwater!" I shouted.

An hour later, Tyson found a seat near the bus lavatory. Reid patted me on the arm as he climbed aboard.

"Thanks for having my back, Mr. U."

Reid and his girlfriend, Skylar Lund, took seats across from Tyson. I began to protest...

"Don't escalate it," Ms. Waylon insisted.

I watched Tyson lean back and begin scribbling in his faded brown diary, the one he carried everywhere.

"Cut him some slack, Mr. U," Sara pleaded. "He's been to hell and back."

"Yeah," I retorted, "and he's dragging me with him."

Skylar whispered something to Reid, who laughed out a wad of gum. He winked at me; it sat like lead in my stomach.

Fifteen minutes later, I listened in as the storm turned:

"You can't be serious," Reid charged. *"Prove there's still slavery."*

Tyson snickered. "You think slavery is cotton-picking? You think segregation is separate water fountains? Not all masters crack whips. Not all slaves wear chains. White people just don't get that."

Skylar elbowed in. "Tyson, isn't your mom white?"

"What's my mom got to do with this, Karen?"

"Do you hate her, too?"

Tyson ignored her. Reid jumped in. "Bro, aren't we on our way to the Martin Luther King Memorial?"

"Yeah," Tyson fired back. "On the Jefferson Davis Highway. Your point?"

"You still haven't proven yours. Prove slavery exists today."

"Okay. Ever been to prison?"

"Uh, no, I hadn't planned on it."

"Neither do innocent black men."

Reid choked. "You mean criminals?"

"Does your naïve ass really believe everyone locked up is guilty? You think a white man and a black man tried for the same crime both get a fair trial?"

"Cry all you want, but it's a fact that black people commit more crimes than any other race."

"You get those 'facts' from your dumbass D.A. daddy?"

There's the line. I slowly moved toward the back.

"That's right," Reid snorted. "My dad's the District Attorney. He works late every night fighting scum, and he'll tell ya, it's mostly blacks and Mexicans. Putting thugs away isn't slavery, it's justice."

Tyson sniffed. "By 'working late,' you mean your daddy's on the office floor bangin' his ugly-ass secretary. Right?"

Reid seethed. I hovered over Tyson. "Knock. It. Off."

"Hear no evil," he snarled, putting his Air Pods in, mouthing, *"This is America..."*

Later that night the storm rolled into our hotel. Colonel sat in the corner reading a book about Gettysburg while I watched the replay of the Angels-Indians spring training game on my iPad. There came a loud knock on my door.

"MISTER UPSON!!!"

It was Tyson's roommate, Alex Wong.

"Come quick!"

Colonel and I booked it down the hall toward Reid's wide open door and the sound of struggle. We entered to find Tyson straddling Reid at the foot of the bed, pummeling him. Instinctively, I linked my arms under Tyson's and peeled him off as Colonel pinned Reid down. My left knee gave out; Tyson fell on top of me, sobbing in my arms, as the air almost imperceptibly turned dark and heavy.

"You're trash, Tyson!" Reid yelled. "Like father, like son!"

Someone called 9-1-1; I convinced the police to stand down over Reid's loud protests for justice. He stuck his phone in my ear so I could hear District Attorney Shane Collins screaming for my job *"for letting that thug off so easy."*

I told him to pound sand and slapped the phone against Reid's chest.

"Your daddy has no jurisdiction here," I quipped.

I found Alex and Zane Nighthorse in the hall, surrounded by gossiping students.

"Someone spill the tea," I demanded.

"We just got back from the 7-Eleven," Alex explained. "Tyson found this under the door."

Alex handed me a printout. My heart stopped.

It was a one-way United ticket for "ATWATER TYSON I," paid for with an Amex card, from Washington-Dulles...

IF YOU HATE IT HERE SO MUCH...

...to Nairobi, Kenya.

...CRAWL BACK TO YOUR SHITHOLE

In the corner of the page, someone had drawn a cartoon of an ugly green frog.

"Tyson went over to Reid's room," Zane explained, "and sucker-punched him."

I'd have done the same. "He needs to control himself."

Zane shook his head. "I mean, can you really blame him, Mr. U?"

I found Tyson on a bench outside in the drizzle, holding Sara's hand as she leaned on his shoulder. Neither seemed to notice the rain. I asked Sara if I could speak with Tyson alone. She gently squeezed his hand and walked inside.

Tyson's eyes fluttered. In his left hand he clutched his diary tightly, almost angrily. The thing was ugly, old and worn, seemingly held together by a miraculous thread.

I put my hand on his knee. "Don't sink to his level."

Tyson stood and whispered with disdain. *"Speak no evil."*

I sat alone and watched the rain fall to the ground, fiddling with my wedding band.

What am I gonna do with this kid?

My phone buzzed. It was a text from a blocked number; I had to read it twice:

The Angels dance, though the Devil stirs the flame...

What in hell...

I noticed something in the trees across the street, an object faint and shadowy...

...I squinted to make out the silhouette of a horse with a cloaked rider. The horse neighed lightly, and the rider shifted the reins; otherwise, the two remained deathly still. I couldn't see the rider's eyes, but I felt them. Burning. Penetrating.

I shuddered and looked away. A Metro bus passed, and the rider was gone.

Jet lag. It's just jet lag.

I closed my eyes just after midnight...

...*when the sky turned a shade of crimson darker than black...*

~

25

I opened my eyes. The Rotunda was empty, illumined only by a dim glow. The sky was dark at...*11:08?*

"Hello?" I called.

Silence.

"Where is everybody?"

"Where you left them, Benjamin."

Pearl snuck up from behind. In the dim light, the old woman looked grayer and more worn. Her hands trembled and her lip quivered.

I stammered. "My kids..."

"...are all safe," she assured me, her voice cracking.

I guffawed. "What is this, ransom?"

Pearl glowered. "Only a monster holds children hostage, Benjamin."

"You playing games with me, Lady?"

Pearl's eyes searched the ceiling. "Perhaps," she said, her breathing belabored. "You were a ballplayer once, no?"

I winced. "Yes..."

"Now it's time to play a more serious game."

I stared at her...then I broke. "Heh...hehe...hehehehehe!! *Colonel?!* Come out, lose the tin foil hat and turn the lights back on!"

Pearl tisked. "You'll need a sharper eye for this game. Would Samuel really resort to cruel japes after your visitor this morning?"

I froze. "I...didn't tell you..."

"No. But let us not speak falsely, Benjamin. The hour is late, and the Champion of Liberty must be on his way."

"Champion?" I choked. *"What are you playing at?"*

Pearl sized me up. "I've known many like you. You strain your eye, but cannot see. You incline your ear, but cannot hear. You loosen your tongue, but dare not speak the evil right in front of you. Mr. Atwater sees much that you don't."

"Tyson," I exhaled. "Enlighten me. What don't I see?"

Pearl stepped closer, speaking barely above a whisper. *"That Liberty is nearly ashes..."*

...a single tile came loose from the dome...

CRASH!

...shattering to powder on the floor. I yelped as another tile fell.

"The beast they call Tyranny is a breath away," Pearl continued. "He targets Liberty's most vulnerable children and blinds the rest. You believe you're safe in this fortress. You refuse to believe it can happen here. Now. *Today.* Yet it lurks beneath the headlines and menaces your children and theirs. What happened at Mount Vernon, on the bus, at the hotel launched nothing less than the decisive battle of the American Revolution. Tyranny has taken from us the one weapon that can defeat him. Unless you wrest it from his hands..."

Pearl paused to re-compose herself.

"...our Revolution dies. Today."

I leaned in to Pearl's level. "You're certifiable. Now, I have to get twenty-five people on a bus to Philly. You need a 'Champion?' You have three million to choose from."

Pearl shook her head. "It must be you."

"Why?"

"No time. Unless you accept, Liberty will surely fall."

"Wha – what does that even *mean*? When will 'Liberty fall?'"

"Precisely one second from now."

I tapped my leg. "*One-Miss-i-ssipp-i.* Welp! Time's up! Tell 'Liberty' Mr. Upson doesn't accept late papers, so...she'll just have to *repeat history.*"

I clapped.

"What's the best way outta here?"

Pearl looked skyward. *"Up."*

I looked with her...

KABOOOOOOM!!!!

...the ceiling ripped free from the Rotunda, taking the fresco with it. For the briefest moment the sky turned a shade of deep crimson, darker than black...then a vortex of golden light punctured the sky, revolving clockwise above me. I panicked and reached for Pearl.

"We have to get out of here!" I yelled.

Pearl remained steady. "Be still, and nest in the eye of the storm."

The walls cracked to their foundations. From the floor, another light whirled counterclockwise. My mind fought as my body surrendered to forces surreal. Pearl turned sallow and stiff, flecks of gray swirling in her emerald eyes. Outside I heard an ungodly *growl*...

"What is this?" I demanded. *"Who are you?"*

"A messenger," the woman replied, breaking into a coughing fit. "Time is of the essence. Do you accept?"

"I…I don't know…"

Pearl's breathing became increasingly shallow. "You swore…an oath…to the boy's mother. Will you…honor it…Today?"

My throat went dry. "Yes."

Pearl dropped a small, heavy object into my front pocket.

"What is that? Lead?"

"Keep…it on you…at all times. If ever…you are lost…it will show you…the way home."

The twin lights collapsed together, whirling around me as a phantom hurricane.

"Where am I going?" I demanded. "What am I supposed to do?"

Pearl strained. "Arthur…will show you…the way…to Excalibur."

The centripetal and centrifugal forces of light rapidly increased in velocity and sound.

"And remember, Mr. Upson," she shouted, *"there are two sides of the coin!"*

"What?! I can't hear – "

BOOOOOOOOOOOOOOOOOOOOOOOOOOOOOOM

The room exploded…

…into a sea of fire…

…and faded to black.

Three

History's Block Party

The sun hung low like a chandelier, heat pounding through relentless humidity. My ears buzzed and my heart beat *thwump! thwump! thwump!* as a flurry of concussive echoes pulsed through my body...

...inhale...exhale...

...inhale...

...

...where am I?

My eyes adjusted, slowly, and my surroundings came into focus. I caught the street sign from where I lay flat on the lawn:

CLEMENTINE LANE

I sat up on my elbows; I spotted my satchel and pounced on it. *Wallet. Phone. Everything's here.* I emptied my pockets.

Pearl's object: a thick dark gray coin, an inch-and-a-half in diameter...and heavy. *This might actually be lead.* A sun with human features hovered over the horizon; thirteen stars encircled the inscription tracing the outer ring:

NOW IN THE COURSE OF HUMAN EVENTS

I flipped it over; the other side was identical.

It's a military challenge coin. Dad collected these when he was in the Navy. The coin's possessor has to produce it on demand or otherwise owe his challenger a drink. Colonel coined me constantly, though the challenge is lost on one who doesn't partake.

I stood. *Too fast.*

The dizzies faded, and I scoped the scene on the street.

Something's off.

An American flag flew from every porch; palm trees stood at every entryway; red-white-and-blue pinwheels dotted every lawn. The Glenn Miller Orchestra lightened the mood from a scratchy phonograph. Amidst a row of white tables and chairs, a Don Draper doppelgänger worked the grill as kids swung hula-hoops, fathers schmoozed and mothers set dishes on a long table with a banner that read:

HAPPY INDEPENDENCE DAY!
from the
Palm Beach County Daughters of the American Revolution

...how long was I...?
...no...
...every car on the block was a classic. A '57 Bel Air. A '59 Edsel...
...they all look new...
...a girl hopped by on a pogo stick...
...
...oh...no, no, no, no, no...
I scrambled around, searching for...*there it is...*
...a rolled-up newspaper, perched on the doormat of a blue house.
I unwound the bands, unfurling the broadsheet:

THE PALM BEACH POST
Vol. LIV; No. 122
West Palm Beach, Florida
Wednesday Morning, July 4, 1962
24 Pages Today ~:~ Price 5 Cents

Bull. Shit.
Instinctively, I pulled one of the rubber bands taut around my wrist...
...snap! "Ahhh!"
...this is real...
...this is 1962...
...no...it can't be...
...I flopped back onto the lawn and closed my eyes...
...counting backwards from...

...10...

...9...

...8...

...7...

...6...

...5...

...4...

...3...

...2...

...1...

((...get up, Benji...))
I pressed myself up. On the street, not a soul had stirred.
I'm invisible...
...he...hehehe...hahahaha!
I laughed for a solid minute as I came to grips with the reality before me.
...I...am...in...nineteen...sixty...two...
I grabbed the newspaper and perused the front page. The County Commission had approved funding for a new baseball park. *That must be Municipal Stadium.* That rusty dive had been shuttered by the time I arrived for Spring Training in the late Nineties.

I read on, fascinated. Nationalists seized control of French Algeria. A "negro woman" received a 35-year sentence for murdering another "negro." A state legislator railed against the Soviet "Red Menace" at last night's Kiwanis meeting. An—

"WHERE THE DEVIL IS MY PAPER?!"

I jumped to my feet. The octogenarian in the doorway wore only a bathrobe and briefs, his white wisps reaching maniacally in all directions. I opened my mouth to explain myself when he stared right past me and yelled:

"MISSUS CARRR-MIIICH-AELLLL!!!!"

A reply came from across the street: *"Claude, don't get your pants in a wad, I'm comin'!"*

Mrs. Carmichael emerged from a pack of housewives, striding confidently across the lane. A tall hourglass woman with strawberry hair, a red blouse and long white skirt, she possessed the spirit of a Queen Matriarch holding sway over all comers.

"Dorothy, he stole my newspaper again!" Claude insisted as she reached the lawn.

Dorothy rolled her eyes and called back across the street:

"James Timothy Carmichael!"

In the front yard of a two-story tangerine house, a cardboard-armored knight jumped, dropping the broomstick he wielded against a four-eyed pipsqueak. The boy clumsily dragged his feet across the lane; Dorothy rested her hands on his shoulders.

"Jimmy darling, did you take Mr. Granger's newspaper?"

Jimmy furrowed his brow and shook his head.

Claude shook his finger at the boy. "You lyin' red bastard!"

Dorothy closed her eyes and exhaled. "For Pete's sake, Claude, Jimmy's eleven. He isn't stealing your papers and for the last time he is *not* a Russian spy!"

Claude spat on the ground, cursed and slammed the door.

"Bitter old codger," Dorothy bit off.

She knelt and studied Jimmy's armor.

"This get-up is new. What happened to Davy Crockett and the Alamo?"

Jimmy kicked a pebble. "Nah. Now we're Knights of the Round Table. I'm Lancelot. Wam-Bam is Galahad."

"Who's King Arthur?"

I perked up. Jimmy shrugged.

"Well," Dorothy continued, "do your queen a favor and tell *her* Arthur to come out and entertain her…subjects, or whatever."

Jimmy quickly beat feet back across the street.

((...Arthur will show you the way to Excalibur...))

I tossed the paper onto Claude's doorstep and followed the boy into 2445 Clementine Lane. Nobody on Earth saw me...save whoever piloted that black convertible to the curb as I closed the front door...

~

Castle Carmichael was spotless, and its patriarch a royal mess. I reclined on a green sectional, perusing an issue of Life magazine with Richard Nixon on the cover and watching the six-foot-four Wayne Carmichael down Scotch like a gangrenous Union soldier. With every sip he closed his eyes, swirled and savored, then opened them again suddenly, eyes wide open, as if awakening from a nightmare.

Rinse. Repeat.

He's a drunk.

I set the magazine on top of the wood-paneled Magnavox tube broadcasting the Independence Day parade in Philadelphia. Wayne couldn't peel his vacant eyes from it. "Arthur," as it were, was useless.

Time to look for "Excalibur" myself...

I started in the garage and worked my way around the house. I had no idea what I was after. Soon I found myself unpacking the world's least interesting time capsule: the story of the Carmichaels.

From an old photo album I learned that Dorothy Jane Tucker married Wayne Alan Carmichael in Reno, Nevada on September 22, 1945. Wayne was a factory manager for Gould Industries; Dorothy was a church organist and local chapter president of the Daughters of the American Revolution.

Their eldest, Tiffany Lynn, was born on April 4, 1946. Her bedroom walls were plastered with posters of Bobby Darin and Ricky Nelson; a lipstick heart framed a boy's black-and-white photo tucked into the corner of a vanity mirror.

James Timothy arrived on October 7, 1950. Every inch of his room was covered with toys, including the pile of green Army men I stepped on. One of the G.I.s I split in two held a walkie-talkie in his hand, likely to radio for backup to fight the giant invading Jimmy's room. *Or maybe he's calling the police.* After all, the authorities must be notified of all these issues of *The Palm Beach Post* padding the back of Jimmy's cardboard shield.

After more than an hour of searching, I was no closer to anything approximating "Excalibur," whatever that was supposed to be. Exhausted, I plopped down at the foot of the stairs, cursing under my breath. My mind wandered back to the Capitol, watching the dome rip away. *What did I witness?* I shuddered at the thought that a lifetime from now everything I held dear had been reduced to ashes.

And then there was Pearl.

Probably a witch. Not a very good one, of course. After all, she'd sent me on a wild goose chase through time to retrieve a fictional sword from a functional drunk. It didn't seem like a well-laid plan.

I glared at Wayne as he lifted the Scotch to his mouth. This time, he paused. He wiggled his nose, then turned his head toward me. I froze.

Shit. Shit. Shit.

Wayne's eyes watered…and his jaw slowly dropped…

Shhhhhhhhhhit. He can see me.

…he took a deep breath…

I slowly stood, ready to explain myself. "Mr. Carmichael, I just needed to use the rest—"

…Wayne sneezed *hard*…

…sending the cherry red memento box tumbling onto the shag carpet.

I didn't see that before.

Wayne took another sip; as he did I swooped in and snagged the box, spreading its contents out on the coffee table.

It was a cornucopia of World War II memorabilia. A rainbow-strapped Victory Medal. A Purple Heart. A Silver Star. A patch from the 285th Battalion. A challenge coin bearing a torch above the motto: CONSTANT VIGILANCE. A black-and-white photo of a younger, sober Wayne in uniform with his arm around a shorter soldier with bushy eyebrows; there was writing on the back in faded pencil:

so great a sacrifice
laid upon the altar
4-4-45
'til next year in jerusalem, hank

Underneath was a pair of dog tags:

FINKELSON, HENRY ELI
BROOKLYN HEIGHTS, NY

Finkelson?

On the Magnavox, President Kennedy spoke soundlessly as Wayne looked on; only now could I see the shadows of melancholy breaking across the man's face.

The soft moment quickly hardened.

"I cannot wait to get out of this house, you controlling hag!"

Outside, a blond girl in a lime green dress stomped toward the house. *Tiffany.* The door burst open and Tiffany stormed to the kitchen, Dorothy on her tail. I tiptoed after them.

"This isn't fair!" Tiffany sobbed. "Joel and I are supposed to go to Delray Beach, but I'm stuck at your stupid block party for this stupid holiday!"

Dorothy slapped Tiffany hard. "Ungrateful bitch!"

Good God.

Tiffany quivered, a fresh welt on her cheek. She looked away bitterly.

"HEY!" Dorothy snapped. "Listen to me! Do you know what this day means to this family?"

Dorothy paused to wipe a tear.

"Your great grandfather's great grandfather died driving the British from Boston. Your father nearly froze to death in a Belgian forest while I waited for him, *chaste.* They risked themselves at the altar of freedom to protect you from foreigners who want to take everything from you. *Faith. Family. Flag.* Not so you could be some...*shiksa* whore!"

Tiffany stared coldly out the kitchen window.

"Wayne! Get in here!"

Wayne sauntered in apathetically, setting glass and bottle on the countertop.

"Have anything to say? Or do you want that Aarons boy to knock up our little girl on the Fourth of July?"

Tiffany fumed. "Your *'little girl?'* That's rich."

"Tiff," Wayne hiccupped, "listen to your mother. Flirt with your neighbors...hell, flirt with Claude, he's lonely. And Dorothy? *Keep your Goddamn voice down.* Some of us are trying to think."

35

Wayne downed the last of the Scotch as Jimmy and Wam-Bam bounded in.

"Mom!" Jimmy panted. "There's a baseball game at the park, with…a priest guy or something. Can we go, please, please, please?!"

Dorothy smiled weakly. "Be back in two hours."

The boys high-fived and bolted.

Tiffany shot Dorothy an icy glare. "I can't go to the beach with Joel, but your precious dweeb can go to the park with a priest?"

Dorothy looked away.

"Well," Tiffany steamed, "since it appears I'm stuck here…"

She slung her beach bag over her shoulder and stormed off.

"…maybe I'll just flirt with the priest, right Dad?"

Tiffany slammed the door.

Dorothy leered at Wayne. "How did a coward like you survive the Battle of the Bulge?"

"Schnapps," he replied, staring deep into his empty glass. "And Betty Grable."

Dorothy groaned and pulled her husband outside.

What an absolute cluster. I was alone in this nuthouse and out of options. I threw myself on the couch, praying for lightning…or Capitol paramedics…

…bzzzzzzt.

Impossible. I retrieved my phone from my satchel. Against all logic, I had a text:

Look for a sword. Find a battle-axe. LOL.

Outside, an engine roared…
…chig-chig-chevroooom….
…bzzzzzzt.

Your Uber has arrived.

I sprinted outside.

It was a '61 Lincoln Continental convertible with an extended cab and two miniature American flags standing stiff at the back corners…and no driver…

...

...it started itself...

...

...I stooped under the grill, looking for God only knows what, as the radio hammered the bass chord:

Dada-doom-doom-doom-doom!

SMACK! I hit my head on the license plate frame...

"Gahhh!!!"

...as the radio played...

Dadala-doom-doom-doom-doom!

...and on and on it rocked and rolled, a Bob Dylan cover playing six years before it was recorded. I caught the license plate. *Texas?*

"Yes, Mr. Upson. It's the same car."

I gasped in disbelief. That nasal Boston affectation was unmistakable. It belonged to a man elsewhere in this time and dead in mine. Shaking like a leaf, I stood.

He wore a white open-buttoned long-sleeve shirt, with faded scarring on his neck and above his right temple. Idling in the driver's seat of his last ride was the thirty-fifth President of the United States.

John F. Kennedy.

Jimi Hendrix crooned:

"...all-a-long-the-watch-tow-er..."

"Quit staring," Kennedy said drily. "Jump in."

I moved slowly, timidly around the fender. I struggled to open the passenger door, then plopped down and stared straight into the dashboard.

Kennedy shook his head. "I said *jump* in."

"Bad knee," I muttered.

"I get it," he chuckled. "It takes some getting used to – eternity, that is."

Eternity. "Am I dead? Is this...hell?"

"No."

Kennedy released the brake.

"This is Florida."

Kennedy engaged the clutch and drove off, as the eyes of an old man clutching his newspaper followed us off Clementine Lane.

Four

Print the Legend

Kennedy drove through Palm Beach like a man possessed, weaving his way in and out of traffic that couldn't see him. It took me fifteen minutes to muster the courage to poke his arm...

"Is that how you greet a dead President?" he asked.

...it was him...in the flesh...*how?* I was incredulous. There was simply no way I was sharing an automobile with the man who would be shot by Lee Harvey Oswald in that same vehicle a year-and-a-half later.

"Ben?"

"You're John *Fucking* Kennedy."

"No, Ben." Kennedy lowered the volume on the radio. "Not 'fucking.' *Fitzgerald.* An old family name. Did you know we once ruled all of Ireland?"

Ruled. "King Arthur."

"Yes?"

"You're Arthur."

"Okay."

"You're going to help me find Excalibur."

"Perhaps."

"This is Camelot!" I laughed. It all made sense now. Jacqueline Kennedy once compared her husband's brief presidency with the mythical kingdom of Avalon.

Kennedy nodded. "I am Arthur indeed," he proclaimed, sweeping his arm dramatically. "Welcome to Camelot!"

On the sidewalk I watched a smiling ice cream vendor give cones to a young boy and girl in exchange for nickels and thank yous. The girl's strawberry cone dripped onto the sidewalk, and a tail-wagging beagle swooped in to lick up the spoils. The scene was delightful. This Palm Beach was warmer and more provincial than the version I remembered – America as my grandparents knew her, before she shed her innocence. The very air smelled like bubble gum.

"Camelot seems idyllic, Your Majesty," I observed.

"Call me Jack."

"Okay. Where are we headed, Jack?"

Kennedy picked at something in his teeth. "You like parades?"

"Not particularly."

"Ever been in one?"

"What do you mean?"

Ahead on Dixie Highway, Kennedy was on pace to plow through a high school marching band buoyantly playing *You're A Grand Old Flag.*

"Jack, slow down."

The bastard whistled…and *accelerated.*

"Oh, *shhhhh….*"

Inexplicably, the Lincoln glided under the police tape and wedged between the band and the Mayflower float behind them.

"…what the hell was that?" I demanded.

"Magic," Kennedy replied. "Er…quantum physics, or so Einie calls it."

"Einie…you mean Alb – "

"The same."

The scene on the sidewalk was a tinderbox of nostalgia. The crowd waved flags. Lovers held hands. Men in uniform basked in the adulation of the crowd.

"Behold the subjects of Camelot!" Kennedy crowed.

He pointed to a late middle-aged brunette cradling an infant.

"Mildred Schwartz, a nurse in Lake Worth. She began her career at a clinic in Northern California sterilizing Mexican teenagers."

"She's a eugenicist?!" I taught America's eugenics movement, which sought to "cleanse" America's "racial hygiene," as a footnote, an exception to the rule of American goodness. It sickened me to put a face on it.

"Indeed. Did you know many Nazi ideas about white supremacy…"

"…originated in American eugenics." It was true. Before we fought the Nazis, we armed them with the very racial propaganda they employed to destroy their own people.

Kennedy proceeded to divulge a series of dark destinies. A draftee who would fall in Vietnam. A runaway who would overdose at Woodstock. A gambler who would lose his family fortune. Kennedy nodded at a man in a flight suit.

"That particular asshole is Barry Cronshaw. Air Force mechanic…and Soviet spy."

"Shut up."

Kennedy shook his head.

I slunk down into my seat. "This is depressing."

"Welcome to Camelot," Kennedy deadpanned. "Hungry?"

"No…are…are you?"

"You think a ghost never craves a cheeseburger?"

"Never really had to think about it."

Kennedy slipped off the parade route. As he turned the corner I spotted the marquis on a small theater and did a double take:

THE MAN WHO SHOT LIBERTY VALANCE
JIMMY STEWART   JOHN WAYNE
1100   130   400   630   900

"Print the legend," I whispered.

"Here in Camelot," Kennedy opined, "the legend has always been fact."

~

Hopper's Diner was packed with patrons, from ceiling fan to checkerboard floor. Kennedy and I squeezed into two open seats at the lunch counter, where, somehow, two plates awaited us. Watching a dead Kennedy devour a cheeseburger nearly gave me an aneurism. The other customers at the counter stared right through him at the young black woman two seats to my right, who might as well have been a space alien. Other than *Pink Shoelaces* blaring from the corner jukebox, you could hear a pin drop.

"Zora Gates," Kennedy said casually, chomping on a dill pickle. "Sociology major at Bethune-Cookman and dedicated Freedom Rider."

Interesting. The Freedom Riders were student activists who disrupted the segregated bus systems of the Deep South. Zora was presently buried in a thick book, ignoring her soup as it cooled, blissfully unaware of the palpable discomfort she induced in the diner's otherwise all-white clientele.

The door jingled. A slick-haired white man in his late twenties entered and made a beeline to the lunch counter. He straddled the stool between Zora and me, strangling me with his cheap cologne.

"Billy Asher," Kennedy belched, setting down his Coca-Cola.

Billy sniffed at Zora like a wild dog. "Whatcha doin' at this counter, coon?"

The slur was jarring. Zora ignored him. Billy dangled a Lucky Strike cigarette from his lips.

"The hell you readin'? You literate?"

Zora turned the page. Her poise in the face of her harasser was impressive.

"They teach y'all to read over at Coon Carver High?"

"Jealous?" Zora posed quietly.

Furious, Billy snatched the book from her hands.

"Ridiculous," he muttered between puffs. "Spendin' the white man's hard-earned taxes on lazy niggers. What's this horse shit?"

Billy held the book out in front of him and read the title of the essay.

"*The Meaning of the Fourth of July to the Negro.* Frederick Douglass."

Billy chuckled in amusement.

"What *does* today mean to you people? Color me fascinated."

Billy drew a puff and read mockingly:

"*'What have I, or those I represent, to do with your national independence? Are the great principles of political freedom and of natural justice, as embodied in the Declaration of Independence, extended to us?'*"

He skimmed and muttered.

"Ooh, listen to this: *'The rich inheritance of justice, liberty, prosperity and independence bequeathed by your fathers is shared by you, not me. The sunlight that brought life and healing to you has brought stripes and death to me. The Fourth of July is yours, not mine!'*"

Billy snapped the book shut and smashed his butt in an ashtray.

41

"Ungrateful nigger. Better a slave in the greatest country on Earth than a dumb spear chucker in Africa. Don'chu agree, Choc'late Puddin'?"

Zora stared Billy down, her façade slowly cracking.

"Can I help you, Billy?"

A young, pretty auburn-haired waitress in a blue headband scowled from across the counter. The jukebox switched tracks: *"Papa loves Mambo..."*

Billy grinned. "Hey, Sugar."

"Don't call me that," the Waitress snipped. "Why are you here?"

Billy took a drag and motioned at Zora. "Just here to help you take out the trash, darlin'."

The Waitress clapped. "Wonderful! You can dump yourself out back where the rats screw."

Billy laughed. "You ain't mean that."

The Waitress rolled her eyes and began wiping the counter. Billy clamped down with an iron paw.

"Stop that. Make the nigger clean that up."

Zora bit her lip, tapping her iced tea. The Waitress looked away.

"You got somethin' to say, darlin'? Say it. I been comin' here for a year jus' for you. Tell me how to love you."

The Waitress looked sideways at Billy; a wry smile slowly crept across her face. She leaned in and placed her free hand over Billy's, brushing against his cheek and whispering breathily:

"You'll never know how to love me. It will be a cold day in hell before I call you mine. You know where the door is, see yourself through it."

The Waitress pried herself loose and drove her left elbow *hard* into Billy's nasal cavity, somersaulting him onto the checkerboard floor. He staggered to his feet, nose bloodied. Impulsively, Zora splashed her tea in his face.

"Bitches!" Billy cried, stumbling into the hot Florida afternoon.

The diner teetered on edge. Zora quivered. The Waitress grabbed her hand.

"Your soup is on the house," she said tearfully. "I am *so sorry* this happened here."

"I can take care of myself," Zora replied.

The Waitress smiled. "If my sister isn't free, I'm not free."

Zora raised her eyebrows. "You're a Freedom Rider?"

The Waitress winked. Zora erupted in cathartic laughter.

Kennedy finished his burger, then plucked mine off my plate. "Let's go. We're on a tight schedule."

As we exited, a middle-aged man grumbled to his wife: *"Why does she get free soup?"*

~

I overheard a police dispatch on the street outside:

"Officer Kettlebeck?"

"Go ahead, Cindy."

"Mr. Granger has called six times in the last hour about his newspaper...can you please get him off my back?"

"10-4. Who took it today? Julius Rosenberg?"

"...Jack Kennedy?"

~

CRACK! The horsehide sizzled to right centerfield; Wam-Bam pedaled backward and fell onto his backside. The ball hit the fence on the fly as the Kid rounded first...then second...another outfielder tossed the ball to the second baseman as a young collared priest in a Red Sox cap barked from the mound.

"¡Tercero! Lanzala a la tercera, Ramón!"

The ball squirted out of Ramón's glove and rolled to Jimmy at shortstop as the Kid rounded third. Jimmy lobbed the ball off target as the Kid slid into home and tipped his tattered Pirates hat to the girl in the lime green dress on the third base slope. The Kid grabbed his glove from the backstop and skipped out to left field, pulling off Jimmy's Yankees cap and mussing the boy's hair *en route*.

"Diego Reyes," Kennedy said. "Seventeen-year-old Cuban refugee and student at St. Michael's School for Boys."

We sat with a bag of peanuts on the bleachers of a Dixie League field two blocks from Clementine. Father Charles O'Brien had taken the field with nine *peloteros*; a throng of neighborhood kids came to watch. Jimmy and Wam-Bam, who had the athletic prowess of a calf in live birth, somehow weaseled themselves into the game.

43

"Nothing more American than baseball on the Fourth of July," Kennedy mused. "It's almost religious...all apologies to the College of Cardinals."

O'Brien pitched to the next batter.

"Speaking of Cardinals, I hear you were a hell of a ballplayer."

"In another lifetime," I lamented, squeezing my left knee.

"Baseball is a game of lifetimes. Only game where you score by returning home."

Kennedy spat out a shell.

"It's uncanny how baseball's history parallels our country's. Labor and economics. War and peace. Religion...and race."

"Jackie Robinson was more than a ballplayer," I admitted. "He was a civil rights legend."

Kennedy chuckled. "'Legend,' he says. Speaking of legends, Mr. Upson, who invented baseball?"

I cracked open a goober. "Well, the legend says Abner Doubleday in 1839, from scratch in Cooperstown, New York. But that's not true. Doubleday was a Union general during the Civil War, and baseball needed a patriotic origin myth. It was actually a volunteer firefighter named Alexander Cartwright who adapted baseball from English games like cricket and rounders. His team actually *lost* the first baseball game ever played."

"The legend *is* sexier, you have to admit," Kennedy surmised. "A victorious war hero or a guy who couldn't win his own game? Easy choice, that is."

Diego snared a fly ball and zinged it to second as he jogged to the slope, flopping onto Tiffany's blanket. He picked a dandelion and held it out to her. Tiffany blushed.

"Do you know the name of the New Jersey park where they played that first game?" Kennedy asked.

I paused, searching, but the name escaped me. "You got me, Jack."

Kennedy leaned back and closed his eyes. "The Elysian Fields."

His words hung wistfully in the breeze.

"Paradise of the Greeks and Romans," he continued, hints of excitement and melancholy in his voice. "Free of death and decay. Baseball is the pastime of heaven. That's an unassailable fact."

The *peloteros* joyfully whipped the ball around the diamond.

"Playing the game," I conceded, "often felt like heaven."

Kennedy studied the teenagers on the slope.

"This is the closest to heaven Diego's ever been," he said. "A year ago he was in Havana, in front of a firing squad."

I coughed out a peanut.

"*El paredón.* 'The Wall,' they call it. Thousands of suspected dissidents executed at Castro's whim. Diego was the only one of ten to survive. They spared him to send a message."

I swallowed hard. "But that's all behind him. Now he's safe. Now he's free. Now he's in paradise."

Kennedy peered over my shoulder. "There's always trouble in paradise."

I turned to see Dorothy Carmichael exit the driver's seat of a white Impala. She flushed hot when she saw Tiffany sharing the blanket with something much worse than Joel Aarons.

"Get your dirty hands off my daughter, you mongrel bastard!" she shouted.

Tiffany rushed Diego to his feet. *"Go! Vamos!"*

Diego put his hands up.

"¡Señora, solo somos amigos y nada mas!"

Dorothy shoved Diego hard, sending him tumbling toward the field. She followed swiftly after.

"MOTHER! WHAT ARE YOU DOING?" Tiffany cried. Behind her, Wayne stood frozen in shock.

Every decent educator has an innate protective instinct, reflexive and automatic. This madness sprang mine to action.

Dorothy jumped on top of Diego. He kicked her away; she somersaulted backward and landed on her stomach. Dorothy, bleeding from the brow, spat grass and pressed herself up as Diego backpedaled on all fours.

"¡No quiero pelear!" he yelled.

Dorothy ignored him and grabbed a wooden bat from the backstop, kicking off her platforms. She took a few steps toward Diego, lifting the Louisville Slugger above her head. With full force and no mercy, she brought the bat speeding down toward the young man's chest.

I caught it flush in my hand.

Dorothy shrieked and backed away. I lay on top of the hard-breathing Diego, holding the bat aloft, my left knee screaming in pain.

"Thanks…" Diego whispered.

I sat up to a dumbfounded chorus:

"Who is he?"

"Where'd he come from?"

I yelled for Kennedy. "Jack!…"

But JFK was nowhere in sight.

"Look at you, *Jack,*" Dorothy spat. "A grown man watching *boys* in the park."

"Dorothy," I panted. "Diego and Tiffany—"

Her eyes turned to fire. *"How do you know our names, Jack? Were you spying on us?"*

"What? No, you—!"

A police siren cut me off. Dorothy lit up as the officers from outside Hopper's exited the squad car.

"Norman, thank God! Arrest this man!" Dorothy rained crocodile tears as the cops approached, hands on holsters.

"Sir," Kettlebeck commanded, "put down the bat please."

I dropped it on command.

"You got a name?"

"Jack…eh, Bauer?"

"Care to explain what you're doing here, Mr. Bauer?"

"He was spying on my daughter!" Dorothy sniffed, wiping blood from her forehead. "Then he tried to kill me!"

I balked. "This is a public park. And *she* attacked *him!"*

I pointed to Diego, now attended to by Father O'Brien.

Kettlebeck stroked his chin. "Where you from, Jack?"

"Boca Raton," I lied.

"Got a car?"

"Uh, yeah," I laughed nervously. "A Lincoln."

Kettlebeck's mouth widened to a grin. "Black? Whitewall tires? Texas plates?"

He pointed back toward the parking lot.

"That one?"

Oh hell. The Lincoln, once invisible, was now in plain view.

"Hey, Officer Kettlebeck," his partner said. "Isn't that the car Claude said was parked in front of the Carmichael house earlier?"

"Indeed it is, Officer Montero," Kettlebeck responded.

"And doesn't this asshole match the description of a *passenger* in a Lincoln driven by a man resembling JFK?"

"Yes, sir."

"Does this asshole have anything to say about that?"

I recalled Dad's most critical legal advice. "Officers...am I under arrest?"

Kettlebeck turned to his partner. "Lucas?"

Montero scratched his neck. "Beatin' the broad and nickin' the news?"

Kettlebeck turned me around and cuffed me. "Jack Bauer, you're under arrest for petit larceny and assault with a deadly weapon."

The *peloteros* howled in protest. Father O'Brien sprang up and hounded Montero as he walked me toward the squad car.

"Officer," he panted, "Mr. Bauer merely defended my student from that vile woman! Is it *justice* to side with the *unjust*?"

Montero roared. "Father, Dorothy is a saint. And *this* asshole," Montero flicked me in the ear, "*this asshole* stakes out her house, stalks her kids at the park, he has a bat in his hand and she's bleedin'? I think we know which one you'll see in confession."

Wam-Bam approached as Montero lowered me into the cruiser. The boy stared at me blankly from behind thick coke-bottle lenses as he handed Kettlebeck my coin.

"Now in the Course of Human Events," Kettlebeck read.

Montero snickered. "He's in a cult. See? Asshole."

As we pulled away, Dorothy cozied up to Wayne for comfort. He didn't move a muscle, his bloodshot eyes fixed on me.

They were filled with terror.

Five

Magic Bullets

"Mr. Bauer!"

The jailer slid open the bar doors, rousing me from my daze on the dingy cell mattress.

"You've been sprung."

I rubbed my eyes. *Beelzebub must've recanted her story.*

I couldn't say I'd miss those walls, the convalescing drunk on the floor, or the oddly oppressive black mold in the corner that somehow grew three inches over the course of my turn in lock-up.

The jailer led me to the lobby and pointed at a row of chairs populated by one Florida miscreant or another.

"Take a seat," he grunted.

There was one available, wedged between a Steve Buscemi doppelgänger and...

...the Waitress?

She was still in her work uniform, holding a bag of frozen peas against her left elbow as she perused *The Palm Beach Post*. I took the seat to her right, and noticed the faint silhouette of a reddish-pink handprint on her right arm. *Billy.*

"I bruise easily, Mr. Upson," the Waitress said without looking up.

I sat in stunned silence. Before I could speak, a bubble-popping secretary dropped a stack of papers in my lap.

"You're free to go," she said. "Oh...*this*...is yours."

The secretary warily held out my phone, like it was a nuclear device.

"This too."

She tossed me the coin. It was lighter...and warmer, flecked with silvery tin.

The Waitress tisked. "Didn't I tell you to keep that on you?"

My stomach turned inside out. Her eyes shimmered like emerald pools, and I caught a glimpse of her nametag:

PEARL W.

Young Pearl stood. "Our ride's waiting."

~

Dusk had descended on Palm Beach County. In the back corner of the police station parking lot, I spied Kennedy casually leaning against the Lincoln. My blood rose to a boil...

That vanishing son of a...

"Jack?"

That wasn't my voice. I turned to see Wayne Carmichael approach tepidly, his hands in his pockets.

"I, um," he pointed back at the station with his thumb, "I told them you didn't attack my wife."

"Oh," I replied, surprised. "Thank you?"

Wayne's voice shook, his eyes blood red. "No, Mr. Bauer. Thank you."

I paused. "I...don't understand."

Wayne drew closer. "Thank you...for showing me who she really is."

He extended his hand. I hesitated...then clasped it...

...and the world dissolved around me...

...into a green forest in springtime...

...

"Töte den amerikanischen! Töte den Juden!"

I, Tech Sergeant Wayne A. Carmichael, lay on my back, waiting to die...the Nazis captured and executed my division four months ago...Hank and I escaped and hid under that dead reindeer in the snow...Betty Grable, we called her...

...they found us, took us to Buchenwald...we saw what they did to the Jews...the homosexuals...the crippled...heard it...smelled it...felt it, until we felt nothing...I swapped our tags to save Hank's Dodger-lovin' ass...

...I was a useful Jew...I fixed their radios, so they spared me...

...I heard the Allies were coming...we escaped before the Krauts could torch us with the place...no weapons...no provisions...we hid in the trees...their hounds smelled us...

...this Ugly Beast tackles me, eyes like steel...I kick him off; he tumbles backward...enraged, he brings a rock over his head...

"Ich bin der Jude! Töte mich!"

...Hank catches the rock...they wrestle...the Beast's revolver blows through my tags into Hank's chest...

...the Beast stands...an American bullet zips through his ugly head...

...Hank doesn't look so good...he'll never buy Lynn that diamond from Tiffany...

...I swear upon the altar of God I'll buy it for her...

...

...the forest faded away. My entire nervous system was on fire.

"Mr. Bauer?" Wayne asked.

I released my handshake and hugged Wayne hard.

"Thank you," I trembled, "for showing me who *you* are."

Wayne released and walked back to his car with fire in his eyes.

He was born again.

~

War rattled through my bones. I gripped the sand between my toes, staring out into the dark Atlantic. The air was thick and heavy, weighed down by the presence of an evil I couldn't define. At that very moment, some hundred miles south in Cuba, the tyrant Fidel Castro plotted with the Soviets to park nuclear warheads on his island and point them at Washington, D.C. In three months' time, the Cuban Missile Crisis would engulf the planet in panic and define the presidency of the man whose...*ghost?*...stood twenty feet away. My mind raced forward to my time, to the ghastly vision of holocaust at the Capitol...

They're connected. I sensed that same nebulous evil in the German forest, at the diner, on the Dixie League field...in that vision at The Quicksilver. *All the same.*

A chill swept through me. I turned to Pearl and Kennedy, leaning against the Lincoln. A thousand questions swirled; I started with the first one on my mind.

"How could they see me at the baseball field?" I asked.

Kennedy folded his arms. "You crossed the threshold."

"...threshold?"

"The barrier separating the seen from the unseen, time from the timeless. You witnessed a young man in terrible danger. You could have let it befall him. Instead, you chose to act. And so you entered the Course of Human Events...and shaped it."

"What's Excalibur?"

Kennedy brightened and smiled. "The sword in the stone?"

I set my hands on my hips, frustrated. "Don't play games with me, Jack."

Kennedy changed the subject. "What happened when you shook Wayne's hand?"

A cold surge iced my nerves. "I was him. Everything that happened to him happened to me."

"And what happened to him...to you...beyond the veil?"

I spoke of Wayne's capture, his escape, of Hank's sacrifice and Wayne's enduring guilt.

"It's weird," I confessed. "Wayne's fight in the forest played out just like mine on the ball field."

Kennedy nodded. "Different theater...same war."

I scoffed. "Dorothy might be evil incarnate, but she's no Nazi."

"I never said she was. But evil is more pernicious than that. It takes many forms, and our endless War on Tyranny is fought in closer quarters...against legends camouflaged as truth."

"So you're telling me Dorothy has fallen for a legend."

Kennedy shrugged. "She's the daughter of a Revolution she doesn't understand, the wife of a warrior she doesn't understand. The spirit of Camelot..."

Kennedy stopped on a dime. He turned his head and scanned the beach, his voice wavering.

"...Jacqueline didn't call my presidency that until after I was shot..."

Kennedy brushed at the scarring on his temple.

"Camelot is nothing without its true knights – those who swear upon the altar of God eternal hostility against Tyranny in all of his forms. They don't pour tar and pitch on those seeking refuge behind their walls as their real enemies destroy the kingdom from within. A true Champion – "

BANG!

The fireworks boomed. Startled, Kennedy careened over. Pearl steadied him and set him on his knees. I lowered myself to meet them; Pearl pressed me back gently.

"Where there is dust, there is rust," Kennedy mumbled, eyeing the sand, seeming to count every speck. *"Where there are seeds, there are weeds."*

Kennedy whipped his head to me.

"I'm not afraid of bombs bursting in air," he said, voice shaking. "I'm afraid we won't make it through the night."

He gripped me with his trembling hand.

"Come and see…"

Kennedy pressed his thumb against my temple as the sky imploded…

…

…ten thousand sparks ignite my crown…the pain is indescribable…

…forty-six years pass before my eyes…

"Jack, can you hear me?"

…Jacqueline's tears fall like bittersweet nectar on my skin…

"I love you, Jack…I love you…"

…a light flashes…my spirit releases into the sunlit screams echoing through downtown Dallas…

"The President's been shot!"

"From the knoll!"

"No, from the warehouse!"

…below, Jacqueline cradles my broken body…

…a voice whispers into the madness…

((…you dodged a bullet, Jack…))

…I soar past the branches through a sixth floor window…the rifle sizzles like cigar ash…

…my scream echoes through the cosmos. I fly into the bore and will the shot back into its chamber…sparks blow me back out…

((…I said you dodged a bullet, Jack…))

…the shooter quivers.

((...he missed...))
Liar! He killed me!
((...he meant only to snuff you out...))
What difference does that make?
((...come and see...))
...and so into gray-and-hazel eyes I fly...into the mind of Lee Harvey Oswald...a madman and a menace...

...a frail teenager rocks in the corner of an empty room...black tar drips from white walls...he cries for a father he's never seen...

...the doctor whispers to his mother...violent fantasies churn...Lee will cause great suffering...he needs treatment...

...Marguerite Oswald draws hot tar into her lungs...there will be no rush to judgment, she says...not for my boy...not for my boy...

...a dark cloud descends upon Lee...it consumes and ravages him...

((...their peace means war...their freedom is slavery...they are ignorant, but you are strong...))

...time flies through the Looking Glass...

...a boy becomes a man...

...first, United States Marine...

...now an acolyte of the Soviet hammer and sickle...

...adrift, he struggles to feed wife and child...

...

...he meets a man in a darkened alley...

...a White Hat Man...

...he drops a cache of bullets in his hand and crosses his heart...

"Snuff him out," the White Hat Man growls...

...Oswald exhales...my spirit flies back into the Texas sunlight...

...I see it in his eyes...he missed...

...he panics...

...he's a dead man...

((...you dodged a bullet, Jack...this isn't over...))

...

...my body dangles over Eternity's edge as Jacqueline watches over...the doctors cut in vain...

...I'm coming home...

...light floods through the windows at Parkland Memorial...over the loudspeaker, the countdown begins...

((...time is short, Jack ...ninety ...eighty-nine ...eighty-eight ...))
...my heart shatters for Jacqueline ...
...I can't leave her ...not here ...
((...let her go, Jack ...seventy-six ...))
...I whisper good-bye to my love ....her breath catches, ever so slightly ...
...I follow the light to a barren plain ...

...the sky is a shade of crimson darker than black ...

...the mountains resound with the growls of beasts and cries of children ...

"Fifty-seven seconds to spare, Jack."
...a man in Army green idles in a black Lincoln ...
"Who are you?" I demand.
"Call me Hank," he says. "Your brother and keeper."
...the passenger door opens ...
"You're in the Army now."
...I take my seat, awash with sorrow ...
"If I come with you," I ask, "will I live?"
...Hank nods into the mirror. "Ask not."
...I turn to see a single lifeless form, tarred and feathered, dangle from a Great and Mighty Elm ...a silent chorus echoes through the valley ...

> *You came to set our house ablaze*
> *((But you will not replace us!))*
> *To teach our young your wicked ways*
> *((But you will not replace us!))*

A Bluebird flies into the Elm and drapes a flag of fire around the hangman. Stars and stripes burn away to scarlet and gold; the tar melts like candle wax. A charred body hangs in the breeze, eyes wide open ...he whispers ...
((...as for me and my house, we choose to remember ...))
...six Shadows gather around the tree ...a seventh holds the scepter ...

...he strikes the ground with fury...

...the mountains catch fire...

... the Earth cleaves in two...

...a river rages in the abyss...

...from the depths comes a low, vicious hiss...

((...at water he drinksssss...))
((...at water he drownssss...))
((...at water he diesssssss...))

...I turn back into my seat...shaken to my core...
"Oswald's employer," Hank says casually. "You spurned him. Now he's angry."
...the radio bursts with white noise...
"What you said last Fourth of July," Hank continues, his voice changing pitch. "Do you mean it, Ben?"
...I panic. "What did you call me?"
"I want to know, Jack," she says, "if you really mean it..."
...

I gripped the dashboard tight, heart racing.

"Well," Pearl called from the backseat. "Do you?"

The radio crackled, and the living John F. Kennedy thundered from the steps of Independence Hall, that very afternoon:

...for that Declaration unleashed not merely a Revolution against the British, but a Revolution in human affairs. Its authors were highly conscious of its worldwide implications. And George Washington declared that liberty and self-government everywhere were, in his words, 'finally staked on the experiment entrusted to the hands of the American people...'

Kennedy clutched the steering wheel, covered in cold sweat. Hesitantly, he held out his hand to me.

55

"With all my heart," he whispered.

I grasped his hand…

…the sky ignited in sound and fury…

…and dissolved to nothing.

Six

A Course in Human Events

That smell...that warm, savory smell...like a thousand Saturday mornings. Saturdays have always had a telltale scent. When I was a kid, it was those orange rolls Dad made from scratch. Now it's that briny, succulent ham and eggs...and that sharp cheddar Michelle spreads all over that sourdough bread. A "croque monsieur" she calls it, sliding it off the griddle and onto my plate.

"You're so cultured," I tease.

"And you," she jests in Gaulish affect, "are so much swine."

I take a bite. Those flavors dance on the tongue.

"Shell," I say with delight. "You've outdone yourself."

She doesn't answer. She sips her coffee and gazes into the yard.

"He's playing in the Sycamore again," she says after a beat.

I turn and look. So he is, dangling from the strongest branch.

"Drink this, Benji."

I turn back...and she's gone. All that's left is a dark, bitter cup of coffee...

...

((...Drink...))

...

I snapped awake at daybreak.

"Drink, Benjamin."

Soft hands slipped a hot cup under my lips; a peculiar blend of honey and citrus slid down my throat.

"Quite a brew," the calm voice assured me. "Dredged straight from Boston Harbor."

"Boston Har–?" I lurched over, suddenly ill...

"Oh, dear. Let me procure a receptac–"

...too late.

"I'm sorry," I gasped, the taste of bile burning in my throat.

I felt his steady hand on my back. "Not to worry, Benjamin. The Harbor tonic is cleansing, but it packs a vicious punch."

The fog cleared on quaint country chambers. In the corner, a single crack wound down the canary yellow wall from floor to ceiling. A stand-alone wardrobe pressed against the opposite wall; a feather quill and candlestick adorned the nightstand.

I've traveled back at least two centuries.

The pudgy middle-aged man before me went flush with embarrassment, his pinkish face accenting gray streaks flaring through raven locks.

"Where are my manners?" he began. "Allow me – "

"There's no need, Mr. Mason."

His brows arched. "You mark me?"

"I do."

George Mason smiled. The Forgotten Founder and catalyst behind the Bill of Rights seemed to relish the recognition, like a bashful child who quietly craved it.

"You warm the heart," he said. "Welcome to Gunston Hall, my familial estate. A hot Virginia breakfast awaits you in the Little Parlor."

Mason stood and walked to the door.

"George?" I called. "What's the date?"

"Today is the twenty-fourth of March."

"Year?"

He smiled. "Sixty-six. There's a change of clothes in the wardrobe. Today is the day you join the Revolution."

1766. It felt as if my feet barely touched ground in the *nineteen* sixties.

Outside the window the sun peaked over the Potomac, illuminating the nightstand…and my coin, with its new inscription:

WE REMEMBER FIRST LIGHT

Just roll with it.

I found a riding hat, coat, knickers and boots in the vestibule. I changed, then grabbed my satchel and slung it over my shoulder. A small brown object fell out of the side pocket onto the hardwood floor.

Tyson's diary.

I seized it and opened it to the bookmark. The Sandburg quote was gone.

I flipped through the entire thing.

Nothing. Every page was blank.

Odd. He writes in this thing every day.

I stuffed it back into my satchel and descended to the Little Parlor. At the breakfast table, Kennedy sat absorbed in the morning paper, wearing garb similar to mine.

"Morning, Jack," I announced, sitting down to a steaming plate of ham and eggs. I devoured it so ravenously that I didn't notice Kennedy get up and leave. I scanned the title of the paper he left behind...

...

...The Liberator...?

...

...a 19ᵗʰ-century abolitionist paper in 18ᵗʰ-century Virginia?

I snatched it up, and did a double take.

The photograph is...moving...

Inside the square a young white man in a suit with curly black hair gave a rousing speech from what looked like the Capitol Rotunda, a black man in judges' robes stirring beside him. The caption read:

> "LIBERTY AND NOTHING LESS!" – Rep. Thaddeus Stevens (left, 1792-1868) and Justice Thurgood Marshall (right, 1908-1993) address the threat posed by König (Ansel Adams: U.S. Capitol/Today).

König?

I read the date on the header:

Tuesday, March 10, 2020

That's today...in my time.

Mason called from across the hall. "In here when you've finished, Benjamin!"

I shoveled down the rest of breakfast and took the paper with me to the ornate Palladian Room. Mason leaned over a long oak table, flanked by a young man with a reddish ponytail and a woman with long, messy brown hair. The woman held a compass and ruler over a parchment map of a winding river.

Mason glanced up. "Ah! Benjamin Upson, meet Ellen Harper and Abraham Woodhull. Two of our finest operatives in the Sons of Liberty."

I knew Woodhull to be one of George Washington's spies during the Revolution. Under cover as a loyalist named "Samuel Culper," Woodhull had passed valuable information on British troop movements to the Continental Army. As historical figures go, Woodhull was a deep cut. Harper, on the other hand, was a complete mystery to me.

Evidently, so was I.

"This is our Champion?" Harper smirked.

Woodhull snickered. "König prepares the finishing blow, and this is our hope? Are the Sisters mad?"

"Perhaps so," Mason replied. "But as Ms. Parks reminds us, the line between reason and madness grows thinner by the hour."

Somewhere between "reason" and "madness," I watched a squiggly ink line move across the map. I jumped.

Mason laughed. "Benjamin, this can't be the first time you've seen a living document... or...no, I suppose it is..."

It was a flurry of activity. The undulating river wound from a mountain waterfall on one end through cities and ports and rapids to uncharted territory on the other. Two steep waterfalls divided it roughly in thirds. Each of the three segments of the river was labeled with a single word, in Latin:

Vita

Libertatem

Beatitudinem

I furrowed my brow. "What exactly am I looking at here?"

Mason smiled broadly and swept his arm over the map. "Behold, Benjamin: the Course of Human Events."

Human Events. "It's a map of time," I breathed. "Like…history is a place."

"History isn't *like* a place, Benjamin," Mason corrected. "History *is* a place. In this realm we loosely call 'Eternity,' time and space are one."

Mason pointed to the river's origin.

"From the Revolution 'til now, 'ordinary' time as you experience it flows in one direction. But here, on the riverbanks, all of history happens simultaneously: Today."

Today? "March 24, 1766?"

Mason shook his head. "What's the date on *The Liberator?*"

I gave him the date. He pointed at the other edge of the map.

"That date…the date you entered this realm…is *Today.* The End of History, a point beyond which even we cannot venture, because those events have not yet occurred. But everything else – all of history – represents the theater for this, the last battle of the American Revolution."

Mason narrowed his eyes.

"It is where Excalibur lies."

Harper nervously eyed an hourglass on the mantle. "George. Do you mind?"

Mason hung his head. "Apologies, Ellen. You have work to do."

Mason turned to me and set his tricorn hat on his head.

"We have business in Fairfax. Let's get you in the saddle."

Saddle?

Mason walked me to the stables outside Gunston Hall, where Kennedy quietly brooded as he readied our horses. He shot me an uneasy look as he assisted me onto an exotic silvery mare with a golden mane.

"This," Mason said, "is Noxie. There is no finer horse on Earth, dead or alive."

I hadn't ridden horseback since my honeymoon in Vail. Noxie's tempo was surprisingly even and smooth, as if she sensed my unease and adjusted to it.

I surveyed the Gunston Hall grounds as we rode out. They were eerily quiet; no one tended to the fields, which had gone fallow…

…strange…

…it wasn't until we reached the trailhead that I heard the war drums. Around the bend, a battalion of blue jackets marched in formation under an American flag with thirty-six stars. I chuckled.

"Something funny?" Mason asked.

"Yeah," I replied. "You said Today I'd be joining the Revolution. But this is *eighteen* sixty-six. Those are Union troops; the Revolution ended eighty years ago."

The undead Mason grinned. "As sure as the sun rises, Benjamin, there is *always* Revolution."

~

For the next hour Mason regaled me with tales of the American Revolution, his role at the Constitutional Convention – and afterwards, when he fired the ultimatum heard 'round the world:

"I refused to sign the Constitution without a Bill of Rights, and I still wouldn't. What good is democracy if those in power can silence the rest, or deprive a man of Liberty without a fair trial? If we don't shackle Tyranny, assuredly Tyranny will shackle us."

I was captivated. "Thomas Jefferson was right. The Convention really *was* an 'assembly of demigods.'"

Mason turned sour. "Honestly, Benjamin, you believe that drivel? Listen to yourself!"

I was taken aback. Mason cursed.

"Apologies. Even death hasn't defused my temper. Regardless, Thomas had a knack for exaggerating our generation's talents. The Revolution was indeed a miracle, but we were merely mortal players on a grand cosmic stage, no less prone to error or temptation than any other. Fertile soil, but choked – "

Mason stopped, cocking his ear at the faint sound of singing.

Kennedy nodded. "I hear it, too. Beyond the tree line."

We came upon a clearing where ten outsized Conestoga wagons circled, each flying the Virginia battle flag – the infamous Stars and Bars of the Confederacy. Rifle-armed overseers on horseback shouted at lines of black men loading onto the wagons. The overseers were drowned out by the call and response of an elderly Song Man and his chorus:

> *Let virtue reign, Lord, hear our prayer!*
> *(Vict'ry be ours and freedom theirs!)*

A guard jammed the Song Man with the butt of his rifle. *"Quiet!"* he shouted.

"George," I whispered, "why are these men still in chains? The Civil War is over. Slavery is – George?"

Mason and Kennedy were frozen, saline streaming from their eyes.

"Tyranny doesn't care what year it is," Mason said ruefully before galloping off.

I lingered on the scene.

"Quit staring," Kennedy snipped as he rode away.

In the field, Song Man staggered back to his feet, and momentarily we locked eyes. In that moment I heard static…then a high pitch…and then the chorus of Song Man's heart echoed loudly into every chamber of mine:

((…Vict'ry mine and freedom yours…))

~

Four years had passed since the Army of the Potomac cut through Fairfax like tissue paper; still its red bricks bore the black scars of "Northern aggression." Though Robert E. Lee surrendered the lost Confederate cause to Ulysses S. Grant at Appomattox the year before, the damn Yankees would remain for nearly another decade to enforce the Union's new anti-slavery laws and despoil the proud Southern way of life. Local resentment against Union "oppression" ran high.

On Old Chain Bridge Road, an amputee in gray Confederate rags limped by a Union soldier with a gouged eye petting the stock of his gun. The thick cold between them was palpable.

"No love lost between Uncle Sam and Johnny Reb," I commented.

"The amputee is Silas Ewing," Mason explained. "A poor Virginia farmer with no slaves conscripted by wealthy and powerful men to risk life and limb for their 'property.' The one-eyed man is William Morrill, a brutally racist Maryland planter."

"Ewing and Morrill, you say?"

"A Union slaver and a Confederate tilling free soil. A peculiar historical oddity. It doesn't undermine the rightness of the Northern cause, but it's instructive: Tyranny can take root anywhere. I mean, just imagine how the South could have spun that story if they had the technology in your pocket."

I reflexively felt around my pocket, just to make sure my phone had survived the ride.

We dismounted at the sprawling colonial Fairfax Court House. I gazed up with unease.

"Something the matter?" Mason inquired.

"No," I insisted. "Just...my dad was a lawyer...courthouses stir up memories, that's all."

Mason studied me intently. "Understandable. But we won't be long. Listen and observe. You're here to learn."

As Mason and Kennedy traipsed up the courthouse steps, I stopped to read the torn remnants of a poster affixed to the wall:

Whereas it is represented to the general assembly, That there hath lately been a great increase of idle and disorderly persons in some parts of this commonwealth, and unless some stringent laws are passed to restrain and prevent such vagrancy and idleness, the state will be overrun with dissolate and abandoned characters, to the great detriment of the public weal...

Be it enacted by the general assembly, That the overseers of the poor...or the special county police, or the police of any corporation...shall be and hereby empowered and required, upon discovering any vagrant or vagrants within their respective counties or corporations...to require a warrant for apprehending such vagrant or vagrants...

The Vagrancy Act? This law effectively made it a crime to be black and unemployed – "idle" – in the Commonwealth of Virginia, even after slavery had been abolished under the Thirteenth Amendment. Vagrancy Acts represented an early attempt by embittered Southerners to re-constitute slavery under another name.

The wagons. I tore off the parchment and followed my colleagues into the commotion of the courthouse lobby.

Flanked by six Union soldiers and a bearded deputy, an elderly white man with a curly black wig sobbed as he clutched a spirited brown-haired girl of three with penetrating hazel eyes.

"Thaddeus," Mason said warmly. "It delights me to see Emmaleigh unharmed."

The elderly Thaddeus Stevens steadied his clubfoot against his cane.

"Her Mother's spirit she has." Mason squeezed Emmaleigh's cheek. She swayed like Shirley Temple, fiddling with the red ribbons in her hair.

"May it never be far from me again," Thaddeus replied, kissing Emmaleigh on the forehead. "Run along, flower. Uncle Thaddeus has business."

Emmaleigh took the hand of a Union soldier and skipped away.

Thaddeus brushed his coat. I was awestruck. The Pennsylvania Congressman was a pillar of righteous fire, co-author of the Thirteenth Amendment. At present he lent his hand to drafting the Fourteenth, guaranteeing equality and due process to every person on American soil – a broadside against "Black Codes" like Virginia's Vagrancy Act. The moving photograph in *The Liberator* that morning had depicted a younger and more energized Thaddeus Stevens. The version before me was aged and worn, though no less zealous.

Thaddeus turned to the deputy. "I wish to examine the accused."

The deputy led us into the adjacent jailhouse. In a corner cell, a black man in his early twenties lay curled on the floor. In the next cell, a young black woman in her late teens wearing a blue tie scarf hunched against the wall.

"Morgan brought them here on kidnapping charges," the deputy announced. "But he also claims them as vagrants. He'll fight tooth an' nail to bring 'em back to Carolina, no matter what you say."

Thaddeus scowled. "Let me mind that cursed bounty hunter."

The deputy departed. Thaddeus turned to address the prisoners.

"Tell me your names."

"Immanuel," said the man, rubbing his eyes. "That's my wife, Mariah."

"She can't speak for herself?"

Mariah sat up. "I can."

"Good. I am Congressman Thaddeus Stevens. I would very much like to help you out of this predicament, but first I need answers. Understood?"

They nodded.

"Where are you from?"

"Sparta," Immanuel answered. "Tennessee."

"Tennessee? How did you come to be arrested in North Carolina?"

Immanuel sat up. "We, uh…we 'scaped the plantation after we heard Lincoln set us free. Met Miss Moses at Combahee an' she took us to General Hunter at Port Royal. We followed 'em for the rest o' the war but when it ended we couldn't find work. So we went up into the Waxhaw Mountains to hunt."

Thaddeus pointed at Mariah. "Did you take my niece?"

"Yes sir," Mariah answered plainly. "We took 'er."

Thaddeus swallowed. "When?"

"Two weeks ago. From the cabin, while Morgan's guards were sleepin'."

"Morgan…" Thaddeus echoed, contemptuously.

Mason interjected, his interest piqued. "A cabin, you said?"

Mariah nodded.

"This cabin: was there anything unusual about it?"

"They tarred it," Immanuel said.

"Tar, you said?"

"Bled through the walls," Mariah added. "We went inside and found lil' Emmaleigh huddlin' in the corner. We din't know how long she'd been there, but I knew we couldn' just leave her for the Devil."

Mason narrowed his eyes. "It is not the Devil who haunts that cabin," he whispered.

Thaddeus continued the inquisition. "How did you know that Emmaleigh was inside?"

Mariah's eyes went out of focus. "Whispers. Same ones that told us to flee the Atwater plantation."

I jumped to life.

"Atwater?" I started before Kennedy shushed me.

"What happened at the plantation?" Mason probed.

Mariah shivered. "I worked in the house. One day a foreign man came – a Prince, he called himself – an' gave Mr. Atwater gold an' silver to use the barn and slaves for an experiment. They coated the inside with tar, jus' like the cabin, took the slaves into the barn, one, sometimes two or three at a time, an' lock 'em in for days. When they came out, they were...different. Killed their minds, it seemed. Like it split 'em right in two."

Immanuel interjected. "Not jus' black folks. Poor white folks, too. Came out chilly cold, no warmth in 'em."

"Ev'ry night we heard 'em," Mariah continued.

"What did you hear?" Mason pressed gently.

"Bad whispers. Demons that twis' a man's mind. Thas' why we 'scaped. Thas' why we took Emmaleigh. Ain' no way we were gonna let her suffer like that."

Thaddeus' eyes watered. "You have my gratitude."

Thaddeus turned to leave and motioned for us to join him outside. His façade broke.

"It's beginning. Grant may have subdued the Confederacy, but König's war has only begun. Here..."

Thaddeus pulled a clipping from his coat pocket.

"...this is circulating in Pennsylvania, infectious as a plague."

It was a political cartoon, one I'd shown in class countless times as an example of widespread white opposition to the Freedman's Bureau, which fed and clothed newly emancipated slaves. It depicted an oversized black man with exaggerated lips lounging while a smaller white man chopped wood at his feet. It claimed that the Bureau was an attempt to "keep the Negro in idleness at the expense of the White Man."

Thaddeus handed me the cartoon, and I grasped it...

((...spendin' the white man's hard-earned taxes educatin' lazy niggers ...))

What the hell was that? It was faint yet audible...like a silent echo resonating deep within.

I shook it off. Mason peeked over my shoulder as I studied it.

"It bears the mark of König's Censor," he observed. "Down to the exaggeration of a black man's 'undesirable' physical traits. If I didn't know better, I'd almost believe the Bureau is the scam of lazy black vagrants."

"A lie!" Thaddeus thundered. "The Bureau does the work of Christ! Northerners underestimate the brutality of the freedman's condition, his need for aid. Our ignorance renders us vulnerable."

Mason and Thaddeus parlayed as they walked back to the courthouse, Kennedy in quiet tow. I began to pace, ensconcing myself in the cartoon, turning those whispers over in my head. Unconsciously I wandered back into the cells...where my heart broke.

Immanuel and Mariah leaned into the bars, gripping one another by the hand. Mariah tried in vain to bury her head in her husband's chest. It was so real...so tender...so desperate...I had to say something – anything – to give them hope...

"It won't always be like this."

Immanuel scowled. I fumbled for clarification.

"What I mean is...it gets better. I promise."

Immanuel laughed. "Who are ya? John Brown?"

"John Brown," I breathed.

"Yeah. John Brown? Harper's Ferry? Crazy cracker promised to take on the Army by himself an' free us all, then got himself hung. A promise ain't but piss in a bucket. Hell, I 'spect when I get to the Pearly Gates, Saint Peter gonna call me a nigger and send me to the fields. So g'on believin' in yo' fairy tales. As for me an' my house, we choose to remember."

My knees went weak. "C-come again?"

"I ain't got the air in my lungs to say it again."

Mariah studied me. "Y'ain't never seen two Negroes in a cell who done nothin' wrong?"

I stammered. "Where I'm from...everyone's equal."

Mariah's eyes fluttered. "I don' believe ya."

I swallowed my tongue.

"Lotsa times, even good white folks like you think, 'Thank the Lord I am so good, I fed some scraps to a damn dog.' We ain't people to you. We're a problem."

"Lincoln said he freed us," Immanuel added. "But it's still happenin'."

((...see no evil...but it's still happening...))

I slid down the bars. I couldn't take my eyes off Immanuel. His caustic and dismissive wit echoed a young man who defied me at every turn.

These are Tyson's ancestors.

The couple returned to their comfort. I slogged back outside and paced around the grass, trying to make sense of what I had seen and heard. The world never felt so small...

((...as for me and my house, we choose to remember...))

...as I brooded, I noticed something thin and shiny sticking from the grass...

...a hairpin, tied to a red ribbon. I knelt to examine it.

Emmaleigh...

"You mutton-shunting hornswoggle!"

Thaddeus' voice rose in ire from the town square. I quickly dropped the hairpin into my satchel and raced around the corner, where my heart skipped a beat.

At the base of the courtyard steps, Thaddeus, Mason, Kennedy and two Union soldiers stood toe-to-toe with three men on horseback...two deputies...

...and a lawman in a White Hat...

...teeth stained corn yellow...

...

...*that's him.*

I had only seen him in visions, but I knew it was him. His leathery face was covered in white stubble, a bayonet scar tracing from his left temple to the corner of his right lip. I watched Kennedy shake with rage at the presence of this man, lifeless and hollow, seemingly animated by nothing.

"Congressman," the White Hat Man rasped with a drawl. "I know you don' respect the rights o' the states, but Carolina has a lawful claim on these niggers what stole your kin. An' I know..."

The White Hat Man laughed.

"...I *know* y'all wanna see 'em hang for it."

Thaddeus ground his teeth, full of nervous tension. "I see through your charade, Mr. Morgan. These are not Emmaleigh's abductors. *You are.*"

Morgan spat. "*Sheriff* Morgan. An' you think a lawman kidnapped a Senator's niece, or lazy niggers lookin' for ransom?"

"A lawman, you say? Spare me your sophistry! Emmaleigh disappeared the very night your man Booth shot Lincoln. That's no coincidence. Or am I to believe freedmen targeted the niece of a devoted abolitionist?"

Morgan smiled. "Desp'rate folks *always* bite th'hand that feeds."

Thaddeus drew within an inch of Morgan's nose, studying his scar intently.

"I know who you really are. This," he handled the star-shaped badge on Morgan's lapel, "is a false flag. You're as lawless as Hell itself."

Morgan whistled. "Quite the legend, Congressman. That soothe yer conscience? Knowin' youse a lawmaker that spits on the law?"

"Some men," Mason charged, "serve a Higher Law."

"An' some men," Morgan replied, shooting Kennedy a devious smile, "find they'selves dead 'pon it."

Kennedy boiled, teetering on his toes. "You missed."

Morgan narrowed his eyes at Kennedy. "Sooner or later, that lead in yer head gon' gitcha. Tick tock, Jack."

The taunt rocked Kennedy to his core. He clenched his fists. Morgan laughed and turned his head, locking eyes with mine. They burned hot with recognition.

"You too, John Brown," Morgan laughed. "Tick. Tock."

My flesh curled. Morgan looked the Union soldiers up and down, tipped his hat, and rode away.

"Corporal Bishop," Thaddeus said to one of the soldiers, "instruct the sheriff's deputy to release Immanuel and Mariah into federal protective custody, to be transported to any destination in the North they choose."

Corporal Bishop hesitated. "Sir, we don't have the authority to so command…"

"Did I stutter, Corporal?"

"No, sir…"

"Our authority comes from on high. Leave these innocents in Virginia lock-up, and they're as good as dead."

Thaddeus pressed his cane into Corporal Bishop's chest.

"I demand their release. Is. That. Clear?"

Corporal Bishop swallowed and saluted, then flew back to the Court House. Thaddeus exhaled as he watched Morgan and his men disappear around the corner.

"He's one of them, isn't he, George? One of the Brothers. One of the *Six*."

Mason nodded silently. Thaddeus shuddered.

"I've never been in the presence of a greater evil."

"You held your ground," Mason assured him. "That's the measure of resolve we need for this fight."

Thaddeus coughed and leaned against his cane.

"Fight," he said, ponderously. "It seems all we do is fight. This bloody war..."

He waved his hand in the air in frustration.

"...this *bloody, stinking war*, and all that came with it. But emancipation won't be the end, equality under the law won't be the end. The damn war..."

Thaddeus looked to me, sorrowfully, bitterly.

"...the damn war *widens*. Now I'm not fighting gray-clad slavers or copper-headed cowards, but the dark force behind them. And *you*..."

Thaddeus pointed at Mason.

"...a slaver dead three quarters of a century, you come with all your ghosts and call me to fight a war that never ends against an enemy who never surrenders. How..."

Thaddeus wiped the sweat from his brow. Mason approached and steadied the aging man with his hand.

"...how is a weary old man supposed to rest?"

Mason smiled. "With a stiff drink."

~

A spectral speakeasy lies just beyond the backdoor of the wood-and-sawdust Wilcoxen Tavern. It exists in another realm altogether, beyond space and time, its patrons jovially imbibing spirits that smell nothing like liquor.

Hours had passed since our confrontation with Morgan. I sat alone with Kennedy at one end of a long table, eavesdropping on Mason and Thaddeus on the other:

"You're telling me that was Jackson's cabin?" Thaddeus whispered.

Mason nodded, *"König's first true American Apprentice...his spirit lingers..."*

König again. A thousand questions swirled.

Thaddeus threw back his drink and set it down hard. *"Miserable wretch."*

"Of all the Faces of Tyranny," Mason continued somberly, *"König's is undoubtedly the most hideous…"*

As the two droned on, I watched Kennedy quietly rifling through a stack of photos. He stopped on one I knew very well…of his own son, saluting his casket in 1963.

"Your son was a great man," I offered.

Silence.

"I mean, John Jr. was – "

"I stole these from Jackie," Kennedy said drily.

"Pardon?"

"From Hyannis in '64. She…"

Kennedy paused to gather himself.

"…she was having another nightmare about Dallas. I whispered that everything would be okay. I sat by her all night. I knew she couldn't hear me. I just wanted her to sleep easy."

Kennedy flipped to a photo of his bride in her wedding gown.

"Ever been madly in love, Ben?"

A lump rose in my throat. "Yes."

Kennedy looked longingly into the photo. "What's her name?"

I fiddled with my wedding band. "Michelle. But she's g–"

The doors swung open. Harper and Woodhull made a beeline to Mason and Thaddeus, parting a sea of patrons. Harper whispered into Mason's ear, and his eyes turned grim. The two spies ran out of the club as Thaddeus lowered his head. Mason stood and loomed over me.

"There's been an ambush."

Seven

The Gospel of Independence

We rode hard in pursuit of the marauders who killed the four Union soldiers transporting Immanuel and Mariah to safety in Auburn, New York. They absconded with their captives southwest, likely *en route* to the Atwater plantation in Tennessee.

"For God knows what purpose," Mason noted somberly.

We caught up to them outside Charlottesville and made camp two miles north at the edge of a flowing creek. Through a powerful spyglass I watched two guards harassing Mariah by the fire. Fifty yards away, Immanuel shivered in a Conestoga wagon piled with shackled black men.

"Why do they have so many?" I asked.

"Insurance," Harper said cynically. "Many will freeze crossing the Appalachians."

I paced anxiously by the fire that night, fretting over the fates of the newly re-enslaved.

"There's nothing we can do for them tonight," Mason insisted. "Get some rest."

I retired to my tent; for the first time the world seemed to slow down. A dull, throbbing headache crept in, and I could hear my heart pulsing between my ears; between *thwumps!* the whispers rose to the surface…

((… the decisive battle of the Revolution…))

((…Today, you join the Revolution…))

…Today.

The day I left Washington, thirty-six hours ago and more than a century-and-a-half from now.

Armageddon, the End of History, dangling off the edge of the river of time.

March 10, 2020?

None of it made any damn sense.

If time is a river, then I'm the rock God skipped upstream…

…the adrenaline ebbed…my eyelids dropped, and all I could see was that violent shade of crimson drenching the sky…the babbling sounds of the rushing creek brought me deeper…

…and deeper…

…until the crimson dissolved…

…and the skies turned baby blue…

…

…over the grassy banks of the South Platte…

…Michelle snatches the essay from my hand.

"Benji!" she bites, hints of her native French rolling from her tongue. "We had one rule for today!"

"Shell, it's one essay."

Michelle flips through the thick stack like playing cards, as if to say, "Really?"

"I'm a first-year teacher. I'm gonna grade papers on Saturdays."

"Not at a picnic, you don't."

I pick grass at the edge of the blanket. "You know how stir crazy I get."

"Fine." Michelle sighs and leans into my lap.

"What are you doing?"

"We'll grade this… 'Peter Collins'… together."

She taps my cheek and reads aloud:

"'Our rights come from God. We're free like our pioneer forefathers to defend ourselves and property from people who would take it from us. This land is America's inheritance, our Promised Land, that God gave us."

Michelle sits up.

"So…God commanded Americans to conquer Natives?"

I feign indignation like Foghorn Leghorn. "Of course a godless French commie doesn't understand America's Manifest Destiny."

"You need to correct this, Benji!"

I grab the essay back. "I can't tell a kid what to believe. First Amendment, babe."

"No, but...you can expose him to better ideas...or challenge his logic? This is a really dangerous idea for someone so impressionable. Did his papa teach him this?"

I roll my eyes. "Drew warned me not to marry a shrink."

Michelle punches me in the chest. "I'm serious!"

"Okay! I'll fix it! I'll save Peter Collins from himself."

"Yeah?"

I toy with a strand of her hair. "Yeah."

She pulls me in for a soft kiss, holding it for a beat before releasing.

"But not today," she says, nuzzling into my chest.

"Then what are we gonna do all day?"

"Pursue happiness, dumbass. Together."

We repose in silence. The South Platte runs its course...

...on the other bank, a man bats a lazy fly ball into the air. His boy snares it and tosses it back.

The father beams. "Nice catch, John!"

My breath catches...

...it won't release...Michelle feels heavy...

"Sweetheart?"

...her eyes are still, her arms a millstone around my neck...her skin fades to gray...

...a Bluebird rests upon her head...

((...chirp, chirp, Benji...tweet tweet...))

...Michelle crumbles to dust...

...a child screams...

...

"JOHN!"

...

...I awakened in a cold sweat, just as a shadow passed my tent.

"I saw it, George," I heard Kennedy say bitterly. *"I can't help him. We're finished."*

Moments later, horse and rider galloped away.

I stared at the ceiling of the tent, pondering Kennedy's words...

Bzzzzzzt...

...impossible.

I pulled my phone out of my satchel:

You need to correct this, Benji. You need to make this right.

I inspected the phone. No cracks, no dings.

How is it drawing power? Where is the signal coming from?

I stuck it back in the satchel; my hand brushed against another object.

The hairpin...

...a thousand whispers flurried...

...and the seed of an idea took hold...

...

...I found Mason next to the campfire, buried in a thick, self-illumined book. Above him rose a tree with leaves like white flowers.

"George, is this a tree or a flower?"

"Both," he replied. "The dogwood is a tree *and* a flower."

"Kind of a contradiction."

"A paradox. Like how the light from this book is both wave and particle, or so that funny little German tells me."

"Einstein?"

"Yes. Strange fellow."

I pushed the logs to let the fire breathe.

"Out with it, Benjamin."

I hesitated. "Jack isn't fully dead, is he?"

Mason peered over his book. "No. But it's only a matter of time."

"So this is...an out-of-body experience?"

"Something like that. Isn't that what you saw? Through his eyes?"

I shuddered. "I've never felt pain like that."

"I imagine a bullet to the head might do that."

"No. I mean mental. Emotional. Separated from his family, neither dead nor alive. He's miserable."

Mason cut to the chase. "Don't take his griping personally, Benjamin. He'll return before dawn. He knows the Gospel is his last best hope."

I laughed uneasily. "Thaddeus speaks of Christ, now you with the Gospel. Am I the only one not catching religion?"

"I'm not talking about the New Testament."

Mason set his book aside.

"I crossed over two centuries ago and still don't understand all the Mysteries of Nature's God. But the Gospel we preach is not sectarian; it reflects a universal truth, the last best hope for all humanity: the Gospel of Independence."

"That's both sanctimonious and sacrilegious," I said.

Mason shook his finger. "Another paradox, no? As it is, 'gospel' merely means 'good news.' And what is the Declaration of Independence if not good news for all?"

"*Is* the Declaration," I observed. "Present tense."

"You're catching on. Few grasp that the Revolution is still ongoing Today...or what it really means."

I squinted into the fire. "A Masonic treasure?"

Mason laughed. "Nothing so esoteric. This Gospel is plain as day to those who have eyes to see. You know the basics: all human beings are by nature equal in worth, free to live and enjoy the fruits of honest labor. The people create a constitutional government to protect those natural rights against those who would lay siege to them, so we may pursue our highest and best desires. So it is written...but words alone can't pierce the darkness. The Gospel reflects a Higher Law inscribed on our hearts and minds. It is only when Liberty's people choose to live by that Law that we overcome this malevolent world she was born into."

"A Higher Law. How could we possibly know it?"

Mason leaned in. "Isn't it self-evident?"

The crickets ceased...the birds of morning took up their song...

"It consists of four cardinal principles...

...the Law of Dust...

...and the Law of Rust...

...the Law of Seeds...

...and the Law of Weeds."

Mason opened his book to a familiar decree.

"You've read the Declaration. But has it ever read you?"

As Mason read, the words floated off the page:

*"When in the course of **human** events it becomes necessary for one **people** to dissolve the political bands which have connected them with another and to assume among the powers of the earth, the separate and equal station to which the **Laws of Nature** and of **Nature's God** entitles them, a decent respect to the opinions of **mankind** requires that they should declare the causes which impel them to separation."*

Mason studied the effervescent phrases.

"There is a pattern here. Do you see it?"

I nodded. "Human. People. Mankind. Nature and Nature's God."

"Naturally, people come first," Mason insisted. "'Democracy' means *demos kratos*: 'people ruling.' We, the people, determined to shake off the yoke of Britain and assumed our separate and independent station as masters of our own lives. Why? Because by nature, each of us is sovereign, and none may compel another to stand or kneel before them. Follow?"

I nodded.

"The political is personal, and vice versa. We experience life as individuals. Persons. But together, by the contract of the Constitution we comprise a people, equal stakeholders in our 'republic' or *res publia*, 'property of the people.' Historically, peoples have been defined by blood, tongue or creed. Many believe America is such a nation, but Independence contemplates something radical: a people defined solely by their love of Liberty, forged together by bonds of mutual affection."

"Such affection is in short supply," I offered.

"True. My generation was no exception. We received the Gospel message even as we enslaved millions. The Revolutionary seed grew alongside centuries of weeds: noxious practices that proved most resilient, as a virus against a host. But even in our darkness, Liberty showed us what we truly are."

Mason closed the book.

"Nothing but *dust*."

Mason blew a layer of dust off the cover. It carried to the edge of the clearing and separated into eighteen pillars, twisting into barefoot boys and girls of every color. One boy held a broken tree branch; fifty feet away, a girl tossed a smooth stone in his direction. The boy swung and sent the stone skyward as the children chased after.

Their game of ball was glorious.

Mason read aloud:

> *"We hold these truths to be **self-evident**, that all men are **created equal**, and endowed by their Creator with certain **unalienable rights**, that among them are **Life**, **Liberty** and the **pursuit of Happiness**."*

The batter crossed home plate.

"Walker is his name," Mason said. "The field's best player…and most valuable person."

I winced. "How?"

"Isn't it obvious?"

"He's a talented player. But he's dust, like the others."

"Like you."

I raised my brow.

"'For dust you are, and to dust you shall return.'"

"So I'm nothing?"

"Not nothing. *Everything.*"

Mason pinched my arm.

"Your mortal body is comprised of the same elements of the soil from which all life grows. Your inherent worth is natural. If we stripped you of your house, your papers and effects, your identity, heritage, and accomplishments, and set you upon one side of a fence, you would be no greater or lesser than any on the other. Your humanity does not begin or end at any border."

"If I'm on the other side of the fence," I countered, "I'm not entitled to the rights of another people."

Mason sighed. "Don't confuse the privileges of citizens with the natural rights of persons. A man may lock himself in his own home, but he is not entitled to inflict suffering on the beggar outside, nor ought he close his doors to innocents fleeing bandits. We are all limbs of Adam, arising at every compass point to pursue the one thing we desire above all else."

"Happiness."

"Yes! And its pursuit is futile without the Greatest Love."

I flinched.

"Only the loveless heart kills, steals and destroys. Liberty's great paradox is that we either live free together or die alone in chains. This is the Law of Dust: Love your neighbor as yourself, and you will both be free."

A determined baserunner took off for second. Walker moved to dodge the runner as he slid hard at his legs, flipping him over to land flat on his stomach. The field erupted in savage violence as the sky turned cardinal red.

In the end, only the base runner's team remained. He took to the mound and spread his arms outward, as his teammates danced around him singing his praises.

"Anson," Mason said. "A devilish boy. A shame there are no umpires to hold him accountable."

"They called their own balls and strikes," I said.

"They governed themselves until – "

" – Anson claimed the game for himself."

"Rules. Umpires. Foul lines. They protect against cheats who play in the Shadows, who defy the Law of Dust."

Anson crowed from the mound.

"That Shadow haunts us both, Benjamin."

I balked. "I'm no saint, but I never spiked an infielder. I've never killed anyone either."

"No, but to deny your Shadow exists is to see it persist. Remember, evil has no substance of its own. As darkness is the absence of light, evil is the absence of good. Where light and darkness meet lies the realm of the Shadow where Liberty and Tyranny contend: *this* realm, *this* world. The Shadow both makes government necessary and requires its limitation, a balance to protect us against those who would destroy us: ourselves."

Anson's teammates knelt before him; Anson moved around the mound extending a chain from his belt, fastening metallic binds around their necks.

"*I, alone,*" he hissed.

Gratefully, they sang: "*We, alone!*"

"The so-called 'virtue' of selfishness," Mason breathed. "Tyranny never returns affection. Like Narcissus, he favors only those in whom he sees himself, and then only until they impede his ends…"

The singing grew softer as Anson's teammates grew weaker. Enraged, Anson struck the earth with a branch. One-by-one his teammates fell into the abyss; the weight of their falling chains squeezed the air from his lungs as he crowed:

"*I, alone!*"

Anson choked his last and turned to stone, then crumbled to ashes.

"Liberty and Tyranny begin and end in our hearts," Mason continued. "And for nearly fifty-seven years the spirit of John Fitzgerald Kennedy has, in his difficult state, placed his hope in humanity choosing Liberty…so he may find peace."

Bonkers. That makes absolutely no sense.

"That," I thought aloud, "is a doozy of a JFK conspiracy."

Mason closed the book, its pages still gleaming. "I certainly didn't write the rules of this absurd game, but I know this one for certain: a willing Champion is essential to setting the world right…"

((…you need to make this right…))

…my thoughts turned to Thaddeus. As a history teacher, I had always been impressed by his devotion to the cause of abolition. To meet him in the flesh was another matter entirely. His zeal, his compassion for the downtrodden was something I'd only seen in one other person in my life. He wasn't merely a righteous orator; he had courage to match his conviction. In that moment before the fire, a fresh boldness stirred inside me.

I studied the ground. "You said Today I would be joining the Revolution. That means I obey a Higher Law than the laws of men. Just like Martin Luther King said. Right?"

Mason nodded slowly. "In principle, yes. A Champion of Liberty takes direct action against Tyranny…not for his own selfish ends, mind you, but to defend his neighbor."

"As you took action against King George."

"Of course. Principle demanded we correct a gross violation of our rights."

"What about your slaves?"

Mason cocked his head. "Pardon?"

"Would the slaves who worked Gunston Hall have been justified in taking direct action against you?"

Mason squirmed. "You test me, Benjamin. Of course they would have."

He looked away, sorrowfully.

"I inherited my slaves. I thought it abhorrent, but I was comfortable and lacked the courage of my conviction."

"Right," I said, growing bolder. "And your cowardice had consequences for my generation. You demanded a Bill of Rights for those already free, but left slavery intact. You violated the Law of Dust."

Mason grew teary-eyed. "It's true. In Liberty's name slavery ought to have been abolished from the start, but we compromised to keep the South in the Union, in the name of 'states' rights'…"

Mason trailed off, staring into the middle distance.

"I am no demigod, Benjamin. My hands are no less filthy than any other from gripping the chains of bondage. I know we failed millions, and millions more have suffered in turn. But I must ask: who are you, of all people, to pass judgment upon my head?"

I drew back. "Excuse you?"

Mason leaned in. "I know my sins. Death has sharpened my sense of them ten thousand-fold. I marched boldly to my grave waving the flag of my own righteousness only to find it a filthy rag. I have been weighed upon the cosmic scales and found wanting. That, my dear boy, is why I am here with you in this forest: like you, I strive to redeem myself in her eyes."

"Whose eyes?"

Mason trembled, ever so slightly, on the verge of tears. "Why are you here, Benjamin?"

I slunk back, pulling the hairpin from my pocket. "To alter the Course of Human Events. To clean up the mess your generation left me."

Mason scoffed. *"The mess that we left?* Did you truly glean *nothing* from this lesson? Take the plank from your own eye! Or do you truly believe yourself incapable of the cruelty I inflicted upon my brethren?"

He watched me playing with the pin; his eyes widened with sudden realization.

"Benjamin," he said nervously, "what do you plan to do?"

I shrugged. "I plead the Fifth."

Mason squinted, pinching the bridge of his nose. "Agents Harper and Woodhull are scouting the road ahead. Be patient. Don't act rashly."

"You know, George," I said, "I've never been good at keeping promises to people I love. But I promised Tyson's mother I would look out for him as if he were my own. Last night through Jack's eyes I saw that young man, who hasn't seen his own deadbeat father in three years, hang from a tree. Today I saw him alive in Immanuel, and something clicked. Now I see his chains. I see his evil inheritance."

I twirled the pin.

"I saw the Capitol fall and the sky turn red. Some way, somehow, that can be traced back to the Atwaters' misfortunes. But Jack said I can shape the Course of Human Events. Tonight, I can set the captives free...I can make things right...and somehow, against all logic, save the world in my time."

Mason removed his bifocals. "Let me see if I understand: you believe your role as Champion is as some sort of...self-anointed Savior?"

"I have a duty to obey a Higher Law, don't I?"

"I don't believe for a second that your motives are so noble. Who do you 'love?'"

"Excuse me?"

"You said you wanted to keep promises to 'people you love.' Then you mentioned the boy's mother."

I fumed. "Tread lightly. I still love my wife."

Mason laughed. "Michelle? When was the last time you even spoke to her?"

I stood and paced, resisting the urge to punch George Mason in the face.

"Assuming you succeed on this suicide mission," he continued, "how will you display your trophies? Hmm? Do you expect your beloved to believe you when you tell her you emancipated two slaves in 1866? Or will she read about your tragic death in some obscure volume of history? I've known hare-brained schemes, but even John Brown had the sense to ask for help before he attempted to end slavery in one night!"

Mason turned his head and laughed.

"I should call upon him for moral support... and to say 'I told you so' as *you* hang from a tree."

I spat. "If I hang, I hang."

Mason grew somber. "Benjamin. Please. You are not here merely to play hero. The battle is deeper; there is so much more at stake."

"So I'm told. I've also been told to take direct action against Tyranny."

"Benjamin, I forbid – "

"I dare you to stop me! You may be a 'ghost,' but I know you're bound to that pudgy body..."

Mason threw his hands up in exasperation.

"You are the Champion," he sighed. "Do what you must."

He retrieved his belongings and entered his tent.

"And live...or die...with the consequences."

I tamped out the fire and woke Noxie, saddling her up for a midnight ride.

I left everything behind save the hairpin, a canteen and the coin. When I was fifty yards out, the dogwood burst into flames, sealing itself from the forest as if in a bubble. It was ash in seconds.

A sign of good fortune. I rode off.

I had a tyrant to overthrow.

~

I tip-toed up to Mariah, who lay between Morgan's guards, both deeply unconscious.

She awoke suddenly. I covered her lips and mouthed instructions.

"Can...you...ride?"

She nodded.

"Silver horse," I motioned. *"Follow the creek north."*

She murmured. *"Imm-n-ml?"*

"We'll...be right...behind you. Do...you...trust me?"

Mariah nodded. I held her hand as she carefully extricated herself from between the deep-slumbering henchmen and set her bare feet on the ground. As I expected, the henchmen were too drunk to notice.

"Go."

Mariah looked to the wagon, then scampered away.

I quietly stole away to the wagon. The arrangement inside was shocking: ten men lined on each side, crammed like sardines. Immanuel slept on the edge across from Song Man, shackled by the wrists and ankles. I inserted the pin into his ankle chains and sprang it with a *pop!* Immanuel startled awake; I quieted him before he stirred the others. He glanced in panic toward where Mariah slept.

"She's...free...we...need...to...go...now!"

Immanuel held out his hands. I worked the pin into the keyhole until I heard it *click!*

The others awoke. From the crevice between sleep and wakefulness escaped their silent whispers:

((...you gon' free me too?...))

((...white ghost gonna get us killed...))

((...he can't take all of us...))

((...Vict'ry Man, give me water from the fountain...))

Song Man eyed my canteen. I brought it to his lips and he drank. His heart whispered again:

((...I get it, Vict'ry man. Freedom is for you, not for Elijah Gates...))

Gates? I paused above him for a moment. I fiddled with the hairpin, hesitating.

"Don't even think about it," Elijah whispered. *"I won't trade my life for your conscience."*

My breath caught. Immanuel nudged me, and we set off into the woods...

...

...ten minutes passed before Immanuel spoke.

"Where's my wife an' baby?"

Baby? "Mariah took my horse back to camp."

"Only reason I'm comin' wit' ya is because y'already freed her. Until we safe it's a bucket o' hot piss."

"Relax. The guards are asleep."

We stepped down an embankment and came face-to-face with the awakened.

"Lucky for me, John Brown, I ain't *never* asleep," Morgan announced on horseback, pistol drawn. His deputies flanked him with long rifles.

Immanuel's eyes widened.

"It really must be you. Only John Brown would die twice tryin'a free niggers."

I stammered. "Y-you couldn't kill Kennedy."

Morgan growled. "Lucky for you, I'm a better shot than that pussy Oswald."

He turned to his deputies.

"Let's give these critters a head start."

Morgan flashed his yellows.

"Sixty…!"

At fifty-nine, we fled.

~

Oomph! I tripped and hit the ground. I hobbled forward, knee on fire, then stumbled over an anthill and fell again. I wheezed and rolled onto my back.

The grass rustled. Footsteps crinkled and crackled, nimble and quick.

"Hello?"

They slowed down. Emmaleigh stepped out of the grass, panting. A ribbon was missing from her hair.

"Emmaleigh? What are you doing here?"

The whinnying of horses echoed through the trees. Morgan barked at his lackeys.

"John Brown's mine. Niggers are yours."

Emmaleigh pulled the coin from my pocket and closed her eyes.

"Where's Uncle Thaddeus?" I asked.

"There he is!"

My heart leapt to my throat.

A hundred yards away, Immanuel cried the terrible lonesome cry of twilight. I couldn't bear to listen. I had no choice.

"Niiiice straight line…ain't you know to serpentine, nigger?"

One shot…

...one yelp...

...one splash of his black body, dead in the creek.

"Tom!" Morgan crowed, *"why cain't ya kill Yanks like that?"*

"I don't know, but y'ever tried to shoot a nigger at night? Can't see shit!"

I dry heaved. Resolutely, Emmaleigh stood and yelled.

"OVER HERE!"

I panicked. "What are you doing?"

"There's John Brown!" the White Hat Man yelled.

Emmaleigh knelt and locked her hazel eyes with mine.

"Go! Leave!"

"Where?" I sobbed. "How?"

Emmaleigh stuck the coin on my chest as Morgan yelled, *"Bye-bye, John!"*

There was a blinding light...

...and a shot in the dark.

Eight

Underground

The sound of gunfire is far worse than the sight. To see is to *know*; to hear is to *imagine*, a torturous sliver of uncertainty. I *saw* that Nazi; I *heard* Immanuel. The scream. The splash. The perverse joy of his killers. Morgan's sick cackle as he sent me packing for midnight:

"Bye-bye John!"

That's all I heard.

All day. Every night.

For three months.

"Fire!" Muskets rang through rusted bars; another traitor dropped like a sack of flour as the Star-Spangled Banner reigned above. She presided over every execution and every one of the General's damn parades. When the Gulf winds stilled, her stars wept and stripes bled.

Her colors do run.

I awoke in the bayou on December 21, 1814, to croaking frogs and the sharp end of a bayonet. They dragged me to this dungeon where they stripped me and soaked me, then introduced me to Titus.

"Where's Cochrane's fleet?" growled the tall man with cruel eyes.

I trembled.

"Stop shakin', ya stir crazy sum'bitch! What's yer name?"

Shake. Stir. The dam broke. I began laughing hysterically.

"The hell is so funny?"

"Bond," I spat, cackling like a crow. *"James* Bond. *Hahahaha!"*

One punch, and the wind fled my lungs.

Titus made other visits over the weeks, each more cruel and unusual than the last. He grew strangely obsessed with me and my likeness, staring into my face for hours, telling me what I looked like now. I had no mirror; I could only see myself through his eyes, as relayed through his lips.

"Ugly as sin," he would mutter. "Like a mangy mutt."

"Why are you doing this?" I would plead. "Just let me go."

"Me?" he would reply. "I ain't doin' nothin'. You're doin' it to yourself."

It was a mind game, and he won by flaying my wits to their last end – all in the name of the General. The General saw himself in the violent Tennessee farmhand, or so the guard whispered when the night lay still. The boy showed me some measure of mercy, but fear tempered his pity for an alien from the swamp. So the good soldier Abner Collins played along that I was spy and traitor, lest he incur the wrath of Commander Titus Atwater.

Another man died in New Orleans today. I didn't know his crime against the reign of Major General Andrew Jackson. I couldn't have cared less.

~

I adjust the pamphlet. An array of coffins illuminates the overhead, proclaiming "An Account of Some of the Bloody Deeds of General Jackson."

"This so-called 'Coffin Handbill'," I say, "represents eighty-four Americans Andrew Jackson is alleged to have executed without trial during the War of 1812. John Quincy Adams distributed this as campaign literature during the 1828 Presidential Election. When we see a claim like this, what do we do?"

"Trust, but verify," the class repeats back.

"That's right. Vet it and source it. Those are your marching orders for your essay, due next Friday."

I write the prompt on the whiteboard.

"Hell yeah he was!" Reid exclaims.

"Eight hundred words using five primary sources, plus the Handbill. Questions?"

Ethan McQueen raises his hand. "Why are you doing this to us?"

"Personal spite, Ethan."

The bell rings. My students herd themselves into the hallway. I catch Tyson.

"Detention's here again today."

The jackass smirks and slumps out. What a waste of natural ability.

"Mr. Upson?"

Mackenzie snaps me out of my daze.

"Ms. Masuda!" I exclaim. "What's up?"

Mac points at the Handbill. "If all this is true, how did Jackson win?"

I spread my hands. "Do we know it's true? You could get away with a lot before the Internet."

"You can get away with a lot through the Internet."

"Perhaps."

Mac purses her lips. "Do you believe in Truth, Mr. Upson? With a capital 'T?'"

"I believe in facts, supported by evidence. As for 'Truth,' I'll leave that to philosophers."

"So do you want facts or Truth?"

"Both. Build your opinion on the facts."

"Not my opinion. The Truth."

"Okay, Mac. Get after it."

Mac turns to leave. A sudden realization dawns on me.

"Mac, wait!"

She turns around. I hand her a twenty.

"For the girls' golf fundraiser."

Mac smiles and hands it back. "The raffle was last Friday. It's cool, Mr. U."

I shove the bill back into my wallet as I read the prompt:

WAS ANDREW JACKSON AN AMERICAN HERO?

~

Drip. Drop. Drip. Drop. Rainwater hit the waste bucket.

"It'll dilute the stench."

((...what stench?...))

"Right. There is no stench."

((...all is well, Mr. Bond...))

"Call me James."

((...as you wish, Mr. Bond...))

Isolation took its toll. Madness crept in. My stony cell was cold, every crack sealed tight. I longed for the sounds of battle and that damn bugle boy's reveille. I tried in vain to recall the lesson of that book Michelle gave me, about meaning in suffering. Every morning I awoke cloaked with guilt over Immanuel, and what might have befallen Emmaleigh...and Mariah...*and their child.* Tar bled through the stones as the whispers cut sharp.

((...you're a killer, like your father and his father...))

"Shut up."

((...you're a man...men kill...))

"No."

((...by the thooooouuuuusands you kill...))

"I SAID SHUT UP!!!"

((...it's you or them...it's you or them...they'll take it all away, it's you or them...))

"SHUT UP! SHUT UP! SHUT UP! YOU TOOK EVERYTHING FROM ME!"

I sobbed. I slept. I awoke, and the cycle began anew. Hope vanished.

Then in March came the vision, *ex nihilo,* out of nothing: a spectral visitor in a gown of scarlet and azure and snow. She was compassionate and good and sorely misunderstood. She frightened her suitors, who never truly loved her. Jealous, they raged over her, destroyed one another for her affection. One wrote a song for her, though he sang it out of key.

Once she met a boy who could not love, for all he knew was pain. He charmed and subdued her. She tried to flee, but she was his; no other could have her. So he sent her to hang in the breeze.

"Would you really love me, Benjamin?"

I felt an intense ache. "I don't know how."

She twirled. *"Isn't my gown beautiful?"*

"It's radiant."

She dropped her eyes to the floor.

"It unravels," she cried. *"Time grows short. Will you dance with me in the flames?"*

"How?" I protested. "You are beyond my reach."

"Is a spirit contained by walls? Is a phantom bound to the Earth?"

"I don't know. I'm nothing. I'm nobody. I'm..."

"...only dust?"

91

I knocked the back of my head against the wall. I was dehydrated and emaciated, resigned to die in my own stink. I had neither strength nor patience for the mind games of a hallucination.

"Listen!" she called. *"He's coming."*

She vanished into footsteps. The cell next door opened for an angry Frenchman. *"This is madness! Why am I here?"* Titus answered, *"You know why, Senator."* The Frenchman called Titus a "lap dog," then came throttling of flesh and bone. The door slammed; my neighbor pounded it.

"You have to knock louder," I cackled.

"Tu t'appelles comment? How long have you been here?"

Bond, I answered, James Bond. For centuries. Who are you?

"Louis Louaillier of the Louisiana Senate."

Why are you here?

"Mon stylo."

Louis explained that Jackson's forces arrived in December to defend New Orleans against the advancing British. Jackson declared martial law, suspending civil liberties and jailing all "suspicious" persons. Some were executed on the spot. Conditions were intolerable, *"but we tolerated them so long as a foreign enemy was at our doorstep."*

The British attacked on December twenty-third. Jackson's forces held them off until January eighteenth, when news arrived from Washington that the war had ended.

"Jackson refuses to restore civil government," Louis explained. *"He claims that enemies still lurk, enemies deep inside this state. I fear he'll never leave, so I objected in the Louisiana Courier anonymously. Now I am betrayed by the quill."*

Two days later another neighbor arrived.

"Dominick! Why in God's name are you here?"

"I ordered your release."

I coughed. I heard whispers, then Dominick grew excited.

"This is the one!"

"Nonsense!"

They argued. Dominick prevailed.

"Mr. Bond is it?"

"James Bond," I replied.

"I am Judge Dominick Hall. We are members of the Sons of Liberty, and we oppose Jackson's occupation. Our leadership alerted us to a missing contact with the initials 'J.B.' It must be you. Unless James Bond is an alias?"

"No," I replied, eyes shifting to and fro. "That's my name."

"It is certainly no coincidence. We will secure your release, James. I promise."

I laughed. "Promise is a bucket o' hot piss."

Night fell silent. Soon thereafter Louis and Dominick were gone.

And so I waited...

...and waited...

...until one night...

...I gave up.

Then the Earth moved.

It happened the night Abner incessantly whistled *Turkey In The Straw.* The intruder dislodged the stone, spewing debris onto the floor. She grunted and vaulted into a seated position, dangling her legs into the hole. She adjusted her yellow bandana and shed layers of mud and silt from her overalls as she softly sang:

> *Little Bird fly*
> *Through the Devil's eye*
> *Tarred and feathered with the Devil's dye*
>
> *Black as Cain*
> *Right as rain*
> *Ridin' to glory on heaven's train*

She was young, black and fit, barely five feet tall. Intense and focused, her left eye drooped. Even in my terror, I knew her for a ghost: this Underground Railroad conductor they called "Moses" was yet unborn.

She strode to the corner I huddled in and knelt, picking debris from my beard.

"Goodness, child. Who did this to you?"

I cocked my head. "Who…what?"

She sighed and stood.

"Call for the guard."

I screwed my face. "Why the hell would I do that?"

She placed her fingers in her mouth, emitting a high-pitched whistle. The door flung open; Abner froze.

"Abner Collins," the intruder said. "You wanna be free?"

Abner nodded slowly.

"Tell Commander Atwater you caught Minty."

Abner hesitated.

"Do it now, before I change my mind."

Abner slammed the door. "Minty" turned back to me.

I coughed. "Dominick sent you?"

Minty shook off another layer of silt. "Expecting someone else?"

"I wasn't expecting Harriet Tubman."

~

Abner couldn't keep from gawking at Minty as he rowed us into the veil of fog on Lake Pontchartrain. He had been at a loss to explain to Titus how she managed to tunnel into the airtight facility. Now the four of us sat in silence *en route* to a rendezvous with a higher authority.

"Ahoy!"

The shroud lifted…on a massive battle-scarred frigate. A thirteen-starred Betsy Ross flag flew above the crow's nest; above it, a red banner depicting a golden seven-headed dragon clutching a spear and staff in each claw.

I read the name on the bow as we moored: *L'Insurgent.*

"Impossible," I muttered.

"What's impossible?" Minty inquired sheepishly.

"*The Insurgent* vanished in the Bermuda Triangle in 1800."

Minty laughed. "They ever find her?"

"Quiet!" Titus snapped, nudging us up the rope ladder.

"Tell me, Commander Atwater," Minty asked once on deck, "is the real General aboard? Or do we have to settle for your boss?"

"They both outrank you," Titus spat. The crew barked at one another in foreign tongues and escorted us to the captain's quarters at stern. Titus flung open the double doors. It was immaculate, lined with gold and tied together with a red rug with the seven-headed dragon depicted on the flag. Floor-to-ceiling, the aft window framed Lake Pontchartrain and the distant lights of New Orleans.

At a small port side table sat a woman in her thirties, her golden hair tucked in a bun, bangs falling upon rich brown eyes. Two strands twirled to her collarbones, where an aquamarine pendant dangled from a golden chain. She shifted uncomfortably in her white dress.

"Titus, I told you the lady and I would dine alone tonight."

Gazing into a cracked mirror on the starboard side was a man in his mid-forties. A scar traced the left side of his face under his dark Bedford mane. Bedecked in regalia from crown to boots with golden epaulettes on his shoulders, Major General Andrew Jackson approached and addressed us with a pronounced Tennessee drawl.

"Who are these stragglers up from the muck?"

Titus jostled me. "This is the spy we captured in the bayou before Christmas last."

Jackson picked at my beard. "Bond, is it?"

"James Bond," I rasped.

"Titus, why is this man still alive? The British have fled, he is of no use to me."

Titus nudged Minty. "The Negress tunneled into Mr. Bond's cell."

"Impressive. Why is she breathing?"

"Because she belongs to her." Titus pointed at the blond woman.

Jackson faced his dinner guest. "Aurora, darling! It appears your confederates have arrived just in time for supper."

Nine

Kingdom of Rust

Awkward silence ruled the hickory table on the torch lit deck of *The Insurgent*. To my right sat Jackson, fourteen years before his inauguration as the seventh President of the United States. Across from me sat Minty; Titus and Abner stood behind her. Across from Jackson to my left sat Aurora.

A prisoner.

Aurora had been secretly dispatched by President James Madison in the spring of 1814 to monitor General Jackson's prosecution of the Creek War, a proxy conflict between American- and British-backed tribes of the Deep South during the War of 1812. Madison worried that Jackson's attacks on Creek civilians would undermine his Administration's efforts to "assimilate" and "civilize" Natives. To her dismay, Aurora discovered that Jackson's brutality was merely a prelude to conquest, as he forced even his Creek allies to cede large swaths of modern Alabama in the Treaty of Fort Jackson.

In response, Aurora assembled a Resistance of militia deserters, Cherokee, Choctaw and Creeks, free blacks, escaped slaves and other cast-offs to foil Jackson through nonviolent sabotage. In one instance, the Resistance fell upon ten militiamen *en route* to loot a defenseless village. The next morning the soldiers awoke tied to a tree and disarmed. Enraged, Jackson promised to shoot the leader of these agitators on sight.

Thus it came as a great shock when Aurora rode into Jackson's camp under a white flag, offering on bent knee to assist in the impending defense of New Orleans against the British. Charmed by Aurora's grace and wit, Jackson agreed to a parlay in his tent, where the renegade delivered her own spies' incisive intelligence on British movements.

"I ought to hang you for treason," Jackson intimated. "Yet my enemies are yours. You are a complicated woman, Aurora."

"I beg to differ, General," Aurora replied, sipping whiskey from the bottle. "I'm a simple woman. It's the men in my life who complicate me."

Jackson laughed and pissed himself to sleep. When he awoke and found that Aurora hadn't killed him in his sleep, he accepted her surrender and brought her to New Orleans as his personal prisoner. As Aurora guided Jackson to victory, the two dined twice weekly during the course of their stay in the Crescent City.

"Now," Jackson said, mouth full of rump steak and hollandaise, "we feast upon victory and drink glory."

"Victory," Aurora replied. "Not glory. Not with blood in the soil."

Jackson laughed and took a long sip of bourbon. "This one fancies herself my conscience. The people will judge me."

"And their verdict?"

Jackson swirled his glass. "What is already on their tongues – that I am the Hero of New Orleans, the Savior of the Republic!"

"Only a braying jackass calls himself a hero, Andrew."

Jackson went cold. He folded his hands, biting between thumb and forefinger. His eyes darted, his breath steadily climbing.

"A jackass," he said softly. "Hmph."

It was jarring to watch a persona writ so large rendered so small. Jackson caught my eye.

"Mr. Bond, where are you from?"

I picked my birthplace. "Annapolis, Maryland."

"What was your profession in Annapolis?"

"I…was the local schoolmaster."

"A learned man? Bless you, sir! I imagine you love those children as your very own."

"Of course."

"Would do anything to protect them?"

"I'd give my life for them," I said, sincerely.

Jackson squeezed my shoulder. "This here is a good man. Loves his country and kin. That's no sin. Let nobody say otherwise."

Jackson pointed his steak knife at Aurora.

"Do you know the terror the Redcoats inflicted upon your servant's home? The Governor fled, and Annapolis became a haven of black marauders! Yet I defend America against such savagery, and I am a *'jackass'?"*

The way Jackson turned Aurora's insult around on her was rattling. She seemed unfazed.

"Forgive me, Andrew," she said, "how does seizing our neighbors' land and stealing their children constitute 'defense?'"

Jackson scoffed. "I'd thought you a patriot. The fathers of those babes massacred your people at Fort Mims! Two hundred fifty butchered without mercy by red devils, and you would extend it to their progeny?! If you are not for your own people, *you are against us.*"

"I have no 'people,' Andrew. I'm an orphan. Like you."

Jackson's cheeks collapsed inward. *Another blow.* Aurora was inside his head.

"At least you knew your father," Jackson seethed. "And my mother died treating Continentals on a Redcoat schooner. *She* is my people, now and ever. No woman gave greater warmth than Elizabeth Hutchinson Jackson, least of all not you...nor the *bitch* who suckled you."

Aurora sipped her wine. Minty held her stare at Jackson. Titus caressed his holster, shifting his eyes between Jackson and me. Abner had the besotted look of a mind in conflict, a Jackson admirer now saddled with doubt.

Jackson waved his knife. *"None of you has suffered as I have."*

Minty broke her silence. "I find that hard to believe."

"Minty, is it? Know your place. I ordinarily don't allow Negros at my table. Mind your tongue before I have it out."

Jackson turned to Titus.

"Commander Atwater, I wonder if Minty here might be a sound investment for your plantation? She's mouthy, but sturdy. What say you?"

Minty grinned. "I promise you Mr. Jackson: I can't be bought."

"Did I address you, child?"

Aurora squeezed her glass and shattered it clean.

"Do not speak to her that way," she seethed.

Jackson sneered. "Why do you care how I speak to those on my ship?"

Aurora leaned back, amused. "Your ship? Andrew, this vessel is General Travers' prize."

"General Travers answers to König's Apprentice, young lady."

König again.

"In any event," Jackson continued, "this insolent Negro is not meant for freedom."

Jackson waved at Minty.

"I mean goodness, her skull is misshapen! Free her, and she will slit our throats in our sleep!"

Jackson whipped his head to me, sticking his finger in my face.

"Don't misunderstand me, Mr. Bond. Some Negroes are wonderful people – *if* properly supervised. But they will rape our women and burn our cities to the ground should they walk free among us. They must never be weaned from the whip."

((...you can never wean a welfare queen...))

I seized up as my eardrums rumbled. *Where is that coming from?*

Jackson rambled on. "Doesn't the Declaration say that a free and independent people ought to assume the *separate* station to which the laws of nature entitle them?"

My head spun. *Is that what Jefferson meant by that?* Something deep...*deep* within...drew me to Jackson's words...they were dark, and...

...*beautiful*...

...in a hypnotic, irrational way I couldn't explain...

...I gazed upon Jackson, and the two of us met eye-to-eye...

...in that moment I hated him for what he had done to me...

...and loved him for what he would do to *them*...

"The Declaration speaks of an American people," Aurora countered, "drawn out from among the nations, living free together. Speak not of things you don't understand."

Jackson pointed at her. "Oh, I understand. I see with absolute clarity what God Almighty intends for this people...and *this continent*..."

From the center of the table a single point of golden light swirled clockwise; a pillar of black smoke moved counterclockwise. The light and smoke wove together in a whirlpool of black and gold dancing in perpetual motion.

"You speak of empire," Aurora said.

"An Empire of *Liberty*," Jackson declared.

From the eye of the storm a topographical map of North America unfolded on the table, like a three-dimensional game board. Jackson stood and placed his hands on the edge of the table, leaning in, meeting Aurora eye-to-eye.

"Your friend Thomas Jefferson has long dreamed of an 'empire of liberty' stretching to the Pacific, living space for our kinfolk where savages now roam. America shall be a fortress of civilization in a sea of barbarism."

An army of wagons moved across the Mississippi, settling lands throughout the American West.

"You say we can make peace with savages? Only a *fool* so divides his house! Madison's efforts to teach these hunters agriculture have failed. Look what destruction Tecumseh brought to Ohio! Nature demands they make way for our heaven-defended race. If the violent Indians wish to hunt, let them not scalp us!"

Another group of wagons crossed to various locations across the Mississippi...then dissolved to powder. The land turned from desert brown to forest green, as crops were harvested from their ashes.

"America will be a citadel for the loyal, courageous and strong."

((...like you, Benji...))

Another light appeared at the foot of the Rockies. It spun outward and exploded onto Lake Pontchartrain as night turned to day...

...

"Hello, Benjamin."

...Jackson pulls me off the ground...

"General..." I begin...he holds his hand up...

"Call me the Apprentice."

...the sky is crisp and blue; the sun shines upon Springland...and a garden, a spectacle of twisting trees and weeping willows overlooking a crystal blue pond...rising above them all is a Great White Manse upon a hill, a glorious house of many rooms...joy abundant springs forth from a well deep within...

...I feel my face and my shoulders and arms...I'm clean shaven...wearing a green Army officer's uniform...

"Where are we?" I ask, clicking my spit-shine heels...

...Jackson extends his arm to the garden. "There's no place like home."

...next to the pond stands a pristine white gazebo, a swing bench hanging from the ceiling...there sits a beautiful sandy-haired woman in an orchid summer dress...and a boy...

...a boy with brown hair and a face full of freckles...

...John...

"Pop! Pop!" he cries...my heart leaps and he runs and jumps into my arms...

...we hug and weep, for I was away at War...

...I fought them all...I fought those dirtbags for him...

"How many hajis did you kill?" John asks...

"Thousands," I brag...

...John beams... I set him down as Michelle slides her arms around my waist...

"You made it right," she whispers. "Now make me happy."

...night falls...the garden fills with living statues of white alabaster and ivory, familiar faces to greet this weary warrior...flags wave and fireworks fly...

...it is the Fourth of July...

...Michelle sets the table, a bounty from the land...all gather for the feast, to eat and drink and give thanks to the General, the Hero who saved the Republic from the savages and abolitionists who threatened to split us in two...

"To Jackson!" I cry, raising my Scotch in salute...

...Jackson raises his in turn. "Long live the Apprentice!"

...we raise our glasses and drink, all of us...

...except for one...

...he is alone, near the water's edge...kneeling before that tree, that Great and Mighty Elm, bearing fruit of many colors...he says nothing, and drinks nothing, still and silent as the sky ignites above us...I approach him, torch in hand...

"Mr. Atwater," I say...

"Mr. Upson," he replies, coldly, stoically...

...I extend the glass to him. "Drink," I command...

...he says nothing, and drinks nothing...he is ever stubborn...since the day we purchased the boy at auction, he has ever been stubborn...

"Drink," I command...

...he turns his head and meets my eye. "No," he says. "I don't kneel for him. Only for her..."

...a collective gasp...

((...insolent shit...))

((...brazen, and uncivilized...))

((...he dishonors you...he dishonors him...))

...I kneel to meet Mr. Atwater, face to face. "Pick your battles," I say. "Die not upon this hill," I say...

...Mr. Atwater doesn't flinch...Mr. Atwater doesn't move an inch...his eyes move through me...past me...fixed on something behind my shoulder...

"Come and see!" he cries. "All who love Liberty, come and see what the Apprentice has wrought on that great and terrible day!" he roars, as a lion...

...I turn...the statues remain, still and silent...

...only one answers the call...

"No," I tremble...

...John leaves his mother's arms...she falls to the ground and weeps as our boy...our flesh...our blood...ascends that hill, to that Great and Mighty Elm...

...he kneels before that Elm...Mr. Atwater takes his hand...

...in the cool waters of the pond, a Bluebird circles in the starry and spacious skies...it circles and circles and descends upon the Elm, perching upon its strongest branch...

...with a new song on its lips...

((...chirp, chirp Benji...tweet, tweet...))

...the Bluebird opens its beak...smoke pours forth...that Mighty Elm catches fire...

"John!" I cry. "Get away from there!"

...

...the world engulfs in flame...

...the sky turns a shade of crimson darker than black...

...he's gone...

...she's gone...

...they're all gone, reduced to dust and ashes...

...

...Mr. Atwater kneels before that Great and Mighty Elm...still...silent...stoic...

...rage stirs within...the pond boils and bubbles with black crude...

...I have nothing...nothing but despair...

...I am nothing...nothing but hatred...

"You took them away!" I cry. "You took them all away from me!"

...then I hear that subtle whisper...that soft and silent echo...

...

((...at water he drinksssss...))

((...at water he drownssss...))

((...at water he diesssssss...))

...

...Jackson hands me a whip...for education...

"Fifty lashes," he says, eyes mad with sorrow and terror. "Rule your servant. Rule him with the cowhide."

...so I tie Mr. Atwater to that Great and Mighty Elm...

...I close my eyes...

"See no evil," Mr. Atwater says...

...beneath the tree I whip my servant, the night growing colder with every crack...

...Shadows gather 'round me, six of them...a White Hat Man gives me a scepter, a golden scepter with the head of an axe...

"G'on, John Brown," he growls. "Judge his killer. Avenge him with the fasces of fire..."

"Law and Order!" Jackson cries.

...Law, yes, and Order...

...and in their names I raise the scepter...

...Mr. Atwater looks upon me with no pity...no shame...no love...

...so he shall have none in return...

...

...the silent chorus sings...

> *You came to set our house ablaze*
> > *((But you will not replace us!))*
> *To teach our young your wicked ways*
> > *((But you will not replace us!))*

...no...he never will...

...I strike the ground with ferocity and focus...thunder tolls, and lightning rolls...

...and there he hangs, tarred and feathered, dangling from the strongest branch...

...it is done...

...

...I weep...Jackson laughs...

"Look now, my Apprentice," he crows, pointing to the sky. "Look what you have wrought..."

...the Bluebird, charred black, circles again above the Elm and perches upon the strongest branch...it sings a new song...

> See him dangle from a tree
> See how he breaks in two?
> You sing, you dance, but don't you know
> That John Brown is you?

...as tar drips from the night sky onto my shoulders...

...I look up...

...another dangles from the strongest branch, tarred and feathered beyond recognition...

...I know...in an instant, I know...

...

...John...

...I weep...the Bluebird swoops and cuts him free, dropping him at my feet...

...I collapse and cradle the boy in my arms...tears fall like fire from my eyes and smolder to ash on his pale skin...

...John...

...how did this happen?...why does God claim the Innocent and the Other alike?...

...it is unjust...

...Jackson laughs. "Hang together," he bellows...

...he points his scepter...the Shadows point theirs, raising an army from the earth, soldiers in silhouettes of black oil and tar...

...he has betrayed me...the Apprentice has betrayed me...

...he has betrayed us...

...

...the Shadows march uphill toward us, closing in like the rings of Saturn...Jackson smiles at me, menacingly, from behind his minions...I clutch the boy tight and gnash my teeth at the invading hordes...

...from among them she emerges, an apparition, a phantom, in dark shrouds and chains...she is melancholy and lovely, ascending the hill step by painful step, eyes dripping the colors of roses...they fasten upon John...

((...let him go, Benji...))

...I grip the boy tight. "No...you can't take him from me..."

...lifelessly she raises her wrists, bound and shackled...

((...I wore these for you...now I wear them for him...))

...I hold him closer...willing my own life back into his...

Live, I command, live!

...the Shadows march, and the cold wind blows...speck by speck...and fleck by fleck...the wind dissolves John to white ash and carries him away into the crimson night...I curl into nothing, hollow to the bone, shaking and shivering on the ground...

"John," I cry. "John..."

...the Apprentice rides uphill on his pale horse of death...he swoops in and steals the phantom, then vanishes into the ether...the Shadows lower their bayonets and march, collapsing upon me from all sides...

...I am lost...all is lost...I will die upon this hill...

...

...a Song Man sings from the strongest branch...the mountains echo his refrain...

> *Know this Mama! Know this Papa!*
> *Do not this loss deplore!*
> *Don't see, don't hear, don't speak its name!*
> *For the child's in pain no more!*

...then a new chorus sings, voices rising in unison...the sounds of the dead and dying wafting up from the ground...

((...comes now the True Champion, riding upon the Night Horse...))

...a fierce warrior rides in, an elegant woman with black skin and jet black hair, on a silver mare with a mane of gold...the Rider leaps from her steed and drives a white feather deep into my heart of stone, pulling out a sword of fire...

"Because Tyranny had his way!" *she cries...*

...the charred bird descends on Mr. Atwater's lifeless shoulders...

Jackson had his way!
The Apprentice had his way!
All falls to ashes
'Cause Tyranny had his way!

...all around the Elm, her Warriors arise from the dust...each one shackled...each one chained...joined one to another they circle the hill, marching silently, solemnly, leaving a trail of tears in their wake...

"Your living space," the Rider crows, "is our burial ground forever..."

...the Trumpet sounds...

...and all together they shout...the earth quakes...the Elm falls into the chasm, and I with it...the Rider catches my hand...in the darkness I hear the violent rushing stream...the Rider speaks...

"Do you hear? Have you seen? Will you speak?"

"Yes," I weep bitterly. "I do. I have. I will..."

...the Rider releases me into the abyss...

...

...as whitecaps smashed the deck of *The Insurgent.* I clung to the table, locking eyes on Betsy Ross as the battle of wits reached a fever pitch.

"Your Empire is a delusion!" Aurora proclaimed. "Liberty will not survive your kingdom of rust!"

Jackson snarled. "You invite a Trojan Horse to destroy us from within! These savages and slaves will be our end!"

"You are blind, Andrew! You destroy your own life, and blame those who saved it!"

Jackson winced. "What the *hell* are you talking about?"

Aurora, exhausted and drenched, stood tall. "You speak of the loyal, courageous and strong! I speak for the stranger, the fatherless and the widow!"

The storm ceased, the waves calmed, and the drenched crew emerged from hiding below deck.

Jackson's breath quickened. Aurora's words held meaning for him.

"It was *you,*" he said. "You came to my cabin...in the Waxhaws...with that Negro woman. But you...you were only a girl."

"Natalie was my wet nurse," Aurora continued, nearly breathless. "I was five, and you fourteen. Though you were wounded, your mother gave us shelter in your cabin. Natalie treated you, and I stitched you…"

Aurora pointed to Jackson's scar.

"You refused to clean a Redcoat officer's boots. That's when you learned to hate. You told me blood was all that mattered. I cried and said…"

"*'What of the stranger, the fatherless and the widow?'*" Jackson finished, his lips trembling, his coat drenched in salt water. "I remember…clear as day. I asked mama if you were angels. That was the measure of your kindness…such simple gifts you gave…"

"Today, you mark us foes."

Jackson's mind absorbed a bright whisper…

((…remember first light, Andrew…))

…light wedged in the cracks of Jackson's stone heart. A coin teetered…

"I would not mark you foes," Jackson said…

…then the whispers cursed and menaced, overpowering Jackson with neither force nor reason. The coin fell.

"I *respect* my foes."

Jackson shook with rage.

"Your wet nurse healed me, then convinced my mother to join her on that Redcoat schooner…she died there…*my mother died there…your shallow mercies sent my mother to her grave!!*"

Jackson plunged his knife into the hickory.

"I will not free her!"

Aurora watched, crestfallen, as Jackson dissolved into anger and fear. He clutched his sidearm, eyes shifting like a cornered animal.

Then a veil tore open, and I saw it.

A Shadow. The dark, rayless silhouette of an unspeakable monster laid its hands – no, its *claws* – upon Jackson's shoulders, emitting a low, pulsing, guttural growl.

It's claiming him. Just like it claimed Oswald.

Jackson boiled over.

"You will not replace us!" he proclaimed. "I, alone am König's Apprentice! Renounce your treason and pledge your allegiance!"

Aurora looked down and wept.

"I'm sorry, Mother," she muttered bitterly. *"I failed you."*

"Answer me!" Jackson cried.

Aurora gathered her strength. "No, Andrew. To Caesar we render nothing. You have no love in you, and you are lost."

"Lost, you say," Jackson replied, barely above a whisper.

Veins popped in his forehead, and his hand trembled as he raised his shaky finger at Aurora.

"No. It is *you* who are lost. Only I know the way to Elysium..."

Jackson swiftly drew his pistol from his holster and pointed it square at Minty. She remained perfectly still, not flinching, not moving an inch, staring right back through him.

"America will only be great if we crush our enemies!" Jackson cried. "Beginning with her."

Jackson pulled back the hammer...

CLICK!

...the gun jammed. In the split second Jackson pulled it back to inspect it, Minty reared her head back and spat, flinging her spittle all over Jackson's face. His eyes rolled into the back of his head and he collapsed in a heap to the deck, motionless. Titus rushed to his side.

"General? General!"

Jackson remained deadly still. Enraged, Titus turned and raised his pistol at Minty. He looked at me, his finger shaking as it hovered over the trigger...

"Traitor!" he seethed. *"You've betr...oomph!"*

Abner bull-rushed him, knocking the gun from his hand and driving him to the deck, unconscious. A crewmember fired on Minty; the shot ricocheted off her sternum and splashed in the water behind him. Astonished, the crew dropped their weapons in surrender.

Aurora rushed over to Titus and removed an object from his jacket pocket, the size of a small brick and wrapped in brown paper. I looked up to the crow's nest, then back at Minty.

"Capture the flag," I said.

Minty grinned from ear to ear. "That's my favorite game."

Abner trained his pistol on the crew as Minty deftly climbed the mast and retrieved the flag. I folded it as Pop taught me, awestruck anew at the scarlet and azure and snow.

"These are *our* colors," I said as we unmoored the rowboat. "Never his."

Abner rowed us east into the descending fog, giving us cover from Jackson's flotilla.

A hundred yards out, I turned to Minty. "Did you just *assassinate* Andrew Jackson?"

Minty cocked her head. "You think I'm a killer?"

"That wasn't poison you spat...was it?"

Minty grinned. "A truthful tongue is always poison to a liar."

She tossed a small object at me.

"Think you can keep it, now?"

The coin was lighter than ever, pure tin shining, declaring brightly:

AS WE SAIL INTO NIGHT

~

The essays are stacked high on the breakfast table, next to the papers from Michelle's jackass lawyer. The papers I refuse to sign. I read Mac's essay for the fifth time:

"...Andrew Jackson was no hero. His jailing of Judge Hall and Senator Louaillier demonstrated contempt for checks and balances and a free press (see, e.g., Op-ed of "A Citizen of Louisiana of French Origin," <u>Louisiana Courier</u>, 03-Mar-1815). This foreshadowed his defiance of the Supreme Court after <u>Worcester v. Georgia</u>...

"...In 1828, Jackson framed President Adams as an 'elite' who conspired to win the presidency through a 'corrupt bargain.' But Jackson was far more corrupt. His 'spoils' system gave government jobs to sycophants and, after the Eaton affair wiped out his cabinet, he relied on a 'kitchen cabinet' of incompetent cronies and relatives...

"...Many say Jackson expanded democracy by appealing to common people devoted to their Hero of New Orleans. But democracy without equality isn't democracy; Jackson instead practiced <u>ethnic nationalism</u>, 'democracy' for only a few...

"...No matter how we sanitize him, Jackson was an outspoken white supremacist. He said it was God's will that Indians be 'annihilated or melted away to make room for the whites.' (Jackson Message to Congress, 1830). He turned white farmers and other workers against blacks, Indians and Spaniards, blaming them for economic problems. Somehow, that message got under people's skin, and the result was the expulsion of Creeks, Cherokee and Choctaw from Georgia. Thousands of innocents died on this Trail of Tears...

"...The Trail of Tears hits me hard, personally. As a girl, my great grandmother told me the story of how she was forcefully relocated from Torrance, California to a Japanese-American internment camp in the dead of night...I cried for a week, afraid that maybe one day my government might do that to me. Now at seventeen, it feels possible...

"'When America ceases to be good, America ceases to be great.' (Tocqueville, Democracy in America). We cannot make America great by emulating Andrew Jackson, because Andrew Jackson was never good. Still, we made a national hero of a broken bigot who blamed the 'other' for his mother's death. Jackson's intense desire for personal vengeance soon became a thirst for conquest in all areas of life, to serve himself alone. He thought he embodied the American dream; by trafficking in slavery and genocide, he shackled America to a long national nightmare...

"The Truth is, we're still living it..."

~

In the cabin of *The Phillis*, Captain Marco Reyes deftly carved three months from my face. It had been eleven years since the Cuban eschewed the smuggler's life to move Aurora and her "Sons of Liberty" all over the world on a schooner once used to ferry captive Africans across the Atlantic.

Minty knocked at the door. "Marco."

"Polo," he replied, his face deadpan.

Minty rolled her eyes and pointed at me. "You done with this mess?"

"Sì, señora. But I have to powder him, too. Make him look pretty." He made a kissing suction sound, then laughed at his own wit.

Minty lowered her eyes, dipping into a deep and devious smile. "I'm no angel, Marco. Keep messin' with me, and you'll be at the bottom of the Gulf."

Marco shrugged, unfazed by Minty's semi-playful threat. Minty shook her head and exited.

"She's truly terrifying," I said.

Marco waved his hand. "No. She has a pure heart, amigo."

"She does," I admitted. "One of the greatest heroes our country has ever known."

Marco nodded. "So I have heard."

I pursed my lips. "But I know nothing about Aurora."

Marco brushed my neck. "Oh, my dear man, but you should. Aurora is a miracle worker, my friend. Her people will make the world anew."

"The 'Sons of Liberty,'" I laughed. "Tell me, Marco: why are we called 'Sons' if more than half of us are women?"

Marco chuckled. "The lady has a sense of irony, I think. Whatever we are, we will leave a better world for my sons *and* daughters to live in."

I giggled.

"You mock me?"

"No," I answered, thinking of the Kid who would fly around the base paths in Palm Beach one hundred fifty years in the future. "Say, Marco: you don't happen to play cricket, do you?"

Marco grinned. "I am the *best* cricketer in the Caribbean."

After Marco finished, I slung my satchel over my back and returned to deck, where Abner played dominoes with a motley crew. The mood on the deck was joyful yet somber, as if the living here were haunted by ghosts. I had felt that heaviness when I first stepped aboard after our night on *The Insurgent,* and it still lingered. This ship carried a curse, even as it blessed me.

I made my way starboard, where Aurora and Minty stood watching the sunset. Aurora wore a blue coat and tricorn hat, and clutched a black cane with a golden Liberty cap on the handle.

I nodded at Abner. "He looks just like Reid."

Aurora smiled weakly.

"For me," I continued, "this began with Pearl confronting me about Reid and Tyson. She said it was bigger than that. That it marked the last battle of the Revolution. What did she mean by that?"

Aurora played with the Liberty cap. "My Sister has a knack for seeing the forest for the trees. She and Mother have that in common."

Sister. Mother. I hesitated. "That thing with Jackson...I heard it speak to Kennedy, too..."

I fiddled with the coin.

"Its vendetta against Tyson, the Atwaters...it's personal."

Aurora reached into her jacket pocket and retrieved a brown leather diary. It was nearly identical to Tyson's, though less worn and weathered.

"That's what you took from Jackson," I breathed, piecing together a puzzle in my mind. "That's what you were after. To keep it away from that...thing."

Aurora flipped through the pages of the diary.

"His name is Tyranny," she replied, stopping on a page written in foreign glyphs I couldn't decipher. "He has many Faces. His vengeance works corruption of blood, and knows no borders."

A single tear fell from the corner of Aurora's eye.

"Andrew understands neither the Gospel nor the Revolution. He will rule for a time, but for good or evil, nothing fashioned by human hands endures forever. That is the Law of Rust."

Her voice grew tense as she gripped the railing.

"Yet the spirits of Tyranny's Apprentices linger for generations, as Jackson lingers in the shadows Today. I fear that in your generation Tyranny may extinguish Liberty forever."

Aurora squeezed my hand.

"Unless her Champion seizes Excalibur by the hilt."

I was overwhelmed. Aurora, like Pearl, was a master of wordplay.

"Aurora," I said, "I don't know where it is. I don't know *what* it is."

"Yes, you do. Only Fear veils it. And you have nothing to fear but Fear itself."

Minty grabbed my shoulder from behind. Aurora touched my chest.

"Rise, Son of Liberty."

The heavens opened and thunder clapped like cannon fire. Gale forces whipped through the air as a silent scream rose from the eye of the storm.

Then my journey began anew.

II

A Cold Civil War

Ten

Down River

I don't remember when the crack in the mirror first appeared. Maybe it was always there.

"I don't care how it got there," Michelle demanded. *"Just fix it."*

It didn't bother me the way it did her. I brushed my teeth in it, washed my face in it, downed those nightly shots of ruby red syrup in it. Broken, unbroken. It was all the same.

Until it split us in two.

They say to stave off the curse one must bury a broken mirror under the light of a full moon. It's a lie. Curses always find you in the dark.

I gazed out the passenger window upon the Tahoe National Forest, deep in the heart of the Sierra Nevada…

((…it's still buried out there…))

…I shuddered, prompting my partner across from me to turn onto his shoulder. Kennedy was a light sleeper, or so I'd learned. The way he slinked against the seat – arms folded over his lapels, Homburg hat resting on the bridge of his nose – one could be forgiven for assuming the man enjoyed a deep slumber. I knew better. This one's demons never let him rest.

Neither will this clatter. The car had been raucously loud since we pulled out of Oakland's 16th Street Station that morning – Thursday, July 1, 1910, according to the *San Francisco Chronicle*. The train was headed eastbound for Reno, Nevada, packed to the brim with spectators for the "Fight of the Century," slated for the afternoon of Independence Day three days hence. In one corner would sit the new heavyweight World Champion, Jack Johnson, the Negro they called the Galveston Giant; in the other the former World Champion, James Jeffries, known the world over as The Great White Hope.

Jeffries had been coaxed from retirement by a sense of racial duty, *"for the sole purpose of proving that a white man is better than a Negro."* Not just any Negro. *That Negro*, the brash, uppity bastard with the audacity to steal the white man's crown – and women. Needless to say, this train carried a partisan crowd:

"No way that gorilla lasts three rounds."

"Ten before Sambo falls!"

"Put a wager on it?"

I felt a tap on my shoulder.

"Ya put yar dollars on the black feller, haven' ye?"

The heavyset Irish passenger to my right grinned, crinkling his pink dimples.

"Ye've been quiet all the wee mornin'," he pressed. "Figured ye an' yer partner wouldn' wan' to earn the ire o' all these white folk, no?"

I creased the *Chronicle* and set it in my lap. "I'm afraid we're in Reno strictly on business."

"Ahh," the Irishman winked. "Nice feller setch as yerself wants to stay hidden. Say no mar!"

I smiled. Truth was, we actually *had* been invisible until at least Sacramento. I'd been sitting next to the Irishman all morning, reviewing dossiers and sketching notes on a moving map of the Course of Human Events; my neighbor had been none the wiser.

Moving in and out of view at will merely by steering my intention was one of many tricks I picked up at The Academy – the clandestine training compound of the Sons of Liberty, accessible through a rip in space-time just outside Culpeper, Virginia. There, I learned under the tutelage of the Sons' Spymaster-in-Chief, who welcomed me into her office with open arms.

"You're three months late. Never pull that hero shit again."

Araminta Harriet Tubman – a.k.a. "Minty" – evoked a respect born of admiration and terror, even as I loomed over her by a foot. This, after all, was a woman who escaped slavery in Maryland at twelve, then spent the remainder of her life risking it to rescue others from bondage. She served first as a "conductor" on the Underground Railroad that snuck thousands to the North and Canada; later as a Union spy in the Civil War who liberated seven hundred fifty slaves in a day at the Combahee River; later still as a warrior for the rights of freedmen and suffragettes alike. She was ever tenacious, not relenting in her fight for freedom and equality even after drawing her final breath in 1913.

Remarkably, she did all this with her skull caved in at her left temple, the gift given her as a young girl by a vicious foreman who threw a metal weight at another escaping slave. Minty stepped between the foreman and his target, taking the full brunt of the weight and sustaining permanent brain damage. She was cursed with violent seizures and bouts of deep depression for the rest of her natural life.

Yet wrapped within that curse was a deeper blessing. Minty was always acutely tuned into this quantum realm, the recipient of frequent dreams and visions that inspired her to see beyond her hardships, to live with a transcendent purpose and secure the blessings of Liberty not merely for herself, but for her posterity. It also made her deeply, preternaturally humble, a lesson she drilled into me from Day One.

"There're no 'saviors' here," she spat, pacing around me in a drill sergeant's circle. "Certainly not you. Understand?"

I swallowed. "Yes ma'am."

Minty scowled and grabbed my face, studying it to the last pore.

"I *knew* it. I *saw* it in that cell."

She wagged her finger at me.

"You made me an idol. 'Harriet Tubman, Ol' Moses!' Thought I was gonna take y'away on a gold-plated chariot? Ol' black mama gonna dispense her wisdom and solve all your problems, *that it?*"

I stammered. Minty broke, and doubled over in laughter.

"Oh, Lordy, that look on your face…precious!"

Minty grabbed my hand and held it against the divot in her head. Her spectral body was warm; in lieu of a pulse, it *hummed*.

"When I took that weight to the head, I didn't do it for hero's glory. I did it on impulse, because deep down I valued my brother's life more than my own. Know what my reward was?"

I shook my head.

"Exactly! *Nothin'*. I was damaged goods! I'm *still* damaged, toilin' on this earth with the same scars. Why? 'Cause until my work is finished, I don't want to see glory in the mirror. Scars keep me *humble*."

She stuck her finger in my chest.

"In your baseball games, everybody cheers when you hit that ball outta the yard. In this game, the Champion doesn't do this for applause. You do it for duty. You're a warrior…"

Minty reached into her pocket and pulled out a chess piece, a small horse fashioned from Elmwood.

"…a *knight*."

She nodded at Kennedy, seated impatiently in an office chair.

"He's your squire."

Kennedy had harbored misplaced guilt for abandoning me in Virginia. Still, since my rescue he kept me at an emotional distance. I had to earn his trust.

"This is going to be intense," I admitted.

"We don't do this because it's easy," he retorted.

For the next five months I was stretched to my limits. I learned the finer arts of espionage and psychological warfare – with "quantum" twists – from the Sons' best agents: Benjamin Tallmadge, leader of Washington's Culper Spy Ring during the Revolution; Julia Child, the celebrity chef who served as an OSS agent during World War II; and Minty's partner, Marine Corporal Ira Hayes, the Pima tribesman who famously raised the flag at Iwo Jima. This star faculty challenged my mental acuity and whipped me into the best shape of my life, all to forge me into a worthy "Champion of Liberty."

"The most vital piece on the board," Minty said, placing the knight on a moving map of the Course of Human Events, "in the most dangerous game of all. *History*."

A dangerous game indeed. Dad always taught me that history was more than a sequence of events, that there was order and purpose to our days. *If he only knew how right he was.* As I had witnessed first-hand in New Orleans, history itself is a cosmic battlefield between two sublime – yet *personal* – forces: Liberty and Tyranny. These two entities, each transcending political ideology and tribal loyalty, had been locked in a perennial tug-of-war over the ultimate fate of humankind since the dawn of time.

The clash of these ancient enemies was behind every significant geopolitical event ever recorded, with the agents of each threading needles back and forth through all of them to weave together a coherent tapestry. With each move one side made, the other adapted and countered, neither giving quarter to the other. The ultimate and inevitable outcome of this worldwide conflict was clear: either Liberty would prevail, enabling humanity to pursue endless happiness in peace, or we would all succumb to the darkness of Tyranny…

…I grabbed the knight and twirled it around my fingers, my eyes locked on the far edge of the map – the End of History. My thoughts lingered on that terrible crimson sky…

"Pearl told me Liberty would fall within the second she met me," I brooded. "It's been months since I left the Rotunda."

Kennedy leaned over the map, intently watching the tiny squiggles move across the yellowed parchment. He rested his index finger on a narrow leg of the river due north of the waterfall representing World War II. There, the wide rapids funneled into a whirlpool that seemed to stymie the river in its tracks before spitting its passengers out into rougher waters with cresting caps. Kennedy's finger shook ever so slightly.

"Time," he said, barely above a whisper, "has a way of stopping on a half-dollar."

Minty calmly placed her hand over Kennedy's. It was clear that the two of them shared a deep rapport.

"It'll be over soon, Jack," she said lovingly.

Kennedy watched the clock ticking on Minty's bookshelf. "That's what I'm afraid of."

((…I'm afraid we won't make it through the night…))

Kennedy's fears weighed on me throughout my time in Culpeper. I kept revisiting that afternoon at Wilcoxen Tavern, watching him clutching at those old photographs like a drowning man reaching for a life preserver. The assassination had been a national tragedy, the loss of a beloved public figure; but Kennedy had suffered a fate worse than death. Armed with special rounds supplied by Nicholas Morgan – the ageless White Hat Man – Lee Harvey Oswald had blown him head first into a netherworld between life and death, where he had lived for more than a half-century on the edge of perpetual twilight. I remember how cold…how vacant…how *hollow* I had felt in those thirty minutes I spent behind his eyes. I couldn't fathom being in that state constantly, as I imagined he was.

But as my training unfolded, the coldness between us thawed. He increasingly sought me out to ask me about my personal life – my loves, hopes, and fears – as if he had come to live vicariously through me. I wish I could say it was flattering for John F. Kennedy to take such an interest in me; truth be told, it was unnerving. We were both men out of time, but his was running out, and it was somehow up to me to carry his wounded soul across some celestial finish line I still couldn't define.

I knew only this much: that these ghosts had inexplicably named me their Champion, and if I kept my head down and did as I was told in their time, I would somehow save my own.

No matter how I tossed that around in my brain, it was still completely insane.

One afternoon late in my training I took a walk in the forest to clear my head. Near the creek bed I heard the sounds of a deep and beautiful female voice singing and humming. I rounded the bend to find Minty dangling her feet in the water, muttering something indecipherable in tonal melodies. The song was altogether joyful, yet there was a tinge of melancholy beneath it. I watched her sing from afar for several minutes when I heard footsteps crunching the forest floor behind me.

It was Ira Hayes, dressed from head to toe in the Marine Corps uniform he never seemed to change out of.

"It's beautiful, isn't it?" Ira offered. "Her daily prayer."

I nodded. "What is she saying, Ira?"

Ira closed his eyes. *"'I go to prepare a place for you.'"*

"A place," I repeated. "For whom?"

Ira half-smiled and touched me on the arm, then turned and walked away. Soon after, Minty finished and paced barefoot down the trail toward me.

"It's time, Benji," she said. "The Champion must be on his way again."

"Where am I going?"

Minty wiped her muddy hands off on a rag hanging from her belt. "Down from this mountaintop, back into the valley of the shadow of death."

I exhaled. "What's my objective?"

"To recruit another Champion to our cause."

That was two days before Kennedy and I boarded this train, whose passengers had already settled on a different Champion.

"After Jeffries knocks that nigger flat," cried a young mustachioed haberdasher, "I say we hang it from a tree!"

Amidst the hoots and hollers of agreement, the Irishman spoke up.

"Come now, lads," he said. "Thar's no need s'long as he knows his proper place."

((...know your place...))

Jackson's spirit lingers. Just as Aurora said it would. The seventh president died in 1845, just as the phrase "Manifest Destiny" entered the American lexicon. Like a virus, the notion that the white man was "freedom's heaven-defended race" spread far and wide, backed by popular pseudosciences like phrenology. Millions of Americans came to view the entire continent as their divine inheritance – its "redskin" inhabitants be damned. Southern slave-drivers particularly salivated at the prospect of annexing arable Western land to extend their power. The resulting conflict over the expansion of chattel slavery into new territories culminated in a bloody Civil War that formally ended the practice, at the steep price of three quarters of a million dead.

Thaddeus Stevens had once dreamed of a free, integrated and peaceful society rising from the ashes of the Confederacy. Yet as he feared, Tyranny's wider war on Liberty had just begun. In the South, legalized racism continued under the policies of "Jim Crow": blacks were segregated in every conceivable sphere of life, faced ever-present violence at the hands of lynch mobs and the Ku Klux Klan, and were effectively re-enslaved by "sharecropper" arrangements with their old plantation masters. The millions who migrated North fared little better, as the titans of industry pitted white and black workers against one another to keep both at poverty wages in squalid working conditions. This, in turn, drove nativist backlash against the rapid influx of immigrants from Southern and Eastern Europe, Latin America and Asia, culminating in a series of laws like the Chinese Exclusion Act designed to curtail the growth of the non-white population.

Yet even as white Americans sought to exclude others from their own land, we had no problem intruding upon the land of others. With the Western frontier closed, and Native Americans driven to poverty on reservations, white America's sense of "Manifest Destiny" transcended our borders, transforming into a universal "White Man's Burden" to civilize "savages" all around the globe. In just over a century – a cosmic blink of the eye – the Revolutionary decree that all are created equal was warped into the idea that Liberty was the sole inheritance of the white man, the apex of creation destined to rule it…

…but there were those who resisted…

…and when Jack Johnson stole the crown from Tommy Burns in 1908, it exposed the hidden undercurrent of transnational white supremacy...

…Fear…

((…you came to take our house away...))

…and a desperate need to wrest the title back from the son of a Texas sharecropper who didn't know his place...

((…but you will not replace us…))

The echoes had grown stronger, always accompanied by that tinnitus-like buzzing in my ears.

I gazed back out the window, into the forest. Hundreds of feet below, an ice blue lake emerged from the forest green. The air grew thick and heavy.

It's still buried out there.

I dropped my hat over my eyes...and drifted alive into a distant memory...

...

"Dreams are mirrors, Ben," Grandma says. "Don't bury them. They reflect our deepest longings, even the ones that haunt us."

My chin rests on my arms as I stare out the cabin window at the Donner snows.

"I hate this dream," I say.

Grandma's white hair moves in sync with the whipping spoon.

"You have to remember the bad dreams to remember the good ones," she says.

I'm trying to remember the good ones...of beaches and palms...of a white house and a pond with a great big tree...of hitting a home run to win the World Series, where Dad greets me at home...then he disappears...

...and the nightmare resumes...

On TV a Navy cruiser fires a missile. A CNN reporter casually talks over it, like it's all a dream:

"...twenty-two days from the President's red line date for Hussein to withdraw from Kuwait, war looms in the Gulf..."

Grandma scowls at Grandpa. She's furious. "Jacob Ascorro! Have you lost your mind? The kids don't need to see that!"

Grandpa turns around in his recliner, confused. Grandma grits her teeth and nods to the Christmas tree in the corner of the living room.

"Change. The. Channel."

Grandpa spots Rachel huddled under the tree, her head buried between her knees, on the verge of tears.

"Sorry, Patty," Grandpa says ruefully, and flips to a re-run of Quantum Leap. He invites my little sister to come sit in his lap. She sniffles and obliges, burying her head in his chest.

I'm still in my head, stuck on the nightmare...one ship rams another....the sharks circle him...he's chum in the water...

...Mom and Uncle Craig enter with groceries.

"Benji." Mom says. "Auraq's outside. He wants to play catch. Rachel, you can go, too. Fresh air would be good for you."

"Sweet!" I grab my glove from my suitcase and bound out into the Donner snows...

...

SCREEEEEECH!

The engineer slammed on the breaks, knocking me back into this realm.

"I. Have. Never!"

A Powdered Woman barked at the Chinese busboy lying prone in the aisle with fragments of broken wine glasses littering the floor.

The busboy snapped up, flush with embarrassment. "Sorry! Sorry!"

"Mr. Wong, is it?" the Powdered Woman snarled, her white corset stained red. "How will I get this stain out?"

Mr. Wong rubbed her corset with a rag. She pushed him away, demanding he fetch the conductor.

"You'd think a Chinaman would know how to do laundry!" she exclaimed to scattered laughter.

Kennedy yawned, the noise rousing him from his slumber.

"Welcome to the land of the living," I quipped.

Kennedy sat up and rubbed his eyes. "Where are we?"

"Donner Pass."

The Powdered Woman continued to joke with her friends, mockingly pressing down her eyelids.

Kennedy groaned. "No better place to eat each other alive."

~

The thermometer at the red brick rail depot registered 108 degrees.

"At least it's a dry heat," Kennedy joked.

"This sea of bodies can't help," I replied, surveying the mob of people on the platform. The Biggest Little City tripled in population that weekend, far more than the makeshift outdoor 22,000-seat arena would hold.

A poster clung to the brick wall of the station, entitled "The Incomparable Prize Fight," depicting the bald and brawny Johnson squaring off against an equally stalwart Jeffries. Below it was a cartoon depicting a grinning, big-lipped black man in a top hat threatening a poor, injured slave driver with his cane. The caption on the cartoon read: "UNCLE TOM'S CABIN – AS IT WILL HAVE TO BE TOLD IF JOHNSON WINS."

I glanced at the inscription on my coin:

WE HANG TOGETHER

I slipped the coin back into my pocket. "Is this where we find Excalibur, Jack?"

Kennedy squinted, shielding his eyes from the hot sun. "Maybe. But remember: a sword is nothing without a whetstone."

I cocked my head. "What does that mean?"

Kennedy patted me on the shoulder, saying nothing. Behind him, a throng of black riders poured from the last car. One man emerged struggling with three large suitcases for a Powdered Woman, who scolded him for his "laziness."

"Let's go," Kennedy said.

We weaved south on Virginia Street through a thicket of Belle Epoch pretense. Once we reached the banks of the Truckee River, a five-story black brick building seemed to materialize from thin air. The sign on the door identified it:

THE SILVER BULLET SALOON & INN

"Our accommodations," Kennedy said, leading me through the doors.

The interior was breath taking. The open atrium was equal parts tavern and French steam punk curio shop. Its walls were lined with glass cabinets of silver trinkets. *"Gifts from Fréderic,"* Kennedy explained. Assorted silver gadgets and musical instruments adorned the walls; balconies overlooked the tavern floor, where four silver mash tuns brewed beneath a sunlit glass dome.

Michelle would love this place.

A black man in a navy blue jacket played "Yankee Doodle Boy" on the piano against the far wall; three men and a woman played cards at a center table. The woman glanced from under the brim of her black cowboy hat, her black boots kicked up on a chair. She was deeply tanned, in her thirties or forties; a faint scar traced in a straight line from the corner of her left eye and tapered off just below her dark brown hair. She stared daggers at Kennedy.

"You *dare* darken my door," she sniped.

Kennedy swallowed and went flush, breaking into a sweat.

The woman moved quickly across the floor and stopped an inch from Kennedy's nose.

Kennedy cleared his throat. "Listen, if this is about the incident at Tammany Hall …or, Kitty Hawk, I take full respon–"

The woman roared with laughter, wrapping Kennedy in a bear hug. "Good to see you, *Jack*," she said sweetly.

Kennedy let out a huge exhale, setting a hand on my shoulder. "This is my partner, Benjamin Upson."

The woman's breath caught. Her eyes lingered on me for an uncomfortable few seconds, studying me up and down.

"John Brown," she whispered faintly. "As I live and breathe."

John Brown…

"Uh," I replied. "Excuse me, miss, but…do I know you?"

She smiled and tilted her head. I looked deep into her eyes…

…her hazel eyes.

The woman clutched me tightly and pulled me in for a kiss on the cheek.

"Come on, Benji," she said. "Don't you remember lil' Emmaleigh?"

~

Emmaleigh Stevens was alive and, as of 1910, the leader of the Sons of Liberty. Slack-jawed, I studied the unmistakable scar on her face, the trace outline of…

…a bullet…

A light-skinned bald black man with a curly mustache and goatee interrupted my thoughts.

"Our hostess forgets her manners," he said. "W.E.B. Du Bois, at your service."

I shook his hand. "Co-founder of the National Association for the Advancement of Colored People. It's an honor."

"You've heard of the N.A.A.C.P.?" He turned to Emmaleigh. "It seems our little upstart outfit is gaining some recognition."

Du Bois studied me, stroking his chin pensively. The native New Englander had long been one of the Civil Rights Movement's more enigmatic characters. At a time when conservative blacks like Booker T. Washington had resigned themselves to the ascendancy of white supremacy, Du Bois was considered a radical. Not only did he reject the compromise of "separate but equal," he also supported the liberation of Africa from its European colonizers. The racism he experienced as a young boy in the North convinced him that emancipation alone was an inadequate remedy; a more aggressive defense of the universal rights of all was required.

Du Bois struck a match and lit a cigar, then waved it to snuff it out.

"This is the man you spoke of, isn't he Miss Stevens? Your 'Champion' so to speak?"

Emmaleigh nodded. Du Bois furrowed his brows and drew a long puff.

"He's not from around here, I can tell. And yet..."

Du Bois picked a thread from my lapel.

"...I think he'll fit right in."

I cocked my head. "How do you mean?"

Du Bois smiled, tapping ashes into a tray. Emmaleigh cleared her voice and introduced the other two men at the card table. One was an aging Cheyenne tribesman named Sage Nighthorse, the other a shy thirty-something black man named Teddy, nicknamed "Growler" because *"he blows that trumpet like a dream."* Each nodded perfunctorily.

Emmaleigh motioned, and I followed her to the bar.

"I hope you're ready for tonight," she began, setting a shot glass in front of me. "What's your poison?"

I hesitated. "Um...nothing, thank you."

Emmaleigh raised a brow. "You don't partake?"

I shook my head. Emmaleigh smiled and shrugged.

"I suppose a real man knows his limits."

Emmaleigh downed a shot and set it back hard on the bar. I was still in shock to see her alive; for eight months I had been wracked with guilt that Morgan's bullet had taken her. The visual evidence in front of me – that long, streaking scar – gave rise to another story that begged telling. As I leered, the ponderous silence between us became palpable.

"You know," Emmaleigh began, twirling her shot glass on the bar, "I saved both our hides that night."

I opened my mouth to speak. Nothing came out.

"I induced Morgan to waste his only shot on you."

The room spun. *She was only three. How the hell could she have known that?*

"Wait," I interrupted. "Why would Morgan want to kill *me*?"

"Not kill. Snuff out."

I furrowed my brow. "What's the difference?"

Emmaleigh pursed her lips. "Follow me. I have something to show you."

Emmaleigh's fifth floor chambers were spare, save for a watercolor portrait of her late Uncle Thaddeus. Atop a chestnut dresser sat a small white porcelain box and three books: *Common Sense, Poems on Various Subjects,* and *Two Treatises of Civil Government.*

"Some of Mother's things," she said. "Aurora spent years tracking them down. My Sister is tenacious like that."

Emmaleigh pulled an ivory drawstring bag from the box, then waved me onto her balcony overlooking the Truckee.

"Hold out your hand."

Emmaleigh dropped a white seedling in my palm.

"What kind of seed is this?" I asked.

"Dogwood."

"I haven't seen a dogwood since..."

I trailed off. The seed looked...*burnt. That tree.*

"How – ?"

"I burned that sucker down."

"I don't understand. You were three years old, I..."

Emmaleigh adjusted my collar. "Our Champion didn't know his limits. I sent up a smoke signal. I had hoped you would come back to your post."

I fell into a chair, annihilated. "I don't know who you are, but – "

"What round were you drafted?"

My breathing slowed, and my heart accelerated. "What?"

Emmaleigh sat down in front of me. "The St. Louis Cardinals drafted you out of high school in 1997. What round?"

My mouth went dry. "Thirty-third."

"Ever make it up to the big club?"

I swallowed. "One game."

"Avalanche took your knee and your dreams, am I right?"

127

Inhale...exhale... "Yeah."

"Do you have anything left?" she asked pointedly. "Or did you bury it all on that Tuesday morning?"

I grit my teeth. "Part of me died that morning. It died again in that forest with Immanuel."

I looked into Emmaleigh's eyes pleadingly.

"Don't make me die all over again. *Please...*"

Emmaleigh leaned forward and touched my left knee.

"Unless a seed falls to the ground and dies, it abides alone. But if it dies, it yields a tenfold harvest."

She looked out onto the river.

"Harvest always comes at sundown. Even from the seeds we sow in darkness."

I looked down at the Truckee, and I saw the first fruits.

~

The sun dipped behind the Sierra in a blaze of orange and pink. The woman perched on a boulder overlooking the river, legs dangling, reading from a faded brown leather diary.

"I made it back, John Brown."

Mariah looked up from the diary. At sixty, she still looked sixteen to me.

"Boy, I'll tell ya," she continued. "Mr. Mason was mighty sore atcha for leavin'."

I approached the rock slowly, short of breath. As I drew closer, I broke down. I slunk forward into her arms and burst into tears.

Mariah rubbed my back as I sobbed into her shoulder.

"I'm sorry," I cried. *"I'm so, so sorry. It's all my fault. I shouldn't have..."*

"You're right," she whispered back. "You shouldn't have. But you did, and I lived. So...thank you."

I released and pulled back *"Why*? Why would you thank me?"

Mariah shook her head. "You think I ever would have escaped that plantation? You think they ever would'a let me keep my boy? You think Immanuel would'a lived?"

"I..."

"Josiah Atwater was...*jealous*."

I looked Mariah up and down. "Oh, God...Mariah, I – "

She held her hand up. "It's over. I got to raise Ezekiel Immanuel Atwater on my own terms."

I wiped my eyes. "Why Atwater? Why would you keep that name after everything..."

"I could'a been a Stevens. Thaddeus offered when he took me in as Emmaleigh's nanny. But I couldn't forget my hard beginnings, or where my husband fell."

Mariah watched the river wistfully.

"At water."

Mariah closed her eyes, meditatively.

"The Law of Seeds: new life from death, the hope that a son might be greater than his father. Now that Zeke is gone, I hold out that hope for my grandson, Teddy."

"What happened to Zeke?" I asked.

Mariah didn't flinch. "They hung 'im. They say it was for beddin' a white girl, but it might as well've been for sport."

My spirit dropped.

Mariah sighed. "White man, you can't save everyone. What you did was mule-headed, but at least I'm alive. Cut that burden loose an' let yourself rest."

I went to bed that night split in two. When I emptied my pocket, the seed was gone, carried away by wind and water.

Eleven

Two Champions

Jack London glared contemptuously over his cards at the Galveston Giant. All night, Jack Johnson had kicked London's ass up and down the table with house money – chips of pure silver – to the point that London could barely cover an ante.

That wasn't what perturbed the famed author of *Call of the Wild*. After all, he had personally witnessed Johnson's competitive fire two years earlier in Sydney, when Johnson pummeled Tommy Burns into submission. It wasn't that he won. No. It was the *way* he did it, flaunting himself in his bespoke black pinstripe suit and white bowler hat, taunting the other players with every victory, flashing gold rings and a golden smile…

…with that *bitch* dripping from his arm.

Belle Schreiber, a buxom blond Chicago call girl, gave London a wink. He steamed.

"Tell me, Miss Schreiber," he said, biting his lips. "What draws you to such a beast as this?"

Johnson lit up a Cuban cigar and leaned back.

"Because I eat cold eels," he answered for her, "and think distant thoughts."

Belle giggled. London sat back, eyebrows knit together in puzzlement. I studied Johnson as he exhaled, filling the table with smoke.

He's Looney Tunes.

Johnson, London, and I were the only remaining players in a high-stakes poker game in a private upstairs parlor at The Silver Bullet. Among the defeated seated in the bar area were Du Bois; Tex Rickard, a fight promoter who co-sponsored Sunday's fight with London; Archibald Gould, a walrus-mustached British industrialist who underwrote Tex's insurance policy on Johnson; and Cecil Barton, a scrawny, muckraking journalist who I sensed was only present to dig up dirt on Johnson.

There was no shortage of demand for it. When Johnson arrived in the packed bar earlier that evening, with two bodyguards and Belle on his arm, a hush of contempt fell over the crowd. With a daft smile on his face, Johnson moved through the crowd toward the bar and ordered drinks for all.

"For all my new friends," he announced confidently, lightly punching the angry white man in the bowler hat standing next to him. The barkeep, Teddy, pointed to the banner hanging over the bar:

ALL SPIRITS FREE!
Kitchen Full Price

"People are gonna die here tonight," I warned Emmaleigh.

She waved me off. "Get under his skin. We'll do the rest."

And so as Teddy and Sage served libations downstairs, the revelers melted to wax, even sobbing in each other's arms. Meanwhile, as Kennedy dealt a heavily stacked deck upstairs, I waited for the opportunity to get inside the skin of the most cocksure man I had ever laid eyes on.

"Bet's to you, Mr. London," said Kennedy.

London grew hotter under the collar.

"Mr. London?"

"I fold," the writer said. Johnson smashed the butt of his cigar in an ashtray and set his finger on one of the chips in the center of the table. He flicked it back toward him, repeating the motion until one-by-one they had all been absorbed into his victory pile. Belle gestured at London with a drooping finger, drawing a hearty chuckle from Du Bois sitting alone in the corner.

London grit his teeth. "Have you no decency?"

Belle touched her finger to her lips sensuously. "A gal can really go places being indecent, can't she?"

"So," London bit off, "you enjoy your white slavery?"

Du Bois took a seat to my right. "White slavery, you say, Mr. London?"

London ignored him as Kennedy dealt the next hand. Du Bois pressed gently.

"My parents endured 'black slavery,' and by their telling it was so brutal even free blacks were considered slaves. Just ask Dred Scott."

Du Bois' voice deepened.

"But I cannot *imagine* the horrors of 'white slavery.'"

London adjusted his bowtie. "Mr. Du Bois, you wear the badge of freedom, as you ought. Do you think that entitles you to the keys to civilization?"

"Civilization? Why, I learned all about Egypt in school."

Du Bois rested his head on his fist.

"Tell me more, Keeper of the Keys."

"You're a smart man," London replied, studying his new hand. "Truly, a credit to your race. But can you say the same of your brethren?"

"Can you of yours?"

London snickered. "I see with my own eyes that white men have advanced further than any other people. Do you contend a Negro brain designed the train that brought you here?"

Johnson remained stoic, arranging and re-arranging his chips. I watched him closely as a new bartender named Chen Wong asked to fill my glass. I declined as London pecked at Du Bois.

"Be thankful the burden of civilizing the world doesn't rest on your shoulders," he said. "It is a bloody climb upward to master nature."

Du Bois smiled. "Bloody climbs. Mastery. I thought you were a socialist, Mr. London?"

"I am first of all a white man, and only then a socialist."

"Two people at once. It must be maddening."

Kennedy cleared his throat. "Bets, gentlemen?"

London jumped. "All in."

"I fold," Johnson declared.

"I call," I said.

"Show 'em!" Kennedy cried.

London presented a straight flush, Eight through Queen of Spades.

"One color," he bragged.

Du Bois smirked. "All black."

I laid down three Queens and two Jacks: a full house.

Belle squealed as I hauled the silver chips in.

Johnson slow-clapped with a stogie in his mouth:

"Well played, Mr. Upson. Smooth as silk."

"Some people play poor hands well," I said.

I grasped London's shoulder.

"Others play good hands poorly."

Belle giggled. London stormed toward the door, snatching his jacket from Mr. Wong.

"Give me that!" he snipped and exited the suite.

Moments later there came from the stairwell an audible *"oomph!..."*

...clunk...

...clunk...

...clunk...

...CLUNK!

...ooooooooommmph.

"Sounds like he has a bloody climb ahead of him," I quipped as Kennedy dealt.

Du Bois smirked. Johnson flashed a smile. "So do you."

I smiled hesitantly. Over Johnson's shoulder I watched Gould whispering to Barton, who furiously scribbled in his notebook. Gould saw me and stared back vacantly. A chill ran down my spine.

"You cold, Mr. Upson?" Johnson said, eyes narrowed. "You haven't had a sip all night. I think a nice bottle of whiskey ought to warm you right up."

Johnson blew a smoke ring out over the table.

"Before I take all your chips."

I perused the new cards Kennedy dealt. "I'm not drinking tonight, Mr. Johnson."

Belle rolled her eyes. "Choir boy."

I laughed. "No…let's just say I prefer to be sober before I run this nice gentleman off the table."

Johnson roared with laughter, eyeing my significantly smaller stack of chips. "That so? It'll take you all night."

I said nothing in return, catching a glance at Kennedy. Johnson leaned back in his chair and yelled at Gould.

"Hey! Papa! I'll be home past my curfew tonight. Don't wait up for me!"

Johnson broke into laughter as Gould stroked his mustache. Gould pulled a gold pocket-watch out of his breast pocket and glanced at it briefly, then whispered something else to Barton, who closed his notebook and exited.

Johnson continued to badger Gould. "Oh, so, Mr. Barton's also on your payroll? Is there a damn soul this side of the world you don't own?"

Gould stuffed the watch back in his jacket. He whispered something else to Tex. Tex began to sweat and shifted his eyes nervously, then nodded his head and abruptly left the parlor. Gould grabbed his black cane from against the bar and sauntered over to the table. He leaned in to within in an inch of Johnson's face and spoke just above a whisper, so all in the parlor could hear it:

"I own everything."

Johnson's smile slowly faded, and he began to anxiously tap his hands on the table. He shifted uncomfortably in his chair before replying, with a slight rasp in his voice, "You don't own me."

Almost imperceptibly, Gould's mouth twisted upward into a smile. "My dear boy. I will always own you."

Gould turned, looked me in the eye and smiled. Without saying another word, he walked out of the parlor, leaving the gallery in cold silence.

Johnson was visibly shaken. Belle slid up closer to him for comfort. He pressed her away.

"Damn it, let me breathe, woman!" he blurted, slamming his fist into the table. Belle gasped and quivered, then slapped Johnson across the face before storming out of the parlor.

Gould did a number on this guy.

Johnson surveyed the parlor, and the uncomfortable looks on the onlookers' faces. In an instant he snapped back into his jovial self, as if nothing happened.

"Come on, Mr. Upson," he said, brushing his lapels. "Time to put you out of your misery."

I shot a knowing glance at Kennedy as he dealt the next hand. I nodded silently at Johnson, and the game resumed.

For the next hour, I beat Johnson hand after hand, slowly withering away his once insurmountable chip lead. To be fair, Kennedy stacked the deck in my favor the entire time, but winning wasn't my primary objective.

Get under his skin. And so I did, lightly taunting Johnson after every win. For a man as competitive as he, it was a slow drip of torture. So I piled on.

"So, Mr. Johnson," I said, counting up the chips I had taken from him. "What truly makes you the World Champion?"

Johnson narrowed his eyes, rubbing his thumb and forefinger together. "I knocked a white man on his ass. Not for the last time."

"So you did," I continued. "But Burns was only the Champion by default after Jeffries retired. Jeffries has never lost a fight in his life."

Johnson cracked his neck, menacingly.

"What makes you think he'll fall on Sunday?"

Johnson bellowed in laughter. "The hell are you trying to do, get under my skin?"

I stared back at him and smiled.

"Alright, alright," he said, tapping the table. "How about I knock you on your ass right now?"

Johnson turned to Kennedy.

"Deal, Irish."

Kennedy nodded and promptly dealt the next hand.

Johnson reviewed his cards and set them down. "I'm all in," he said, shoving his chips to the middle of the table.

Kennedy looked to me.

I nodded. "Call."

We each threw down our hands. My three-of-a-kind beat Johnson's two pair.

The gallery politely clapped as Kennedy pushed the chips toward me. Johnson fumed, cursing under his breath.

I flipped a chip in the air. "Wanna win it back, Champ?"

Johnson cocked his head.

"Real Champion never lets another claim victory."

Johnson cackled. "Aren't you just another cocky white boy."

"You backing down from a challenge?"

Johnson leaned back. "Go on."

"Name your game."

No hesitation. "Billiards."

I shook my head. "I didn't see any open tables downstairs."

"Not on your turf. Mine."

I laughed. "Yours?"

Johnson clamped his teeth around another stogie. "Yeah," he said, lighting it up. "Mine. Rick's Resort. Right now."

I looked to Kennedy, whose face went blank. Du Bois clapped his hand on my shoulder.

"I think you should take the World Champion up on this offer, Benjamin," he said. "I'm curious to see which one of you bends the knee to the other tonight."

I nodded slowly. "Alright, then. Let's roll, Champ."

Johnson stood, and his muscle followed after. Du Bois motioned to me. "I'll drive."

Du Bois and I exited downstairs and hopped into Emmaleigh's Model T. Du Bois engaged the clutch and drove west onto Old Verdi Road.

Bzzzzzzt.

I reached into my pocket and tilted my phone so only I could see it:

Keep stirrin' the flame, you might get somebody killed.

I exhaled and shoved the phone back into my pocket.

"Is something troubling you, Mr. Upson?" Du Bois inquired.

"Nothing," I answered. "Just a little tired."

"Well, wake up. You still have work to do."

The road ahead turned bumpy. I turned to look back at the lights of downtown Reno; I blinked, and saw another set of lights.

~

Auraq's errant throw sends us scrambling for a white ball in the snow. I'm anxious, and a little irate: that was Dad's Curt Flood autographed ball. Auraq doesn't know who that is, or why that ball is so valuable. He isn't from here, and he doesn't know baseball. He's a couple years older; his dad rented a cabin near Grandma and Grandpa's for the holidays. He saw me tossing the ball in the yard with Uncle Craig the other day and couldn't stop asking questions. It turns out he sucks. Now I have to look for Dad's ball while Rachel skips ahead cluelessly, singing as annoying little sisters do.

"We bounce it in cricket," Auraq tries to explain. "That is why I threw it on the ground."

"Cricket?" I ask.

"Pakistan's game."

"Pakistan. Is that in the Gulf?"

"No, it is next to India."

"Oh," I say, disappointed. "My dad's in the Gulf. He's on the USS Blue Ridge. He's a JAG and tells them when it's legal to fire missiles at the Iraqis."

Auraq stops in his tracks. I turn.

"Did you find it?"

He shakes his head slowly.

Idiot. "Well lo—"

"Your father is a killer."

Rachel stops in her tracks. So do I.

"What did you say?" I seethe.

"I said," Auraq proclaims, "your father is a killer."

~

Nestled on the edge of town off Old Verdi Road, Rick's Resort was the last place one would expect a heavyweight champion to train for a prizefight. It was a small, quaint two-story inn, not much bigger than a bed and breakfast. For the past week, it had been host to Jack Johnson and his entourage as he prepared for Sunday's fight in an outdoor ring. Tonight, the fight took place upstairs, on a different mat.

"Side pocket," I said, burying the eight ball. "Winner, winner, chicken dinner."

Johnson cursed. "Two-out-of-three," he said, struggling to rack the next game. His hands trembled lightly as he carefully placed each ball, one-by-one, into the triangle. He dropped the solid green six ball onto the mat and scrambled to put it back in place. Du Bois spoke up from the corner table.

"Mr. Johnson," he said, sipping whiskey neat, "you seem flustered."

Johnson exhaled through his nose. He looked to me. "Break," he said as he finished the triangle. "Ain't gonna wait 'til sunrise to whip your ass."

I knocked three stripes in on the break. "You might have to."

Johnson knocked his cue lightly against the table. Du Bois pulled up next to him, whiskey in hand.

"Boy, Mr. Johnson," he said, "that marionette has your number."

Johnson furrowed his brow. "What the hell are you talkin' about?"

"Mr. Gould. That robber baron said something to you back at The Silver Bullet that spooked you something special. What was it?"

I missed on the two ball. Johnson took over and buried two stripes. He said nothing to Du Bois.

"So these walls have ears, do they?"

"He's not my puppet master," Johnson bit back as he sank the thirteen ball into the corner. "And I have no strings. I'm a self-made man."

Johnson knocked the eleven in, slowly gaining confidence.

Du Bois laughed. "I know you feel them, brother."

Johnson quietly dropped the rest of the stripes in one swoop.

Du Bois pantomimed. "Up and down and side to side, you just dance to their tune."

Johnson lay his cue on the table and stepped up to Du Bois, leaving barely an inch between them.

"*I. Am. The. Champion!*" Johnson belted. "My blackness is my excellence, mother fucker! You think it's a curse? You think I'm still a slave? Look at me!"

Du Bois lifted his glass to his lips and drank. He sipped and swallowed, then pointed out the window. "To them, your blackness is *unforgivable.*"

Johnson laughed. "You think I'm just another house Negro, don't you? Ain't got no schoolin', brother. *This* is *my* ladder."

"Until your body breaks. And what then? You advance *yourself*, but do you advance the Cause? How does a sharecropper profit from all of your preening?"

Johnson slammed down his glass. "You want me to be a *real* race man, is that it?"

He pointed his finger at me.

"I've taken my lumps! I've heard them cry *'nigger, nigger, nigger'* every time I step into the ring, every time I step out of my damn house! Don't think I don't know this is a white man's world!"

Johnson pounded his chest.

"But I'm gonna conquer it!"

"They'll never let you," Du Bois retorted.

Johnson's ire reached its zenith. Du Bois cut him to the nerve.

"You're still flustered, aren't you? Here."

Du Bois pulled a flask from his jacket.

"Like Mr. Upson, I'm not much of a drinker. Liquor, after all, is destroying the land of our ancestors."

Johnson demurred.

"There is, however, a homespun elixir I turn to in distress. A powerful tonic, soothing to the nerves. It's never failed to clear my head, but I'll bet your constitution won't stand it."

Johnson's low laugh crescendoed to a roar.

"Or will it?"

Johnson wiped his nose. "You're a funny man."

Du Bois shrugged.

"Pour!"

Du Bois pulled two shot glasses from the table. Du Bois poured the amber liquid into the glasses. It smelled like whiskey.

"What shall we toast to?" Du Bois asked.

Johnson pondered, then grinned devilishly. *"House Negroes."*

Du Bois laughed. They clinked and drank. Johnson shattered his glass against the dartboard.

"Still standin'!"

Johnson grabbed his cue and lined up for a shot on the eight ball.

"Corner," he called.

Johnson pulled back and tapped the white cue ball into the eight ball. The eight ball sank into the corner pocket…followed quickly by the cue ball.

Angrily, Johnson snapped the pool cue in half.

I struck. "I suppose we should make it best three-of-five?"

Johnson slowly turned his head, then ambled toward me, tensing his eyes and jaw. He stepped into me and stuck his finger in my chest.

"I'll bury you."

((…I'll bury you…))

I seized up; my heart leapt to my throat. Johnson slid past me and exited, descending the stairs in a huff.

My breathing rapidly increased. Du Bois stepped up behind me.

"You did well," he said. "Now go after him."

I nodded and exited, descending the stairs into the downstairs parlor, which Johnson's trainers had long deserted for bed. Johnson turned the corner into the men's restroom. I followed after.

Inside, Johnson leaned over the sink, staring at his hands. I soaked mine under the faucet next to him, fiddling with my ring.

"Everything alright, Champ?" I asked.

It took him a beat before answering. "Mr. Upson," he said, woozily. "Why…are there two of me?"

He looked at me.

"Why are there…two of you?"

Johnson lowered his head…

"Jack – " I began.

…and I saw something flash in the mirror.

"JACK!"

I spun and caught the assassin's knife arm with both hands. The momentum knocked Johnson into the mirror, shattering it. I rolled the assassin onto the floor; he spun me onto my back, and I froze. So did he.

He was young. Deep brown eyes. Dark brown hair. He looked exactly like…

"…Titus?" I whispered.

He hissed in a Tennessee drawl. *"They took it all away…everything…"*

My arm spasmed; the assassin slipped, lacerating my left temple.

"Shit!" he yelled, then prepared the killing strike.

THWAP!

The assassin flew into the wall, unconscious. Johnson stood stone-cold sober in a fighting stance. My vision blurred as Johnson dropped to his knees and collapsed.

The last thing I saw was the assassin's dagger of pure lead, lying on the tile floor, its red hilt emblazoned with a golden seven-headed dragon.

Twelve

Bonds of Affliction

"...Your father will kill Iraqi women and babies. He is a bad man," Auraq says.

No. He tells them to shoot the bad guys. He doesn't kill babies. He doesn't.

"My father is a Stanford professor, he is not wrong! Allah will punish your father for the murder of his people."

Who is Allah?

"You guys, STOP!" Rachel bawls.

Go back to Pac-Man Land, Auraq.

"You are a child. You don't understand."

I clench. There is nothing to understand...

...I'll bury you...

...I'll bury you right here in the snow...

...

I snapped awake just before daybreak to Mariah pressing a hot towel firmly against my forehead. A bowl of blackened water sat on the nightstand of a bedroom at Rick's Resort. Downstairs, I heard Johnson shouting:

"Who the hell was that guy?"

I jerked up. Minty pressed me back.

"Relax," she said. "You did your job."

I balked. "My job was to get under Johnson's skin, not to get in a knife fight with – "

I bolted upright and fled the suite.

"There goes Mr. John Brown," Mariah quipped.

I heard Emmaleigh replying to Johnson as I limped downstairs toward the parlor:

"An agent of chaos..."

Titus. His name is Titus Atwater.

Johnson sat silently across the table from Emmaleigh, who twirled a lead dagger with a red hilt in her hand. Belle, with visible tears in her eyes, stood behind Johnson, gripping his shoulders tightly. Kennedy and Du Bois stood behind Emmaleigh. Several of Johnson's trainers looked on nervously in the background, anxious to know more about the attack on their prizefighter.

Johnson waved them out, then dropped his head into his hands. "So Mr. Gould is not who he says he is."

"Nor Mr. Barton," Emmaleigh added.

Johnson leaned back in his chair, a bead of perspiration forming at his brow. I could feel his heart beating from across the room.

"Mr. Gould found me at the race tracks in Dallas when I was a boy," he explained, staring into the middle distance. "He's been there ringside at every fight, always with Mr. Barton by his side. I've made a lot of money as a fighter, and that man's bloody handprints have been over every dollar."

Johnson bit his lip, shaking his head.

"I'll do it."

Emmaleigh nodded slowly. Strength sapped, I fell into the nearest chair. Kennedy rushed to my side.

"Easy, partner." He inspected my head wound closely. "How do you feel?"

"What do you think?" I snapped.

Kennedy whistled and held a rag against the cut. "Son of a bitch cut deep."

"Sorry." I wasn't. Every thought burned as the blackness coursed through me.

Ira approached from the kitchen with a tray of two shot glasses and a Jack Daniel's bottle of amber whiskey, the same color as Du Bois' elixir. He set the glasses out in front of Johnson and me and poured.

I cocked my head, suspicious. "What is that?"

"Our medicine," Johnson answered.

He whipped a chair around backwards and took the rag from Kennedy, pressing it against my temple.

"We need our strength for our mission."

My ears rang. "What do you mean *our* mission?"

Johnson sighed and nodded at Emmaleigh. "This fine lady here has just explained to me what you, Mr. Kennedy and Mr. Du Bois have been up to. With all the things I saw last night, I know there's a lot more at stake on Sunday than just a prize fight."

"What – what did you see?"

Johnson nodded at Du Bois. "I saw double."

Ira placed a shot glass in Johnson's hand, then turned to hand me mine. I refused.

"No," I said, shaking. "I don't drink. I haven't touched that shit in nineteen years."

"He won't mind," Emmaleigh said softly.

I swallowed. *"What did you say?"*

Emmaleigh took my hand.

"You have acute lead poisoning," she explained. "We need to flush it out."

Lead poisoning? What is she rambling about?

Johnson grabbed my hand...

((...I know what she has planned, brother...trust her...))

...I looked to Kennedy and Du Bois. Each of them nodded at me.

Uneasily I grabbed the shot glass. The odor was heavy but pleasant, with hints of honey and citrus. *This doesn't smell like Jack Daniel's.*

I closed my eyes and reached into the darkest place within...

...forgive me...

...we clicked...I drank.

...that definitely wasn't Jack Daniel's...

~

It was 110 degrees outside, and I desperately needed water. Someone poured it down my parched throat. I looked down to see my hands wrapped in tape and covered in leather boxing gloves.

"It's alright, Mr. Upson," Teddy assured me, tapping my face. "Just focus and breathe."

It was Sunday, July 4, 1910; I had been out for sixty hours. I was in the outdoor arena for the Fight of the Century, and it was nearly empty; only a tenth of the 22,000 spectators were present. Every now and again the scene would flicker, and I could see all of them. But not through my eyes...no...through the eyes of a shadow companion riding along inside me.

I'm two people...

In the opposite corner sat my opponent. At once he was Jim Jeffries, the Great White Hope, come to take back his crown...at another he was nobody, the vague outline of a man without a face...

...I'm in the fight.

Kennedy crouched in front of me.

"Jack," I said, "what is this?"

"The sword needs a whetstone," he replied.

I touched the scar on my head. It no longer burned...

"To yield a harvest, the seed must die. For the seed to die, it must split open. And for the seed to open...it must *crack.*"

I eyed my opponent coolly...rage built within, unbridled rage, and with it strength. Strength to carry on. Strength to *fight.*

The world flickered. A brass band of horns appeared ringside. Cecil Barton held up a baton to conduct them, a shadow conductor, ready to craft the music in his own image, and his own way...

...and behind Tex, in the center of the ring, Archibald Gould stood guard as shadow officiant. His eyes were cold and cruel, and he raised his cane high into the air, a black cane with the golden head of an axe, the ancient *fasces* of Rome, the power of the patriarch who strangles the world in the palm of his hand...

...my shadow passenger whispered...

((...time to dance, Mr. Upson...))

...as Gould struck the ground with fire and fury.

CLANG!

"NIGGER!" went the hue and cry as Barton struck up the band.

I stepped into the ring, one man split in two, afraid for both of my lives...

...

Auraq walks away. Nobody walks away.

I drive him into the white snow, painting it red under a blue sky...

...

...Round Four. We clinched and circled the first three rounds. Jeffries is stronger than I, but I'm quicker. He has never lost, but now he is vulnerable. Nervous. He'll never let go. If he lets go, he'll never reign again...

((...it's you or him ...))

One slip. Drive it home.

WAPPPP!!!!

I land a stinging right to his face, sending him to the ropes. Even I felt that. The old ship is sinking.

((...we drown together...))

22,000 went silent as the band played on. I, World Champion Jack Johnson, landed the first heavy blow against the Great White Hope...

...

...the white snow turns red as I punch Auraq in the nose a second time. Everything within me shouts "KILL! KILL!" My conscience rises, and I shove it down. That dirtbag Auraq has to pay...

...he has to pay...

...

...Round Thirteen. It's cold here, fighting these ghosts, Battle Royale. I feel every punch I throw as every punch I've thrown a thousand times over. Dock Boys. Candy Man. Black Hercules. Ol' Joe.

((...you're worthless...you're nothing...))

Candy Man said that with his eyes when he kicked me out of his store. Ol' Joe said it, too. Come to Texas to kick a nigger's ass, he said. They threw us in jail an' made us fight bare knuckle.

SMACK! Jeffries lands a side blow, *POP!* I counter.

You can't kill me, White Boy.

((...don't call me a killer...don't call my daddy a killer, you're a liar...you bring it all on yourself, you dirtbag...))

Yeah. I brought it on myself. I hung those nooses at the Nashville church. I prayed for my own death. That's why I fight.

((...Crisis...this is no fight, it's a Crisis...))

Amen. *POP!* I nail Jeffries in the jaw.

((...this is my Crown...now you want to take it from me...it's you or me, dirtbag...))

You're tired, White Boy.

((...sit down and stay down!...))
BAM!!

I *won't* cower! I *won't* stop struttin'! Call me uppity 'cause I beat your game, call me a liar when I tell it plain? Stir the flame, Devil. I'll dance 'til I dangle from that tree...

((...the world was mine...you took it from me ...))

I'm done with this White Boy.

Feel my pain! Feel it!

Only one Champion wins Today.

Left-right-right-uppercut!

Sweat flies...and I send this White Boy into the heart of another...

...

"...STOP FIGHTING!!!" Rachel's shrill screams vanish into the tree line. Auraq punches me hard in the shoulder. He's stronger, but I have the fire. I roll him... he flips me over....one shot to my gut knocks the wind out of me...I shiver in the snow...

...

...Round Fifteen.

"Don't let the nigger knock him out!"

Too late. Jack Johnson has worked me up, down and around. Punch. Counter. Weave. He has attacked me from angles I can't defend. Not in this heat. Not at these heights.

My legend will fall.

((...your daddy is a killer, Jeffries...his daddy was a killer...killed my daddy...and his daddy...))

Fuck you, Jack! You wear *my* crown!

((...you kill my son...your son kills his...generations come, and all my children go...you take everything...everything...take it high, take it low...))

Fuck you, Tyson!

((...Angel?...you look like the Devil to me...))

Fuck you, Auraq!

((...you or me...never we...))

He's killing me. Fast and slow, he's killing me...

...

((...I see you, Benji...I see what happened...is your pain mine?...))

No. It is mine alone.

((...then here comes the train...))

147

Right upper!
Left hook-left hook-left hook! BOOM-BOOM-BOOM!
Down I go.
The Champion took my Great White Hope away…
…I am replaced…forever replaced…
…
…*Auraq flees as Uncle Craig carries me away.*
No. It's still buried out there, I whine, dangling from his arms…
…

…I dangled on the ropes three feet from Jeffries, convulsing. I'd never felt so dark or terrible. I was Johnson, and I was Jeffries. There were other passengers, too, Shadows I couldn't tell one from another. I felt them all as my rawest self. Nothing could dull the pain as ancient animus crushed from all sides.

I hate myself.

In the ring, Johnson donned the flag and danced another day as World Champion. I knew he saw me there, with his tired eyes, wounded and scared. It was a fleeting glance, but I knew. I lived beneath his skin now, and he mine.

"We own you still, Benjamin."

A chill swept through me. Gould pushed through the crowd toward me, eyes like cold steel, stinking and reeking of tar. He pressed the axe end of his cane into my chest and pulled himself forward to meet me nose-to-nose. Black smoke curled from the corner of his mouth. My body convulsed in his presence, just as it did with Morgan. I swallowed hard.

"I don't know what the bitch is up to," Gould continued. "But I see through you. Your heart is one of darkness, and you will never wield Excalibur against us. You have accomplished nothing Today."

Gould released the cane and dissolved to black ash, fading into the air. Behind him, in the press pool, Barton whispered to journalists as they typed to their wire services. What looked like tongues of fire appeared over their heads as Barton swept through like a whirlwind, fading to black and vanishing as Gould had.

I fell back against the ropes, exhausted, when I felt a hand on my shoulder.

"Come on, brother," Du Bois offered, extending his hand to mine. "She's waiting."

Du Bois pulled me through the crowd and we slipped out of the arena, invisible, as the whispers of 22,000 echoed into the ether.

~

From the rooftop of The Silver Bullet, Reno smelled like a Texas oil rig.

"What do you see, Benjamin?"

Emmaleigh nodded at the throngs below. A few celebrated their Champion; many more mourned their Great White Hope.

"Look closely."

I relaxed my eyes. I saw.

Incredible.

Everyone was double: their physical selves …and a Shadow, an echo from deep within, both in terrible conflict. In many the seedling of conscience rose, only to be drowned out by racial vitriol. Others in their spirits saw anew the veil between them and their brothers, who had always lived in a house divided.

There was pushing. Shoving. Punching. The Shadows scattered in all directions, engulfing a continent in flames.

I stared agape at Emmaleigh, awestruck. "Who are you, Emmaleigh Stevens?"

"Only a messenger," she replied curtly. "Same as you."

Messenger. "Johnson and I…we were…*conduits*…."

"Those who drank from our fountain saw in our Champions their own reflections."

"Empathy. The people who drank at The Silver Bullet…they saw the fight in double."

" '*Labor to keep alive in your breast the spark of celestial fire called 'conscience.'* My uncle's last words to me."

Emmaleigh turned to Du Bois.

"Thank you for your services this week," she said. "Inform Mother that the seed has been planted."

Du Bois bowed. "May the walls come tumbling down."

The man saluted, then vanished into thin air.

Emmaleigh handed me my satchel, and Kennedy placed his hand on my shoulder.

"A long and bloody century begins," Emmaleigh whispered bittersweetly.

She touched my chest...

...near, a gunshot dropped a man into the river as a seed floated by...

...far, bodies broke and cities burned. A serpent declared, *"The Champion is weak..."*

...eighty years coursed with fire, as ancient enemies set the world ablaze...

...it drew me in as a moth to the flame.

Thirteen

Prometheus

The capital burned with fire and fury. Thousands took to the streets, singing and chanting songs of newfound freedom. The riot police staked out positions throughout the city, on every street corner, and made no moves. It was no use fighting a fire that didn't start here.

Minty surveyed the Wall. A single tear rolled down her cheek.

"A seed broke open on the Fourth of July," she said. "And now harvest has come in East Germany. Right here. Right now."

It was the evening of November 11, 1989. The twentieth century had been a time of unthinkable war and bloodshed; Liberty and Tyranny collided on fields far and flung. Nation rose against nation, kingdom against kingdom. There were world wars and fell famines, one never far from the other. A hot war ended in Berlin in 1945; soon thereafter, a cold war between nuclear superpowers arose in its place. As humanity came to grips with the horrors of a Holocaust that claimed the lives of millions, there arose a new consciousness of the dangers of bigotry, sparking demands for justice and the overthrow of empires in the name of freedom.

I watched as Berliners dripped through the fissures in the Wall separating communist East from democratic West since 1962, a monument to Tyranny that finally came crashing down.

"We did this?" I breathed. "How does a punch thrown in Reno in 1910 bring down the Berlin Wall in 1989?"

Minty watched a man wailing away with a pickaxe, joined by a half dozen of his brethren. "Not alone. It took many blows from many instruments."

She clasped my shoulder and descended into the BTR-60 we "commandeered" from the *Nationale Volksarmee*. Atop the Wall, a Berliner drank champagne from the bottle and breathed back fire. The memory tumbled like an avalanche, of father and son watching this very scene unfold live a world away, on a living room couch in Okinawa...

...

"The Evil Empire is crumbling," the father whispered, hugging his son...

...

((...may the walls come tumbling down...))

I shivered as I climbed down into the tank. As I closed the hatch the fire extinguished, an echo drowning in a sea of forgetting.

~

The Pacific laps gently against Huntington Beach Pier. We arrived at sunset to pay tribute to an officer and a gentleman. A family man and a patriot. A tenacious warrior and a generous soul.

The beloved John Eric Upson.

Orphaned at fourteen, the Long Beach native and son of James and Esther Upson worked his way through college and law school. He enlisted in the Navy as Judge Advocate General and married Marie Leanne Ascorro, a nurse from Reno. I, Benjamin John Upson, joined them in Annapolis on January 16, 1979, before the world or I were ready. Dad taught me to see the world beyond my own, and to embrace the better Angels of our nature...

...and now he is gone to be with them...

"Benji, do you want to say something?" Mom strokes my arm lovingly.

"There's nothing to say that hasn't already been said," I softly reply.

Michelle buries her head in my chest. Rachel grips my arm. I stare deep into the ashes.

I'm sorry, Pop. I'm so sorry.

I give him back to the sea. Tears rise like the tide; I shove them back to the surf.

I must be strong. Too strong to cry.

Mom breaks down. Grandma and Uncle Craig take her for a walk down the pier.

Michelle kisses me on the lips.

"Talk to your sister," she says, wiping away a tear and following after Mom.

Rachel and I stare silently at the ocean.

"How's your knee?" she asks.

I shake my head and look away. "I'll never play baseball again."

She wipes a strand of brown hair from her face. "I'm sorry. Should we sit?"

"Probably."

We sit facing away from the Pacific. A light turns on inside Ruby's Diner.

Rachel pulls a flask from her Sun Devils hoodie.

"Cinnamon schnapps?"

I shake my head. "I'm done with that."

"Do you have a problem?"

"No, no, it's just...I haven't had a drop since...since that day."

Rachel grimaces...then tosses the flask over her shoulder into the Pacific.

"Shit, Rachel!"

"Today only. All bets are off when I get home."

"Yeah? How's Phoenix?"

Rachel cracks her spine. "It's hot, and so are the guys."

I snicker.

"Although," she says, leering down the pier, "if you don't put a ring on Michelle soon, I will."

Rachel Elise Upson is the only person who can make me laugh in a moment like this.

"What? Has she said something?" Rachel purrs and licks her lips.

"No. But you're right. She's the one you never let go."

I look at my feet.

"I'm going back to school in August."

"George Mason U?"

"Yeah. Secondary ed. I don't want to be a lawyer like Dad...but I want to pass on what he taught me."

Rachel smiles. "Yeah?"

"He was a man on a mission wherever he went."

"So are you. You were his little protégé."

"Yeah..."

My mind drifts elsewhere as the tide washes against the Pier.

"Do you remember when that kid Auraq jumped me on Christmas Eve? When Dad was in the Gulf?"

"I remember when you jumped Auraq."

"Whatever. Dad blew me up over it when he got back. 'There are always two sides of the coin,' he said. He always tried to imagine himself in someone else's shoes, even if they hated him. He was so compassionate..."

The waterworks flow.

"...that fucking lemon farmer...he wasn't one of us...he wasn't supposed to be here, and he killed him..."

Rachel hugs me punitively. "Benji, stop it!"

I let it rain. "...but I drove him there, Rachel...I drove him..."

~

I felt for the guy.

"What are you? A phantom? A demon?!"

"Neither," Kennedy replied. *"Ich bin Berliner."*

Antosha Khramtsov dissolved. For twenty-two years, the KGB Directorate S agent wrought havoc as Air Force mechanic Barry Cronshaw of Atlantis, Florida. In 1962 he began a torrid affair with Air Force One flight attendant Bethany Campbell. One night of pillow talk yielded the President's itinerary for an upcoming trip to Texas, intel Khramtsov relayed through Mexico City to an unhinged Russophile named Lee Harvey Oswald.

So please forgive his confusion. After all, his interrogator *did* look a hell of a lot like Jack Kennedy.

"Do they all scare so easy?" I asked Minty. She shrugged.

Kennedy traipsed over to us, leaving Khramtsov to wail.

"Dresden," he said. "I – "

Khramtsov's crying reached a crescendo.

Minty raised a finger. "Excuse me."

She marched over to Khramtsov and licked her hand.

"I can't hear Mr. Kennedy."

Minty reared back and slapped Khramtsov unconscious, then returned to the conversation.

"Anyway," Kennedy continued. "This rogue agent's codename is Platov. He's been meeting his handler behind the Iron Curtain – Warsaw, Kiev, Prague – but also in the West. Places like Munich – and Biarritz."

"Biarritz?" I echoed. "In France?"

Ira Hayes glanced up from the radio. "König has a new Apprentice."

"It appears so," Kennedy said. "Platov routinely visits a prisoner in Dresden named Erna Petri. Someone we'll want to talk to."

"Signal Pearl," Minty instructed Ira. "It's time to haunt the castle."

Ira punched what looked like Morse code into his radio.

I cocked my head and squared up to Minty. "Haunt the castle?"

~

To the uninitiated, the status quo ruled *Gedenkstätte* prison. But the dreaded Stasi – East German secret police – had for days been mere puppets of a fiery middle-aged Yankee redhead. She'd teased ranking officer Torvald Geist for weeks, until one evening he let her into the facility.

"Bears love honey," Pearl explained, *"especially when it's just out of reach."*

As Torvald lusted after the honeypot, fifty undead Sons of Liberty invaded *Gedenkstätte* and played a high stakes game of peek-a-boo with the Stasi, appearing and disappearing at will. Meanwhile, Pearl and I negotiated surrender with Torvald in his own office against a soundscape of shrill screams and sporadic gunfire.

"Dies wird als nächstes passieren, Torvald," Pearl told the frightened officer. *"Diese Einrichtung wird jetzt von den Sons of Liberty kontrolliert."*

Twelve hours later, the elderly Erna Petri waited in the interrogation room. I stood behind the two-way mirror watching the old woman when Minty tapped me on the shoulder.

"You need to see this."

Erna's cell was covered in thick layers of odorous black tar. It felt grim and angry inside. My knife scar pulsed.

"It's like Jackson's cabin," I said.

"And your cell in N'Orleans," Minty added. *We've got to get her out of here.* "Let's give her some fresh air."

So we secreted Erna across the Elbe to Waldpark. She muttered from under her bag as Ira leaned her against a spruce tree:

"Ich nehme an, das ist die Gerechtigkeit, die ich verdiene, oder?"

I removed the bag. Erna looked much older than sixty-nine. Her stringy blond hair was matted over deathly white skin. Save her shifting blue eyes, there were few signs of life. Minty handed her a cup of coffee. Erna looked at the five of us – me, Minty, Ira, Kennedy and Pearl – and settled into a deep belly laugh.

"Oh my," she managed in a heavy accent. "The American rainbow has returned."

She took a sip of coffee, then cradled the cup to her chest.

"My appeals have been denied, I see. One last taste of my own hospitality?"

She scanned us again.

"None of you are armed. Poison, then?"

I shook my head. "We're not here to punish you for your crimes."

"Then what?"

"What does Platov want?"

Erna swallowed. "I see. I'm in the middle of another Soviet-American conflagration."

She eyed me closely.

"Platov drives a harder bargain than you. Perhaps when your blood is colder…"

Erna coughed violently.

"I grew up among Third Reich monsters. I know monsters, and I am one. Yet nobody chills me like Platov."

Ira spoke up. "He did something to you."

"No," Erna spat. "Platov is a gentleman…and a mastermind. So I must tell you, whoever you are, that you will lose."

Pearl stepped forward. Erna studied her fire red locks and frowned.

"Fraulein. Ich weiß nicht, für wen du dich hältst, aber– "

"Wann haben Sie das letzte Mal das Motorrad Gefahren?"

Erna scowled. "What about my motorcycle?"

"It was your father's gift to you," Pearl continued. "She had quite the horsepower."

Erna was perplexed. "I don't understand."

Pearl leaned in more closely. "What did it mean to you?"

Erna looked away. "I used it for farm business in Gotha. We had nothing before the Reich. No one would buy from us, so our harvests rotted..."

Erna retreated into the recesses of her mind.

"...the *Jews* did that to us. Not the ones I knew, but the others. The bankers. *The Christ killers.*"

Erna set down her cup and leaned back, wistfully.

"Then God gave us the Reich. We contained the cancer and we prospered. I met my husband, Horst. Oh, but he was wild! Masculine, yes, and *disciplined.* He was everything that a man should be, and we fought our enemies together. I loved him to the end. *Rode* him to the end and beyond. And that is *exactly* what my motorcycle meant to me: freedom. Freedom from those who would take it from me. Aryan freedom. *A taste of American freedom.*"

I winced.

Pearl studied her closely. "You witnessed a miracle on that motorcycle."

"Yes," Erna said.

She closed her eyes, audibly tingling.

"I rode late at night, a week before my wedding. I came across a spruce that caught fire, but consumed only itself."

"My Sister lit that fire," Pearl said drily. "It was meant to convey one message. You took it for another."

Erna opened her eyes.

"I took it," she said bitterly, "as a sign from God that the love Horst and I shared would ignite the Master Race. He was the new Moses, and this Burning Bush commanded us to go to the Promised Land of Ukraine, new living space for the Aryans..."

((...your living space...our burial ground...))

...

"Moses," Minty said flatly. "Liberator of Hebrew slaves."

Erna growled. "There were never any 'Hebrew slaves,' do you hear me? *We* have been slaves to them for centuries! And now the elders of Zion will enslave us all – through the banks, through the universities. It's all in the *Protocols*. You Americans could have joined us, but Roosevelt's internationalists betrayed you."

"Internationalists," I said. "You mean 'globalists.'"

Erna grinned. "Globalists. Hmm. That's a good word for them."

"Tell us what happened in Ukraine," Pearl demanded.

Erna hesitated. "No."

Minty placed her hand on the nape of Erna's neck. She relaxed.

"I found six children on the side of the road, escaped from a train. *Juden.* They were tired and hungry. Like a good mother, I took them home and fed them."

Erna strained under Minty's hand.

"I couldn't keep them. I knew Horst wouldn't allow it. It was against everything we ever staked our lives on. I knew if I truly loved them…"

Erna let out a light, nervous laugh.

"So I lined them up in the yard…"

A mix of disgust and morbid fascination welled within.

"…they didn't cry. They just moaned. I took my pistol and ended their suffering."

She was shockingly cold and mechanical, her heart buried under ice and stone.

"It was legal. And *merciful.* Don't you see? I saved those children from the camps."

She believes this.

Pearl caressed Erna's cheek. "That's not why Platov came to you."

Erna shivered. "One of you must have a cigarette."

Ira pulled a lighter and pack of Camels from his pocket. He lit one and handed it to Erna.

"He came with guests. Six 'Brothers.' A rich man. A cowboy. A news man. A general. A priest. And a prince. They asked about my childhood, my favorite color, my favorite foods, making love to Horst, how I felt when the *führer* spoke…what it meant to be Aryan."

Erna puffed.

"They said there were people like me all over America: *'Erna, they are asleep. Help us awaken them.'*"

Erna watched the birds flying overhead.

"Why are you bothering me? Why should I help you?"

I smirked. "We can throw you back in the tar pit if you'd like."

Erna narrowed her eyes. "Tar pit? What are you talking about?"

She can't see it.

"What is your name?"

"Benjamin."

Erna took a drag. "A Semite's name. You remind me of Horst."

I stiffened. "Your husband. The SS officer."

"You have his fire. You will no doubt ruthlessly defend your own against the invading hordes."

My stomach dropped.

"I believe Frau Petri has had enough," Pearl interjected. "You've been most insightful. We may call upon you again."

Erna looked Pearl up and down.

"You're Pearl, aren't you? The youngest Sister. The *weakest*. You will not survive the onslaught to come."

Erna reared back in laughter.

"I told you that Platov brought me a Prince. The Master of Thrones. The Crown Prince of Biarritz!"

Erna slowly raised her fist into the air.

"Heil König!"

Fourteen

The Mark

No one could see the red-orange BMW 325i parked opposite the Soviet Rezidentura at 4 Angelicastraße in Dresden, an hour south of Berlin. Nothing was happening, and at a frenzied pace. That wasn't the case an hour earlier, when fifty East Germans, emboldened by the fall of the Berlin Wall and the Soviet puppet state, stormed the gates and shook them. They were scared off by the man in the *Ushanka*, face warmer and heavy coat firing a PSM semi-automatic pistol into the air. The way the man shot it, with steel in his eyes...just one impulse, one firing nerve, was all it would have taken for him to lay waste to all of them. No remorse. No mercy. It chilled me to the bone.

"Everyone's on edge here," I said. "Everyone but him."

"Think he's Platov?" Dutch asked from the driver's seat.

"He's our mark," Kennedy said from the backseat.

That was around two p.m. Three hours later, only one light remained on in the Soviet Rezidentura. As Pearl explained, *"while other Russians will be distressed by the collapse of their East German ally, Platov will have the calm confidence of a backer like König. He will not look over his shoulder; he will not be afraid of ghosts."*

This man fit that profile. I watched his office light up as Dutch and Kennedy tackled deeper things.

"It was embarrassing," Dutch said. "Olivia said Errol kissed like a prince and I kissed like a penguin."

Ronald Reagan – a.k.a., "Dutch" – looked younger these days, fresh out of the Golden Age of Hollywood. The fortieth President and former B-list actor had been an agent of the Sons of Liberty for fifteen years, and a close friend of Kennedy's the entire time. The Gipper had that same twinkle to his eye. But up close, there was something else buried behind it...something deeper...

Kennedy cackled. *"Santa Fe Trail* was an awful film."

"The worst," Reagan sighed. "Made John Brown out to be an evil madman. Truth is, he had the right idea."

"Yeah, well, *Hellcats of the Navy* was worse."

Reagan guffawed. "There you go again, Jack."

"Come on, Ronnie. You used stock footage of an American boat as a Japanese flagship."

"That was post-production! I didn't splice the damn thing together."

As the old Presidents bantered, I tried to focus on Platov. What Erna said haunted me as a dull migraine pulsed under the scarring on my temple.

Kennedy tapped on the center console. Reagan opened it and tossed back a bag of black licorice jelly beans.

"Hey Ben," Kennedy said as he shoveled beans into his gullet. "Your pop was in the Navy, right?"

I nodded. "JAG Corps. More than twenty years."

"Always love a Navy man."

"Kiss all the ass you want," I said. "Ronnie here was Dad's favorite President."

Kennedy smacked me with a file.

"What?" I yelped. "You're *my* favorite!"

"Ass-kisser."

Reagan gripped the steering wheel tight.

"Ronnie," I said. "You okay?"

He grimaced. "I don't deserve that."

"Deserve what?"

"To be your father's favorite President."

He looked out the window, tapping his thumbs on the wheel.

"I didn't take the cliffs on D-Day any more than I knocked down the Berlin Wall. A great man doesn't take credit for the works of better men – war heroes like Jack here."

Kennedy shifted.

"Or John Upson."

I did a double take. "You knew my father?"

"I met him once, and I'll never forget it."

Reagan exhaled.

"John came to my ranch up near Santa Barbara with Under Secretary Goodrich to ride horses. He was still reeling over his Angels blowing that 3-1 lead to Boston in the ALCS."

"Halo Nation will never forget," I sighed.

"Anyway," Reagan continued, "At one point John and I rode alone for about fifteen minutes. He said, 'Mr. President, permission to speak freely.' I said, 'John, I am your civilian commander-in-chief, not your XO. Speak your mind, sailor.' What he said next changed the Course of Human Events."

I was in shock. "What did he say?"

"He said, 'Mr. President, the cat's about to come out of the bag on these illegal weapons sales to Iran. I know that you know about it. You know that I know about it. Come clean now: the American people deserve to know.'"

I was shocked. "That sounds like him, but...who speaks to the President like that?"

"A *patriot*, that's who," Reagan said with moral certitude. "John Upson's words rang in my conscience for months before I came clean about Iran/Contra. No one in my orbit ever dared to speak to me so candidly. Save for maybe the Duke, but you can only take that white supremacist with a grain of salt."

I furrowed my brow. "You mean David Duke? The Klan leader?"

"No. Not that lunatic. John Wayne."

I was taken aback. "No. Sorry. John Wayne was no Klansman."

Reagan threw his hands up. "There you go again, Benjamin."

Kennedy joined in. "Remember what I said in Florida: Dorothy Carmichael isn't a Nazi, and John Wayne isn't a Klansman, but both are white supremacists. Hell, you heard Jack London in Reno. That virus has been with us since the Revolution, Jackson accelerated it, and even the Civil War couldn't stop it."

"You're bonkers, Jack. We've made a lot of progress. Racism is still a problem, but it's not the norm anymore. It's an outlier."

"Is it? Tell me, have you ever thought, even fleetingly, that you were better or smarter than a person of color? Ever tried to help a person of color because you assumed you had greater wisdom or insight?"

I rolled my eyes. "That's bad, but it's not intentional, and benign by comparison."

"Malevolence often starts 'benign,'" Reagan continued. "As the Duke told *Playboy, 'I believe in white supremacy, until the blacks are educated to a point of responsibility.'* From your vantage point, was he 'benign' to want to 'educate' them?"

"You're twisting my words."

Reagan whistled. "Talk about printing a legend, Ben."

I threw up my hands, exasperated. "I don't know. That just seems like an exercise in gnat-straining. Why focus on small potatoes like that? I mean, we have problems with real white nationalists. Think back to those guys marching in Charlottesville back in 2017. *Those* are the people that Jack Johnson fought against. That's the *real* threat."

"I thought they were just 'outliers?'"

"It was...I...just think our race obsession only fuels the real racists' fire."

"Does chemotherapy fuel cancer?"

"I...I mean you just...I..."

...had nothing.

It started to drizzle; Reagan turned on the wipers.

"Look," I said. "I'm tired. It's been a long journey. I just want to find this elusive 'Excalibur' and return to my life. Until then I'm just along for the ride, and living on blind faith."

"We're all living on faith," Reagan said, "but not blindly. Trust the process. I know that's hard, but the Champion has no choice, not with Aldric König's target on his back."

I exhaled. "The so-called Crown Prince of Biarritz, whatever that means."

"Potent puppet master and influence peddler. For centuries, König has whispered in the ear of every tyrant in the world: Napoleon, Mao, Castro, Hitler, Stalin, Noriega, Kim, Hussein, Pinochet, Erdogan and Chavez. He is the preeminent of six Brothers who implement Tyranny's will the world over. I wish I heeded Fred Douglass' warnings about him earlier."

"Here, here," Kennedy added as he flipped through files.

"Wait," I said. "You both knew Frederick Douglass while you were President?"

"He's been our White House ambassador since the McKinley Administration."

"Although," Reagan laughed, "in 2017 the president didn't know who Fred was. Fred pops into his bedroom at 9 a.m. while he's watching TV, the guy spills McNugget sauce everywhere and now the Secret Service is involved."

I leaned back. "So that's what that tweet was about…"

"I always enjoyed Fred, but he pulled no punches with me."

"Like how?"

"For one, he challenged my support for the apartheid regime that segregated South Africa. He lambasted the racial sentencing disparities that arose under my War on Drugs. Fred insisted that achieving *full* racial equality preserves Liberty for *all* people. If you say 'all lives matter,' but don't protect the most vulnerable lives, you're a fraud. You expose our soft underbelly to Tyranny's claws. Think about it: if a father has four children and he invites a thief into his home to ransack one of the kids' rooms, he's practically begging the thief to steal from the others, too. Decent people don't openly embrace monsters, but if the monster appears benign…"

Reagan trailed off. Kennedy hovered over the center console.

"Cozy?" I asked.

"No," Kennedy replied. "What did you think of Du Bois? Before the fight, I mean."

"Why?"

"Curious."

"Charming…and disarming. Combative, but not militant."

"Why 'combative, but not militant?'"

"I don't know. I'd always seen him as a radical compared to pacifists like Dr. King."

"An honest answer. Wrong, but honest."

Kennedy blew warm air into his hands.

"Would you consider Zora Gates radical or combative?"

"From the diner? Not at all."

"I thought she was radical. Subversive, even. A national embarrassment."

"Wh – how?!"

"That's what I called all the Freedom Riders. Zora. Pearl. All of them. Mixed-race group of college kids got on buses and sat where they weren't supposed to. Segregationists dragged them off and beat them, even set their buses on fire. And I said the *Freedom Riders* were the embarrassment."

Kennedy pulled a typed letter on yellowed paper from his pocket and cleared his throat, then read from the first page:

"'You, Mr. President, have said that our country has lost prestige in the councils of the world. We believe that this is true and that there is a definite relationship between this fact and the attitude of government toward us, its Negro nationals. Some of us cast our vote impelled by the hope your words generated, and guided by the fact that we cannot live as formerly.'"

He turned to the second page:

"'Mr. President, the time is right for a new Emancipation Proclamation...Abraham Lincoln showed the way. But the task was left unfinished. Our democracy will embrace all or it will embrace none.'"

Kennedy put the letter away.

"A 93-year-old W.E.B. Du Bois wrote that right after my inauguration. He never sent it to me. It was found amongst his papers after he passed on."

Kennedy touched his scar.

"I wish he had. It took a long time before I put my money where my mouth was and fully committed to the Revolution. It's not enough to be non-racist. If we aren't actively *anti-racist*, we undercut the Declaration's core message of human equality, which is both our national identity *and* our international mission."

I cocked my head. "International mission?"

"You don't find it curious," Reagan added, "that Jefferson uses the phrase, 'among the powers of the Earth' and values a 'decent respect for the opinions of mankind?' It's a Declaration to the whole world. That's what inspired me to win the Cold War, but even then I didn't fully understand it."

"What do you mean?"

"I thought the 'shining city upon a hill' simply meant Judeo-Christian capitalism defeating atheistic communism. So I unleashed carnage in Latin America, and real people suffered. But the *real* perennial war between Liberty and Tyranny transcends party, ideology and borders, even politics itself. It concerns the dignity of every human being, regardless of birth status. It's about every American's oath upon the altar of Liberty to vigorously combat Tyranny over the heart and mind."

Reagan scratched his neck.

"I fought Tyranny in some theaters, and allied with him in others. I've paid dearly for the latter."

He turned.

"Don't make the same mistake I made in Philadelphia. Guard your heart. Stay vigilant."

I pulled the coin from my front pocket. Pockets of iron marked the tin on either side. I read the inscription that first appeared in Berlin:

IN CONSTANT VIGILANCE

"What happened in Philadelphia?" I asked.

Reagan sighed. "I blew a very loud whistle."

The office light went out. Kennedy taunted:

"Heeeeere, commie, commie, commie."

Eight minutes later Platov arrived at the gate, carrying a briefcase.

"Добрый вечер, Платов," the guard said.

"Да," Platov replied curtly, turning right down Angelicastraße.

"Either he lives nearby," Kennedy offered, "or he's meeting someone."

Reagan rolled out after a yellow Peugeot skirted by. The Beamer crept along at a snail's pace, maintaining a distance of about thirty yards. Any closer, and our intention to act upon the living could expose us.

Platov entered a footpath between two housing developments. Two other agents appeared from around the corner, picking up his tail.

"Let's see what Minty and Ira cook up," I suggested.

Reagan pulled over. I flipped on the radio. Peter Gabriel was playing:

"Games without frontiers..."

A half hour later, Ira tapped my window. I rolled it down.

"He lives there," he said. "Bastard went straight home."

"We peg the wrong guy?" I asked.

"No," Minty said, hands on her hips. "He's our man."

"How do you know?" Reagan asked.

"I saw his second apartment."

"*Second* apartment?" Kennedy added.

"It's a knockout, a dummy. One floor below his. He put everything in the dryer."

"The KGB isn't paying for that," I said.

"No. Gould is," said Minty.

Reagan nodded. "König."

"Game on, Platov," Kennedy added.

Reagan turned the key and drove back to Stasi headquarters. We had a break-in to plan.

~

Platov left his apartment at 7:45 a.m. the next morning. Once we got the all clear, our party of five entered in the guise of a gray-clad cleaning crew. We cracked open the dryer safe; files were stacked on three different shelves. Some were marked "KGB" – Platov was stealing from work.

We split the contents among the five of us and spread out throughout the apartment, photographing each page. I worked alone in the bedroom. The bulk of the files I found were in Russian and German. At about two o'clock, I came across a thin red folder, with 25-30 bound pages. The cover read in Cyrillic gold:

Королевские предметы

I opened to the first page. It was a short letter, written in English:

11 November 1989

My Dearest Platov,

Here is the dossier of the gentleman I spoke of during our last meeting regarding Silent Echo. We will eliminate him in due time.

~ A. König

...

"Platov," I whispered, "what secrets do you hide?"

…

I flipped the page…my knees buckled…

…

"UPSON, JOHN ERIC"

…

…No…

…

…my hands went clammy…

…no…this isn't…

…no-no-no…no…

… I steadied myself against the bed…

…Daddy no…

…God damn it no…

…and resisted the urge to vomit…
Bzzzzzzt.

I told you to correct this, Benji. I told you to make this right.

The radio crackled in the living room: *"The Redcoats are coming…"*
"10-4," Ira replied. "We copy, over and out."
Ira turned off the radio.
"Re-assemble all files and return to the shelf. Ben?"
My ears rang…and the room spun…
"Ben!"
"Copy!" I slipped the Red File into my satchel.
We quickly restored the dryer shelves to their original condition and scurried out to the van. Reagan slid the door closed.
Reagan's partner, Julia Child, turned from the monitors. "Goodness, Ben. You look like you've seen a ghost."

~

I couldn't sleep that night. The Red File burned a hole in my satchel. I couldn't bring myself to open it. Instead I let my imagination run free...to the crash...to the fire and smoke...to the face of that dirtbag at the wheel. They said in another life he was just a lemon farmer, an immigrant nobody at the mercies of forces larger than himself. The dossier had thrown that into sharp relief. I was twenty-two when my father was killed, and every night since had been a contest against deeper darkness and hidden anguish. Now the darkness threatened to surface, as my anguish on the rising tide...

...

...I kicked myself out of bed, eager for a distraction. I wandered down to the Stasi dark room, where photographer Ansel Adams developed the negatives we took with a solution that translated any text into the language of the viewer. Making idle conversation, I asked him about his photo book, *Born Free and Equal: The Story of Loyal Japanese-Americans,* which once sat on our family's coffee table on a Navy base in Okinawa.

"They called me a traitor," Ansel lamented. "But I considered exposing Manzanar to be aiding the war effort."

"Yeah, well," I said, "different theater."

"Same war."

Same war. It raged inside me the next morning. Kennedy noticed and offered a hot toddy. I passed.

"Suit yourself," he said. The man was constantly eating and drinking, like he had the metabolism of a teenager.

That afternoon I went for a walk in Waldpark, propping up against a spruce tree. I pulled the Red File out of the satchel to review it...I shut my eyes; my hands trembled, and my breath drew short and fast...*3...2...1...*

I jumped in headfirst...and I exhaled...

...it was uncannily accurate: height, weight, birthplace, personal tastes, habits and neuroses, next of kin and even how, where and when he would die. My bones shook. I jammed the Red File back into my satchel.

...inhale...

...exhale...

My pulse eased off the gas as my breath returned to rhythm. It was all too much...

...it was way too much...

..."Pop," I muttered as I drifted. "I miss you, Pop..."

...

"Pop!" Michelle laughs like a lunatic. "His name is Pop! Get it?"

My giggles sputter like the outboard motor we don't have.

I can't control myself. "Hehehe...because...he's an otter..."

"An Otter Pop!"

The late September sun is cruel. Our raft beached on this Potomac sandbar south of Harper's Ferry an hour ago. The river nymphs sent us a friend to keep us company. His squeaks are so adorable we adopt him on the spot.

"What were you gonna name him?" Michelle asks, toying with my hair.

"Haha. Mel Otter."

Nothing.

"It's a baseball joke."

She rolls her eyes and pulls sunscreen from the cooler.

"Before today," I say, *"I thought SPF 500 was a NASCAR race."*

Michelle zings the tube off my chest. *"Lather up, Casper. I don't want you to get sunstroke."*

"Oh, the unbearable whiteness of being."

Michelle winks and kicks me lightly. She scrunches her nose and feeds Pop string cheese. He nibbles politely.

"Pop's a cute kid."

Michelle leans against the raft. *"He looks like his papa."*

"I'm not that furry."

"No, the eyes."

"Mine aren't that far apart."

Michelle is beside herself. *"Squeak for me, Pop."*

"You're pretty funny for a French girl."

She sips her Capri Sun. *"Well. We did invent Jerry Lewis."*

"Jerry Lewis isn't funny."

Shell gasps. *"Take. It. Back."*

"No."

We play bicker for twenty minutes. Pop grows restless. Cheese and grapes aren't forthcoming, so this otter is outta here.

"Benji!" Shell cries. *"Pop is gone!"*

I remove my cap as the critter floats away. *"He was a good son. He never asked for money."*

"He always finished his supper."

Michelle flips over to "sob" in my arms.

"There, there," I say. We repose forever.

Michelle nuzzles against me. "Want to know why I love otters?"

"Tell me, so I can become one."

She blushes. "They fall asleep holding hands so they won't drift away."

I'm over the moon for this woman. "I miss Pop already."

"We'll see him again."

Michelle scratches my chest.

"Maybe one day we'll have a Pop of our own."

"Wouldn't that be something?"

And so we rest...

...overhead, I hear the terrifying squawk of a bird of prey....it circles and circles...black smoke billowing from its beak...it turns south...down river...

"No," I whisper...

...it spreads it wings and soars southward along the Potomac...it disappears over the horizon...

"Get away from there!"

...the world erupts in fire and flame...the sky turns red, a shade of crimson darker than black...

((...get up, Benji...))

...

I snapped awake to the biting cold.

In my periphery, an auburn-haired woman in a jumper slowed her jog.

"What weighs on you, Benjamin?" Pearl asked, approaching cautiously, hands on her hips.

I sat up, nervously. "I just needed fresh air."

Pearl sat down next to me, waving her arms in the air. "It's thirty-five degrees."

She rolled up her sleeves and tied her hair back. Her right elbow still bore the red marks I saw back in Palm Beach...the ones Billy inflicted on her...*twenty-seven years ago...*

...how?

"I told you I bruise easily, Mr. Upson," Pearl said with a weak smile. The way her eyes creased...I noticed for the first time a faint scar streaking from her left eye.

171

Pearl put her hand on mine.

"It's always been your cross to bear, hasn't it?"

I squelched the rising tide of anxiety. "I don't know what you're talking about."

Pearl brushed back my hair, lovingly, as a mother would.

"You know it wasn't your fault."

I felt a tear well up. I shoved it back down. "I know who is."

I looked Pearl square in the eye.

"Once I find Excalibur, I'll run him through with it."

Pearl exhaled. "I said it's your cross to bear, not your axe to grind."

A white bird flew overhead, flying south for the winter. I shuddered.

"Nothing flies forever, Benji. Gravity always prevails."

Pearl pecked me on the forehead and jogged back onto the trail.

I slept under thirteen stars that night. I needed their reassurance, their permanence.

These colors don't run.

Fifteen

Active Measures

"Silent Echo." Pearl tapped her fingers. "That's what König calls this operation."

It took three days to sift through the thousands of photos littering the conference table. The majority was fluff: profiles of Soviet heroes, love letters of Catherine the Great, a program from the 1972 Olympic Men's Basketball Gold Medal Game. Platov knew someone – Mossad, CIA or MI-6 – would come snooping and buried the lede.

Soon the pieces came together: advanced network maps of the Internet and ARPANET. Old propaganda posters from the Soviet Union, Nazi Germany, fascist Italy, and even the United States. Footage from *Birth of a Nation*, the 1915 film that resurrected the KKK in the South, and *Triumph of the Will*, a 1934 Nazi propaganda film chronicling the Nazi Party Congress in Nuremberg, a hate rally with 700,000 Germans in attendance yelling *"Heil Hitler!"*

There were reports of riots in Watts in 1965 and 1992; another in Chicago in 1968. A 1928 *New York Times* article about a Klan rally in Queens. Historical records of a long-forgotten race massacre in Tulsa in 1921, leaving scores of residents of "Black Wall Street" dead. And there was an article from *The Daily Gate City* of Keokuk, Iowa, dated July 5, 1910, describing whites murdering blacks across America after losing their Great White Hope.

There was a panoply of political cartoons, including a familiar etching from 1866, with a big-lipped lazy black man and a white man chopping wood, decrying the Freedman's Bureau. There were amateurish drawings of the likes of Mickey Mouse, Bugs Bunny and an ugly frog spewing racist and anti-semitic tropes.

I caught Pearl lingering on an 1872 painting by John Gast titled "Spirit of the Frontier," depicting the golden-haired goddess Columbia leading civilization's conquest of the savage West. Pearl gripped the edges of the canvas tight.

"They mock you, Mother," she muttered.

And then there were The Platov Letters, addressed to "My Dearest Platov" and signed with the initials "A.K." for Aldric König:

October 3, 1986

General Travers and I were happy to receive you at my estate in Biarritz...we heard good things about you from our associates in Leningrad...we were not disappointed...

November 19, 1986

...the Natural Order is the strong ruling the weak...it was this way for millennia, until the one they call "Mother" re-established Liberty's stronghold in North America...

...we must eliminate the Sons of Liberty...

December 14, 1986

...patience...the Soviet Union will fall within five years...unencumbered by communism, Russia will rise from the ashes like the phoenix, the centerpiece of our Eurasian Empire, with America as her client state...

March 15, 1987

...Aristotle knew politics is more than government, that it is an extension of man's inner life...the political is always personal...to conquer a people, you must conquer its persons...their thoughts, but more importantly, their emotions...the ultimate kompromat...

June 19, 1987

...the Declaration has infected billions with the democratic disease...yet democracy properly exploited can be used to secure power...

...as the Revolution unfolded, we raised a counterfeit...distorting the original as Shadows bend Light...the proud colonials, steeped as they were in the Natural traditions of slavery, provided a ready toehold...we appealed to their basic self-interest and convinced them that Liberty had chosen them by virtue of their heritage...that Liberty was theirs alone...

...thus may Liberty be made to serve Tyranny, wrapped in their flag...best personified in my Apprentice...Andrew Jackson...

July 18, 1987

...the American I met in Moscow craves power and attention...like Jackson or Nixon, but with even greater vanity and stupidity...a low I.Q. individual...in time he could be a valuable Apprentice...a Trojan Horse to infiltrate Liberty's house, and rally her children to our cause...a useful idiot...

November 16, 1987

...we have lost soil...West Germany and Japan...East Germany, the Soviet Union and her satellites are next...in her Mother's name, Pearl has caused us more grief than her Sisters combined...

...Liberty has spread like weeds...billions reject the Natural Order and embrace this perverse "equality"...soon Russia will be infested...you and I will pull it out root and stem...

...we will not fully restore our Order in our lifetimes...humanity will not easily surrender their own Liberty...instead, they must be enlisted to take Liberty from others...in the very name of Liberty...

December 8, 1987

...many events precipitated our defeats over the last century...world wars and social movements...black veterans returned to America and demanded their "rights..."

...overlooked was the Negro's prizefight in 1910...Mr. Barton spun the Negro's victory to incite violence against other primitives...Mr. Barton lobbied to ban footage of the fight all over America...censorship shapes the narrative...

...Emmaleigh counter-spun our efforts against us...one-tenth of the crowd had hallucinations by her hand...turnabout, as we say, is foul play...

April 20, 1988

..."soft" bigotry is the easiest to exploit...even Liberty's friends ignore it, as it grows undetected through trauma and crisis...

September 6, 1988

..."equality" is a threat to our Order, because the "equals" have only the Order to fight...one group must always dominate...the stronger faction will expend its energy fighting the weaker on our behalf...we exploit them both...

...economics, geography and chance have positioned the white race to dominate...they would be fools to believe they are truly superior, but this is the hand we play...we must take active measures...

November 1, 1988

...enemies can be useful...Reagan, like his predecessors, served us in Grenada and Nicaragua...

...Reagan heard about lazy blacks and coined the phrase "welfare queens"...a subtle message conveyed as a "dog whistle," sub-text that is plausibly innocent to many, but which our target audience understands...

...in Philadelphia, Mississippi the police and KKK killed three "civil rights workers" in 1964...Reagan opened his general election campaign in Philadelphia speaking of "states' rights," a Civil War euphemism for opposition to federal "civil rights" laws...

March 23, 1989

...use their strengths against them...as General Travers says, let your enemy shoot himself, and you will save money on bullets...

June 17, 1989

...the aim of Silent Echo is to saturate the American mind to the point they question their own perception of reality...behold, the power of the gaslight!

...advances in technology, the power of propaganda will be in the hands of all...understand the science of memetics...from the Tower we will unleash a plague of frogs...

...we call this "the long con"...we will lead America by the bloody jaw to its own demise; they will come willingly because they love the taste...believe they assert independence from the world they despise, and when their fists are in the air, we shackle them...

177

September 12, 1989

...when Berlin falls, the liberal West will believe it has triumphed forever...we will collapse America's own history upon itself...we will dismantle Pearl's post-war regime, and Tyranny will reign everywhere...

November 5, 1989

Khramtsov is on your tail. Commence Omega Protocol...

...

Nothing of any use to me. *I need answers.*
Pearl's office was unlocked. I sifted through the papers on her desk.
Nothing. I looked on the chair...
...*bingo.* Pearl snuck a letter out of the pile...

...

23 November 1989

My Dearest Platov,

1 December at 2:00 a.m. Dresden airport. Hangar behind P3.

~ A.K.

...December 1st...
...
...tonight.
König was in Dresden *tonight.* The man behind my father's death was here *tonight.*
And Pearl knew it.
She knew.
She knew, and she hid it from me.
I screamed silently.
Who the fuck *does she think she is?*

I slammed my fist on the desk; a baseball rolled toward me and into my hand.

The ball was signed:

Curt Flood.

You're kidding...

Enraged, I fired the ball into the corner locker handle, popping the door wide open. Torvald's uniform hung inside, including his standard-issue Makarov pistol...

...

...rain fell outside. I peered through the blinds...

...the Beamer...

...

I fetched the key from Pearl's desk and retrieved the flag from my quarters.

Bedecked in Stasi tan, I slid behind the wheel in full Stasi regalia and keyed the ignition.

The rains came down. The clock read *1:08*. Plenty of time.

I had a tyrant to overthrow.

~

The Beamer flew north on Königsbrucker at 174 kph, wipers on full blast. My blood ran hot with anger...*raw...fucking...anger.* I hoped to God that my uniform kept the *Volkspolizei* out of my way. *For their sake.*

I got to the airport in six minutes flat. *P3. Up ahead, to the left.* I rubbed the barrel of the Makarov as it lay across the center console – next to the coin.

The sun in the center scried into my soul:

((...do you rise, Son of Liberty, or do you set?...))

"What do you care? If I set tonight, I'll take these sons of b–"

... THA-DUNK-DUNK-DUNK-DUNK...

...

...my right tire rode up the divider...

...

...DUNK-DUNK-DUNK-DUNK...CLANG!

...

179

...the fender caught on a spike and ripped off; the car spiraled upward like a Hail Mary. Time slowed, and my heart with it. In the smallest possible opening between space and time, I heard those whispers...

((...choose, Benji...you can't have both...))

This! I choose this! Let me have this!

((...as you wish...))

The Beamer spat me out; I landed *THURMPH!* on the grass between the road and the terminal, the Betsy Ross flag floating gently after. The Beamer skid down the road, igniting sparks and spilling radiator fluid.

"Oh sh...."

KABOOM!!!

"Shiiiiit!"

I rolled into the drainage ditch as shrapnel flew overhead....

...

...after a few moments I stood, panting. The car was now three bright orange flames...first one...then the next...and the last...slowly extinguished, each leaving a pile of ashes in the middle of Königsbrucker.

I stepped toward the ashes. My foot brushed against two objects.

The coin.

And the Makarov.

"Choose, Benji."

Pearl paced calmly across Königsbrucker, her hands behind her back, irate but patient.

"Vigilance...or *hyper*-vigilance. You can let your spirit lead you...or your wound."

My adrenaline surged. "Is that another *bullshit* aphorism your 'Mother' taught you?"

Pearl stopped cold in her tracks. Her usual stoic calm dissolved with the rain. Her eyes shifted to and fro; I felt her pulse from ten feet away.

Pearl hesitated. "She's your Mother, too, Benjamin."

I laughed anxiously. "Yeah? 'Liberty,' right? An *abstraction*. Well, guess what? My father was *real*. He was flesh and blood and marrow and...*fuck!*"

I doubled over at a jabbing pain in my side. I took a deep breath and stood.

"He was John Upson, and I loved him. He lived and breathed Liberty. I always thought he was just in the wrong place at the wrong time, but now...I know...there's finally someone alive I can blame...someone *I* can hold accountable..."

I watched the rain fall from above. "...Jack says the sword needs a..."

I laughed.

"...a *'wet stone.'*"

Pearl bit her lip. "Benji – "

"Don't call me that."

I spat.

"You don't have the *right* to call me that. You are *too familiar.*"

I gripped the Makarov tight.

"It won't bring him back," Pearl said.

"It might."

Pearl quivered and cried, her tears and the rainfall indistinguishable on her face. She stepped close and searched me.

"You choose to abide alone," she said. "The true price of vengeance."

"Justice," I laughed. "Didn't your Mother teach you? Liberty is meaningless without it."

"No Justice flows from unclean hands, Benjamin."

I scooped the coin and flag off the ground. Against all protocol, I draped the flag over my shoulders.

"The Champion wields Excalibur," I choked.

Pearl opened her mouth...then shut it tight.

I grabbed Pearl by the hand; she slapped mine away and delivered a palm strike into my chest...

OOOMPH!

...knocking me to the ground. Pearl gave out a soft moan of pain, and her breath shortened.

"Pearl?"

"You have a plane to catch," she snapped, then walked away.

I jumped to my feet. "Hey – "

And then she was gone.

No turning back now.

I pulled the slide stop on the Makarov and walked toward the hangar.

I had murder in my heart.

~

There they stood, one hundred yards away, at the other side of the hangar. Platov and...

...*König*...

...*him?*...

...the echoes roared as my heart fell to my knees...

((...are you looking for a young man?...))

...he puffed a cigarette, reviewing documents...

((...he came tearing through here a minute ago...))

...talking to Platov as a G5 hummed on the tarmac...

((...a little bird whispered something terrible in his ear...))

...the young staffer...with kind and compassionate eyes...

((...you can call me Al...))

I ducked behind a Cessna. I peaked. Aldric König was the same age he is Today. His blond hair was greased back; he donned a white blazer over a black turtleneck and jeans. Platov had his back turned to me in his *Ushanka* and matching flight jacket.

A chill seized me. *What the hell was König doing in the Capitol?*

I shook it off...

Breathe. First Platov. Then...König.

I snuck closer...and closer...

...the pilot killed the engine. Then Platov turned.

I froze. *Ho...ly...sh...*

"Benjamin!" König raised his hands excitedly, a hint of Bavarian in his accent. "Good to see you! How is your student, uh..." he snapped his fingers. His feigned timidity was gone.

"Tyson," I said shakily.

"Yes! Tyson *Atwater*. A special young man. He means *a lot* to me."

König examined me head-to-toe.

"A Stasi uniform, wrapped in an American flag? Are you *sure* you don't work for me?"

I eyed Platov with a lump in my throat.

I've made a fatal mistake. This man is dangerous.

"Helloooo?" König waved.

He looked to Platov.

"Ich denke, unser Freund ist schüchtern."

Platov took off his hat to reveal a mop of dirty blond hair. *"Wer ist diese kleine Scheiße?"*

"Er ist der Champion."

"Да?" Platov loaded a fresh bullet into his pistol and pointed it at my chest. "Тогда позволь мне застрелить его и покончить с этим."

König steadied him. "Еще нет. Еще нет. Думаю, ему есть что сказать."

Platov scowled.

"We're in a hurry, Mr. Upson. If you wish to come to Leningrad and defect, spit it out."

"I'm no commie."

König laughed. *"Neither are we.* I have *many* loyal subjects in America. I think Erna was right: *you* could be one of them."

König flashed a grin.

"Or do you want Platov to shoot you?"

"You killed my father," I rasped. "Somehow...you were behind the whole thing."

König laughed and pointed at the pilot idling in the cockpit of the G5. "In case you didn't realize, Benjamin, I wasn't at the wheel. But yes...that lemon farmer and his comrades were doing my bidding."

He turned to Platov.

"Schieße den Feurvogel ab. Er hat es uns zu leicht gemacht."

Platov readied to fire. I pointed the gun at him and pulled the trigger.

CLICK

Shit. Safety's on.

Game over.

"Bye bye, John," König growled.

The bullet hit me square in the chest. In the smallest fractal of time and space, I stared down the barrel of the gun and up into the cold gray eyes of a young Vladimir Putin.

There was no soul to see.

Sixteen

Silent Echo

The bullet spun and smoked at the threshold of my heart. The pressure built and built as it compressed the shell like a miniature smashed can. Adrenaline surged...

...inhale...

...exhale...

...that jump felt different...

...like a rock skipping across a pond...

...as footsteps thundered on the cold cement of the arena floor, every voice ringing like a tuning fork. The overhang read:

WELCOME TO UIC PAVILION
Home of the Flames

Flames. There was no more appropriate name for what unfolded in front of me. I floated in a witches' cauldron of conflict. I saw everyone in double, and heard them in duplicate.

"Build the wall!" *((...freedom rings for my kin, **not** yours...))*

"My people are not rapists!" *((...freedom rings for my kin **and** yours...))*

"Go back to Africa!" *((...stay in **your** place...))*

"I was born in Milwaukee!" *((...**this** is my place...))*

Security dragged away protesting students in hijabs.

A shoving match ensued under a sign that read "Love Trumps Hate."

A white man tussled with a black man over an American flag. I clutched Betsy tight.

A news reporter broadcasted from behind a barricade...

"...protesters have taken control of this rally ..."

...where reporters were cordoned off, sitting ducks for the shrill:

"HE ISN'T A RACIST, YOU ARE!! YOU HAVE BLOOD ON YOUR HANDS!"

((...for them to be free, they must take it from me...))

"STOMP MY FLAG AND I'LL STOMP YOUR ASS!"

((...dissent is disloyalty to American royalty...))

"*LUGENPRESSE!* YOU'RE ALL FUCKING LIARS!"

((...it can't be true if it comes from you; hand on the Bible, your words are blood libel...))

Fifteen feet away, a late middle-aged woman in a red hat chewed her fingernails nervously. She was the only one who could see me. She looked my Stasi uniform up and down and hyperventilated...

((...commies...commies...I knew these snowflakes were just commies...))

I felt something on my shoulder...tar dripping from the rafters...

...

...I reminisce on the '97 CHSAA League Championship banner hanging from the rafters of Brien Ochs Gymnasium, Home of the Warriors.

"Look at this, Ben."

Colonel holds up his phone. Eighth grade parent night is over, and we're loitering.

"Ben, look."

It's a live news video of a campaign rally in Chicago gone berserk. A reporter narrates the ugly scene from behind a metal barrier:

"...just gotten word that the campaign has suspended this rally. Thousands of protesters have taken control of this rally. We are told that no security screened any of them, highly unusual for a campaign whose rallies have been defined by the presence of the faithful..."

A Latino man holds up a sign reading, "We Are Not Rapists."

Two women flip each other off; one chants "USA! USA!"

I wave it off. "This'll blow over."

Colonel shakes his head. "I smell Reichstag fire."

"Is there a sale on tinfoil at Safeway?"

Colonel abruptly grabs his phone and walks away.

"Old man, where are you going?"

"Seven o'clock."

A woman with jet-black hair, bronze skin and deep turquoise eyes approaches. I caught those eyes several times tonight. She's even better looking up close.

"Can I help you, Ms...?"

"Oh, hi," she says. "Barrios. Marissa Barrios. You...don't remember me?"

"...should I?"

She covers her mouth. "Oh God, I'm so stupid! I just...all night I thought you were someone I met once. You were both very inspiring."

"Oh. Thank you?"

"I mean, what you said about the need for civic education and democracy up there, to 'keep the Republic.' It just reminded me of something somebody told me a long time ago, and I agree."

"Ahh," I reply.

An awkward pause.

"Sorry," I stick out my hand. "Ben Upson."

"Right. Benjamin John Upson, as you said."

Another pause. I fiddle with the band on my finger.

"So...I just moved here with my kid, and I'd...love for someone to show me around town?"

"Uh, yeah..."

"Can I get your number?"

"Sure, uh...3-0-3..."

...

...I felt my pockets for my phone. I couldn't find it. I didn't need it. The signal came into my head loud and clear:

> *You went and set our house ablaze!*
> *((But you will not replace us!))*
> *To teach our young your wicked ways!*
> *((But you will not replace us!))*

My ears rang...I heard that refrain everywhere, overlaying every sound. I punched at my ears, futilely trying to knock it out of my head. That's when I saw him, near the podium with the "MAKE AMERICA GREAT AGAIN" sign. He wore a gray suit with a skinny black tie, packing away what looked like a recording device.

Cecil Barton. He hasn't aged a day.

Barton saw me and made a mad dash toward the exit. I pushed past Nervous Nelly and raced after out into the bleeding Chicago night, where the chaos was even worse than outside. Barton hustled east on Racine across the expressway, toward the CPD barricade at Van Buren. I started after him when a hand clamped over my mouth.

"Get off me!" I yelled.

The hand released. It belonged to Ira Hayes.

"...Ira?"

"Rooftop!" he shouted. "University Hall! Come on!"

We beat feet down West Harrison. Halfway down the block I watched a white woman salute *"sieg heil"* at a journalist. I dare not repeat the whisper of her heart.

When we came to the thirty-story UIC dormitory, Ira stopped me at the stairwell:

"Fair warning: he's pissed."

~

"You son of a bitch!"

Kennedy flattened me with a wicked right cross.

"You STUPID! SELFISH! SON OF A BITCH!"

Minty held Kennedy back as he struggled against her.

"You think this is a game? Do you know what I have at stake?"

Pearl, gray as the day I met her, stepped between us.

"That's enough, Jack."

Pearl pulled me up and slapped my other cheek.

"You're a damned fool!" she sniped, holding up the Red File.

She handed the file to Ira, who was busy adjusting knobs on his radio.

"Open to any page."

Ira flipped to the middle.

"What do you see?"

"Corporal Block," Ira replied, confused. "What is this?"

"A clever trick. Now flip it. Like a cartoon."

The pages kept turning...and turning...it never ended.

"Thank you, Ira."

Pearl tossed the Red File off the rooftop and it disintegrated.

"König *wanted* you to find that. He gave it to Platov to make sure that you would. It mirrors back an intense emotional attachment to draw the reader out into the open, and you – *the Champion* – bought it!"

I looked away in shame. From two blocks away, all I could see was chaos and confusion.

Two sullen figures watched the mayhem from the edge of the roof.

"It is as we expected." A hipster-bearded Alexander Hamilton lowered his binoculars.

"Let me see." A short German woman took the binoculars. "This is only the beginning."

Pearl's voice cracked. "You have your storm, Alex."

Hamilton groaned. "A storm of König's making, and the Apprentice rides it like a wild stallion..."

...the Apprentice? Jackson...?

...

...the rally...the candidate...

...

...this man occupies the White House...Today...

...

"I didn't think the Sons of Liberty had political rooting interests," I offered.

"We don't," Pearl snapped back. "But we are also not blind to Tyranny, through whomever he chooses to operate."

I paced the rooftop to calm my nerves. I felt around in my pocket...*the coin*. It was lead again. The new inscription read:

WE PLEDGE ALLEGIANCE

I took the flag off my shoulder. Platov's bullet had burned a hole dead center of the thirteen stars. It still smoldered.

"I found the signal!" Ira proclaimed. We crowded around a transmitter designed to pick up more than AM and FM waves.

"Listen closely, Benjamin," Pearl said. "You may hear your own echo."

The radio relayed a flurry of shouts from the hosts below, and that awful refrain:

You went and set our house ablaze!
((But you will not replace us!))
To teach our young your wicked ways!
((But you will not replace us!))

I pinched the bridge of my nose, nauseous.

"This is a test run," Pearl blurted.

"A Reichstag fire," the German Woman added.

Pearl turned to Hamilton. "The Apprentice said law enforcement told him to cancel the rally? Because of the threat of violence?"

Hamilton nodded. "A lie. The protestors were demonstrating peacefully. Local police had it under control."

"*He wanted this*," Pearl seethed. "This is a diverse campus, and he's been provoking minorities for months. He let them stew together in that arena for hours, pulled the rug out and let them go. Now he'll spin it to play victim. Has he called the networks yet?"

Hamilton held up an iPad, where the Apprentice's face appeared over helicopter footage of the streets below. The Apprentice denounced the "violent" protestors who disrupted "law and order." I caught the date in the corner:

Friday, March 11, 2016

"Another pretext to suppress peaceful dissent," Hamilton said. "Something he has already done with the press."

Pearl coughed violently. Hamilton reacted swiftly.

"Pearl…"

She waved him off. "I'm fine."

Another whisper boomed through the radio.

((…these sand niggers will impose Sharia law on all of us…))

"He's using our Fear against us," Pearl said. "And it's working."

~

"Idiot! Fool! Twice!"

George Mason set his hand on my shoulder.

"Yet alive – *in spite of yourself.*"

189

An uncountable number of visitors streamed through the parlor of Hull House, the boarding house founded on Chicago's Near West Side in 1889. In their lifetime, its caretakers Jane Addams and Ellen Gates Starr used it to educate the neighborhood's immigrant population. Tonight it hosted a much more ethereal convocation.

"Come along, Benjamin. You need to hear this."

Mason escorted me up a hidden staircase that appeared to go on forever. We reached the top in seconds.

It was the most breathtaking thing I'd seen in my mortal life.

We were in the Capitol Rotunda…or a version of it elsewhere in time and space, and larger…*infinitely larger.* A grandstand ringed the edge and ascended unendingly to an opening in the heavens above, where a circular constellation of thirteen stars hovered in the midnight blue. The floor was an exact replica of the sun hovering over the horizon on my coin; an Elmwood table ringed the edge, broken only by an ornate entrance of white and gold.

We came to a first-level balcony where Ellen Harper and Abraham Woodhull sat patiently.

"Might I ask you to babysit?" Mason posited sarcastically before scurrying off. Harper nodded; I took a seat next to her.

The grandstand was packed with…good God, possibly *millions*. Nearer to the floor sat my living contemporaries. I spotted one I recognized and pointed.

"Is that Elijah Cummings?" I blurted.

Woodhull nodded. "He and Pearl have been close for many years."

Most of the rest were average and anonymous, and of diverse age, race, sex, orientation and economic status. I estimated less than a thousand of them. Harper read my mind.

"Virtually every living Son is here," she explained.

"The student body of MCHS is more than double that," I replied.

"Few heed the call."

A diverse group of twelve undead patriots – six men and six women – streamed onto the Rotunda floor, finding their seats at the round table. I recognized two of them: Mason and the German Woman.

"Apollo's Thirteen," Harper explained. "Our advisory council."

I shook my head. "Why are you telling me all of this? Am I still the Champion? Aren't I on probation?"

Harper squinted into her cheekbones. "I thought you were weak at first. But I was wrong. You're reckless, but you might be a Champion after all."

I raised an eyebrow.

"I watched my brothers burn alive at the Battle of Long Island. I know wildfire when I see it."

A powder-wigged herald carried a long silver horn into the center of the Rotunda. Pearl followed from the doorway. The herald bellowed...

"Comes now before you..."

...before Pearl gently shoved him aside.

"Enough. You sound ridiculous."

Embarrassed, the herald scampered to the exit.

Pearl scanned the ring until her eyes locked onto mine. Every eye was trained on this woman, this diner waitress, this Capitol docent, this master of spies. Whoever she was.

Who are you, Pearl?

"I wish I came before you under better circumstances," she began, her voice carrying to the stars without the assistance of a microphone. "I wish I could tell you we stand at the brink of a golden age of Liberty. But the Truth is sharp, and I must cut you with it."

Pearl slowly spun counter-clockwise.

"Twelve score ago, Liberty awoke from an ancient slumber because her people cried out for her. For millennia Tyranny ruled this planet as the Leviathan, the seven-headed beast with his Prince and Oligarch, Hierophant and Censor, General and Sheriff. Then Liberty's light shone in the darkness, and darkness has never understood it. Yet as Mother taught us, where there is dust, there is rust; where there are seeds, there are weeds."

She paced the perimeter.

"Twenty-seven years ago in East Germany, our agents uncovered König's plans to reverse the worldwide gains we made after the Second World War. Now, his long con bears fruit, and our Revolution stands at a crossroads. Our mutual affection fuels Liberty's fire, and only when that fire cools may Tyranny snuff it out. That fire nears a critical threshold. Either Liberty will continue her work on Earth...or we will consign her to the Ash Heap."

Pearl extended her arm to the council.

"Dr. Arendt?"

The German Woman stepped down from the dais. Dr. Hannah Arendt was a paradox: a Prussian Jew who grew up despising her heritage, owing to a desire to be authentically German. Ultimately she escaped the Nazis before they fully consolidated power in Berlin and sought refuge in the United States, where she became one of the most influential minds of the twentieth century.

"Confusion. Consolidation. Control," she began. "The Three Conquests in action."

Dr. Arendt waved her hand, manifesting a free-floating 3-D projection of a pudgy middle-aged white man yelling at protesters:

"Go to Auschwitz! Go to fucking Auschwitz!"

The gallery gasped collectively.

"From one of the new Apprentice's rallies in Cleveland. It is not an isolated occurrence."

She snapped her fingers: white Apprentice supporters pushed a black teenager around as if in a mosh pit; then the Apprentice offered to pay the legal fees of those who do violence on his behalf; another Apprentice supporter who punched a black protestor crowed, *"Next time, we might have to kill him."*

Dr. Arendt frowned. "This is straight from the dictator's playbook: condoning violence, raging at minorities, demonizing the 'lying press' or *'lugenpresse'* – a Nazi favorite – labeling political opponents 'enemies of the people...'"

...scenes from the UIC rally played in the air...

"...tonight, however, represented the Apprentice's most insidious attack on Liberty yet. As supporters and protesters alike were herded into that arena, the Apprentice hadn't even left the tarmac in St. Louis. A man who lives and dies for applause doesn't open his doors to a campus that despises him. He had no intention of holding that rally; he deliberately engineered a violent atmosphere to discredit his opponents and present himself as a paragon of Law and Order."

Dr. Arendt stopped in her tracks.

"Now in the Course of Human Events, Tyranny rides to absolute power on the storm of Chaos, yet we refuse to see his hands on our flag. *'This is a democracy,'* we say. *'Our neighbors will stop this before it is too late,'* we say. We look to our neighbors and our neighbors look to us, and while we look the thief robs us blind."

Dr. Arendt wagged her finger.

"My friends, Germany was a democracy! Germany had a constitution! The people elected the Nazis under conditions not dissimilar to ours. Germany was not populated by obvious monsters, but by people we would otherwise see as decent. But our psychic wounds from our defeat in World War I drove resentment toward an easy scapegoat, the Jews. This made Germany ripe for a man like Hitler, who stirred the passions of the ignorant with legends of a Master Race entitled to their neighbors' land for 'living space.'"

Dr. Arendt bowed her head, solemnly.

"I heard a story once of a charismatic and unscrupulous demagogue, who incited his people with fanciful legends of national superiority. He inspired the conquest of a continent and the enslavement or extermination of its inferior inhabitants, all the while convincing his own people to cede their own power and freedom to him alone. He became an autocrat who defied accountability even as he invoked 'Law and Order' to impose his will. This man needs no introduction."

Dr. Arendt snapped her fingers, and there appeared a larger-than-life hologram of Adolf Hitler.

"Sorry. Wrong image."

She snapped harder, and Hitler dissolved into a portrait of Andrew Jackson.

"You say it can't happen here? *It already has.*"

Millions of murmurs swirled. Dr. Arendt held her hand up.

"I hear your objections. You're right. They are not the same; but theirs is a difference of degree, not kind. It is said that he who destroys one life destroys an entire universe. So to the slave it makes no difference if he perishes in the hot box or the gas chamber. To the Creek it is irrelevant if the road to hell is a Trail of Tears or a train to Treblinka. Jew or Creek, slave or free, there is no difference. A universe is destroyed. And the Apprentice of Aldric König will let countless universes die if it means he is master of them all."

Silence ruled the Rotunda.

"Is human nature any different from time to time or place to place? No. No matter where we arise along the Course of Human Events, we all rise from dust, and we are all bound to rust."

In the center, hundreds marched across a bridge in Selma, Alabama in the face of looming brutality.

"We've grown comfortable reaping the harvest of those who planted before us: the abolitionists and suffragists, activists and journalists. We are lulled to sleep forgetting that Liberty's seeds grow in fields rich with Tyranny's weeds. We have failed to uproot them, and they have choked our brethren. Now comes our reckoning: Tyranny's Trojan Horse lays siege from within."

Dr. Arendt snapped, and in the air appeared a younger Apprentice in front of the Kremlin with König. The audience murmured.

"July 4, 1987. The property tycoon who claims he will 'Make America Great Again' once spent Independence Day in the capital of America's greatest adversary. It was on this visit, we believe, that the Apprentice unwittingly became an asset of Russian military intelligence. This was the work of König himself, who has himself held the Russian people hostage for a millennium. König frequently whispered into the Apprentice's ear to run for President. The Apprentice announced his first serious campaign in July 1999. At the same time, König convinced another to ascend to his country's highest office…"

Dr. Arendt conjured a new image: Vladimir Putin meeting with König, Gould and two other men on the beach at a seaside resort in France.

"König engineered Putin's rise from middling KGB bureaucrat to head of its successor agency, the FSB. We captured this meeting between Putin, König, and members of Russian President Boris Yeltsin's cabinet on July 16, 1999, near König's estate in Biarritz, France, once a center of opulence and power of the Angevin kings. Putin agreed that day to serve as Yeltsin's Vice President, a springboard to the Russian presidency…"

Dr. Arendt paused.

"Many of you are aware of the Apprentice's unusual admiration for Putin and his strong-arm brutality. There are deeper connections. This month, the Apprentice hired as his campaign chair Paul Manafort, previously on Putin's payroll advising the puppet President of Ukraine. We have made many more connections between the Apprentice and Russia. As our agents plumb these depths, we would be wise to remember that Russia is *very good* at hiding its tracks. Whether this is a partnership or the Apprentice is merely a useful idiot, we don't know. What we do know is that these strange bedfellows share common cause…*Tyranny's* cause…"

Dr. Arendt continued to detail the parallels between Putin and the Apprentice, including their belief in absolute power and appetite for political violence and suppression of dissent. In spite of those similarities, there was a significant power imbalance between them. Putin's even-tempered demeanor and history of strong-arm rule gave him an advantage in dealing with the emotionally imbalanced Apprentice, a political novice. This made the Apprentice an oddly perfect choice as an American puppet: others would understand how to leverage America's power against Putin. As it was, König and Putin's most important objective for the Apprentice was for him to disengage the United States from the world to allow Russia to expand its sphere of influence. Indeed, only months after the Apprentice returned from Moscow in 1987, he took out full-page newspaper ads calling on President Reagan to reduce our troop presence around the world.

Dr. Arendt shook her head.

"He doesn't have the 'foreign policy brain' to have come up with that on his own. Someone in Moscow taught him that. But why was he talking to Moscow at all?"

Dr. Arendt elaborated on the Apprentice's inability to secure loans from American banks after his bankruptcies in the early 1990s, and his subsequent reliance on Russian-backed investments. Soon, scores of Russian oligarchs loyal to Putin were laundering money through the Apprentice's properties around the world.

"'*Kompromat*' is the old-fashioned Russian name for this."

The most jarring revelation was the Apprentice's and Putin's shared affinity for two dangerous ideas: transnational white supremacy and its political counterpart, fascism.

"And therein, ladies and gentlemen, lies the rub. You ask whether Tyranny will destroy the American Experiment from within or without? The answer is both."

As my jaw slouched toward the floor, Dr. Arendt illustrated the long Russian flirtation with fascism even under the Soviet Union. The godfather of Russian fascism, Nazi sympathizer Ivan Ilyin, favored an Orthodox theocratic monarchy in which the state is considered an extension of the family. Ilyin's ideas served as a template for many Russians hungry for a national identity after the fall of the Soviet Union. The heir apparent to Ilyin's legacy in Russia was shadowy pseudo-intellectual Aleksandr Dugin, an adviser of Putin's who called for total war against the West to build a continental empire spanning Europe and Asia.

My apologies, Colonel. I thought you were nuts.

"Eurasianism," Dr. Arendt explained. "It is Russia's version of Manifest Destiny and White Man's Burden, which may explain why it appeals to the Apprentice's white nationalist supporters: the so-called 'Alt Right,' which may be even stronger in Russia than the U.S. While these groups are openly extreme, their subtle influence on the American mainstream cannot be overstated..."

...something tightened in my core...

"...how on Earth could such ideas possibly capture the White House in 2016? All it will take is a dose of old-fashioned *active measures*..."

...I felt a sting in my temple...

"...used by the KGB in the Cold War to disrupt democracies by inciting political and interpersonal hatred and extremism from within..."

...then a hollow ringing...I doubled over...

"...only now it won't require a single pair of Russian feet on our soil. The only things required are the Internet...and *you*..."

...something like black bile bubbled up from my center...

"...via the nascent science of **memetics**, a virtual army of useful idiots deploys simple icons, catch phrases, slogans and bogus news stories, wrapping old fascist ideas in the garb of American patriotism and machismo..."

...I vomited...the black fluid congealed into smoke in mid-air, and the image of an ugly frog appeared...

((...Kek...Kek...Kek...))

"Abraham," Harper whispered, *"Ben's hallucinating."*

Dr. Arendt continued: "These trolls aim through repetition and emotional provocation to elicit a visceral reaction, triggering the target's personal fears and traumas as their memes spin in their minds over and over until they are subconsciously ingrained...the goal is to create a loyal following of zealous true believers who will spearhead a plurality of the passively obedient... to tip the scales, they only need one-tenth...this is the goal of *Silent Echo*..."

...the frog growled and flashed a row of sharp teeth...

((...CUCK...CUCK...CUCK...))

...then it vanished into smoke...

"...like a virus, the hateful idea not only spreads horizontally through repetition, it is also descendible, transmitted across generations. Though the meme may lay dormant for a time, it cannot be fully cured...once it infects, it can always be revived..."

...weak, I fell to my knees...

"...our Shadow is always with us, a mirror away...amplified by the airwaves..."

...then onto my side...

"...be vigilant we must against Tyranny's **Three Conquests**, three 'cons' deployed sequentially and simultaneously..."

...and my back...

"...*Silent Echo first seeks to* **confuse** *the American people as to the very nature of Truth, drowning it out in a sea of noise, broadcasting legends of a chosen people with a legendary past and glorious future...*"

...and closed my eyes. I dreamed of Michelle, singing from the tallest tower...

"*...in their confusion and Fear the people will yield to a strongman to protect them. He will* **consolidate** *power, jettison the rule of law, treacherously evade accountability and brand his opponents as traitors...*"

...the song became a scream, as black smoke poured from her mouth...

"*...with power consolidated, the Apprentice will exert* **control** *over all of government and society...giving the illusion of Liberty, Tyranny will dominate mind, body and soul before the people even know it...*"

...I struggled to stand, leaning against the railing on the balcony. I began to regain my senses when...*oomph!*

A hand, and

a yellow cloth; it

tasted…

…like…

…honey and…

…cit…*rus*…

Seventeen

Weeds

"Get up, Benji."

Minty rapped my cheek, breaking my spell. I was slunk down in the passenger seat of Kennedy's Lincoln on a side street in the middle of what appeared to be a college campus. Minty popped open the door and pointed toward a modular-shaped building.

"Your partner's inside."

I looked straight forward into the dashboard, saying nothing. I was pissed.

"Come on, Sugar."

Reluctantly I slithered out. I saw Ira looming behind Minty.

"Chloroform, was it?" I seethed. "Real nice, Ira."

Minty pushed me back and stuck her finger in my chest. *"Don't. Start."*

She bit her bottom lip, her eyes welling up.

"Now that you've indulged yourself," she continued, pointing her finger at the building, "do us all a favor and indulge *us.*"

I clammed up and followed Minty and Ira. *This feels like an execution.*

A sign on the building welcomed us to the Illinois Institute of Technology. It looked more like an office building…yet as we neared…one world seemed to dissolve into another…

…and the street teemed with turn-of-the-century Model G's and Schacht Roadsters. The building transformed into a raucous nightclub, with the name emblazoned on a red vertical marquis:

CAFÉ DE CHAMPION

Inside the club was loud, packed with mixed-race patrons. I tripped and stumbled into a waitress…and right through her.

"This is a living memory," Minty called from the stairwell. "October 1911. Pay attention, then tell us what you see in the Looking Glass."

I followed her upstairs where a jazz band riffed away. I recognized the trumpeter immediately.

"That's Teddy Atwater," I exclaimed.

Teddy ripped an extemporaneous solo on a silver trumpet. It said something to the crowd, and nothing to me.

"He reminds me of Tyson."

"Not as brash, but his spirit's in there."

Kennedy leaned against the bar. He looked tired and haggard, and the color drained from his face. This was a weary man.

Nervously, I saddled up next to him.

"How did Teddy get to Chicago?" I asked. "I know Mariah liked to keep her grandson close."

As I spoke, a bold and brash World Champion appeared at the door, decked to the nines.

"Johnson heard him play in Reno after we left," Kennedy said. "Invited him to play here in these digs he opened up on the South Side."

"He plays that silver like he was born to it," I offered.

"That silver nearly snuffed you out."

I swung my head. Kennedy crossed his arms.

"Morgan's lead bullet grazed Emmaleigh's face and stuck in the ground. Then she collected it…and made something of it."

It hit me. "The Silver Bullet. Everything in the tavern. That's all…from that one bullet?"

"Alchemy. What Tyranny meant for evil, Liberty used for good."

Teddy's solo ended to uproarious applause. The bashful man blushed.

"Jazz. A beautiful expression of pain…and redemption. Black men have had to overcome a lot more than slavery to achieve in this country. Each generation is just another round in the prizefight of survival. You can see how that might make a man weary."

I lowered my head. "I think I see it now."

"No. You don't."

I scowled.

"Don't take it personally. I don't either. Admit to your limitations."

Teddy's band finished their set. Minty and Ira applauded as Johnson took to the microphone.

"You fought that fight through his eyes. What did you see?"

I dug deep within. "I saw what drove him, and the hatred he endured. There were things I saw in him even he couldn't see. Like…"

I searched for the words.

"…memories of discrimination he never fully processed. He fought bare-knuckle battles against other black men in front of rich whites like Gould for their amusement. He knew they didn't love him, even as they cheered him. And there was the candy store…"

"The candy store wasn't Johnson. It was Du Bois."

"Du Bois?"

Kennedy mimed drinking a shot.

"Du Bois drank with Johnson…then Johnson drank with me."

"Bonds of affection…or should I say *affliction*," Kennedy said. "Johnson grew up in Galveston, Texas. He didn't really encounter white bigotry until his teens; most of the other whites he knew were as poor as he was, and there was a lot of intermixing. That's what made him so cocksure and confident, the relative safety of his neighborhood."

I watched Johnson laugh and shake hands with a table full of white patrons who looked like Chicago mobsters. He was an able and affable glad-hander.

"Du Bois' upbringing in New England was radically different," Kennedy continued. "From the moment he was shunned at that candy store he was two people: his own man, and the 'black' man the world said he was. The veil cut his soul in two like the Berlin Wall, and it remained in place his entire life."

"Double consciousness," I said. I watched Minty brood as she brushed at her head. She often did that, staring into some vacant space a foot in front of her. It was in those moments I imagined that she was the recipient of some curious vision, when she was a woman straddling two worlds at once.

"It cut Johnson, too, but differently. Two talented black men emerging from the shadow of slavery, worlds apart, bound by mutual affliction. You saw it, and so did 2,200 other spectators that Fourth of July."

"One-tenth of the arena," I exhaled. "What did we drink?"

Kennedy smiled. "Ambrosia."

"Ambrosia?"

"The 'nectar of the gods.' That which courses through the veins of the just."

"That's what you've been eating and drinking all this time."

"It can be medicinal for the soul in concentrated amounts. It packs a mean punch if our hearts aren't ready for it."

I sighed. "Mine clearly wasn't."

The apparition of Belle Schreiber wrapped her arms around Johnson's waist.

"Johnson's downfall," Kennedy continued. "The American government used his proclivity for white women against him."

I grimaced. "The Mann Act. Criminalized transporting women across state lines for 'immoral purposes.'"

"Congress passed it nine days before the fight ostensibly to combat 'sex trafficking,' but it was all about Johnson. It was unthinkable that a white woman would have a voluntary sexual relationship with a black man…and certainly not breed with him."

"White slavery. A hell of a euphemism."

"The government's key witness was the original white slave herself."

Kennedy nodded at Belle.

"Under subpoena. The feds threatened her into cooperating."

"No shit."

"That's how desperate we were to destroy Johnson. It wasn't his fists we feared. It was his presence at our table. In business. Politics. *Life.* If we let that happen, how many other black men would take the white man's job? His woman? How long before the white man is replaced?"

((…you will not replace us…))

"John Arthur Johnson was never the same after his time at Leavenworth."

I paused. "His middle name is *Arthur?*"

((…Arthur will show you the way to Excalibur…))

Teddy finished his set to a round of applause. He quickly descended the stage to glad-hand the white men Johnson embraced earlier. I had a terrible sense of foreboding.

"Jack," I began. "What happens to Teddy?"

Kenned stared at the floor. "When this club shut down, Teddy tried to open his own venue. As a young black man with no collateral or credit, no bank would lend to him. So these loan sharks took a risk. The club floundered, and they called in the debt. Teddy outran them until they caught up to him in Los Angeles in 1921. He sent his wife and son away before overdosing on heroin at thirty-three."

I closed my eyes. "I'm noticing a pattern."

"What's that?"

I exhaled. "Young black men destroyed in their prime. For no good reason."

Kennedy grabbed my shoulder. "Now do you see the evil?"

I nodded. "As much as I can."

"Now that you see how Tyranny digs his claws into your brother's heart, I suggest it's time to get over your personal shit. A lot more than *you* depends on it."

I winced. "Are you serious, Jack? My dad meant *everything* to me. You want to talk empathy? Throw a little my way."

Kennedy's eyes widened. "You're kidding, right?"

He pulled within an inch of my face.

"My baby brother was cut down running for President five years after I was shot. You think I didn't want to slit Sirhan Sirhan's throat for killing Bobby? You think I didn't dive to the bottom of Long Island Sound to rescue my son after his plane crashed? Why is *your pain* so exceptional?"

My bottom lip quivered with Kennedy's. I noticed then that my temple scar mirrored his.

"I know pain, Ben. Believe me. But the Kennedy Curse is a *picnic* compared to the Atwater Curse."

I grit my teeth. I knew he had me. Still, I fought.

"I *want* the best for Tyson," I said. "Believe me. I *love* that kid. But he has to want it, too. Yes, he battles racism. What Reid did to him was disgusting. But he *chose* to let his emotions rule him. Yeah, his dad isn't around; yeah, he has abandonment issues. But now he has opportunities at MCHS, and he still *chooses* to act up. So yeah, I see the evil. I heard Immanuel die. But I also see the other side of the coin: I see how Tyson uses the 'Atwater Curse' as a crutch."

Kennedy bit his lip. "For a history teacher, you have a piss-poor understanding of the Course of Human Events. *Everything* in the river flows downstream. We're only responsible for what we can control: our actions, yes, but not our circumstances or how the world responds to us."

I sighed. "You sound like Michelle."

I looked at the ceiling.

"Sometimes I think she stayed with me so long just to fix me."

Kennedy gulped. "Sounds like Jacqueline."

I cocked my head.

"Let's just say you and I both married up."

"Yeah," I replied. "I know I did."

"I wanted to be better. I also wanted to be all things to all people. For more than a half century I've watched this country build legends around me. You told me once that Jackie Robinson was a civil rights *legend*, but he shed *real blood* to break the color barrier. He was a *real* profile in courage. Me? I couldn't have stomached that. I believed in equality if it was clean and neat. I floated in the clouds, and only one person on this planet kept me remotely tethered to it. And time and again, I betrayed her…"

The ghosts of 1911 dissolved. In the same room at the long-abandoned *Café de Champion,* a young black-tied John F. Kennedy stood arm-in-arm with a beautiful brunette photographer born Jacqueline Bouvier. They clinked champagne glasses with a man in a white tuxedo.

Aldric König.

"Jack," I breathed. *"You didn't."*

"No," he replied. "I didn't. This is 1955, my third year in the Senate. König got to me through my father, who found him mildly charming but didn't know who he was. Archie Gould threw me a fundraising dinner at the Café de Champion long after it shuttered. They offered me the world. König even said he believed in my vision for spreading democracy around the world."

A blonde bombshell brought Young Kennedy a tray of Cuban cigars. He gleefully picked one out and stuck it in his mouth, his eyes traveling the bombshell's every contour. As Kennedy and König schmoozed, Jacqueline withdrew to a corner booth, watching König with suspicion. A young teenage waitress with auburn hair offered to take her empty flute.

"Yes." Jacqueline placed her flute on the tray. *"Thank you."*

Young Pearl offered Jacqueline a glass of colorful fruit juice.

"Your stomach is in open rebellion, Mrs. Kennedy," she said. *"I promise this will quell it."*

Jacqueline laughed and took the glass.

Across the room, König leered at Pearl. She blew him a defiant kiss.

"An ancient rivalry," Jack said. "Between Brothers and Sisters."

"Brothers and Sisters," I repeated.

"While the War on Tyranny is fought on history's big stages, its battles are fought in more intimate quarters. I declined König's offer at Jackie's insistence, but he still had his hooks in. He convinced me to focus on 'law and order,' not equality. I didn't tell my brother to stop marching; but I did tell him to slow down...even as the lynch mobs sped up to catch him. It all began here, where König and I danced in a Champion's ashes. König shackled my mind even as he worked against me...until *she* broke my chains."

The *Café* dissolved into the Oval Office. President Kennedy sat at his desk lecturing two young women.

"I want to see equality as much as you do, believe me," he said. *"But there's a right way to do it. The Freedom Rides weren't it. Civil disobedience has its limits."*

Zora Gates spoke up. *"You're telling us not to fight segregation, Mr. President?"*

"I'm telling you to pick your battles."

Pearl interjected. *"Can we join yours?"*

President Kennedy stammered.

"Did you really mean what you said last Fourth of July?"

"With...all of my heart," the President said weakly.

"No." Pearl stood. *"Not all of it."*

As Pearl turned, Zora splashed Kennedy's tea in his face. Secret Service moved on her before Pearl raised her finger. The Secret Service stood down, and the women left untouched.

"That was in the spring of 1963, right before Birmingham caught fire," Kennedy said. "Zora stirred something in me. That night I spoke with Jacqueline and the dam broke."

In the bedroom of the First Couple, Kennedy buried his head in a visibly pregnant Jacqueline's chest; dried tears caked her face. An empty pill bottle lay on its side on Kennedy's nightstand, its contents scattered over the surface.

"I told her it was time to lead, to begin the great work. We talked about what it would be like to live in the America I envisioned at my inauguration – truly free and equal. What became the Civil Rights Act was truly born that night. I announced it on national television on June 11, 1963, the night before Medgar Evers was killed. König was done with me after that."

I heard a scream…a gunshot…a cry and a whisper…

((…I love you, Jack…I love you…))

Kennedy quivered. "Until Agent Hill shielded her, Jackie was still in Oswald's line of sight. Her life was not so precious to her that she wouldn't trade it for mine. Me. A womanizer. I inflicted so much pain on her…even after that night in June, idiot I was. *She had just miscarried for Christ's sake…*"

Kennedy buried his face in his hands and lost all control. I awkwardly put my arm around him and brought him into me. After a few minutes, he regained his composure.

"Sometimes I wish Oswald hadn't missed," he moaned. "Sometimes I wish he had lodged that bullet right in my heart and spared me all these years of pain."

I hesitated. "What if he hadn't missed?"

Kennedy exhaled.

"Jack?"

"My heart wasn't pure yet. I would have lived…with lead in my heart, König's puppet forever. His Apprentice. I would have caved on the Civil Rights Act, and legal segregation might have continued for a decade or more."

"Lead, you say." I fiddled with the coin.

"The heaviest of metals, the substance of corruption and darkness. The legend says that the alchemists could turn lead into gold and other precious metals. But beyond that, alchemy is a metaphor – for transformation of the heart."

Kennedy stuck his finger in my chest.

"That, Benjamin Upson, is what your journey is about. You want to find Excalibur? *Look within.* You won't find it playing 'hero.' You won't even find it unraveling this whole Russia mess. You'll find it when *you experience* the Greatest Love anyone can have for another, and not a second sooner."

Kennedy slunk back, exhausted from teaching an obstinate student.

"Jack," I started. "What is it that you have at stake?"

"You're the last Champion left," he replied. "If you fail, Liberty will be imprisoned again in the Ash Heap...everything she has built in heaven and on Earth will fall. And I will wander this world alone, forever."

Kennedy stared at a spot on the wall.

"We now have less than a second left. Please, Ben...."

...the dinner party faded into a sun-drenched hill...

"...I just want to dance with my French girl again..."

...a newlywed Kennedy spun Jacqueline around...

"...don't you?"

...and her short brown bob gave way to long, curled sandy blond locks. I went weak at the knees. Michelle was rapturous in that white dress. The Man in the Looking Glass spun her and pulled her in, kissing her softly as lightning struck...

...

...a golden-haired girl spins like a top in a dress of red-and-white. Downhill a Powdered Man surveys the landscape while a Stout Man marks parchment with compass and square. The girl laughs under the noontime sun.

"Pierre!" she shouts at the Stout Man, "nous allons le construire sur cet endroit!"

Pierre chuckles. "Pourquoi la-bas, Mademoiselle?"

"Bien sur, parce que c'est l'axe du monde!"

The girl spins again, as another man...a Man in the Looking Glass...approaches on bended knee, offering the band on his finger. Delightfully, the girl accepts.

"Papa!" the girl shouts. "Will you watch me dance in the flames?"

The Powdered Man stands tall. His eyes turn beet red as the Man in the Looking Glass raises Aurora's arm and cradles her waist. He storms uphill, blade drawn.

"Aurora, no!"

"Monsieur Washington!" Pierre cries. "Arrêtez-vous!"

Tar oozes from the pores of the Man in the Looking Glass. In seconds he is covered from head to toe...then the tar recedes, revealing a blond man in a suit.

"Stir the flame," he hisses.

Violently König spins Aurora on her toes. As cold blue flames erupt at her feet, her butterscotch vanilla hair whips around...to dark chocolate brown...then cinnamon bittersweet auburn. The flames consume her and rend her to stone, her deep emerald eyes the last of her luster to go out. The sky is a shade of crimson darker than black.

König laughs. Washington weeps, tearing at his clothes...

...bright light spins from the axis of the world, collapsing to a single point...

...

...I surveyed the empty computer lab.

"Jack," I whispered. *"Who is she?"*

Kennedy told it plain. "You know exactly who she is."

Eighteen

Adversaries

Nothing to bury tonight, I thought. Outside, there was neither light nor sound to speak of. Two days after the new moon it still hid from itself, keeping the howling predators at bay. I sat alone at the kitchen table, illuminated only by the artificial light of an old hand-held TV set playing an exposé of the infamous Central Park Five at a low volume.

"Still up, Benji?"

Pearl stood robed at the entrance. I looked at the clock.

3:21.

Pearl turned on the overhang lamp and sat down. She swept her hair back over her left ear and placed her right hand on my arm. The surge of cold electricity was soothing. I raised my eyes to meet hers.

"When did you die?" I asked.

"You take me for a ghost?"

She grabbed my left hand and pressed it against her chest. It pulsed hot.

"Life is for the living, Benjamin."

"So you're human."

"What else would I be?"

I sighed.

"A sprite? A goddess?" she laughed.

"That – or maybe a witch."

Pearl laughed. "Then burn me at the stake and be done with it."

"Whatever you are – whatever your 'Sisters' are – it's above my pay grade."

Pearl sighed. "Alright then. I'll tell you."

She adjusted her gown and went to the freezer. She pulled out a carton of Ben & Jerry's Mint Chocolate Cookie and two spoons. She sat back down and offered me a spoon. I declined.

"I'm an orphan," she said as she dug in. "I lived with my aunt and uncle in Sacramento until I was eleven, before we moved to Washington for my uncle's job. I never finished high school. I joined the civil rights movement when I was twelve and came to lead the Sons of Liberty at eighteen. I've traveled to every single country on Earth. When I was thirteen, I snuck into Disneyland before it opened and rode the teacups. When I was twenty-five, I saved Janis Joplin from an overdose in Haight-Asbury. At thirty-eight I sharpened skates for the U.S. Olympic hockey team. I keep score at every baseball game I attend. My favorite flower is the petunia. I have inherited more money than God has ever seen, and there are days when I would trade it all for this."

She savored a bite of ice cream.

"I never married, but I've never lived without love."

"You and Michelle would get along great."

"Of that, I'm sure. I'm a notorious Francophile."

"I meant your stubbornness."

"That's why you love her, right? An irresistible force needs an immovable object."

"Right."

I sat up.

"I've learned the hard way not to get ahead of my skis. But I'm getting impatient. It's been nine months since the Rotunda. I never asked for any of this. Between Tyson and the Apprentice and all this noise, I need to know: what is my end game? Where am I supposed to be?"

Pearl leaned back in her chair. "Has it really been nine months? I'd lost track of time."

I noticed again the red marks on her right arm, and the streaking scar on the left side of her scalp. It was less of a scar than...

...*a silhouette*...

...*a Shadow*...

...*a Silent Echo*...

...of some injury sustained by someone else long ago. Pearl caught me leering at it.

"Let me first answer the question I know is on your mind," she said. "Yes, Benjamin. I had the scar when we first met. You just didn't see it."

I marveled as she continued.

"I'll answer your others in reverse: you're *exactly* where you're supposed to be. Everything that has happened already happened. You always saved Diego from Dorothy. You always freed Immanuel only to hear him die. You always confronted König in that hangar, and you always ended up here, tonight, with me. Nothing has changed. The Course of Human Events had its shape long before you entered it."

My eyes shifted to and fro.

"As to where you are going: to where you've already gone."

I closed my eyes.

"An unsatisfactory answer, I see."

"It's no answer at all. Why won't you just level with me?"

"You want a red pill to open your eyes?"

I frowned. "Did you recently watch *The Matrix*?"

"My favorite film without a Hepburn. And unfortunately a touchstone for many acolytes of the Apprentice."

I cocked my head in surprise. Pearl sealed the ice cream and marched to the freezer.

"Those disaffected by this reality often seek refuge in another. Not everyone has the courage and honesty to confront inconvenient truths. Yet König and his Brothers have millions chasing after an illusory escape hatch, a 'red pill' to show them a set of 'alternative facts,' a fantasy to liberate them from the hard truths of reality."

"So you offer a blue pill," I said. "To be blissfully ignorant."

"There is no blue pill. There is no red pill. There is only Truth. We can only lead the horse to water. We cannot make him drink. That itself would be Tyranny."

Pearl sat back down.

"Tyranny, after all, commands you to reject the evidence of your own eyes and ears."

"Orwell," I said. "*1984*."

"Confusion. The first of the Three Conquests."

I looked away. "I haven't thwarted any of them yet…have I?"

Pearl slowly shook her head. "No. Not yet."

My heart sank. "I'm afraid it's too late to do anything about them."

"We have nothing to fear but Fear itself. Because Fear *never* tells us the Truth. It clouds our minds with anger and hatred and pain and fantasies of vengeance against those who have wronged us. Fear of the new and unfamiliar often masquerades as 'love' for the old and familiar. Just as the seed begins to bear fruit, Fear is the weed that crowds in and chokes it."

Pearl stood to leave. At the staircase, she bent over into a terrible coughing fit.

"Pearl? Are you okay?"

She sniffled and her cheeks glistened.

"I'm only human," she replied. "And like you, in the grips of a terrible Fear."

She motioned upstairs.

"In your closet, there is a suit tailored to your particulars. Wear it in Wheaton on Monday."

"What's in Wheaton?"

"The front lines of the War on Tyranny."

~

The jury had already decided, and so had I.

Guilty.

"Ladies and gentlemen, welcome to the front lines in the War on Terrorism."

Adam Shaughnessy, DuPage County Assistant State's Attorney, stuck out his chin as his co-counsel, the perspiring Douglas Kaine, sized up opposing counsel, frizzy-haired Assistant Public Defender Adhita Parvati. The thirty-year-old Parvati rubbed sleep from her eyes as she finished writing her opening statement. She hadn't had time for the client who foolishly refused a plea bargain, the black man in the blue suit and glasses to her left.

Abdul Haq Salaam.

Radical Islamic terrorist.

In a packed courtroom an hour west of Chicago on Monday, March 14, 2016, Shaughnessy retold the tragedy of the Trinity United Methodist Church Bombing in Aurora, Illinois. Salaam planted the bomb during a meeting of the Aurora Interfaith Council on Friday, May 23, 2014 and detonated it remotely that Sunday morning. The bomb wounded thirty and killed eleven, including a three-year-old girl named Hope.

The jury was moved by Shaughnessy's opener, and they pitied Parvati, who spouted truisms: *"It is better that ten guilty men go free than that one innocent suffer."* That one didn't land well: the famous "Blackstone's ratio," meant to bolster the presumption of Salaam's innocence, sounded more like his own attorney's admission of his guilt. After all, these weren't Salaam's peers. Under the oversight of the stern Judge Walter Lawrence, the attorneys whittled a diverse pool of one hundred fifty to eleven white people and one Asian man. Juror Number Twelve was none other than Nervous Nelly herself, the one who spotted me at the UIC rally. As I watched her take her seat, I recalled Dad's lesson on juries.

"'Jury' is from the Old French jurer, meaning 'to swear,'" he explained. *"A man's peers swear an oath to protect the innocent against false accusations."*

"What about the guilty?" I asked.

"If a man is guilty, prove it. Tyranny thrives on false accusations. That's why John Adams defended the British soldiers involved in the Boston Massacre. Everyone is presumed innocent, even the ones you don't like."

Salaam's innocence unraveled quickly.

"What time did Salaam enter the bathroom, Ms. Valentine?" Shaughnessy asked the visibly uncomfortable church secretary.

"Between 3:30 and 4:00," she answered, clearing her throat. "I was chatting with one of our deacons. The son of a bitch smiled at me."

Three AIC members testified that Salaam left early with a small black duffle bag.

"He was unusually anxious," said Reverend Paul Guilford.

Joe Parker of the Aurora P.D. bomb squad testified, "The battery, casing and wiring all came from RadioShack."

"And the detonator?" Shaughnessy pressed.

"Same."

The detonator was in the bed of Salaam's pick-up when Officer Jason Giovanni arrested him later that evening.

"When I held it out to him," Giovanni testified, "Salaam called me a 'subhuman sack of shit' and threatened to kill my family."

Rod Casey was Salaam's manager at RadioShack, two blocks from the church, where Salaam worked that Sunday morning. Casey testified the radio for the detonator had a radius of two miles. When asked if it was possible for Salaam to have carried it around the store without drawing attention, Casey replied, "Of course."

Salaam's neighbor Sean Marinski described a part of Salaam's garage, near his prayer rug, where he "worked on all kinds of electronic devices." Marinski also recalled several times Salaam denounced the American government for its "crimes against the Iraqi people."

Each night that week I reviewed my notes. *"Pretend that you're on the jury,"* Pearl instructed. *"Only I want you to cheat. I want you to read articles and watch the news. I want you to connect what you see there to the world around you."*

The media didn't help Salaam's case. One local newspaper reported the testimony of the State's witnesses as established fact. Jennifer Valentine's testimony that Salaam had entered the bathroom sometime after 3:30 became *"Salaam placed the bomb in the bathroom at 3:30."* On a popular sub-Reddit, someone claimed Salaam was an Army deserter personally trained by Osama bin Laden.

One night in the Hull House kitchen I watched a prominent bow-tied cable news host denounce Salaam as *"a radical Islamo-fascist hell-bent on jihad"* and declared, *"Why go on with this charade of a trial? He's clearly guilty. Just execute the guy."*

A talking head rebuffed him: *"There's no death penalty in Illinois. So by law..."*

"Law? Screw the law! What we need is old-fashioned mob justice..."

((...amen to that...))

Amen.

Pearl entered the kitchen.

"Pearl, this Salaam is a piece of – "

She clamped down on her ears and spun back around.

I shrugged and drank my coffee. "A piece of work."

The State called its last witness on Friday, March 18, an elderly Catholic priest named Carlo di Lorenzo. Father Carlo was frail, all skin and bones. He shook as Shaughnessy assisted him to the stand. I wondered if Parvati would object, that this man was clearly in no state of mind to testify. As Shaughnessy pulled that sweet high falsetto from Father Carlo's mouth, Parvati seemed loathe to challenge him. Shaughnessy asked Father Carlo about a conversation he had with Salaam a month prior to the bombing:

"Salaam...confided...in me... that the...day...was coming... when America... would need... to... take acc..c..count...for her sins..."

"Did Salaam say what he meant by that?" Shaughnessy pressed.

"He...told me...that one day...the Capitol would be...set ablaze...and that...our old ways...of living...would be cast into...the Ash Heap. He said...that...Americans would...have...to sacrifice...before...entering a new...era."

Motive and intent. That seals it.

On cross, Parvati tried to challenge Father Carlo's memory, but gave up when he kept asking her to speak up.

The State rested. Judge Lawrence conducted business with counsel at sidebar. My pulse accelerated as I watched the stone cold Salaam sit motionless...*remorseless.*

I imagined Salaam building that bomb in a laboratory of death, proclaiming American heroes as killers, setting that device in the bathroom, slaughtering the innocent from two blocks away as he shouted "Allahu Akbar," rolling me onto my back as he punched and shoved, assailing everything I know and love and hold dear, sniveling as he called my father a killer, then murdering him.

He *must* be punished. *He fucking must.*

I caught the eye of the Foreman, a young man in a lacrosse jacket.

((...don't worry, brother...we have your back...))

He winked. It sat like lead in my stomach.

~

Marissa answers on the first ring. I invite her to Blackstone Coffee.
"I don't think that's such a good idea."
"Oh – "

"Coffee is a first date for college students. Take me to dinner on Friday?"

So on a Friday night in March Marissa and I find ourselves at Victor's Cantina. Marissa orders a margarita.

"Diet Coke, Ben?" Jorge asks.

Marissa wrinkles her nose, holding back laughter.

I cringe. "Yes, Jorge. Thank you."

Jorge scoots back to the bar. Marissa clears her throat.

"Diet Coke, huh? That's adorable."

"Very funny."

"I try."

Marissa tosses her hair over her shoulder as Jorge sets our drinks down.

"So," she begins, sweeping salt onto her finger. "Ben Upson doesn't drink?"

"Not since my dad died."

She stops cold and covers her mouth. "Oh my God. I...I'm so sorry."

"It's okay. It's been almost fifteen years."

Marissa's eyes water; she grabs a Kleenex from her purse.

"Look at me," she says. "Crying at the drop of a hat. You must think I'm a lunatic."

"Absolutely not," I assure her. Truth is, I find her sensitivity attractive. Still, I fight hard not to think of Michelle.

Marissa clamps her hand over mine. "You're really sweet, Ben."

She studies my face

"You look so much like him."

I tilt my head, puzzled. "Who?"

She whispers lightly. "John..."

I freeze. "What did you say?"

Her eyes begin to dart back and forth as she pulls back, cursing under my breath.

"John. John Upson. John Upson was my father. You...you knew my father?"

Marissa exhales. "When I saw you last Friday, I thought you were him. John was like my knight in shining armor."

I let go of her hands. "Explain."

She looks me up and down, then the realization hits. "Oh God no! It was only one time I met him. He came to my engagement dinner and..."

Her lip quivers.

"I need your help."

~

On Monday, March 21st, Parvati was surprisingly upbeat, considering the drubbing her client took the week before.

"Ms. Parvati," Judge Lawrence began. "I understand you have only one witness."

"Yes, your honor," Parvati answered. "The defense calls Pearl Warren."

Warren?

The double-doors opened. Pearl looked dazzling, striding in wearing a red skirt suit and white heels. As she approached the stand I realized why she had avoided me in the kitchen: she didn't want me spoiling her testimony. How she knew this despicable man was beyond me.

The clerk swore Pearl in. The jury subtly quaked in her presence.

"Good morning, Ms. Warren," Parvati began.

"Good morning, dear."

"Can you state your name?"

"Pearl, P-E-A-R-L, Warren, W-A-R-R-E-N."

"How old are you?"

"I turned seventy-four on the seventh of December."

"Do you know a man named Abdul Haq Salaam?"

"I knew him once by another name, but yes, he is the gentleman in the glasses and blue suit."

"How do you know Mr. Salaam?"

"I've been his godmother since birth. March 29, 1974."

"Who named you his godmother?"

"Keith's mother. My best friend, a wonderful woman named Zora Gates."

Zora? My heart rose, and the blood rushed from my face.

Shaughnessy stood. "Objection, I'm sure Ms. Gates is wonderful, but it's irrelevant. Move to strike."

"Sustained." The judge said. "The jury will disregard the statement about the wonderfulness of the defendant's mother."

Parvati pressed through. "Ms. Warren, who is Keith?"

"Oh, dear, my mistake."

Pearl looked straight at me.

"Abdul Haq Salaam," she said, "was born Keith Immanuel Atwater."

~

Marissa crumbles under an invisible weight. I stand to console her; she runs away into the cold mountain air. I find her on a bench outside.

"It's my son," she says, tearfully. "Ever since we moved from Chicago he's been so lost. He's only fourteen, for God's sake, he doesn't deserve this!"

I hesitantly place my hand on hers. She doesn't recoil.

"What happened in Chicago?" I ask.

She shivers and pulls back. "My...ex-husband got mixed up with...a hate group. We received death threats. So we moved here, to get as far away from all that as we could. My son...he doesn't have any friends, he just...sits in his room and cries. He was a straight-A student before this. He was an amazing baseball player."

She barely staves off the full flow.

"His father is out of the picture. He needs a real role model and, lo and behold, John Upson's own son teaches at his high school? That's not a coincidence."

I sit up tall. "Boy, um. I'm flattered. But I'm not sure I'm the right guy for that job."

She closes her eyes. "No. I mean, yes...I like you...yes...but this is...independent of that."

I nod. "It's just that...well my wife left me in January."

Marissa scowls. "What kind of ditz would do that?"

"A ditz who knows me too well."

Marissa studies me. "Did you have kids?"

My stomach turns. "Um...no. We tried, but...no."

Marissa wipes at her eye. "I'm sorry. I really think you'd make a great dad."

This is uncomfortable. "Listen, whatever you thought of my dad, and it's probably true, I'm not him. I don't have his wisdom to impart."

Marissa guffaws. "Bullshit! I've asked around about you. You're one of the most popular teachers at Milton Clark. You connect with those kids."

She sticks her finger in my chest.

"Connect with mine."

I exhale. There's no way I'm getting out of this. "Okay. So you say your son plays baseball?"

"Yes."

"Not to brag, but I used to play for the St. Louis Cardinals. Minor leagues, anyway. 40-man roster. One Spring Training game. Anyway...maybe I can take your son to a Rockies game? Or maybe the batting cages?"

Marissa blushes. "He would love that."

"I've seen the incoming freshman roster. There isn't anyone named Barrios."

"That's my maiden name."

"Your son?"

Marissa beams. "Atwater. Tyson Immanuel Atwater."

Nineteen

Immanuel

The world spun around me like a top.

This is Tyson's father.

I did the calendar math in my head. Now I understood why Marissa acted the way she did at Victor's. Her ex-husband was on trial. *Tyson's father is a terrorist.* They fled from Aurora to Springland and never told a soul. *Not even me.*

They were ashamed of him.

((...you're trash, Tyson...like father, like son...))

What did Reid know about this?

"How well do you know your godson, Ms. Warren?" Parvati asked.

"Very well. I have visited him many times over the past twenty-two months as the county held him without trial."

Shaughnessy, up like a rocket: "Objection!"

"Have I said something wrong?"

Judge Lawrence removed his glasses.

"Ms. Warren," he intoned. "I implore you to stick with the facts and leave your personal observations out of this."

Pearl blushed. "I beg your pardon, Walter, but what part of my statement wasn't factual? Is it not true that Mr. Salaam has spent nearly two years in solitary confinement?"

Judge Lawrence prepared to give a stern warning. Pearl held one finger up, and, inexplicably, he clammed up.

"Continue your questioning, Ms. Parvati," Judge Lawrence said nervously.

Over the next hour, Pearl shed light on much that the prosecution omitted. For example, the reason Salaam was so knowledgeable about explosives was due to his Army service in Iraq between 2003 and 2006, where he had converted to Islam.

"Sufism, specifically," Pearl clarified.

"Sufism?" Parvati asked.

"It is analogous to Quakerism in Christianity. The poet Rumi was a Sufi. Sufism emphasizes oneness with God and deplores violence."

"Why did Mr. Salaam tell you this?"

"He was conflicted. He believed his faith could teach his son to be a man of peace. But he wasn't sure how his wife or mother would handle it. Zora was a devout Christian, and he didn't want to betray her convictions in her old age."

Pearl's portrait of Salaam was very different from the monster the prosecution painted. The State's witnesses were credible, but had limited perspective. One good character witness was enough to plant reasonable doubt in my head that Salaam could have possibly bombed a church.

Then the plot thickened.

"Ms. Warren," Parvati continued, "has Mr. Salaam ever spoken about what happened on Friday, May 23, 2014?"

"Yes," Pearl answered. "On multiple occasions."

"What did he tell you?"

Shaughnessy stood warily. "Objection. Hearsay…"

Parvati jumped on it. "It's a party statement, your honor. It's admissible."

"The defendant is circumventing the Fifth Amendment!"

Judge Lawrence rubbed his eyes. "By invoking it? Overruled."

"Which one?"

"Both!"

I wasn't sure if any of this was admissible. Still, Pearl had Judge Lawrence by the gavel.

Almost like she outranks him.

"Go ahead, Ms. Warren," said the judge.

Pearl nodded curtly. "Mr. Salaam had received threatening calls from a 'Christian Identity' group that believes that white Aryans are the true Israelites."

"How serious were these threats?"

"Enough to send his family away."

Parvati shifted gears.

"Did Mr. Salaam explain what his plans were that afternoon of the 23rd?"

"He planned on attending his son's Little League game."

"Was his son with him at the church?"

"No, but he had his son's uniform. It was his plan to leave the meeting early and have his son change in his truck."

"What kind of truck did he drive?"

"A black Chevy Colorado. He didn't want to leave his duffel bag in the open bed, so he brought it into the church."

"What time did he arrive at the church?"

"Between 3:15 and 3:30."

"When did he leave?"

"Approximately 4:30."

"That's when he left the meeting room?"

"Yes."

"When did he leave the premises?"

"Five to ten minutes later."

"Did he tell you what he did during those five minutes?"

"He made a stop at the restroom."

"Did he see anyone else in those ten minutes?"

"Yes. Church secretary Jennifer Valentine spoke with the choir director, Greg Mullins, outside the sanctuary."

"Anyone else?"

"Two other men."

The gallery stirred. Judge Lawrence banged his gavel. *"Order…"*

Parvati pressed. "Did Mr. Salaam describe these men?"

"Both of the men were white, lighter hair, average height. One had Norse tattoos on his arms. They stocked the vending machine from a large black bag."

"Did Mr. Salaam describe anything else about them?"

"No."

"Did you speak to Mr. Salaam that Memorial Day weekend?"

"That very evening."

"Where?"

"Stuart Sports Complex, for his son's game. I watched him pull out his son's uniform for him to change in the truck."

"What did the uniform consist of?"

"A navy blue and gold Padres jersey, white pants, golden yellow socks, his 'SD' hat, his glove, batting gloves and cleats. Also several baseballs, a large water bottle, grape Big League Chew and a pound of sunflower seeds."

"Anything else?"

"Nothing else would have fit. It was bursting at the seams."

The courtroom erupted. I watched the jurors closely, studying each of their faces. I counted ten of them completely engaged, teetering on the edge of reasonable doubt...

...yet two held firm: the Foreman...

((...I'm not buying this bullshit sob story...))

...and Nervous Nelly...

((...Only a dirty Muslim would bomb a church...))

...with an assist from the bench...

((...I'll never be re-elected if this man is acquitted. My instructions will convict him. The jury has to obey...))

...as the courtroom darkened...everyone but Pearl froze.

"The jury has to obey, John Brown."

A chill ran through me. He stood at the end of my row. Scar. Corn yellow teeth. White hair, white beard. Black uniform of the Du Page County Sheriff, radio on his shoulder.

Nicholas Morgan. Cecil Barton slithered behind, muttering to himself in a bespoke suit.

Pearl stood, firmly, resolutely.

"Pearl," Morgan intoned. "It's been awhile."

"You've come for me, Nicholas," she said.

"It's time. You're weak."

Pearl began to cough violently. She plopped down in her seat, exhausted.

Morgan cackled. "Mr. Barton, lay down your mumbo jumbo."

Barton eyed me and mocked, *"Chirp, chirp, Benji. Tweet tweet."*

He passed through the swinging gate and leaned over the witness stand, grabbing Pearl by the cheeks. Furious, I stood. Morgan's Colt .45 clicked.

"Still think you'se a hero, John Brown?"

I stared down the barrel of his gun. "You have one bullet. Make it count, you sick illiterate fuck."

Barton whispered into Pearl's ear. The room rapidly lost oxygen. Tar oozed from every wall, dripping from the ceiling and scalding the souls trapped inside this...

...echo chamber...

...as growling black Shadows slipped from cracks in the air itself and swept toward the jury...and me. The beasts flew into me, knocking me to the ground, seizing me with dark and terrible thoughts. I stared into the abyss of death itself, from which emerged the sound of ten thousand amphibious croaks and that name...

...Kek...

...Kek...

...Kek...

...for the briefest moment, I felt what it was like to be nothing, formless and airless; but the nothingness, the emptiness...was still pain...infinite pain, cold pain, and the naked impulse to destroy everything and everyone in sight...I was darkness discarnate, lost and alone...

...I lost all hope...

...then they came to me, *ex nihilo,* out of the nothingness, a gust of second wind dazzling in scarlet and azure and snow...

...three words...

...three daughters of the rising sun...

"...get up, Pearl."

The courtroom flooded with blinding light.

Morgan and Barton fell to the ground with a thud; the Shadows scattered. The tar evaporated. She was so radiant I was compelled to my knees. I gazed upon her as I would the sun itself.

Pearl was young again, the auburn-haired waitress at Hopper's, the feisty Freedom Rider. She cast her face upon all in the room, reaching her healing hand out to the jury as if to say...

"Come now...let us reason together..."

That's when I knew.

That's when I knew exactly who she was.

Her light shone upon the still-frozen jury and melted lingering resistance to the truth of Salaam's innocence. Then I heard the whisper of Salaam's heart, trapped in a stone cage of bitter regrets.

((...Let me free! Let me see my wife, my boy! Marissa! Tyson! Tyyyyssssson!...))

Inside Salaam broke into agonizing tears, shattering like a mirror in a sonic boom...

...drawing me deep inside his darkest memories...

...

"Out of the car now! On the ground! Hands where I can see 'em!"

Giovanni drags me out of my pick-up and throws me to the asphalt. I hold up my hands. He spins them down and around and seals the cuffs. Strickland yells into his radio:

"Suspect apprehended on North Avenue bridge, Fox River. Request backup."

My twelve-year-old son hyperventilates in the passenger seat.

"Dad? What's going on?" he cries.

"I don't know, Tyson. Be quiet."

Tyson doesn't believe me. When he looks at me, he sees double.

Strickland barks at my son. "Yeah, Tyson. Your daddy has the right to shut the fuck up, and so do you."

No. No you son of a bitch. Not to my son.

I'm not guilty. But he's innocent.

I mutter a prayer.

"What's that Muhammad?" Giovanni yells.

Cold steel jams against the base of my neck.

"I could waste you right here and I'd be a hero," he says.

He pulls the slide stop.

"Stop resisting!"

Tyson moves out of my periphery. No. No, son, no!

Strickland pushes him back against the seat. Giovanni points his weapon at him.

CLICK

Giovanni's breath catches. He's surprised.

...

...I have never felt this before...

...this anger...

...this rage...

"FUCKYOUYOUSUBHUMANSACKOFSHIT!"
Snot flies. Everywhere.
Giovanni knocks me down. "What'd you call me, Muhammad?!?"
I sob, chest heaving. "You'd say...same to me...if I tried to kill the ones...you love."
My glasses are broken. But I see Tyson, hard as plaster.
He splits in two. He'll never be one again.
"You're lucky, Muhammad. Jihad Junior gets to keep his head today."
I hear Strickland rummaging in the glove box. He finds my coin
"He's in a cult."
I don't have to look...I know they just tossed Liberty down the river...
...

...the light receded. Pearl collapsed into her seat. Barton steadied himself up next to the still frozen jury. Morgan stirred in the aisle, searching with his hand for his...
...Colt .45. On the ground...

I leapt. Morgan scrambled on all fours. We collided and wrestled, gun in the air. Morgan kneed me in the groin. *Ooomph!* I let go. Morgan trained the gun on me as Barton slithered up and down the jury box whispering terrible legends:

(((...*foreign...Muslim...terrorist...black...black* is *dark...dark* is *evil...evil...evil...*)))

The jurors' hearts visibly hardened, suffocated anew by the Shadows.

Morgan panted. "I ain't doin' ya dirty today, John Brown. Come find your gift under the tree."

He swung his arm to the right. Pearl's shimmering emeralds stared down the barrel.

Morgan pulled the trigger...

...

...the bullet exploded through Pearl's chest.

No.

Her eyes rolled back into her head in pain as the wound slowly sewed itself shut.

"Bulls-eye!"

In the blink of an eye the interlopers vanished, and time resumed…

…

"Medic!" Judge Lawrence cried. Pearl was out cold; as far as anyone else could tell, she had merely fainted.

Harper and Woodhull burst into the courtroom. I sprang up and leapt over the barricade.

"Move aside! Move aside!"

I put my hand to Pearl's heart. She awoke with a gasp, to the relief of the Court. Judge Lawrence banged his gavel.

"Recess. One hour."

The clerk led the jury away.

"Ms. Warren," Parvati pressed, anxiously. "Can you continue?"

Pearl cast her gaze away.

"No, dear," she said. "I don't have the strength."

Crestfallen, Parvati delivered Salaam the bad news:

"You'll have to waive the Fifth and testify yourself."

Salaam's head dropped, and he began to cry.

"Tyson…" he sobbed. *"They're killing him. They're killing my boy."*

Harper and Woodhull propped Pearl up by her shoulders and walked her out of the courtroom. Salaam and I locked eyes, his weighed down with despair…

…then something passed between us…

…a familiarity…a kinship…

((…help me, John…you gotta help me…))

…

…and then I remembered my oath…

…

…I have no idea why I'm wrapping my pinky around Marissa's. I don't really know her. I have no obligation to fulfill her strange request. Yet, somehow, I feel compelled to do this…

"Marissa, I promise you I will look after Tyson."

She shakes her head. "Not good enough."

"No?"

"Do you swear upon the altar of God that you will guide and protect my only son, Tyson Immanuel Atwater, as if he were your own?"

I look deeply into her turquoise eyes and exhale. Fine.

"Upon the altar of God," I say, "I swear it."

~

"Four years, no more. Then the lead poisoning takes her."

In life, Dr. Helen Taussig was renowned for her advancements in cardiology and hospice care. Now she was Pearl's personal physician, tending to her bedside upstairs at Hull House.

Minty raged. "She doesn't deserve this."

Pearl coughed. "You know I can hear you, Harriet. You don't have to talk about me in the third person just yet."

Minty laughed through her tears as she drew nearer. Pearl stroked her left temple.

"Goodness, child. Who did this to you?"

"Whoever it was," Minty squeaked, "he did me a favor."

Pearl lingered on her. "There is no one, dead or alive, who shares in Mother's spirit as you do."

Minty burst into tears and stepped away, sobbing into Ira's arms.

"Where is Benjamin?"

I stepped forward, hesitantly. "Here."

Pearl smiled, the crow's feet creasing at the corners of her eyes.

"You look so much like John," she whispered gently, holding my hand and rubbing it in circles with her thumb. Her eyes had grayed like stony gravel in leaves of grass; her skin turned sallow.

She pulled me closer.

"Come here, Benjamin," she eked out.

I scooted closer, breath fast and shallow, heart pounding out of my chest. Pearl covered my hand with hers.

"Benjamin John Upson, Today I reaffirm you as my Champion. I charge you to carry forth my flame and redeem Liberty from the Ash Heap. Only the Greatest Love will prevail. Hannah?"

Dr. Arendt stepped forward. Pearl eyed the hourglass next to her bed. The sands rapidly neared the end.

"The time of turning is near. In his time, our Champion has a fraction of a second to spare. Execute Camlann immediately."

Dr. Arendt nodded, then indicated for me to follow.

"Benjamin," Pearl said, holding on to my hand. "Answer me this question."

Beads of sweat poured from my forehead. "A-anything."

For a brief moment, her skin flickered like a candle, eyes shining green and bright.

"Will you dance with me in the flames?" she whispered.

I nodded. "Yes."

"Then you know who I am."

I nodded again. Pearl fell into a nasty coughing fit, then shooed me away.

"Go on, Benjamin Upson. Our story is not over yet."

I lingered over her, then turned to follow Dr. Arendt. A number of others followed us downstairs, then up the hidden staircase into the Celestial Rotunda. Minty, Ira and Kennedy gathered around me in the center of the round.

"She will be brought here to the Temple momentarily," Mason said, "and remain under guard until the Champion's heart is fully prepared to storm Tyranny's Gates and redeem her. Here, he will wield Excalibur against Liberty's foe and defeat him. You three have been chosen to accompany our Champion on this quest."

Dr. Arendt handed me a Blue File embossed in gold leaf:

OPERATION CAMLANN

"Camlann?" I asked. "What is Camlann?"

"The last battle of the Revolution," Dr. Arendt said. "We're mounting a counter-offensive, and you're the tip of the spear. First things first: clear the airwaves. Begin with the Tower."

Mason reached into his pocket and pulled out a brand new phone. He opened the timer app and handed it to me.

"As I said, Benjamin," he began. "*Today* is the day you join the Revolution."

I glanced at the timer:

20:23:59

"What does this mean?"

Mason looked grim. "When our Lady first touched your heart in this very Rotunda, she was only a second from succumbing to the poison she sustained Today. In our realm, a second is equal to one year…one full Revolution of the Earth around the Sun. For you it has been two hundred sixty four days. You ought to have one hundred and one left…"

I slowly scanned the faces around the room. I was overcome with shame…

"…but when the Lady struck your heart in Dresden to protect you from Platov's bullet, it drained her of nearly a quarter second – eighty days' worth – of her power. The countdown has accelerated, and now you have less than a tenth of a second – three weeks – to complete your mission before she is gone to us forever. When she is gone…"

Mason grabbed my shoulder.

"… our entire world falls with her. Do you understand?"

I looked again:

20:23:58

"Yes, sir," I said.

Mason scoured me up and down.

"Then at last, you know who she is."

"I do," I answered, choking back a tear.

Mason looked through me intensely. "And?"

"Hail Columbia," I whispered.

Above, the celestial chorus shouted.

"Hail Libertas!"

Mason nodded. "Go."

I gripped my coin and closed my eyes.

The Rotunda whirled to light in silence.

We jumped…

...and my coin turned to iron.

Twenty

One if by Gaslight…

The Copper Queen doesn't rust; hers is a more graceful corrosion. As her mint patina seals her from the alimental air her fire will extinguish. She will be frozen forever, lost to her luster and vitality. Bereft of voice, the profane will speak for her and through her. She will be a pale imitation, sold by the nickel for cheap amusement. No warmth will issue from her flame.

19:22:18

I shivered, watching the sunrise over the Narrows on Wednesday, February 17, 1939. Battery Park, on the southernmost tip of Manhattan, was frigid; three layers deep and the wind still whipped right through me. The Copper Queen stood still, holding her flame aloft. This morning I saw her anew.

She walks among us.

First as Aurora.

Then as Emmaleigh.

Now as Pearl.

The Sons of Liberty call them Sisters, but they are one and the same, and from the most ancient of days they answer to a different name.

Libertas.

Liberty personified, her living presence animates our national spirit, and illuminates the hopes of all.

Until the day Tyranny poisoned her heart.

The day *I* poisoned her heart.

"Her light and ours are interdependent," Dr. Taussig explained. *"When our love for her fades, she becomes vulnerable to Tyranny's assassins. Something tipped the scales during her testimony. Now Morgan's bullet spins in her heart and the process has begun. She will be reduced to stone, a symbol with no substance, and Tyranny will wield her against us all. Only her Champion can redeem her now."*

That was March 21, 2016, four years before I arrived at the Rotunda, where Pearl had been waiting for her unworthy Champion. Me. Ben Upson. Now I knew why my rash actions in Charlottesville and Dresden generated such backlash.

I was sacrificing Liberty on the altar of personal grievance.

A bittersweet musk filled the air. I threw up.

"You don't look so good, Mr. Upson."

An aging Giant approached, hands in his coat pockets, warmed by a derby hat and scarf. It had been three decades since Jack Johnson and I last met, as his broken body attested. For me, it had been a matter of weeks.

"I'm told you're still a Champion," Johnson said. "I suppose you're still in shape for it?"

"Not even close," I replied, truthfully.

The pigeons scattered as Johnson eased himself, uncomfortably, onto the park bench.

"Lotsa Champions sick these days," he said. "Ol' Ironman Lou Gehrig has some kinda nerve disease nobody's ever seen. Shame. Krauts love that Yankee."

"Speaking of Germans," I said. "I hear you trained Max Schmeling to fight Joe Louis last year?"

Johnson winced. "Yeah. The stories are true. I had a beef with Louis' trainer, goes back years. That gave me cover. Only way a Negro could cozy up to Nazis. Of course, nobody saw it that way. Now black folks hate me, too."

Johnson handed me a manila envelope. I grasped it, but he held tight.

"I sacrificed my reputation with my brothers to get this. Don't waste it."

Johnson let go.

"Y'know, Mr. Upson, I've been praying to meet you again. To tell you the things I saw in you that day that you couldn't see in yourself."

He leaned in.

"You don't have to keep him down there anymore."

I flinched.

"Your daddy didn't deserve what happened to him."

"No," I said. "It happened all the same."

"I'm a flawed man. I have resentments, too. Take a little advice from another flawed man."

Johnson slowly stood.

"Go all in this time."

Johnson whistled as he walked away, hands in his coat pockets.

I reached into my pocket and pulled out my iron coin. It had a new inscription:

TO LIBERTY AND JUSTICE FOR ALL

I flipped it in the air; Ira caught it.

"You got it?"

I peaked inside the envelope, studying its contents. "He came through."

Ira nodded. The Pima was a man of few words, but not because he had nothing to say. One of six Marines who raised the flag at the Battle of Iwo Jima, tourists would later come to his home in Phoenix and ask, *Are you that Indian who raised the flag?* His fame felt like infamy, and he carried it like dead weight. He retreated into himself, so many mistook him for a "stoic Indian." Ten years after Iwo Jima, he died in a snowy ditch of frostbite and alcohol poisoning, an unjust end for a selfless American warrior.

"Tell me, Corporal," I started, "why do you still serve the thankless?"

"I don't do it for thanks. I do it for her."

I studied Lady Liberty again. "You know, in this light she looks tired and poor. Like the huddled masses. Like..."

"One of us?"

"Yeah. Like one of us."

~

She's like nothing I've ever seen.

"She's a lioness," Antoine slurs, dribbling down his Superman costume. "You'll never tame her."

"Just give me that line again."

He whispers breathily.

"Got it."

"She's lost *hiccup* that lovin' feelin'."

"Have another glass of Kryptonite."

I throw on the aviators, adjust the flight jacket and take off across the floor.

The DJ mixes from REM to...Bananarama. Amateur hour. Only at a Georgetown party.

Target acquired. White fitted sheet, bare shoulder. Sandy blond locks curling at the collarbone, foam crown of seven green sun-rays. Light freckles. Radiant.

There's a semi-circle of Clichés around her. Devil. Nurse. Bunny. Another Devil.

Easy pickings. Engage.

I break in and...stand there. Awkwardly.

She smiles, pierces me with those baby blues. The Clichés smell blood and close ranks. A squeeze play. Move fast or lose her forever.

"I'm Ben."

Stupid. Stupid. Idiot. Stupid idiot.

"I'm curious," she says. Her accent is subtle but pronounced.

I stammer. "About what?"

The Clichés snicker.

She sips from her red cup. "What did Superman tell you?"

...um... "What?"

"I asked first."

Shit. Danger zone. Plan B....C?

B. No...D.

"Your costume isn't working," I say. F.

The Clichés laugh in unison. She raises her eyebrows.

"Hold your arm up. Show your...um...fire to the world."

A Devil laughs. "I'll show you fire."

She gives me the bird. You know, the finger.

The Clichés explode. "NICE, DARCY!"

Crashed and burned.

"Hope I didn't spoil your evening," I say. "Good night."
She just smiles. I feel her eyes follow me as I walk away.
Antoine is pissing himself.
"Lioness," he mouths. "Never tame her."
Watch me, Superman.

~

18:11:14

I'd come to see her as Superwoman. From the moment she tunneled into my cell in New Orleans, I'd been awestruck by her. She was pure iron, a fearless warrior, beyond human.

She was never more human than she was that night.

I found her by the window of a backroom at Fraunces Tavern, the red brick restaurant at the corner of Pearl and Broad that served as Washington's New York headquarters during the War for Independence. She sat alone, arms crossed, not drinking, not speaking. She simply stared out at the foot traffic and the city lights, yearning. Paperwork littered the table in front of her, but she paid it no heed. She was elsewhere…and else when…

"Hey Mint," I began, taking the seat across from her. "Are you okay?"

She didn't look back at me. Her face was matted with tears she hadn't bothered to wipe away. She only muttered wistfully, to no one in particular: *"I go to prepare a place for you…"*

I sat in silence. Minty had been spirited away from this world and into another, a world of great pain. My better judgment prevailed in that moment: I had no real comfort to offer to someone experiencing something I simply couldn't understand.

After a few moments she finally spoke up. "Have you ever…"

She paused, regaining her composure.

"Have you ever carried the weight of the world on your shoulders, Ben?"

I nodded slowly. "I have. I feel like I'm carrying it now."

"I suppose you are."

Minty sniffled, and drew her attention back down to the table.

"I carried that weight my entire life. I didn't expect to add the weight of another world after I passed."

She heaved her shoulders and emitted a deep sigh.

"It never seems to end."

I glanced down at the papers on the table, some of which I recognized from Johnson's file. Directly in front of her was a cartoon, a crudely drawn cartoon of an ugly green frog with an insidious grin. The frog was draped in an American flag, placing a Star of David in the oven.

"Do you know what that is?"

I shuddered. I'd seen that frog before, drawn on some of my students' assignments, in the corner of the ticket that Reid left for Tyson. I'd seen it as social media profile pictures, and amidst the litany of racist and sexist cartoons in Platov's file. *And I'd hallucinated it in the Rotunda.*

"I've seen it," I replied. "But I don't know what it means."

Minty gripped the cartoon, staring deeply into it. "Kek."

((...Kek...Kek...Kek...))

"What the hell is Kek?"

Minty leaned back in her seat. "Who I've been fighting since I was twelve years old."

I tilted my head. Minty's bottom lip quivered.

"Kek...is the name of an ancient god of darkness, from Egypt. The Egyptians saw him as a man with the head of a frog. Lord knows why. But it's just another name for Tyranny...that formless monster from the Abyss. Cold. Merciless. Unrelenting."

Minty looked back out the window. She grit her teeth, angrily.

"In my darkest hours, that's what I saw when I closed my eyes."

I looked closer at the cartoon. "These are the 'memes' Dr. Arendt was talking about. A so-called 'virus of the mind.' Circulates through the public over and over until it's like, embedded in our subconscious, our thoughts and emotions. Almost subliminally, until before you know it you've been trained to hate someone."

Minty folded her arms. "They did that to me."

I sat back in my chair, watching Minty visibly shake. It was heart rending to see a woman of such strength so fragile and vulnerable.

"The wanted posters, portraying me as a monster for daring to take away the masters' so-called property. I might be a hero in your time, but in my day I was hated. Just because I wanted to live. Just because I wanted a place for me and my little Gertie..."

Another tear streamed down Minty's cheek.

"I go to prepare a place for you."

She wiped the tear away.

"Mother knows more than anyone, that place isn't here."

I glanced down at the table, at the other files and all the propaganda. My eyes landed on a poster advertising a "Pro-American Rally," a "Mass Demonstration for True Americanism," the location of our next mission. I sat back and gave thought to what Minty said.

"Who is Mother?"

Minty rubbed her eyes, then lay her hands on the table, taking hers into mine.

"Someone who once carried the weight of the world on her shoulders."

~

"Square your shoulders, Benji."

It was embarrassing. Two seasons of minor league baseball, and this Georgetown psychology student from the south of France is dominating me at table tennis. It's a weird place for a first date: pizza and ping-pong. It's weirder that Michelle Deschamps tracked me down after I crashed and burned in front of her on Halloween. It's weirdest after she pumped Antoine's sappy-ass line out of me:

"Tes yeux sont comme les étoiles du ciel."

She laughed: "'My eyes are like the stars of the sky?' Wow. That line is just…wow."

I shrugged. "I mean…it fits."

She rolls her eyes. "You're lame, but cute. Here's my number."

Now I prep my serve.

"Shell, I'm gonna knock you into the basement."

"I don't think this place has a basement, buddy."

I serve. And get served. Game-set-match, Deschamps.

I'm totally good with that. I could drink beer and eat pizza and talk to her about the D.C. squirrel menace and Austin Powers and the French World Cup win over Brazil and growing up a Navy brat and Jungian shadows until sunrise. She's a secret nerd, like me. I'm trying not to fall in love on the spot.

The talking heads on the TV at the bar intervene:

"The President is coming under increased scrutiny concerning an alleged sexual relationship with a White House intern..."

Michelle polishes off another slice. "Poor girl."

I wave her off. "She's a grown woman. She can deal with the consequences of her own actions."

"If she was in any position to choose them."

I'm surprised. I lean back in my seat. "You're saying he forced himself on her?"

Michelle shrugs. "No, not necessarily. Just...gaslighting."

I shoot her a weird look. "Gaslighting?"

She sips her soda. "Powerful people can be hypnotizing. They can bend the truth to their own whim. They can make people question themselves, their reality. You know...get under their skin."

I whistle. "Have you been watching X-Files?"

Michelle picks an olive off the pizza and flicks it at me. "Nope."

"You did not just flick an olive at me."

"Yes I did."

"No. You didn't."

Michelle pauses. "No. You're right. I didn't."

"Good," I laugh. "I'm glad you see it my way."

Michelle giggles. "Hey. What's the President's favorite song?"

I spread my hands.

"Devil With A Blue Dress Off." She sips her cherry Coke to the bottom.

I can't control the laughter. Good God. I've met the mother of my children.

~

17:14:06

George Washington towered over the stage in Continental blue. Different versions of the stars and stripes hung from either side. Deep down, I got chills from the patriotic fervor humming through Tex Rickard's Madison Square Garden, where twenty thousand venerated the emblem of the land they loved.

The Swastika of the German-American Bund.

"Sieg heil! Sieg heil! Sieg heil!"

A chill swept through the Garden as I slipped invisibly through the ranks of the deranged, wearing a black SS uniform in the event of exposure, searching for a signal in the noise:

((…too much crime here, especially the Negroes…))

((…Roosevelt is a corrupt elitist…))

((…the false news, the lugenpresse, comes from the Jews…))

Young men goose-stepped past carrying Nazi and American flags together. Orthodox protesters were barricaded next to the stage, like the press in Chicago.

Up in the rafters I watched Minty deftly balance on the crossbeams as she scoured the floor below where Ira, Kennedy and I swept for König's agent.

A man came to the stage to introduce the next speaker:

"We love him for the enemies he has made: ladies and gentlemen, Mr. Fritz Kuhn!"

The crowd applauded wildly for the Bund leader, a weasel-looking man with a dour disposition and thick German accent:

"Ladies and gentlemen, fellow Americans, American patriots…"

((…hereby proclaim January 20, 2017 as National Day of Patriotic Devotion…))

The kickback was loud. I recognized that voice. *The Apprentice.*

I pressed my earpiece. "Did you guys hear that?"

"Keep your ears to the ground," Minty answered. *"Don't get distracted."*

I moved warily up and down the aisles as Kuhn screeched.

"You all have heard of me through the Jewish controlled press…"

((…the fake news media is not my enemy, it is the enemy of the American people…))

Shit. Focus, Ben.

"…prescribed to us by…the Rabbi Weissmans, Undermeyers and Dicksteins…"

((…my enemies are all corrupt…corrupt…corrupt…))

"…of Hitler…what I read in the papers, that surely he is too busy planning the seizure of the Ukraine…"

((…Putin…is not going to go into Ukraine…))

"...in mentioning this Jewish gentleman, Rabbi Weissman and the others...the aristocrats of the world, let me say that I have the greatest respect for them..."

((...I have great respect for women...the New York Times...African-Americans...))

"...unless you aliens, Nordics and Christians speak up..."

((...we're losing our country...we want immigrants from Norway...not those shithole countries...))

"...our government shall be returned to the American people..."

((...we are transferring power...back to you, the American people ...))

"...and determine to protect our wives, our children against the slimy conspirators..."

((...greatest coup of all time...they could be ISIS...))

"...if you listen to Dicksteins and some other political hounds...in the pay of the Jews...you will have absolutely the most false impression..."

((...totally corrupt...fake news...))

...

"Chirp-chirp, Benji! Tweet-tweet!"

What the hell was that...?

I moved into the aisle. It was a kid. A young kid, a dirty little street urchin in a St. Louis Browns cap leaning against a tall stack of newspapers. Under his cap he had dark brown hair, and under the grime a face full of freckles...

...I know him...

...

...John?

I reached out to him...

...as he rolled a band around a paper and fired it into my gut.

Oomph! I fell to the concrete floor. The kid came charging forward and kicked me square in the nose; the entire arena started to ring and buzz. The kid pressed his smug face against mine. His eyes were gray, and he smelled like tar.

"Chirp-chirp, Benji! Tweet-tweet."

The boy dissolved to smoke, then as a charred black bird he took to the rafters. From the floor arose thousands of frogs leaping and croaking. Each said something, and collectively nothing...

CUCK… SNOWFLAKE… BLACK ON BLACK CRIME…MUSLIMS ARE TERRORISTS…BEND THE KNEE…MAGA…AMERICA FIRST…ILLEGALS…TRAITORS… …WHITE GENOCIDE…

"A real man defends his own people."

I froze.

It was like looking into a mirror. The apparition looming above me was my spitting image, wearing a white polo and khakis. He pointed his gas lit tiki torch at me.

"Look at you, cuck. You don't have anybody!"

He kicked me hard in the pelvis and spat, then dropped a newspaper flat on the ground.

I wiped my bloody nose and fetched it up:

THE PALM BEACH POST
Today
Snowflake Edition

I unrolled the broadsheet:

UPSON GOES ON BENDER, FATHER DIES IN FIERY BLAZE

"Fuck you!"

An image swirled together in the middle of the paper. *Shit, shit, no.*

The wreckage. The carnage. I threw the paper on the ground. It boomeranged back in my face:

MICHELLE DITCHES BENJI: STILL A MAN, OR JUST ANOTHER CUCK?

Ira broke through the smoke and grabbed the paper from my hand, then tossed it to the floor and snapped his fingers to ignite it. He seized me by the collar.

"Clean your ears out, damn it!"

There was commotion on stage, as Bund security piled atop a Jewish protester and beat him.

((…knock the crap out of them…I love the old days…they'd be carried out on a stretcher, folks…))

The ringing and buzzing crescendoed until it nearly blew out my right eardrum…

"Ahhh!!!"

…and then…

((…not much tape left…I hope Mr. Gould pays what he promised…))

I grabbed Ira by the shoulder. "Did you hear that?"

Ira pressed his earpiece. "Minty, do you have the fix on the location?"

"Copy," Minty replied. "Brunette, back row on the floor."

I nodded toward the mezzanine exit. "We do it there."

I moved away from the stage to get a closer look at the subject. I spotted her from a hundred feet out: shoulder length, wavy brown hair, in the brown shirt and tie of the Bund. She packed away in her shoulder bag a recording device identical to the one I saw Cecil Barton with in Chicago.

((…Papa….you haunt me…but I must protect myself…))

"Chirp chirp, Benji! Tweet tweet!"

I turned. The kid was in his Sunday best. He beckoned with his finger. I shook my head. He frowned like a scorned puppy.

"Why do you hate us, Benji?" he said sweetly. "We're your people. *Your family."*

"No," I said. "You aren't."

"We would never hurt you, Benji!" he moaned. "They will!"

Emboldened, I bent over to look the phantom in the eye. *"Fuck. Off."*

He vanished. From behind me came a deep voice like a trombone.

"I'm disappointed in your tone, Benjamin…"

An ugly, slick-skinned frog wore the Freckled Boy's suit.

"What brazen incivility."

Ira clapped in my face. "Come on, man! What's up with you?"

The frog vanished again into smoke. Ira bounded toward the exit. I shadowed the subject, keeping my distance. She put the recording device in her shoulder bag and squeezed out of the aisle. I followed her up the stairs through a chokepoint to the Sixth Avenue exit.

((…once we transmit, I am finished Papa…I promise…))

Out of the shadows a hand clamped across her mouth. Another form came stealthily from below, snaking the bag from her shoulder and pushing out onto the city sidewalk. Kennedy held her gently from behind as I put my finger to my lips…and stopped cold.

"Mildred?"

Her eyes widened in surprise. I looked at Kennedy for confirmation.

"The parade in Palm Beach..."

Kennedy nodded. Over his shoulder I watched Minty and Ira vanish into a subway grate.

"Mrs. Schwartz, we don't mean you harm. Do you understand?"

She nodded vigorously.

"When do you check in with your handlers?"

She held up her hands.

"Ten? At ten o'clock?"

She nodded.

"At ten, call your handlers and tell them, *'ALL QUIET IN KEKISTAN.'* Agreed?"

She nodded, shocked that I knew her codes.

We exited the arena and escorted Mildred into a cab.

"Pearl and Stone, Hank," Kennedy commanded.

The driver, a young Brooklynite named Hank Finkelson, adjusted his mirror. "Yessir."

~

17:05:37

In a corner of our downtown safe house eight floors above Delmonico's, sound technician Ray Atwater analyzed Mildred's recording on a complicated device light years ahead of its time.

"This is incredible," he said, scribbling notes in a faded brown diary. "The B track actually *alters the meaning* of the A track."

"Explain it to me like I'm from the nineteenth century," Minty demanded.

"This tape is intelligent."

Minty squinted. "It can read?"

"In a way...yeah. Paired with any other track, it blends them both into a message that sounds like the A track, only with the B track's undertones."

"It's subliminal?" I asked. "Like hypnosis?"

Ray scratched his head. "No. You can hear the B track, so it's louder than a whisper. Somehow, the B track is powerful enough to convince the listener that it's substantially the same message as the A track...even if they're nothing alike. Like if a beautiful woman whispered softly into your ear that she was gonna kill you, but all you remember is how her breath made the hair stand on the back or your neck."

"Two sources merge into one signal. It has the original track's emotional tone and the new track's message."

Ray snapped and pointed. "You got it."

"Sounds like lipstick on a pig," Minty inveighed.

Ray tapped his pen on his desk. "Except the lipstick turns the pig into something else. This is dangerous. Dig deep enough, I'm sure you could fake entire recordings with this."

"Good work, son," Minty said, clapping Ray on the shoulder and motioning me up the stairs.

In the roof garden Ira knelt in front of Mildred, who sat rigidly in a wooden chair. Kennedy paced impatiently. Minty whispered to Ira; he shook his head and wandered to the railing, frustrated.

Mildred had proven difficult to break.

"Ms. Cohen," Minty told her brightly, "we'll only need a few more minutes."

Cohen?

Minty exited. Mildred's eyes followed me as I spoke to Kennedy out of earshot.

"Jack, she's the eugenicist we saw in the parade in Florida, isn't she?"

"She was...or, at least she will be."

I was stunned. "*Cohen.* How does a Jewish girl get caught up with eugenics and Nazis?"

"Survival," Ira offered, staring off the rooftop. "She married a blond, blue-eyed Aryan so she could be fully 'white.' To fit in. To protect herself."

"That makes no earthly sense."

"Neither did Creek collaborating with Jackson. Free blacks fought with Jackson too, then he sold them as slaves. Tyranny never returns affection."

I stared at the street below. "I met Jackson once. That was enough for me."

"Harriet told me. She said that's when you started to see whose colors they really are."

"Not Jackson's. Not König's, nor his Apprentice's for sure."

"No. Definitely not."

Ira paced over, arms folded.

"I grew up in land the Pima occupied for two millennia before Tyranny conquered it flying those same colors. My ancestors despised them."

I swallowed. "They had every right to."

Ira nodded. "Even so…for some reason, my father saw something in them. 'A diamond in the bullshit,' is what he called it. He fought in World War I as a non-citizen, a stranger in his own native land. Even after Congress made us citizens the State of Arizona kept us from voting until 1948. In spite of all that, my parents hung the stars and stripes from our mantle for years. Not to worship a symbol, but because they chose to see it as a sigil of the unfulfilled promises of Liberty herself. What you do with symbols isn't important. How you respond to Liberty herself is."

The rooftop entry swung open.

"Speak of the Devil," Kennedy remarked, "and an Angel shall appear."

Emmaleigh Stevens dazzled in a long silk winter coat and black beret. I had met her at the age of three, and again at forty-seven. Now, at seventy-six, her silver-gray hair cut short into a blunt bob with curls, she was nearly Pearl's identical, save an inviting pair of light hazels in the place of shimmering emeralds. She set aside the Playbill in her hands to remove her arm-length black gloves. She rubbed her hands together and placed them on Mildred's. Mildred regained color, and she relaxed.

"I saw the most marvelous production tonight," Emmaleigh boasted. "*The American Way*. A German immigrant struggling to adapt in this strange country. I imagine you and your compatriots can relate."

Mildred looked at Emmaleigh sideways. "Why are we doing this outside? It's freezing."

"Why, this wonderful view!"

Emmaleigh stood and spun around.

"I'm a country girl at heart, but even I have to admit there is nothing like the lights of Manhattan in winter. And of course, there is the Harbor…"

Emmaleigh extended her hand southward, where the mint green Statue of Liberty glowed faintly in the dark.

"Forgive my vanity," she grinned.

Mildred shifted her eyes nervously. "So it's true. You really are *her*."

Emmaleigh raised her eyebrows. "Mr. Gould told you?"

"No. Mr. Barton."

Emmaleigh shrugged. "Six of one. They're all the same."

"He told me I worked for you."

Emmaleigh frowned. "You don't. And from the look in your eyes, you don't work for *him* anymore, either."

Mildred remained stoic. "I don't even know who I am anymore."

"You're an American, no? Born in Reno on June 14, 1910?"

Mildred was taken aback. "I...how did you know that?"

"Were those young men you stuck needles in not Americans?"

Mildred trembled. "Yes..."

"And your husband?"

"Dietrich is Austrian."

"That doesn't mean he couldn't be American."

"He is a citizen..."

"...that alone does not make him American."

"Stop it!!" Mildred shouted, exasperated. *"Stop with your mind games!"*

"Dear, I'm not trying to trick you. I am trying to make you see."

"See what?" Mildred gnashed.

Emmaleigh looked on Mildred with unearthly compassion. "That you are dust."

"Excuse me?"

"Your father was a tailor. Saul Cohen. He fled from France in 1903 during the persecution of the Jews in the Dreyfus Affair. He met your mother, Gretchen Hiller, in San Francisco, and they moved to Reno in 1908."

Mildred's bottom lip quivered.

"Your father..."

"Don't!" Mildred cried.

"We *must* tend to the wound, Darling."

Mildred clutched the side of her chair and shut her eyes.

"On the Fourth of July, three weeks after you were born, your father drank himself into oblivion. He'd bet on Jack Johnson that day, and when he went to collect his winnings his bookie shot him in the heart. He died floating in the Truckee."

Mildred doubled over.

"Your mother married Winston Jarvis, a Methodist minister. He refused to adopt you, so you remained Mildred Cohen, a half-Jewish pariah in your own home. Your half-sisters made up a song about you."

Mildred slunk from her chair. The song echoed loudly from her depths.

((...Jew shrew, there she fell; Jew shrew, burn in hell...))

Emmaleigh melted. "All your life you wanted to prove yourself *goyim*. Then you met Dietrich. You moved to Northern California to cut off generations of those you thought unlike you. But they, like you, were *dust...*"

"Forgive me, Papa..." Mildred whimpered. "I am dirt. I am *nothing*."

Emmaleigh lifted Mildred's head. "Not nothing. *Everything*."

Mildred wiped her face.

"You don't belong with the wretched, Mildred. Their weeds are shallow, but our roots grow to the *center of the Earth*."

Mildred ripped the swastika from her arm, tossing it into the fire, where it disintegrated.

"What can I do?" she asked.

Emmaleigh leaned in.

"Tell me König's plans for the Tower."

Twenty One

...Two if by Torch

It was just before midnight on Monday, February 22, 1939. The last time the Germans attacked Liberty was an accident. In 1916, Kaiser Wilhelm II's saboteurs blew up a New Jersey munitions factory; the shrapnel tore through her torch and showered the Hudson with copper debris. The platform was thereafter permanently closed to the public...but not to the Sons of Liberty, who maintain it Today as...

"...an antenna," Ray explained, tilting his head back. "Broadcasts directly into the minds of any who choose to tune in."

Ray was the antithesis of his shy and quiet father, Teddy. He shuffled to keep his blood flowing in the cold.

"It was modeled on the older Sister," he continued. "The blonde. What's her name?"

"Aurora."

"Yeah. The French were *infatuated* with her. Really good friends with Lafayette and Tocqueville. That's why Fréderic build this."

"That explains those trinkets at The Silver Bullet."

Ray laughed. "My daddy told me about that place. I've never been there, though."

I pointed at the torch. "It broadcasts everywhere, you say? Over some subtle electrical field?"

"Everywhere," Ray answered, "and every *when*. Backwards and forwards across time and space, serenading the mind of man with the sweet sounds of Liberty and Justice for all."

"Sounds magical."

"I've managed to sneak in a little Marcus Garvey and Alice Paul every now and then..."

"Good company, there."

"…and occasionally," Ray bragged, "some of my jazz."

"Yeah? You play trumpet?"

"Saxophone." He wiggled his fingers. "All over Harlem and the Bronx."

"Is it silver?"

"You got it." Ray winked. "My daddy played silver. I play silver. Lil' Marcus is gonna play silver and his son and grandson after him."

I sighed. "The Tower is under siege tonight, Mr. Atwater. Are we ready?"

"Ready enough," Ray answered, looking me up and down. "Man, you really do take to wearing that bullshit."

"Right." I sized up my artificially bloodied and shredded SS uniform. "If it's any consolation, it looks like I wore it through the propeller of the *Titanic*."

Ray doubled over in laughter. "Just like a Nazi. Subtle as a shipwreck."

~

"Boy, Tyson, if Skylar is a Nazi, she sure is subtle about it."

He doesn't look at me. He never does. I hold up the tattered yellow sign he tore off the wall.

"How did Skylar's campaign sign oppress you?"

Tyson finally looks up from the desk. "Did you actually read it?"

"Yeah. 'SKYLAR WEARS STARS AND STRIPES – LUND 4 SENIOR VP.' Patriotism is so terrible."

"She underlined the and, Mr. U."

"…and?"

He rolls his eyes. "Mr. U, she's running against Sara Finkelson."

I shake my head. "So it's some coded anti-Semitic message? In a high school election?"

Tyson yanks the toggle on his sweatshirt, closing the hood over his face.

Unbelievable. "Detention's over in thirty minutes."

I lay the sign out on my desk. "SKYLAR WEARS STARS…AND STRIPES."

In the corner, someone had drawn an ugly green frog.

"I just don't see it."

~

15:06:55

Emmaleigh gazed somberly out over New York Harbor. Even the most carefree of the Sisters couldn't shake the weight of gravity. She could read between the lines, and tonight seemed like a curse.

Wearing their own bloody shirts, Harper and Woodhull operated the Crown Command control board. Currently, the Tower broadcasted Abraham Lincoln's Gettysburg Address:

"...our fathers brought forth on this continent a new nation, conceived in Liberty, and dedicated to the proposition that all men are created equal..."

Emmaleigh savored Lincoln's words meditatively.

"König's goons will be here any minute," I said.

I eyed the control board.

"Can we trust Mildred with the ringer?"

"Sometimes a fighter has no choice but to back into the ropes," Emmaleigh sighed.

She looked away, fighting back tears.

"Since 1886, this Tower has amplified the light of Truth all over the world. The tired, the poor, the huddled masses on their native shores; the divided and downtrodden on our own. As long as there are hearts willing to listen..."

Emmaleigh trailed off. I felt around in my pocket for my phone. All those text messages I'd received, for better or for ill, had been broadcast using this Tower as a relay. Some had been Liberty's, some had been Tyranny's; at the time I received them, I couldn't have told you the difference. The phone had gone silent in recent days. *Probably because I've stopped listening.*

A slow, whirring siren rose and fell, echoing through Liberty's inner sanctum.

"The redcoats are coming," Emmaleigh breathed, leaning over the control panel. "Timing is everything."

Harper gave Emmaleigh the thumbs up as Woodhull watched the monitors above.

Emmaleigh took a step toward me, touching my chest lightly.

"John Brown. As I live and breathe."

She withdrew her hand and headed for the lift. Ray saluted and followed after.

"Godspeed, Mr. Atwater," I whispered.

Lightning flashed as a dense fog rolled into the harbor. At the edge of Liberty Island surfaced the dark gray sail and foreplanes of a Nazi U-boat. It docked, and a squadron of black-clad MG-34 toting SS thugs poured out of the hatch onto the island.

Woodhull grabbed the radio. "Mars, this is Sirius, do you copy, over?"

Hank Finkelson came to life. *"Mars copies."*

"Roger. Neptune, do you copy?"

Behind the U-boat, Kennedy's head surfaced from below water. *"Neptune copies."*

"Roger. Pluto, do you copy?"

Minty replied. *"Pluto copies."*

"Roger. Jupiter, do you copy?"

Ira kicked on as propellers whirled in the background. *"Jupiter copies."*

"Roger. ETA?"

"Just have Mercury ready to fire. Over."

"We who have already died salute you. Sirius, over and out."

Woodhull hung up.

"Air, land and sea all accounted for."

I peered at the ground a hundred and fifty feet below. The Nazis swept the island for guards. Not finding them, the lead SS goon spoke into his walkie-talkie.

"Die Entwarnung."

Four faces emerged from the submarine: two more SS scouts, followed by Morgan...and a man in a tan uniform trimmed in red and gold. The whole of Liberty Island stunk of tar.

"Ellen," I asked, "who is that?"

Harper tensed. "Travers."

"That's General Travers?"

Harper looked away, gritting her teeth. "Yes."

"Miss Stevens!" Morgan yelled. *"Y'ain't shy! Come on out, darlin'!"*

Emmaleigh and Ray appeared below with their hands up. Two SS scouts entered the door behind them. *Right into an ambush.*

Emmaleigh addressed Travers. *"A rare public appearance, Mauritius."*

"The business of Empire is grueling," Travers growled. *"I leave the politicking to Aldric…"*

I anxiously awaited word from the downstairs team. Then came the signal.

"Clear down. Mars, over and out."

I whispered to Harper. *"Batter up."*

Harper stood and took a bat to three of the six monitors above, raining glass everywhere. Woodhull ripped out the wires on his right, sparking controlled fires. The two quickly moved to the corner and slumped over each other. I loaded my Walther with six blank rounds. I took a deep breath, pointed the gun at the undead spies, and…

Bang! Bang! Bang! Bang! Bang! Bang!

I heard shouting outside in German. Then Ira came on.

"Mercury, this is Jupiter. Small craft launched from a frigate to the south. Mildred and three goons in black."

I peered outside. *The Insurgent.* König had sent the kitchen sink.

"Be ready, Mercury. Jupiter out."

I re-loaded the pistol, watching the events below.

"Surrender the Tower!" the General commanded. *"Let us have peace!"*

"You've known the Truth for millennia, Mauritius," Emmaleigh replied.

She fell to her knees.

"Peace is mine alone. To Caesar I render nothing."

Time braked on a dime everywhere but Liberty Island.

No waves rolled, no lights twinkled.

"No," I whispered.

Morgan trained his Lugar on Emmaleigh.

She lifted her head.

The light was so powerful it carried as the softest sound over the Tower airwaves:

"Come now…let us reason together…"

In seconds, her light flickered and went out.

Then came the shot.

The Nazis fired in celebration. I dared to look.

Emmaleigh lay flat on her back, unconscious. *Venus down...*

The General yelled in German. The Nazis trained their weapons on Ray.

Shit, Ray. No...

Then the earth moved. With Herculean strength, Minty thrust the grass upward and launched both Morgan and Travers into the Atlantic. Ray took cover as the Nazis fired futilely on Minty as she marched defiantly toward them.

The Earth moved again.

"Huzzah!" Twenty living Sons of Liberty sprang forth from their covered foxholes and surrounded the Nazis, training their rifles on them.

"Lass deine Waffen fallen! Jetzt!"

The Nazis dropped their weapons, raising their hands to the sky.

The drenched, shivering Morgan and Travers slowly climbed out of the Atlantic, steering clear of Minty and hiding in the bushes. Behind them, surface waters rippled away from the U-boat.

Ray crawled over to Emmaleigh and held her hand, gently resting her head against the grass.

Ira came on over the radio. *"Ten clicks up. Jupiter out."*

I whispered a prayer and stood behind the control board, leveling my pistol at the opening. The elevator opened as Ira landed in the frame.

Bang! Bang! Bang!

I blew Ira Hayes into the night.

"Auf wiedersehn!" I yelled, short of breath.

"Fucking savage."

I turned to see a solemn and angry-looking white man step forth from the elevator. He wore his ice blond undercut swept to the side. Mildred stood nervously at his arm with a canvas bag. Two goons carried machine guns behind them. The Taller Goon was older and grayer than the others. He was hideous, his face partially caved in, supported by metal plates. All four wore parachutes on their backs.

"You are Gunnar or Lars?" the blond man inquired.

"Gunnar," I exhaled. "Lars is dead."

"I saw his body."

"You are Dietrich?"

Dietrich nodded.

I made eye contact with the Taller Goon. He lingered on me intensely; it was unnerving.

"Do you have the reel?" I asked Dietrich.

Dietrich looked to Mildred. "Millie?"

Mildred pulled the reel from the bag and handed it over to me. The Goons went to inspect Harper and Woodhull as Dietrich surveyed the control board.

"Amateurs," Dietrich said coldly. "No system damage. They only wanted us to *think* they sabotaged it."

Dietrich turned to the Goons.

"Get rid of the bodies."

The Goons tossed Harper and Woodhull onto the landing below. *CLANK.*

Dietrich waved me over. "Gunnar, tape."

Lincoln's voice continued to carry across the airwaves…

"…a new birth of freedom…the better angels of our nature…a house divided cannot stand…"

I handed Dietrich the reel. He flipped a switch, and Lincoln fell silent. Dietrich unhooked the B track reel from the board and replaced it with the new one. As he fiddled with the soundboard Mildred looked to me anxiously.

Dietrich finished. The loudspeaker inside Crown Command now played two tracks: the Gettysburg Address…and something very different:

"…dedicated to the heritage, identity, and the future of people of European descent in the United States, and around the world…America was until this past generation a white country designed for ourselves and our posterity…"

"I have never heard this man before. Richard Spencer. But Herr König adores him."

I recognized the name. Spencer was one of the Apprentice's chief sycophants in the white nationalist "Alt Right." Hearing Spencer playing alongside Lincoln was nauseating. Dietrich let a crooked smile escape.

"My mother wanted me to be the next Mozart. This is *her* symphony: *Tyranny in USA Minor.*"

Dietrich pat me on the shoulder, flipped another switch and put Harper's headphones on. The Taller Goon loomed over me, breathing down my neck.

As Dietrich listened…

…his smile slowly faded…

…his eyes shifted back and forth…

…he bit down hard on his lip…

…he quaked violently…

…then *SLAMMED!* his fist on the board. He tore off his headphones and trained his Lugar on Mildred's chest. The Goons raised their guns to me.

"When König told me to plug all the leaks," Dietrich fumed, "I should have known he meant *you.*"

Mildred quivered. "Darling…what are you saying?"

"Where is the real tape, Mildred?"

"This is the real tape."

"Like hell it is!"

Dietrich grabbed Mildred by the ear. She yelped as he threw her onto the chair and forced the headphones on her.

"You hear something else, don't you? *WHAT DO YOU HEAR?!?*"

Mildred shook her head. "Two messages. Lincoln and…this Spencer." She removed the headphones.

"I thought I was recording the rally? Where is Fritz Kuhn? Where are the Nazis?"

Dietrich punched his wife in the gut. I flinched.

Dietrich turned to me. "Fucking broads, right?"

Mildred clutched her gut and wheezed. The asshole knocked the wind out of her.

"I told you, *Millie,* you were recording the *whispers* of the *crowd*, not Kuhn!"

Mildred clutched her ribs.

"*My* tape, the one that *you* gave to the *fucking Sons of Liberty*, captures the *zeitgeist* of the rally and seals it inside Lincoln's message, which is then broadcast as *Spencer's* message to the unconscious mind."

Dietrich pointed to his head.

"It's an *undertone,* and if this were my tape, I would hear it with these headphones on *this control panel. But it's not my tape, so it plays both! We can't sneak our message in if it has to compete with Abraham Fucking Lincoln!"*

KABOOOOOM!!!!!

The U-Boat exploded in a ball of fire, rocking the Tower. As Dietrich gawked, I caved in his elbow and spun him to the ground. He gasped as I dragged him up and pulled my Walther on him. Mildred quickly picked up Dietrich's gun, retreating behind me and leveling it at the Goons.

"Drop your weapons over the side!" I yelled at the Goons. They complied, and raised their hands in the air.

I drove my knee into Dietrich's spine for sport.

"Hit her again," I hissed, *"and I'll dropkick you into the Hudson."*

The Taller Goon laughed nervously.

"You," he pointed. *"I knew it was you."*

I stared blankly at him. He pointed at his face.

"Nigger had a helluva right cross."

That Tennessee drawl.

He was thirty years older, hair grayer. Still, it was him.

The assassin from Reno.

Dietrich struggled against my hold. "Mr. Atwater, who is this impostor?"

Mr. Atwater. I knew it. Dietrich twitched.

"Easy, Proud Boy," I said. "Put d – *oomph!"*

Dietrich drove me back into Mildred and against the railing, dropping our firearms down Liberty's guts. Dietrich dropped me with a left hook, then stripped Mildred of her parachute and threw her to the Shorter Goon as "Mr. Atwater" stuck the pointy end of a dagger into my back.

"Leonard!" Dietrich yelled. "George! We run the contingency!"

Leonard Atwater twisted the dagger. It set my nerves ablaze.

"You're the Champion, ain't ya, kid?" he whispered. *"Time to light the torch."*

The Goons pushed us out of Crown Command. We ascended Liberty's arm, with Tyranny nipping at our heels.

~

"Did anybody find the thirteenth hand?"

Ms. Waylon stands at the edge of the Marine Corps Memorial, a bronze-cast of six men of uncommon valor raising the flag.

"You won't. There are only twelve hands on the flag. The thirteenth hand is a legend, but many people believe it's there because they all blend together. But each pair of hands has a name..."

Kathy points at each Marine, front to back.

"...Harlon Block...Rene Gagnon..."

Sara Finkelson stands alone in the back. She's been withdrawn all afternoon. It's out of character for the outspoken musical theater geek.

"...Frank Sousley...Michael Strank..."

At the Holocaust Museum that morning, each of us was given a "passport" of someone who experienced the horrors of the Holocaust. Sara drew Paulina Finkelstein, a Berliner who perished at the Sobibor concentration camp in Poland. Paulina had nearly escaped the Nazis aboard the St. Louis, a passenger liner bound for Cuba with hundreds of European Jews on May 28, 1939. Halfway across the Atlantic, the Cuban government revoked all passenger visas. So the St. Louis sailed from Havana to Miami, to the shining city upon a hill, humanity's last best hope.

It wasn't to be. The U.S. had set hard caps on immigration in 1924; while some in Congress moved to accommodate an additional 20,000 Jewish refugees, the act died quickly under the guise of "national security." And so the nine hundred thirty-seven Jews aboard the St. Louis were turned away, and forced to re-settle in Western Europe. After the Nazis swept through the Netherlands, Belgium and France, two hundred fifty-four of those passengers died in concentration camps.

Two hundred fifty-three, plus Paulina Finkelstein.

"...Harold Schulz..."

Tyson and Sara's best friend Hayley Lisowski give her a wide berth.

I invade her space.

"Hey. You gonna be alright, Sara?"

She shakes her head. "I can't stop thinking about him."

"Him?"

"...and Ira Hayes," Kathy finishes:

Sara wipes her eyes. *"My great grandfather. He died in Germany during the War,"* she said.

I catch my breath. "I...Sara, I had no idea you lost family in the Holocaust. I...I am so sorry..."

"No," she sniffed. *"He was in the Army. Grandpa Ari talked about him every day..."*

"I'm...so sorry."

"It's okay. It's not like I knew him personally. But this, plus the Museum today...it's all just too much."

Kathy shows the group the inscription on the side of the Memorial.

"Know what's really messed up, Mr. U?" Sara pulls a pair of silver dog tags out of her pocket. Each one has a bullet through the middle, making the name illegible:

C-------------------------YNE
BIS---------------IFORNIA

"These are the tags they found on his body. Can't even tell who this is. Might as well tattoo a number on his arm."

We listen in to Kathy's monologue: "Harlon Block originally wasn't recognized...but Ira Hayes fought for the rest of his life to give credit to his brother-in-arms..."

Sara sniffs and laughs. *"I see the thirteenth hand."*

"Where?"

She points. *"Right there."*

I blink. "I don't see it."

"Do you believe in ghosts, Mr. U?"

A stiff breeze blows southward toward Arlington National Cemetery.

"I've always believed there's an invisible hand behind everything, guiding us. Don't you?"

I frown and gaze down the Potomac. "No, Sara. I don't."

~

"Leonard. The dagger."

Leonard relinquished his dagger to Dietrich, the same dagger with the red hilt he attacked me with in Reno; then he trained his sidearm on me. Dietrich placed the knife against the torch; it pulsed with red light.

"Your people failed to account for direct signal interference," Dietrich said. "Put your hand on the torch."

I hesitated, and looked to Mildred, clutching her side, her eyes red and puffy. She had nothing to offer. She looked defeated, like she just wanted to go home…

…home…

((…if ever you are lost, it will show you the way home…))

…

"*Do it!*" Dietrich screamed.

Reluctantly I raised my hand toward the torch. At the same time I reached into my pocket and squeezed the coin. I focused the entirety of myself on the coin – heart, mind, will and emotion. It *hummed* and *buzzed* and warmed in my hand.

"*I said do it!*"

I placed my hand against the torch…the torchlight dimmed; a thick cloud cover descended. Lightning crashed as it spun and emitted a sonic *BOOOOOOM*…the copper convulsed, whirling light and darkness into shades of gray as the lead bled into the torch itself.

I clutched my temple as it screamed. Inside my head a thousand garbled voices spoke at once…one slipped through…like the voice of darkness, it rose from within…

((…answer me this question, Benjamin son of John, before it is answered for you…will you let this First World nation become a polyglot boarding house for the Third World?…))

…I clutched the coin tight, fighting my own personal civil war as Mildred fought hers…

((…the Champion of Liberty is a traitor if he sells her to the stranger…the Arab and the Zulu and the Pima…the lazy Mexican…the idle lemon farmer who killed his own father …))

…tar dripped from very pore…the coin turned scalding hot…

((...they are all spoken for...why speak for them?...who speaks for you when the hordes break into your house gate to take everything from you?...))

...Dietrich grinned gleefully. "If *she* won't broadcast *our* signal, we'll scramble *yours*."

Behind Dietrich, a shadow mounted the railing. The coin sizzled in my hand, and an electric current shot through me, carrying a new message...

((...Benji, you know this nation was founded and shaped by people of many nations and many backgrounds...the rights of all are diminished when the rights of one are diminished...))

...the shadow crept...

((...people of all nations, even the First Nations, fight for your Liberty...are you to say to the world you will not fight for theirs?...the Arab and the Zulu and the Pima, who surrendered his life to preserve yours?...))

...and Corporal Ira Hayes cried, *"Semper fi!"*

I released my hand; the torch spun back in the other direction. The broadcast fizzled out of my head, as the torch blared a triumphant refrain:

From the halls of Montezuuu-uma to the shores of Tri-po-li!
We fight our country's baaaat-tles in the air, on land and sea!

"No!" Dietrich yelled. He dropped the knife and circled to the other side of the flame, pistol cocked...

First to fight for right and fre-edom and to keep-our-hon-or-clean!
We are proud to claim the tiii-itle of United States Ma-rine!

Dietrich fired, puncturing the copper flame. The Marine Corps Hymn crackled out as sparks flew; lightning fried George, dropping him dead to the platform.

"George!" Leonard yelled.

I bull-rushed Leonard, sending his gun to the island below. He kneed me in the groin and flipped me over. He reared back his fist...and stopped. He stared deep into my eyes, frozen in place, his lip trembling...

"Lenny, hands up!" Mildred shouted.

Leonard slowly raised his hands, never taking his eyes off me.

"Stand and face me."

Leonard stood to face his captor.

"You're a traitor, Millie. König's gonna plug all the leaks; it'll be a *massacre.*"

Shaking, Mildred stroked the trigger as death lurked behind her.

"Mildred!" I shouted.

She turned just as Dietrich fired, grazing her left arm. She emitted a shrill cry, dropping her gun off the platform. Leonard moved, giving Dietrich a clear shot at me. I closed my eyes.

I'm coming, Dad.

"Drop it! Drop your weapon!"

Hank Finkelson trained his M1911 on Dietrich, with three Sons of Liberty behind him. He wore the same "bloodied" SS black as I, resurrected after playing dead below as "Lars."

I dragged Leonard back behind the Sons and cuffed him as Dietrich pulled Mildred up and pressed his Luger against her neck.

"You lost to a Jew, goose-stepper!" Hank shouted. "Let her go!"

Dietrich held Mildred close.

"Piss poor excuse for a Master Race, no?"

"Fuck Hitler," Dietrich snarled. "He's a means to an end."

Dietrich fastened a harness over Mildred and hooked her to his chest. He stepped onto the railing. Mildred peered out to the ground below, trembling.

"A plague is coming," Dietrich growled.

He stepped to the top of the railing and positioned himself toward *The Insurgent,* where the drenched Morgan and Travers steered Dietrich's boat. Mildred closed her eyes and shook something loose from her sleeve. It was red-and-gold. And lead.

Oh shit...

"Heil König!" Dietrich stepped out and pulled the cord. The paraglider opened as they sailed away...

…clear of the island, Mildred reared back…

…and stabbed Dietrich in the thigh.

"Aaaaaaauuuugh!!!!"

Mildred unhooked and dropped into the icy Atlantic as Dietrich burst into flames…a missile headed straight for *The Insurgent's* mast.

The panicked crew poured off the sides. Herr Schwartz collided with the mast and set the ship ablaze, fire consuming its flag of red and gold.

Twenty yards out, Kennedy surfaced with a shivering Mildred. Below, the Sons of Liberty escorted captured Nazis into holding cells under the island. I felt my hand for scarring; there was none. I retrieved the coin: it was now pure copper.

"Hey, Ben," came the Tennessee drawl.

I turned to Leonard and wiped my nose. "You have something to say to me?"

"How come you don't age?"

Not engaging this. "Antioxidants," I quipped, and turned away.

"You look like Esther."

Frozen, I turned. "Who?"

Leonard grimaced. "My granddaughter. She got the same wrinkle you got, in the corner of your eyes."

I clench my fists. Leonard grew angry.

"So if you're one of us, why do you fight for the niggers an' Jews, huh? They took it away! We had a plantation! Now our family gots *nothin',* an' the bastards even took our damn name! *There ain't nobody left to carry our name!* They'll do the same to you, you fuckin' idiot! They're tryin' to replace you! They will *not* replace us! *You will not betray us!"*

Leonard started up off his knees. Hank fed him a cold knuckle sandwich, and he dropped to the platform.

"You're welcome," Hank said.

I said nothing. My body convulsed, down to the tendons. Bitterly, head hazy, I descended Liberty's arm.

~

15:03:39

We gathered at the foot of Liberty, nesting in the eye of the storm as Emmaleigh convalesced on the grass.

"I think we got head-faked," said Kennedy, now out of his wetsuit. Behind him, a crew of medics kept a shivering Mildred warm.

Ray covered his face. "This wasn't about broadcasting to the masses."

Kennedy grimaced. "They poisoned the Tower. Anyone who tunes in will have to sift through a lot of noise to find Liberty's signal."

"I heard a personalized message," I offered. "Two of them, actually. One light and one dark."

Kennedy looked me up and down. "Who did you hear?"

"Pat Buchanan...then you."

Kennedy squinted. "Well I hope I won your attention."

I nodded. "It was a close call. But yes. You won."

Emmaleigh coughed violently; Ray set his hand on her back to steady her.

Ira and Minty approached. Both were exhausted.

"I know where to go next," I said. "Leonard let slip about 'plugging leaks,' and a 'massacre.'"

Minty pursed her lips. "You ready?"

I nodded. Saddened, I retrieved my coin and looked to Emmaleigh. I hoped this wasn't our last meeting.

"Go," she said, reading my mind. "Carry the message with you."

I lingered on Emmaleigh and whispered goodbye, leaving her fate to another Champion.

I gripped my coin, watching as its glistening copper transformed to mercurial quicksilver before my eyes. All around, choruses of light and dark dueled over the airwaves to capture the audience of ages. As the sound grew to a crescendo, Liberty's flame shot us out as stars into the night.

Twenty Two

Defiance

07:04:13

The echoes climbed the walls and scaled the ceiling, meeting at the apex and pouring down like rain on the eavesdropper in bronze. At nineteen feet, Thomas Jefferson already towered over the five-foot-nine Secretary of State. By a different tape, the Secretary measured three feet tall.

"I can play it again if you'd like, Mr. Secretary."

Ari Finkelson was toying with the man. It was three in the morning on Saturday, October 20, 1973, and Henry Kissinger was already ground to dust. I could only imagine how grating even the sounds of the Tidal Basin lapping against the marble steps of the Jefferson Memorial must have been. Now, he was also at the mercy of a rogue CIA analyst and his motley companions.

"Agent Upson," Ari Finkelson said, "I think Secretary Kissinger didn't hear the first two times. Should we give him a third?"

"Play it, Agent Finkelson," I answered.

Ari hit PLAY on the recording device:

"...if they put Jews into the gas chambers in the Soviet Union it is not an American concern..."

Ari dramatically hit STOP. Kissinger cleared his throat.

"Where did you get this?" he demanded, his Bavarian accent matching the tape.

Ari shook his head. "Friggin' Deep Throat. Whatever, man. What are you gonna do to make sure I don't give it to Bob friggin' Woodward."

Kissinger scowled. "You understand it is treason to blackmail a cabinet member."

"Is it really, Mr. Secretary?" Zora Gates asked. "My Constitution doesn't permit the powerful to punish dissenting patriots as traitors. In fact, I believe that even threatening to do so is a high crime against the people, is it not?"

Kissinger's self-assurance evaporated.

"As it is," I added, "this recording proves you the traitor."

Kissinger recoiled. *"I beg your unbelievable pardon?"*

"In three hours, you will board a plane for Moscow to engage in détente with Leonid Brezhnev over the Israeli-Arab War. You, Henry Kissinger, a Jew fortunate to escape Germany...*you* were America's concern then. But the Jews facing pogroms in Russia...they're not?"

Kissinger's breathing grew heavy.

"You give aid and comfort to Tyranny, and you accuse the Sons of Liberty of treason? Who do you serve? *What* do you serve?"

Kissinger stammered. "M-my country."

I sighed. "Haunt the castle."

At that moment, Minty and Ira materialized at Kissinger's shoulders. He cursed and raved, staggering backward toward the steps.

"What sorcery is this?"

"On your left, Mr. Secretary, is Harriet Tubman; we call her 'Minty.' She forced Abraham Lincoln's hand over slavery in the Civil War. On your right is Marine Corporal Ira Hayes. When FDR brought him home from the Pacific as a display trophy, Ira demanded to be sent back to the front lines."

Kissinger trembled.

"You see, neither of them would say they are a hero. But both," I paused for emphasis, "are *warriors*. And if you believe they – we – who obey a Higher Law will back down in our defense of Liberty against this Administration's mad quest for power, you are gravely mistaken. You swore an oath, and so did we."

I pointed to the ceiling.

Kissinger tilted his head back to read the inscription encircling Jefferson's crown. He glanced furtively from me to Minty to Ira to Ari to Zora and back to me.

"What do you want?" Kissinger asked, pulling off his thick glasses.

A 31-year-old Pearl stepped forward in her trench coat, sunglasses, and Emmaleigh's black beret.

"Agents Upson and Finkelson need to get into the Oval Office. Today."

Kissinger guffawed. "Who do you think you are that you would make such a demand?"

Pearl took off her shades to reveal her shimmering emeralds.

"To most," she answered, "I am the niece of Chief Justice Earl Warren."

Kissinger shook his head. "You're Justice Warren's niece?"

"To you, however, I am the owner and landlord of the residence at 1600 Pennsylvania Avenue, and I demand that its tenant make it available for inspection."

Kissinger laughed nervously. "Ghosts, and now the insane. My answer is no. I will n–"

A brilliant flash of light engulfed the District, shutting off power everywhere within a ten-mile radius. In the blink of an eye, power was restored, and Kissinger lay flat on the marble floor. He nodded vigorously as Kennedy straddled him reciting demands. When their parlay concluded, Kennedy reached down and pinched Kissinger's cheek.

"*It's good to see you, Hank,*" he said. "*You're a good egg.*"

Kissinger scrambled to his feet and hustled out the backside of the memorial where his car awaited to take him to Andrews Air Force Base.

Pearl approached and clasped my shoulder. "You're speaking truth to power."

"I swore an oath," I replied, looking to the ceiling:

I HAVE SWORN UPON THE ALTAR OF GOD
ETERNAL HOSTILITY AGAINST EVERY FORM OF TYRANNY
OVER THE MIND OF MAN

"I intend to keep it."

~

"Alright, Ben and Michelle, big smiles, say 'cheese!'"
"Cheese!"   *"Fromage!"*
The photographer is peeved.

"Mrs. Upson, that's very funny. But we say 'cheese' to stretch out your smile. You don't want your kids to think you got your tonsils out on your wedding day, do you?"

Michelle is dumbfounded. "I – "

"Of course you don't. Do what I tell you this time."

Under pain of death, she complies.

"This man is ridiculous," she says through grit teeth.

"He's a petty tyrant," I likewise reply.

He finishes. "Better. Alright, maid of honor, best man, bridal party, line up in front of the Tidal Basin! Come on! Chop-chop!"

Thank God. Michelle and I beat feet up the Jefferson Memorial steps to escape the radius of Stefphon's wrath.

"Where," I laugh as we plop down, "did Darcy find this guy?"

"She said he's the best." Michelle removes her shoe to rub her feet.

I motion. "Nope. My job."

Michelle props her leg up on mine to receive the best foot massage of her life.

Down below, Michelle's parents wave. We wave back.

Next to the Deschamps', Mom and Roger watch the bridal party intently; Rachel and Dylan look bored, whispering to each other.

"My sister's boyfriend is an alpha douche," I say with conviction.

"He's nice, Benji. Don't be a turd."

Roger keeps looking up at me, then Mom, then me...nervously.

"Am I a turd if I say Roger's a beta douche?"

Michelle's fist finds my arm. "He's good for Marie. He treats her well."

"He's passive-aggressive. He always compares himself to Pop...and me."

I hear Michelle's eyes roll. "You think he's trying to replace John."

"I know he is. But he won't. Ever."

I tickle the bottom of Michelle's foot. "Stop," she laughs.

"You're not the boss of me," I joke. "I'm the boss of you."

"Hmm," she hums, thinking deeply.

"What are you plotting, Shell?"

She licks her lips. "You know, Roger's a nice name."

I stop rubbing. "We are never naming our child Roger."

Michelle laughs. "Okay, then. You win. No Roger."

I laugh back. "Good! I'm glad you agree."

~

10:13:46
I held the coin aloft:

IN DEFIANCE OF TYRANNY

It's an easy thing to say, that you'll take a firm stand against evil when the time comes. It's something else entirely when it calls your number. It never happens at a convenient hour. It happens when your mouth is cotton and your mind is mud. Fairly or not, posterity will judge you by how you steered the fiery careening cart of your soul through the abyss, when you can't see a foot in front of you.

It's a lot like entering the Nixon White House in the middle of Watergate.

"Richard Milhous Nixon has let König right through the White House door," Zora opined.

It was Tuesday, October 16, 1973. The table of our Dupont Circle safe house was cluttered with Chinese take-out. Ari played *Horse With No Name* on a vinyl record as Zora sorted through banker's boxes. Zora was thirty-one, and an attorney in the new Civil Rights Division of the Department of Justice. Even there, a strong, young black female attorney was a novelty in a field where only a few black men or even white women had trod. The battle-tested warrior was four months pregnant with the child of an artist named Marcus Atwater, and she was made of cast iron.

Zora gave one file to Minty and another to Kennedy.

Then she handed me a copy of today's *New York Times.*

"You asked me about my case. Center column."

I found the story by Morris Kaplan, about a Department of Justice civil suit against a Brooklyn landlord who discriminated against black and Hispanic renters. The story identified the landlord as…

"…the Apprentice." I said aloud.

Ira hovered over Minty's shoulder, scanning the other file with his finger.

"He's represented by Roy Cohn? Wasn't he Joseph McCarthy's lawyer in the Red Scare?"

Zora nodded. "A ruthless practitioner of the politics of personal destruction."

"And our Apprentice is just a mean-spirited power broker in Cohn's image," I muttered.

"More like König's image. Cohn thinks he's special, but when he has outlived his usefulness König will toss him."

I recalled a story that Cohn had been a closeted gay man; when he contracted AIDS in the 1980s, the Apprentice refused to visit his mentor in the hospital, leaving him to die an agonizing death alone.

Minty spoke up. "The Apprentice's company marks the applications of colored people with a 'C?'"

Zora nodded, rubbing her stomach. "Bigots make effective Tyrants. Especially when they've convinced us they aren't bigots."

Zora waved at the image of Richard Nixon on the television in the corner.

Pearl interjected. "Ben, that's why it's critical that you listen carefully on Saturday. Everything you see and hear, we will see and hear."

I exhaled. "I'm a walking antenna."

Pearl snickered. "Welcome to the club."

I was still wary of signal distortion from the Tower, in the wake of Dietrich's attack. "Can't Fred Douglass just bug the Oval Office? I'm sure Jack has people still loyal to him."

Kennedy zinged a water chestnut off my chest. "In the Nixon White House? Are you mad?"

I raised my hands. "You gonna pay Ari for dry cleaning? This is his shirt?"

Ari waved it off. "I use baking soda. Calm down."

Pearl brought us back to focus. "There are a few places around the country where, as a defense against espionage, we've made it impossible for anyone to enter undetected, even ghosts. We can hardly expect candor with Frederick or Jack present, and I can assure you any bugs will be discovered."

"Okay," I said, "But how are we even getting into Fort Nixon with Cox turning up the heat on Watergate?"

Ari cleared his throat. "I've had Kissinger eating out of my hand over the Yom Kippur War in Israel. Don't worry. We'll persuade that insouciant ass to get us through. Besides…I'll have your back."

I swallowed hard. *That's what I'm afraid of.*

~

I've been flat on my back for eight hours.

I haven't moved an inch since I put out for a sub. I don't know how to describe this feeling. Is it mental? Emotional? Physical? All three? Whatever it is, it's like ice and adrenaline shooting through my nerves. It grips me at odd times, when everything else seems just fine, when a sane person ought to be happy. Productivity shot, I'm forced to waste away the hours in the grips of a terrible Fear.

TV hasn't helped. Watching them play the President's speech over and over has only made it worse. His red carpet gloating over his victories won't return fathers to their children.

I switch to the game; the Angels lay siege to Boston. Just as Trumbo launches a moon shot off Lester, a cozy critter drops from the sky. He's brown and gray, and holds a clamshell against his chest. A soft, warm kiss lands on my cheek.

"Get up, Benji," Michelle sings.

That helps a little…but not like it used to. I sit up and hold the plush buddy in front of me.

"It's an otter," I smile.

Michelle plops down on the couch, hair in a bun with black glasses and black pantsuit.

"Remember this little guy?" she asks.

I grin slightly. "Pop."

"I saw him at Build-a-Bear and thought he might cheer you up."

He does a little. "Love this kid."

I pull Michelle in for a kiss.

"Thanks, honey. I needed something to take my mind off things."

Michelle removes her glasses and unravels the bun. She smirks.

"What's up?"

"You've been taking your mind off it for ten years. It's still here."

I slowly sit up, defiantly. "You expect me to just...forget? Like...poof? Gone?"

"No." She puts her hand on my knee. "But you act like you were the only one in the world impacted by it."

I can't believe I'm hearing this. "You didn't drive him there."

"Don't you think it's time – "

"Not interested."

"No therapy? Not even EMDR?"

"Nope."

Michelle purses her lips. "You can't dam everything up inside. Eventually, you'll flood."

That's what I'm afraid of.

"It's like Dr. Frankl says. There's purpose in suffering. But you have to allow yourself to feel through the pain."

I look away. I'm not ready to do that. She knows it.

That night in bed, I turn her words over and over, tossing Pop up and down.

((...maybe we'll have a Pop of our own someday...))

I roll over.

"I thought about what you said. About purpose in suffering."

She puts down her book. "And?"

I softly grab her hand. "Let's have a Pop of our own."

~

06:15:17

Ari's blackmail gambit on Kissinger worked. By afternoon, our names were inconspicuously inserted into the guest log of a White House under siege.

"Over an embarrassing tape," Ari said. "Imagine the leverage you'd have over a president running an international business out of this place."

A local reporter camped outside the West Wing broadcasted a live remote stand-up:

"This afternoon, Watergate Special Prosecutor Archibald Cox spoke from the National Press Club demanding President Nixon hand over tape recordings concerning the Watergate burglary whose existence was revealed during Senate testimony in July, per the District Court's October 15 order. Nixon had steadfastly refused, citing 'executive privilege,' but now offers a compromise. The White House would transcribe summaries of the tapes and submit them to a third party, 72-year-old Senator John Stennis of Mississippi, who would listen to the tapes and authenticate the summaries..."

"Isn't Stennis deaf?" I asked as we entered the first floor through the West Wing Portico, brief cases in hand.

"Yeah," Ari replied. "And a year ago he got mugged and shot in the chest. He's also a Nixon supporter."

"Perfect guy for the job."

"The best, bar none."

In the west terrace in front of the Rose Garden, a black man with a wild mop of gray hair sat on a bench reading a newspaper with the headline, "COX DEFIANT." Ari and I flanked him..

"Hey, pal," I whispered. "Mind if I borrow the sports section?"

Famed abolitionist Frederick Douglass handed me the thin section with the headline, "DEFIANT ATHLETICS LOOK TO FORCE GAME 7 IN OAKLAND." I opened it and slid two thin sealed packs into my coat pocket. Ari picked at the bottom of his shoe as two buzz cuts frantically breezed past. I pretended to read for an appropriate length of time, then handed the paper back.

"Always a pleasure, Mr. Douglass."

"Good luck, Benjamin Upson," he replied. "Welcome to the pit of hell."

"4:30," Ari said. "Almost time for a shift change."

We came upon a small office hidden in the corner of the suite. Curt Gowdy's voice carried from the TV inside:

"Reggie Jackson knocks in a run off Seaver to give the World Champions a 1-0 lead over the New York Mets here in Game 6 at the Coliseum..."

We broke open our packs. Ari knocked and pushed the door. Two Secret Service agents waited for their five o'clock shift to start.

One saluted Ari. "Hey kike. Workin' on the Sabbath, eh?"

Ari scratched his head. "I know, *oy-oy-oy-oy!* I'm not a mensch! And I got lobster all over my handkerchief. Here, smell this…"

Ari and I smothered them with the cloths. Instantly, the two fell silent.

"We just chloroformed the Secret Service," I said as I changed into Steve Colton's uniform.

"That wasn't chloroform," Ari said as he became Marty Dahlberg. "It's a hell of a lot stronger than chloroform."

Ambrosia.

I cracked open the briefcase and turned on the radio. I fit the Secret Service transistor on my right ear.

"Lancelot to Arthur, Lancelot to Arthur, over."

Kennedy's voice crackled in my ear. "Loud and clear, Lancelot."

Ari joined in. "Galahad to Arthur, over."

"Roger. Testing transmission relay from Liberty Tower, let me know if the echo is clear."

A high-pitched whine came through. Then it faded into the voice of Nixon…

((…hits it right on the nose. It's about law and order and all the damn Negro-Puerto Rican groups out there…))

…with an echo from the Apprentice…

((…my administration is…totally determined to restore law and order…))

"We hear it, Arthur. Over."

"Roger. You know the failsafe."

I glanced at my watch. *4:54.*

I looked at Ari. "You ready to meet the most powerful man on Earth?"

Twenty Three

I, Alone

I've never been more powerless. I've never been more alone.

Once upon a time, a stiff drink would have been the doctor's order on a night like this. I wasn't in the mood to take any doctor's advice.

"Your count is too low," Dr. Heller said. "Among the lowest I've seen."

He said they could try and boost my levels, that there were treatments, but that we were both thirty-five and the window was closing fast.

"Have you considered adoption? Or in vitro?"

No, I say now in the dark, bringing the photo closer. It's not the same.

He stares back through me, this Man in the Looking Glass, in his Navy white. His presence is everywhere in this house, in this living room...

...as a loving father...

...as a boy with freckles...

...

((...John...))

...

...but now we've reached the end of the line...no more gardens...no more games...

...only bitter regrets, from now until forever.

Michelle tries to comfort me, wrapping her arm around my neck, kissing the back of my head. It's a moment frozen in time, as I am.

I slink away and climb the stairs, into the bathroom with the broken mirror. "Fix it," she had said, but I never did. Tonight, as all others, I will brush my teeth in it, wash my face in it, down that shot of ruby red syrup in it. Broken, unbroken. It feels the same.

It feels like nothing at all.

I can hear her whimpering downstairs, that wonderful, beautiful French girl. She would have made a good mother, I think.

I gaze out the window at the star-spangled canopy of night, knowing it will never be. There is anger here, rage and fear and sorrow. I can't touch them now. They are beyond my reach.

"You can't do this to me," I whisper.

The stars don't answer, but the mirror does...

((...it is already done...))

~

06:14:40

"You can't do this to me now, Elliot."

President Richard Milhous Nixon sat legs crossed in an ugly mustard chair in the Oval Office. On a matching couch to Nixon's right, White House Chief of Staff Alexander Haig shifted impatiently. Across from him Attorney General Elliot Richardson twiddled his thumbs. His letter of resignation lay on the coffee table.

"I can," Elliot said, "and I will. I have to, Mr. President."

Nixon remained calm. "You cannot allow your commander-in-chief to suffer such an embarrassing blow in the middle of a crisis in the Middle East. Kissinger has been dispatched to Moscow, but there may still be war with Russia. This is not the time for insubordination, is it?"

"I gave you a direct order, Elliot." Haig asserted. "Fire Cox. Failure to do so undermines the chain of command."

Elliot looked at Haig warily.

"Shit, Al," he said. "The chain-of-command begins with the people, and they have already given their orders in the Constitution. Power does not vest in the President alone."

Nixon stirred. "You do realize that Brezhnev could make a serious miscalculation if you throw this presidency into turmoil. I know you don't want innocent blood on your hands."

Elliot folded his hands prayerfully. "Mr. President, I don't think I have a choice here. I can't do it. I will not undermine the public's trust in this office."

Nixon fumed. He adjusted his tie, uncrossed his legs and leaned forward.

"Elliot," he began, "I'm sorry you put your personal commitments ahead of the public interest."

The Apprentice echoed in my earpiece:

((...they didn't applaud me...treason?...they seem not to love their country very much...))

Elliot leaned back into the couch and stared at Nixon, blood rushing and body quaking in indignation. After several breaths, he spoke calmly, with subtle hints of spite:

"Mr. President," he said, rising to his feet "it would appear that you and I have different definitions of 'public interest.'"

At that, the Attorney General walked out the door.

That was around 5:20. Next, Haig called Deputy Attorney General William Ruckelshaus to command him to fire Cox. Ruckelshaus also refused and resigned. It wasn't until Nixon reached the third in line, Solicitor General Robert Bork, that he found an agent willing to carry out his orders. Cox was fired.

The Saturday Night Massacre was underway.

"Torch the evidence," Nixon commanded. "Get the FBI to seal off Cox's office. If anyone asks, he didn't find anything on me. We'll bury our enemies before sunrise."

((...have some pretty good enemies out there, but step by step they're being defeated...they're some bad people...someday maybe they'll love us...))

Haig left. Nixon kicked up his heels on his desk, oblivious to the fact that the two Secret Service agents assigned to the Oval Office broadcasted every word back to our agents arrayed around the White House.

The President's faithful secretary, Rose Mary Woods, appeared in the entryway.

"Mr. President, your seven o'clock has arrived."

Nixon stretched and waved the visitor in...

...the place stunk of tar.

He wore an ostentatious cerulean suit, a red-and-white checkered shirt and a solid cherry tie with a matching handkerchief. His white-and-brown wingtips were well polished, and he drew breath from a slender cigarette that accentuated the musky sulfur smell accompanying his every move. König, like Morgan, Gould, Barton and Travers, was ageless, owing to some dark fountain of youth.

"Aldric," Nixon said. "A pleasant surprise."

König slowly ambled into the room. His eyes darted around the ceiling, never falling on Nixon.

"I thought Mr. Gould was coming to discuss CREEP."

König stood in the center of the room, silently drawing and puffing.

Nixon grinned. "Anyway, my friend and partner, I'm glad you're here. Please take a seat. I won tonight…*we* won tonight, you and I both."

König dropped the cigarette onto the carpet, burying it in the Presidential Seal.

"What's gotten into my favorite kraut?"

König stroked his chin. He opened his mouth, then stopped and wagged his finger. He forced a smile, then walked behind Nixon's desk and swept his feet off the surface.

Nixon sat upright, fuming.

"How dare you," he raged. "Who do you think you are that you can walk into my office and assault me like that. I – " he pointed at his chest "am the most powerful man in the world!"

((…I alone can fix it…))

König broke into low, steady laughter. "I am the most powerful man in the world. I have been for a very long time."

Nixon sneered. "I'm the President of the United *fuckin'* States. There's no higher office on this planet, do you hear me?"

((…the powers of the president to protect our country are very substantial and will not be questioned…))

König brushed lint off his suit. "Who made you President?"

Nixon swallowed. "The people."

"Tsk-tsk-tsk, Richard. The people had *my* help in making that decision…well, with the help of Mr. Gould and Mr. Barton."

Nixon nervously adjusted his tie.

"Where would you be if we hadn't driven the Nazis away from Liberty Island? How would your message of 'Law and Order' be received?"

What does he mean "we?" König sent those Nazis to Liberty Island…

…Nixon doesn't know who he really is.

"We convinced the people that you will make them safe, if only *you* held the power. The people gave it to you because *I* told them to."

Nixon grabbed two glasses and a bottle of Chateau Lafite Rothschild from his cabinet.

"Herr König," Nixon began, "Today was a good day. Let's not ruin it with cynicism, you're beginning to sound like me." He poured red wine into each glass and slid one to König. It was a baleful attempt to re-assert control.

Nixon took a drink. König didn't touch his.

"This is expensive shit, Aldric. Drink it. I don't want it to go to waste."

König grasped the glass by the stem, lifted it in front of his face, and crushed it into a thousand pieces. The wine mixed with blood, dripping onto the carpet together. König slowly opened his hand to Nixon. His wounds quickly faded, skin lacing with skin, leaving no scars. Nixon was terrified.

"What...are...you...?"

König smirked. "Neat trick, eh Dick?'"

He brought his hand to his chin.

"Where were you when I found you, Richard? A bitter former Vice President who couldn't beat that pretty boy John F. Kennedy, couldn't even win governor in your home state. Broken. Humiliated. Aimless. I, alone, resurrected you."

König circled behind the desk and leaned over Nixon. The President sweat bullets, gripping his armrests.

"We had a *deal*, Richard. And through your reckless action at Watergate, you broke it."

Nixon began to breathe heavy. "What are you talking about? You told me to consolidate power! That's what Watergate was! You want someone to blame, blame those muckrakers at *The Washington Post*! This whole investigation is a Goddamn witch hunt!"

((...this whole Russia thing...is fake...total witch hunt...))

König was unimpressed. "I gave you the *will to power*, Richard, so you could use it responsibly, not clumsily. Do you even know your enemy?"

Nixon sat up. "Warren's niece. What about her?"

König rubbed the wooden bust of Abraham Lincoln at the windowsill, wiping away a speck of dust.

"A false prophet," König proclaimed, pacing to the center of the room. "Self-styled defender of Liberty, *she* is the Tyrannical anarchist behind the unrest and rebellion of the last decade. She would upend the sacred traditions that have held free civilizations together for centuries with all manner of perversion and 'tolerance.' Naïve she is, yes. But make no mistake, she is *powerful*. Their civic religion, their heretical 'Gospel of Independence' has grown like wildfire."

König picked up a copy of Tuesday's *New York Times* from the coffee table. The corner of his mouth turned up.

"Only a strong leader – a *savvy* leader – can properly assert the absolute authority to restore the Law and Order that Liberty requires."

König laughed and sighed.

"We haven't seen Law and Order in this country since Thaddeus Stevens destroyed the Constitution with 'equality.' I entrusted you to help me undo his errors."

Nixon shook his head. "Aldric, you're out of your damn mind if you think I agreed to resurrect slavery."

"Of course you did, Richard."

Nixon balked. König doubled down.

"What is 'Law and Order' if not restoring the freedom these wild monkeys destroyed? Come on, Dick. You never meant to make those simians safe in their 'urban jungle.' You mean to protect *your* people *from* the monkeys, and *from* the jungle! Liberty for the lives that *truly* matter! Slavery was ugly, yes! But as a means of civilizing wild beasts, it was *necessary*. Call it slavery if you like, or another name. If there is no plantation to return to, then we need new ways to keep the darkness in check. *To keep the darkness in its place.*"

König pointed.

"You lack charisma, and you lack subtlety."

Nixon looked away.

"You campaigned on restoring all that Chief Justice Warren destroyed once he ascended to the Supreme Court. He was ours once, before his bitch niece bent his ear. A proud Native Son of the Golden West who fought the yellow plague. Now the American frequency has shifted, and Warren with it. Instead of swift and efficient justice, we coddle criminals with free lawyers and tell the police where they can't go. This will soon be the land of Martin Luther King, soft and feminine, incapable of defending itself…and immune to the old ways of power. You never adjusted to this. That is why you have stumbled into this hornet's nest."

König sat down in his chair.

"As a German, I am fascinated with the U-boat." He held his hands apart. "There was a prototype called the U-480, codenamed *Alberich*, for the German god who could make himself disappear…"

König blew and spread his hands out for effect.

"German vessels could detect the U-480, but not the Allies. Friend, but not foe. Like…a dog whistle. You blow it in the street and nobody stirs, but every dog for miles can hear it. Like a…*Silent Echo*."

Nixon's eyes grew wide.

"We do not say, 'Shackle the slave' anymore; we say 'Cuff the criminal.' It echoes through the void, but only *our* people, the Silent Majority, will hear it. And they will know. They will trust us. They will give us power if only we will make them *feel* safe."

König leaned in.

"Soft tyranny, my friend. Before we enslave the body, we first enslave the *mind*." He pointed to his temple.

Nixon ground his teeth.

"Do you really want power, Dick? The power of kings whose word alone is law?"

Nixon exhaled. *"Yes."*

"It is wasted on you. You don't have the discipline to wield it. Your recklessness has allowed Woodward and Bernstein to bleed you out."

"Aldric, that is *not* – "

"And where are your true believers? Hmm? The people who will bleed and die for Richard Nixon? Where are those who would rally to your side as you shoot a man dead in the streets? You need *foot soldiers* to impose Law and Order! You need those conditioned to hang on your every word, who will declare the sky crimson if you say so! You need those who will do violence to your enemies, even those deep in the state itself. Jackson had them. My next Apprentice will have them…"

Nixon went berserk. "Your *next* Apprentice?!"

König held out his arms. "You didn't think this would last forever, did you?"

Nixon gripped his armrests tight.

"I have to admit: in many ways, you have done brilliantly, Richard. It's a shame your plot to assassinate the journalist Jack Anderson fell through. But you forgot yourself. You thought you could govern from your own fears instead of instilling it in your subjects."

König's tone grew darker.

"And so you have committed the unpardonable offense."

König leaned over the desk within an inch of Nixon's face.

"Treason…against…me…"

Nixon swallowed. "You're daffy, Al."

König slammed his hand on Nixon's desk. "What *madness* possessed you to break into the office of the party that nominated George *fucking* McGovern? You had *nothing to fear* from that radical! You would have defeated him in a landslide anyway! And what *insanity* inspired you to fire Cox in plain view of those who despise you? How stupid are you, Richard?!"

Nixon trembled.

"You're afraid, I see. What did I teach you about Fear?"

Nixon shook. "It..it's better to be f..f…feared than l…loved."

"And?"

Nixon hyperventilated. König rolled his eyes.

"Come on, Dick! This is not a trick question!"

Nixon struggled to speak. "It..it…it's b…better to be loved than h…hated."

"*Yesss...very good.* You want to be feared, but not hated. Fear is what enables the Prince to impose Law and Order, to defeat disloyalty in government...to intimidate crooked lawmakers and corrupt judges, to exert leverage, to consolidate power, and *then* control the public, shaping it in your image. Fear is what drives the beast, the one we call Tyranny...the *Leviathan.*"

Nixon was now catatonic.

König grabbed the bottle of Chateau Lafite and poured half of its contents down his throat. He took another swig, swished it in his mouth, and spat its rouge contents onto Nixon. The President didn't move.

"Fear," König raised his finger, "is to be cultivated first and always. But if you must choose between being loved or hated, be *loved.* Because I assure you, Richard, you are soon to be deeply hated in every corner of America."

The air thickened with sulfur. A heaviness beat down from the ceiling. Nixon struggled to protest, like a man in perpetual cardiac arrest. I watched Ari at the opposite door, holding steady in the midst of the torrent. He caught my eye, and I heard his whisper.

((...be still, and nest in the eye of the storm...))

To the south, all time and motion stopped. The night turned a shade of crimson darker than black.

"*Partner,*" König scoffed, "let me remind you of what you really are. You are weak, burning with lust for significance. Overlooked, under-appreciated for your genius, a boy from Whittier College swimming amongst the Ivy League elite. But it's true what they say. *You don't belong.*"

König lowered himself to whisper in Nixon's ear.

"*You will only be, as you say, 'the most powerful man in the world' for another two hundred ninety-two days. You will resign in disgrace. Your name will be anathema for generations to come, and you will go down in history as a two...bit...crook.*"

Nixon croaked. "I'm...not..."

"*Oh, yessss. You arrrre.*"

"Wh...who are you?"

König smiled. "*Let me show you.*"

König seized Nixon by the throat. A sound like a shrill whistle rung in my left ear; my scar screamed with sharp pain. The Shadows rung my bones, and in a flash I leapt into an empty vessel with a dark passenger...

...

...the snow is warm against my ice cold cheeks. Lie still. Very still. When the moment is sprung...strike.

The General is off to preen in front of his men. A glutton for flattery, he is, sitting astride his horse. They say he doesn't desire the power of kings. I know better. All men crave it. Those who deny it are liars or fools. Washington is a liar, and Washington is a fool.

He was a fool to cross the Delaware in the ice. The current should have swept him and his men into the abyss.

But he had the girl with him.

An infant, with a Negress for a wet nurse. I saw them together outside this tent. A black devil suckling a white angel: an abomination. I heard whispers that the child was a miracle. No mother. No father. She descended from the sky, it is said, and gave Washington the strength to repel our British comrades from Boston.

I didn't believe it until I saw her, the little girl, in Trenton. She was glorious, possessed of a power I knew to be mine by right of strength. Washington's warriors weren't fierce enough to run an elite Hessian mercenary force out of town as they did. Not alone. She, not they, powered their victory. She, not they, captured my comrades. I fled not from Washington, but from her.

Then I pursued her.

I stalked them for days. Now, I will take her and claim her power as my own.

The guard nods off. Time to strike.

My knife slowly plows a razor thin canyon in the guard's neck, spilling a shade of crimson darker than black. I don't kill from behind. I am an angel of death; I live for the light that drowns in the eye. I wipe my hands and blade. All must be proper. All must be clean.

Now I enter the red tent.

The Negress is asleep with the babe on her belly. Her nipple is exposed. Disgusting. Women are vile and filthy; I have never known one, though many tried to lure me. Pleasure is nothing next to power. Power I will have in seconds...

...I kneel before the wet nurse; I grip my dagger and raise it over her beating heart...

...something rattles...clink...

...clink...clink...

...clink...

...I hate that noise...I hate it...I hate it...

...the blade runs through my heart, exiting my breast. He slides it from me, and I fall to my side. It isn't clean.

Crimson flows as Washington kicks me over. This is the ugly beast I must see as I breathe my last...I will hate this coward forever...

...red...cardinal red...in every direction...

...my body floats along the icy Delaware...

...for a thousand eternities...

...until I come to a distant shore.

It is a land of crimson darkness and winter flurries. Lightning flashes illuminate a hill of sorrow where Shadows toil, choking and croaking with that disgusting, meaningless sound:

"Kekkk," they choke.

"Kekkk," they croak.

It smells of tar and sulfur.

The darkness peels itself from the sky like dead skin and descends as a Shadow of a man. It...he...growls. He surrounds me in a deep black cloud...lurking...studying...

...I should feel terror...

...I feel nothing.

"Identify yourself," I say, "or I will kill you, too."

The Dark One blazes. "I ammm Turrrrannnos."

It is Tyranny, darkness, evil...known to many as the Leviathan....

...he stands before me in his wildest form.

"What is this place?" I ask.

He replies, "Thisss is noooo place. Noooo time, noooo space. Eeeeeteeeerrrrnityyyyy...."

Lightning crashes again, illuminating the hellscape with ice-cold fire. The Shadows of irredeemable souls are here...where there is weeping and gnashing of teeth...

"Thisssss isssss the Assssh Heap of Hissssstoryyyy."

"You have not bound me with the others," I say. *"Why?"*

He points at me. *"Emptyyyyy vesssseelllll. Iiiiii help youuuu…youuuu help meeeee."*

"You wish to strike a bargain."

Tyranny cracks like thunder and shows me a vision of the child in the arms of her wet nurse, the child with golden crown and brown eyes of fire. I rage.

"You want me to kill the child?"

He moans. *"Noooo… Not killll….snnnnuuffff ouuut."*

In the vision the fire goes out of the child's eyes. The wet nurse screams and drops her to the floor, shattering her into a thousand pieces.

I say to Tyranny, *"What shall I receive in return?"*

He whispers, *"The pooowwwwer of kiiiiiings."*

He pours his darkness into my body, all the malice and avarice of every despot who ever lived and will live, and the power to whisper unto thrones and make empires rise and fall. Tyranny ejects me from the hellscape…

…I awake on a beach in the Old World. There is a castle before me. It is mine…

…mine alone…

…

…I slumped against the wall of the Oval Office, beaten.

König continued to shout dark terrors at a petrified Nixon.

"You are finished, Richard! Another Apprentice slouches toward Washington to restore the Empire of Liberty upon the crumbling ashes of Aurora Wheatley, Emmaleigh Stevens and Pearl Warren!"

König spun around, his eyes swirling gray like cement, and pointed.

"And the ashes of her Champion!"

I felt something seize my throat from within. I went nauseous and cold.

Ari barked out the distress code: *"SUNSET! SUNSET!"*

Something like a Shadow arose from the deepest, darkest part of me, wrapping around my spine and overwhelming my senses with every vile and vicious thought that ever passed through my mortal being: my lust, my greed, my wrath...*especially my wrath*...and my every pain. They coalesced into beastly form and rushed Ari, pinning him to the wall and shorting his receiver. Deep in the throes of torment I gasped for air. König lifted me by the throat.

"Did you get all that? Did you like that part about soft tyranny?"

I struggled hopelessly against his arms.

"I don't have to shackle you, Benji. *I already rule you.* I destroyed your father. I destroyed your marriage. I've nearly destroyed every other Atwater. I destroyed that boy and his father. *Now I'll destroy you.*"

König pulled a dagger from his jacket, one with a red-and-gold hilt, and pointed it straight at my heart.

"Say it with me," he said through clenched teeth. *"Heil König."*

"Not so original, Al."

König winced. He dropped me like a rock and turned to face his taunter. Kennedy stood atop Nixon's desk, open and unprotected. König flipped his knife into a reverse grip, forearm up.

"Ich bin Ihr größter Misserfolg, bin ich." Kennedy continued. *"Töte mich."*

König seethed. "You could have lived, Jack. I offered you everything I gave Nixon and more. But you missed the mark."

Kennedy spread his hands. *"So did you."*

König charged. As I slipped into the abyss I caught Kennedy's eye, beholding me as a brother...

...

I dream of a mountain sunrise, and a Tree like a Mighty Elm. Root to leaf it is strangled by weeds. A noose hangs from the strongest branch. A stone in the form of a child lays at the foot of the Tree, a claymore of silvery steel run straight through it. Morgan's cackles echo through the valley.

"Come find me, John Brown. We'll see who wields it."

The Gates open to a sky of crimson darker than black, where the sun rises no more...

((...seek not silver, but the pearl of great price...))

...

…the light burned through my eyelids.

Pearl stood atop the mahogany desk in luminous glory, flushing a thousand hidden memories from dry, unexplored caverns. König and his Shadows fled from her presence. It was brighter and more intense than in the courtroom, penetrating me joint and marrow. Pearl drew her light inward, and the Oval Office was restored.

I was weak, down to my last cell. König had sapped me of all strength. I was too tired to think…too tired to exist…it was as if I had awoken from a centuries-long slumber under a hot desert sun. As Minty and Ira propped me up, I swept my eyes across the Oval Office…

…Kennedy looked far worse.

No…

Adrenaline surged; I pushed myself up and paced across the Oval Office to kneel in front of my partner…my friend. Ari and Zora leaned him against the desk. A fresh scar on the right side of his chest bled solid black through his white shirt. The color threatened to flee his skin. Every time it did he reeled it back by the force of the deep resolve visible through his eyes.

Ari held a wet cloth against his wound, caking and draining its obsidian contents into a tin bucket.

"Count yourself lucky, Jack," Ari said. "Looks like he missed again."

Jack shook his head. "No," he replied, breathing heavily, "I wanted him to get the heart. He knew what he was doing. He slashed me on purpose."

Kennedy turned to Zora.

"How far did he get, Z?"

"Just far enough," Zora said morosely.

Pearl knelt before him. "Jack, you've done everything you can. Minty and Ira are more than capable of escorting Ben the rest of the way."

Kennedy winced and pushed himself up. "With all due respect, Ms. Warren, I swore an oath."

He turned to me and laughed lightly.

"I'm sorry I punched you in Chicago."

"No you aren't," I said. "I needed the sense knocked into me."

Minty stood at my shoulder.

"Did you see where we go next?" Minty asked.

I nodded. "He has her. Tyranny has her."

I looked Kennedy in the eye.

"Where Excalibur lies."

Kennedy bid Pearl to stand him up. "I don't think I can jump on my own."

Ira squat in front of Kennedy and lifted him on his back. Ira looked to me. "Ben?"

I retrieved my coin. It was pure silver, and pulsed with warmth.

Pearl handed me my satchel. "Go."

I tightened the strap and closed my eyes, as Ira, Minty and Kennedy clung to me.

Lightning crashed through the static. Then the signal broke through, the voice of one calling out in the wilderness. A brood of vipers awaited on the other side of the river, eager and ready to strike.

Twenty Four

Pacific Theater

04:11:17

She worked at a diner on South Edward Street, in a place called Independence. The tiny town began as Camp Independence on July 4, 1862, where the cavalry rested from pursuing Paiutes fleeing into the Sierra Nevada. No rest could be found in California's Owens Valley, an environment so tenacious and unforgiving that its mining outposts were ultimately abandoned to the ghosts. The farmers followed when the Los Angeles Aqueduct diverted the Owens River south, devastating the ecosystem and rendering arable soil infertile.

So as of Thursday, December 21, 1944, only a few hundred declared Independence home. The remnant took comfort in the cold, desolate high desert, away from the noise of California's cosmopolitan urban centers. It was a place where one could spend a lifetime in peace.

Exactly the way Dorothy Jane Tucker liked it.

"How is everything, Captain Carew?" the 22-year-old waitress said, touching my hand.

I'd hardly touched my burger. The woman's presence was unnerving. It had been almost a year since our violent encounter on the ball field in Palm Beach, on my first day in Eternity. After all I'd endured in the intervening time, I'd almost forgotten all about her. Now she was right in front of me, young and innocent, wholesome and vivacious, with none of the bile and bitterness of her 40-year-old self. Her every move behind the counter was irksome to me. The touch of her hand on mine triggered a wave of anxiety I couldn't define.

"It's fine," I replied. "I'm not very hungry today."

Dorothy laughed playfully. "I can see that!"

She turned to Kennedy.

"More coffee, sir?"

"No thank you," Kennedy, a.k.a. "YAZSTREMSKI," said through a cough. He had re-gained enough color to make him presentable. Underneath, though, lead poisoning coursed through his veins, courtesy of König's dagger. Truth be told, he was in no physical shape for this operation. But behind his eyes was a deep resolve to see this thing through, hell or high water.

Minty stirred her soup gently, absorbed in a book by a man named Coates. Her nameplate read "PAIGE," and like Kennedy and I she wore a green Army side cap. She may have been wearing the same officer's uniforms as us, but between us might as well have been a thousand worlds.

"More coffee, ma'am?" Dorothy offered her. Minty waved her off, eyes glued to her book.

"Sergeant Paige has always been hyper-focused," Kennedy explained.

"Must be some book," Dorothy replied, placing the coffee pot back on the burner. "To be so enraptured by it."

"Thank you for accommodating us," I interjected, eyeing the sign above the counter:

WHITES ONLY

Dorothy waved her hand. "I don't believe in that. Let me get your check."

Dorothy worked her way to the back kitchen.

"This isn't the Dorothy I remember," I said.

"This isn't the Dorothy *she* remembers," Kennedy replied.

A Latina waitress named Rita whispered something to Dorothy, and they giggled like schoolgirls. I picked up the editorial page of Tuesday's *Washington Post*. The headline proclaimed in bold capital letters:

LEGALIZED RACISM

It seemed that one Fred Korematsu, 25, of Oakland, California had lost his appeal to the Supreme Court of the United States. Two months after Japan attacked Pearl Harbor, President Franklin D. Roosevelt issued Executive Order 9066, sentencing Korematsu and 110,000 other Japanese-Americans to internment. Korematsu petitioned for a writ of *habeas corpus*, demanding his release.

"'You have the body,' that's what habeas corpus means," Dad once told me. *"More literally, it's a question: 'Why do you have the body?' You can't just arbitrarily restrict someone's physical movement. That's the very definition of Tyranny, son: to control a man in mind, body and soul."*

The Supreme Court sided with Tyranny, citing the threat of espionage by Japanese-Americans who *might* be loyal to Hirohito as justification for taking Liberty from all of them. They languished together in ten different camps across the country.

Including Manzanar. City of ten thousand.

Outside the diner, Ira pulled up in a black 1940 Oldsmobile Series 90.

I tapped Minty. "Our ride's here."

I set money on the counter. As we exited, a solemn Hispanic officer named "CLEMENTE" entered with a card in his hands.

I took the passenger seat next to Ira. Through the window I watched Rita cover her mouth. Dorothy slumped against the back counter, mouthing one word:

"Wayne."

The cook hugged Dorothy from the side; Rita rubbed her shoulder. Dorothy sobbed, and a deep rumbling growl echoed from the greasy spoon.

I read the coin of pure silver:

OUR GREATEST LOVE WE GIVE

As the snow began to fall flake-by-flake onto the valley floor, "Corporal Bender" pulled away from the diner, driving the Sons of Liberty south toward Tyranny's front door.

~

The doorbell rings. I answer it.

"You must be Benjamin."

"You must be Haji," I shake his hand, "and Mazaa," I shake hers. "Come in."

Michelle invited work colleagues over for the game today, a handsome late middle-aged couple from Ethiopia. I take their coats as Colonel and Drew bark from the living room.

"GO! GO! RUN YOU SONOFABITCH! YEAH! TOUCHDOWN CAMPBELL!"

Mazaa looks terrified.

"Army-Navy game," I explain. "It's an intense rivalry."

Michelle embraces her colleagues and introduces them to our friends. Colonel ambushes me in the living room.

"10-7 Black Knights, baby!" he brags, sipping a Samuel Adams Winterfest.

"You know," I countered, "there are freshman at MCHS who have never been alive for an Army win?"

Drew snorts. Colonel waves me off.

Navy opens the next drive with a 35-yard completion.

Haji sits next to me. "So Michelle tells me you teach school, yes?"

Oh no. He's gonna talk during the game. "Yeah. Social studies."

"Excellent! I have a few questions about your pedagogy if you don't mind."

Not now. I'm trying to watch the game.

He rambles on for minutes. I give him perfunctory answers, desperately hoping he'll get a clue. I'm in no mood for small talk. The Middies are on the march.

I hear Michelle, Mazaa and others at the breakfast table...

"...he doesn't want to adopt?"

"...no...he says it isn't the same..."

Michelle sniffles. My stomach tightens, and my head starts spinning in circles...

~

The pudgy little boy of three drew a circle in the snow with a stick. He had pulled the hood of his fur-trimmed winter coat over his white sailor's cap. He plopped on his backside onto the powder, stuck the stick in the middle of the circle and clutched a misshapen brown cloth baseball in his right hand. From his seat he chucked the heavy ball at me. I caught it in my leather-gloved hand.

"You're sure these are the right barracks?" I asked.

"Yeah," Minty nodded. "That's what Sage said."

I scanned the horizon, the sound of a solemn moonlight serenade arising from an unknown point among the rows upon rows upon rows of long barracks hastily constructed from cheap wood planks and tar paper. Somewhere inside the Manzanar War Relocation Center, the three-year-old niece of California Governor Earl Warren was held captive. The only question was where....

...the landscape flickered in and out. A caravan of Army supply trucks...

...*turns to covered wagons. There are Creek, Cherokee and Choctaw in all of them. Most are dying of pox or plague. A golden-haired angel numbers among them. She is sick, and still she tends to their wounds...*

...I shake my head.

"What'd you see?" Minty asked.

"Nothing." *A lie.* These static breakthroughs increased in frequency since König seized me by the throat, live memories I couldn't control. When we arrived the day before, I saw busloads of Japanese-Americans lined up to enter, one-by-one, strangers exiled in a strange land. Their spirits left an indelible imprint in time and space that would echo forever. One committed suicide on the third day of internment. A promising musician would on release become a gambler and heroin addict, dying of cardiac arrest at thirty-four. A woman shot trying to escape hovered over the wall restlessly, half slave, half free, flooding the valley in sorrow.

Now, outside the barracks, a little boy playing in the snow sang:

> *One little, two little, three little In-juns*
> *Four little, five little, six little Nig-gers*
> *Seven little, eight little, nine little Jap-Nips!*

I shook my head. The boy stopped. Tyranny was playing tricks.

"You see somethin' else?" Minty asked.

I nodded. "This kid was singing."

Minty squinted. "I saw and heard things, too, after my head was crushed. Took me awhile to understand that whatever Tyranny knocked loose just made me see more clearly."

Minty turned to the boy and smiled. He smiled back. Minty quickly scooped up a snowball and *zinged!* it into my chest. I watched the snow fall from my shirt as the boy rolled on the ground squealing with delight.

"You're a genius, Mint," I said.

"Let your work be play," she replied with a grin.

I tossed the cloth baseball back to the boy. I grabbed my arms to mock shiver. His smile faded. He scrambled to the door, pushing it open and waving us in.

"Haitte kudasai!"

We followed. It was no warmer inside than out. The "block" apartment was all of 400 feet square with six twin-size cots. From one corner to the other hung a clothesline with wet shirts and slacks, each stealing warmth from a dingy room with no heating or insulation. Three people huddled in the corner, shivering. One teenage girl on a cot contended with sores on her face. Another coughed violently, clearly wrestling with pneumonia.

On the other side of the room, a woman in her mid-20s sat at a corner desk, meticulously drawing on thin paper with a crude pencil. The boy ran up to her and shouted, "Mama! Mama!" She jumped at his shouting, then turned and scowled at him.

"Benjiro! Watashi wa sakenda koto nit suite nani o iimashita ka?"

The boy pointed at us with his stick. His mother's eyes met ours, and she panicked.

"Shohei!" she yelled at the man seated cross-legged on the cot next to her. *"Shohei! Karera wa anata no tame ni koko ni iru!"*

"Rirakkusu, Hanako," the man said, eyes closed. *"Karera wa watashitachi no tame ni koko ni imasen."* He wore only a white undershirt and trousers. In spite of the temperature and his attire, he did not appear to be the least bit cold.

"Sir," I said, taking off my cap. "Do you mind if I have a word with you?"

The man opened his eyes, emerging from deep meditation.

"I just have a few questions," I pressed, "about the whereabouts of a little girl."

Hanako looked up from her drawing warily.

"He means the girl with the red hair, doesn't he, Shohei?" she asked, in perfect English.

Shohei nodded. "Yes. The girl with the green eyes."

Hanako stood up and pointed her pencil at me.

"You know where she is!" she cried. "You're the bastards holding her!"

"Hanako!" Shohei shouted. "I have never seen these guards before; they are not them."

He turned his head to me.

"Are you?"

"No," I said, pulling up a wooden chair next to the cot. "We are the Sons of Liberty. We serve an authority higher than any government, even the government of the United States. Our sole objective is to free the girl from her captors."

Minty stepped forward. "We know you've seen her barracks."

Shohei nodded.

"Do you know who she is?" I prodded gently.

"That depends," Shohei answered.

"On what?"

"On who you really are. Your name is not really 'Carew,' is it?"

Shohei had an indefatigable poker face.

"Okay," I said. "My name is Ben Upson. I'm a schoolteacher in Springland, Colorado."

Minty spoke next. "Araminta Ross. People call me Minty. I'm a railroad engineer from Auburn, New York."

Shohei turned to Hanako, who nodded.

"My name is Shohei Masuda," he began. "This is my wife Hanako and our son, Benjiro. What do you want to know?"

~

"I want to know how you do it."

Colonel is riveted by Haji. He just needs a distraction; Navy is coasting to its fourteenth win in a row.

"How do you guys do what you do in this political environment? All the racism and xenophobia over the last five or six years."

Haji sets down his wine cooler. "The last fifteen years have been very difficult for Safe Harbor. That's why we love Michelle so much. She donates many hours to counseling asylum seekers and trafficking victims. She has such compassion for these children."

Something irrational rumbles deep in the back of my mind.

"It doesn't help when so many Americans view them as threats, when they are not."

On screen, four midshipmen yell into the camera, holding up their "Number One" fingers. All I see is that Navy white.

That irrational thing has surfaced.

"Haji," I say, "did you ever think, maybe, that some of your clients might be threats?"

CLANG! In the kitchen, Michelle drops a pair of salad tongs.

Haji is confused. "No, Ben. I do not. The people we assist have demonstrated evidence of persecution and abuse. We screen out people who would abuse our system."

I nod. "So you agree that a lot of immigrants abuse our system."

"No, I don't agree. As an immigrant myself, I can tell you that most immigrants are good people, just like most natural-born Americans are good people."

A small voice tells me to stop. I ignore it.

"Sure," I say. "As long as they're all here legally, right? All of your clients have all their paperwork in order?"

Haji laughs. "Of course they don't."

Got him. "So why should someone be granted asylum if they aren't here legally?"

Haji takes a deep breath. "Have you ever played tag?"

"Yeah. Got paid to do it, too."

He's confused. "Oh. Right. Baseball. Very clever."

Haji crosses his legs. No socks under his loafers. So weird.

"Asylum is a game of tag, in which the country you are seeking asylum in is like the 'base.' You say, 'base,' and you are safe."

"Why?" I demand. "Why should someone be able to do that? Why shouldn't you apply for asylum in your own country first?"

Haji looks me in the eye. "Because you would die. They would kill you."

He bows his head.

"You talk about legal versus illegal, like a lot of other Americans who say they love the Declaration of Independence. I have to say that your concept of the law is not only wrong, it is un-American."

A violent beast growls inside, though only faintly...

((...your father is a killer...))

"Asylum seekers are fleeing from governments who use the law to abuse them. I believe Martin Luther King said laws that violate the higher law shouldn't be enforced. Anyway, international and American law is clear that you are protected if you can claim asylum however you get here. Just call 'base.'"

Ridiculous. "It's anarchy. I'm sure you'll find people here seeking asylum who end up killing someone. I'm sure there are a lot of criminal illegals taking advantage of my wife's generosity. Oh, and by the way, she immigrated the right way."

Colonel tries to save me. "Ben – "

"Colonel." What, man?

Haji thinks, patiently. "You know that most immigrants you call 'illegals' simply haven't renewed their visas, right?"

"And? Are they any less dangerous?"

Haji sits back.

"Are they?"

Haji rests his arm on the back of the sofa. "Are you suggesting that we treat people who miss deadlines as criminals?"

"I'm suggesting," I begin, "that the law is the law, and if you don't obey, we boot ya. No questions asked. Just pack your bags and go."

Michelle emerges from the kitchen on the verge of tears. She's been listening the entire time.

"No exceptions?" she says, quivering.

I nod. "Right. No exceptions, babe."

The room has cleared out. I'm looking at the woman I love, but I can't see her.

~

"When did you first see her?"

Shohei exhaled. "In the General's Jeep. June, I want to say."

"I take it this wasn't Patton?" Minty pressed.

"No. General Maurice Travers. We call him *'Rikugun.'* Director Merritt is in charge here, but Travers pulls his strings, and Travers answers to someone else."

König. "Where did Travers take the girl?" I asked.

"To the barracks." I detected from Shohei's body language that he was being evasive. We hadn't earned his complete trust.

"Is there anyone else here like Travers?"

Shohei looked puzzled.

"Someone who isn't 'official,'" Minty chimed in.

Shohei understood. "You mean Nicholas Morgan."

Minty tightened. "Among others."

"He is 'hoankan,' the Sheriff of Manzanar. He inspires the abuse of the prisoners. There are three others."

Minty and I leaned in.

"Archibald Gould. He is businessman, or 'kaichou.' He makes a dishonest profit from these barracks. Cecil Barton. He censors the camp news and sends spies to eavesdrop on conversations..."

Shohei trailed off. It occurred to him we might be Barton's agents.

"And the priest, or 'akira gaku mono,' Carlo di Lorenzo."

Father Carlo. My mind reeled as it flashed to the old priest's testimony in Wheaton.

"These are the *waru ma* of Manzanar. The demons. Not everyone can see them. But we can."

"Leviathan," I muttered.

Shohei stared blankly.

"A sort of demon," I explained. "A dragon with seven heads. A Prince and an Oligarch; a Hierophant and a Censor; a General and a Sheriff."

"That's only six," Hanako cut in. "Who is the seventh?"

"I..."

...don't know.

Shohei pulled his son onto his lap and kissed his head. Benjiro only seemed interested in playing with the cloth baseball.

"I am sorry," he said, "but I am not sure what you want from me, or why this girl is so important to you."

I looked to Shohei. "Do you know who she is?"

"A girl," Hanako interrupted as she sketched. "She is just a girl with red hair."

"She is the niece of Governor Earl Warren."

The room went quiet. The three huddling in the corner stared at us, agape.

Hanako fumed. *"Warren.* The Attorney General who stole our home? Who tried to strip us of our citizenship? That *bastard* is *Governor?!"*

"Hanako!" Shohei yelled. "Keep your voice down!"

"Let her starve!"

"Hanako!"

"Mr. and Mrs. Masuda," I said. "Whatever your feelings are toward Governor Warren, I assure you the girl is not truly his niece. She is his to care for, but she belongs to all of us. And if these six Brothers have their way, she will suffer a fate worse than death, as will every man, woman, child, every human being on the face of the Earth."

The barracks hushed as the night winds howled. One of the women huddling in the corner spoke.

"She is *kami?"*

I paused. "I...I don't know what that is."

"Ancestral spirit," Minty answered. "Divine..."

…

...in a flash, the barracks become the Atlantic. From a merchant sloop black bodies are tossed to the waves as chum for the sharks. In the hull, a golden spirit shines upon on a frightened young girl. The vessel is called The Phillis...

…

...the vision came and went in the blink of an eye.

"However you want to characterize her," I said, "she is no ordinary child. And the leader of these *waru ma,* the dark one they call Aldric König, wishes nothing but to see her fire vanquished. Then the world loses the beacon of hope who guided you to these shores."

I paused to let it sink in.

"I've seen what they plan to do to her. I know where we must take her to stop it."

Hanako looked up. "You have seen the Tree?"

My head swiveled. "Yes. Have you?"

Shohei cradled Benjiro into his arms. "When you witness the Tree of Liberty cut down in your own yard, you can hear it crying the rest of your days."

Benjiro grabbed the stick and made circles in the air before Shohei gently took it away.

"I was a dentist. I partnered with Dr. Charles Bolingbroke at a clinic on Emerald Street in Los Angeles. Three days after Pearl Harbor, Charles' lawyer served me with notice that the war with Japan made it 'commercially impossible' to continue the partnership and demanded that I surrender my half of the practice. It was an absurd claim, but no lawyer would represent a Japanese man after 3,000 sailors died."

Something stirred in my gut.

"We had a house on the corner of Hickory and Maricopa. As soon as FDR gave the order, our bank foreclosed. We never missed a mortgage payment, but the bank knew we would be relocated. Hanako and I arrived here with my mother, her parents and her sisters" – he nodded at the other side of the room – "and a nine-month-old son. I work in the orchard for $13 a month. Hanako sews clothing. Her sisters are in school, and her parents are too old to work. My mother died of heat exhaustion and dehydration that first summer."

Shohei looked away, sorrowfully.

"A man came through here last summer to photograph the camp. Everyone was required to smile by Merritt's orders, but there are no smiles here. There is no life when the Tree of Liberty is choked by these weeds."

Shohei's pacific temperament devolved into lingering anger.

"But I refuse to be strangled any further."

"We are meant to be like the bonsai," Hanako said, holding up a beautiful sketch of the Japanese tree. "The bonsai grows wherever planted, and its branches reach everywhere. We cannot control it – only prune it. It is this way with a people who are free."

"We, the Masudas," Shohei continued, "choose freedom no matter our circumstances. They take our bodies, but our minds will not submit. We are warriors, and we will fight until our dying breath."

Shohei gave Benjiro over to his mother.

"When I saw the girl, the day Morgan locked her away in that barrack, I saw the face of a child I dreamed of in Hiroshima. She told me to sail east beyond the rising sun. She is why I am here. She is the one who has brought us together, Mr. Upson."

Hanako trembled as Benjiro played with her hair. The coin pulsed hot in my pocket.

Shohei put on his coat. "I will take you to her."

I pressed my finger to my earpiece.

"You get that, Jack?"
"Every word."

Twenty Five

The Tree of Tyranny

It was a long march to the other end of camp in sub-freezing temperatures. The tower swept its light over the barbed wire. The guards had been given orders to shoot any potential escapees on sight...

((...vindicativ in libertatem...))

Shohei held me back. "Do you hear that?"

"I do."

((...hunc hominem libero volo...))

I pointed down the road toward the middle of a long barrack. "It's coming from there."

"Yes," Shohei said. "That is where they are holding her."

The barracks oozed black with tar. *To suffocate her spirit. To drive her mad...*

...the long train is full to the brim with undesirables: Jews and Gypsies and homosexuals and journalists and Communists. Their spirits are poisoned long before their bodies are marched to the chamber to respire death itself. The boxcar bleeds black...

...

...focus, Benji.

No one stood guard on our side. "All clear South."

Ira came on over the line. *"All clear North."*

Strange. There were guards at Emmaleigh's cabin, but not here...

...no. It didn't matter. She couldn't suffer another second in this echo chamber.

I crept up to the door, Minty at my seven, Shohei at my four. I reached for the door.

ZZZZZAP!

"Shit!" I jumped back, shaking out my hand.

"Are you alright?" Shohei asked.

"I wasn't expecting an electric shock," I panted. "But I'm fine."

Minty's eyes shifted to and fro. Slowly she backed away...

"Mint?"

...she pressed her finger against her lips, then pointed to the door...

"Get inside," she mouthed, bolting around the corner...

"MINT?"

...then she disappeared.

"How are we supposed to get inside?" Shohei asked, eyeing the door handle nervously.

"I'll have to knock it down," I said. "Stand back."

I dug in and charged. I barreled into the door with my shoulder, knocking it flat.

Lightning shot outward in all directions, sizzling through the tar on the walls. There was a blinding light, then I saw her, a specter spinning in mid-air. Rapidly she dissolved into her exhausted three-year old body, clothed in dirty rags with stringy auburn hair and bright emerald eyes.

"Benji!" she cried and rushed to me.

I clutched her and found myself crying deliriously.

"She is kami," Shohei whispered breathlessly. *"Truly."*

Young Pearl grabbed my cheek.

"Don't let the bad men take me again," she whispered.

"Over my dead body they will," I replied.

The rifle cocked.

"That's the idea, John Brown."

Morgan stood on the rooftop, Colt .45 trained on us through an open panel.

"Glad we agree for once!"

I gazed up at the shadow moving behind Morgan. Gently I sang:

"Up-on-the-house-top..."

CLICK

Morgan scowled.

CLICK *CLICK*

OOMPH!

Down to the cabin fell Sheriff Nick as Minty drove him to the floor. She choked him furiously at the base of his neck.

"Nothin' to throw at me, Nick?"

Shohei and I bolted out the door.

"Chū ni haitte!" Shohei shouted at those woken by the commotion.

We ran for a solid minute until we reached a snowy intersection…

"Put the child down!"

The skinny man on the megaphone was Camp Director Ralph Merritt. Next to him General Travers held a pistol against Kennedy, on his knees with his head slumped forward. Between Travers and Merritt, flanked by two rows of soldiers with their rifles trained on us, was a large man in his fifties with a crew cut and cat-eye glasses, California Governor Earl Warren.

"Pearl, sweetheart!" Warren yelled.

He pointed his finger at me.

"Don't you dare hurt her, you bastard!"

"Say something," little Pearl whispered.

"Governor Warren!" I shouted. "These men are not who they say they are!"

Pearl pointed at Travers. "Bad man! Bad man! Bad man!"

Warren looked confused, studying the snow, eyes shifting. He turned to Merritt. "Ralph, you call me saying you've found my niece, and now she calls your general a 'bad man.' What is she saying?"

Merritt stumbled over his words. "Earl, I…"

He turned to Travers and feigned outrage.

"General, I *warned* you what would happen if you let that fool Morgan…"

Travers slapped Merritt across the face.

"Your groveling disinterests me, Merritt," he said, pistol cocked. "Peace and security require sacrifice. Don't tell me now you don't have the stomach for it."

Travers delivered the order to the riflemen in a cold steely tone.

"Fire!"

Then Pearl's light filled Owens Valley, blinding all but those who knew her. Travers recoiled from the light with an otherworldly scream; Kennedy made a break for it as Travers fired blindly…

…*BANG!*…

…*he missed.*

"Shohei!" I yelled. "Where's the Tree?"

"Follow me!"

Shohei led us through the barracks to the eastern edge of camp to an orchard of pear and apple trees. The Tree took my breath away.

It was a Great and Mighty Elm, standing alone atop a rising hill. Its barren branches grew wild like the bonsai, its varicose roots surfacing above the snow. Just below the trunk where I had seen the sword...

...a long stick shot out of the snow.

A stick. A cruel joke.

"Up the slope!" Shohei yelled. "The Tree will protect you!"

Kennedy, Pearl and I sought shelter under the tree. Ira followed, Minty trailing after clutching her temple.

Hanako followed behind us with Benjiro in her arms. *"Shohei!"*

Shohei turned.

"Anata no shiro ni!"

A guard raised his rifle. "Freeze, Nip!"

The shot hit Shohei in the stomach. He fell to his knees, clutching his bleeding mid-section.

"Oh, holy Jesus," the soldier whispered, lowering his rifle.

Hanako screamed. She fell next to her husband at the foot of the snowy hill.

Minty's eyes widened. *"Not on my watch."*

She rushed back downhill, retrieving her bandana from her pocket. She spat in it and placed it on Shohei's exit wound as a tourniquet. Shohei slumped to the ground as his wife and child huddled over him in tears.

The world slowed to a crawl. I grew dizzy. My ears rang. I fell to one knee, watching from the foot of the Tree as Shohei Masuda bled scarlet drop-by-drop into the pure white snow...

...and young Benjiro lost his father...

...over...

...and over...

...and over again...

…that sickly feeling returned, crawling up from my gut through my chest and seizing my throat from within, gripping and crushing my windpipe…

…I couldn't breathe…

((…they took him away…))

((…they took him away from me…))

I dropped to my knees and vomited into the snow.

((…he's gone…gone forever…))

((…and so is she…))

Rage built.

Unbridled rage.

And sorrow.

And shame.

((…never let go…))

((…never…let…go…))

"Stay with me Jack!"

Ira's shout snapped me out of my daze. He propped Kennedy's weakened frame against the Tree and snapped his fingers to start a fire. *Travers got him.*

"Ben! Flag!" Ira yelled.

I pulled Betsy Ross from my satchel and draped her over Kennedy. Pearl fell on top of the flag and touched the dying man underneath. On contact with his skin, the flag seemed to transfer the life in its own seams into Kennedy, giving him a second wind.

"That…that was the kill shot…" he eked.

Travers' leaden shot entered below the scar on Kennedy's throat. His skin had managed to partially knit back together – but not before it oozed black puss.

Ira glanced up at me. "He doesn't have much time left."

My jaw tightened. "How long?"

Ira shook his head. "He'll be lucky to make it to morning."

((...I'm afraid we won't make it through the night...))

I trudged over to the stick. It was no sword; it was only a mirage. A cruel joke.

Below, throngs of prisoners awoken by gunfire swarmed through the orchard. Pearl stood up with a jolt. She sprang over to me and pulled the stick from the ground.

"Hey! Pearl! What – ?"

Pearl made a beeline downhill toward the Masudas. From there she dashed around the foothill, dragging the stick along with her. Within a minute, Pearl had drawn a circle all the way around the hill, the radius extending just outside where Shohei lay. Exhausted, she collapsed. I scooped her up and cradled her.

Benjiro buried his face in the snow to hide away his tears, still clutching the cloth baseball in his chubby fingers. His father, a strong and compassionate man, winced as Minty held the tourniquet against his wound. She returned my gaze with intense sorrow. It was useless.

Shohei Masuda would die, bleeding out upon this hill, fighting a battle I picked for him.

A battle I drove him to.

Shohei reached toward his son and whispered.

"Ki...kitebenji."

Hanako cradled Benjiro to herself and took Shohei's hand. Their eyes locked in place until Shohei's gave up their light.

Young Benjiro wept in silence. *And so do I.*

In a flash, Shohei's body burst into flames, sending Hanako pedaling backward. It consumed itself as it turned to ash, melting the snow around it. Leaves of green grass grew and small flowers bloomed like springtime. The prisoners stood in awe, talking among themselves and pointing at Pearl.

"Kami!"

"Ji yu!"

What happened next was a miracle.

A teenage girl whispered to twelve other prisoners. Quickly they fanned out around the hill and settled in equidistant spots. One-by-one, they sat gently on their heels, forming a ring around the snowy tree skirt. The girl bowed her head. The snow around her slowly melted, and green grass grew underneath her, an oasis in the high desert. The others bowed their heads as well, and the Earth came alive beneath them.

Then a fourteenth joined…and a fifteenth…and on…and on…until one hundred sixty-eight linked arms around the foot of the hill. The soldier who shot Shohei dropped his weapon and trudged to the circle, dropping to his knees in front of me and joining arms with the prisoners beside him. He bowed his head, crossed himself and began to pray:

"O Father, who art in heaven…"

One hundred sixty-nine Guardian Angels held vigil around the Tree.

A wave of energy swept the perimeter of the hill. Inside the circle, all snow melted. The sweetgrass came to life with every variety of flora, an island of beauty in a sea of ugliness. The Tree bore a ripe fruit clothed in many colors.

Ambrosia.

Ira clambered up the side of the Tree to pick the fruit. "Harriet! Quick!"

Minty jammed back uphill to assist him. *Medicine for Jack.*

I followed with Pearl. Where the stick once stood, a small rock outcropping jutted from the base of the Tree, identical to the one in my vision. Exhausted, I set Pearl down on the ground; she scurried to the rocks and sat upon them. Even in her ragged state, she brimmed with life.

Outside the perimeter a Jeep pulled up with Travers, Merritt and Warren. In seconds, at least a hundred infantry surrounded the Tree, weapons drawn on our Guardian Angels. Limping behind them was Morgan, powered by hard piss and sour vinegar. The cold fire in his gray eyes was fueled by the fresh burn marks on his neck, where Minty had strangled him. He set his backside down on a smooth boulder directly in my line of sight and began spinning the chamber of his Colt .45. I looked at my phone:

02:22:36

One soldier pointed at me and fired. The bullet disintegrated just above the circle.

"Hold your fire," Travers commanded coolly. He paced slowly around the circle, menacing the Guardian Angels until he arrived at Shohei's shooter. The General hovered over the trembling rifleman, whose knees fell just outside the circle.

"What is your name, centurion?"

As the soldier opened his mouth, Travers unsheathed his dagger and speared him clear through it. He fell to the ground, dead.

Travers observed the circle again. Not a soul had flinched. Travers growled and hovered over the teenage girl who started the circle. He lingered for effect, to no avail. He returned to the Jeep and seized Merritt by the scruff of his neck, dragging him out of the driver's seat. Warren jumped out to avoid the wrath of the General.

Travers keyed the ignition and barked at Morgan. "I wasted my shot on the Celt, Nicholas. Wait this one out. He'll do it himself."

Travers drove out of the orchard with Merritt. Morgan continued to spin his chamber as Pearl stared him down. She could have cut him in half with her intensity of focus.

Cut him in half.

Like a sword.

A sword in a stone.

I laughed...

...and laughed...

...manically, I laughed...

...as I picked Pearl off the rock...

...holding her tight, rocking her back and forth.

I bubbled over with nervous energy. As I watched the soldier's body turn to flame and ash, I brushed back Pearl's hair and kissed her on Emmaleigh's scar.

"I've found you, Excalibur," I whispered. "And I will never let you go."

Deep within those shimmering emeralds, it was clear she didn't trust me...

...

...I want to weep, but the spigot shut off a long time ago. The Sycamore weeps for me.

Michelle puts her last suitcase in the Cherokee and closes the hatch. I've been sitting in the snow at the foot of the Sycamore for an hour. She steps to the edge of the grass, purse over her shoulder, clutching her keys.

"Benji – "

"Don't call me that."

Her toes turn inward and she nervously bites her lip.

"Just go."

Michelle kneels in front of me.

"I still don't understand why."

"Yes you do," she says.

"You say I'm a child. Explain it to me so I understand."

Her lower lip trembles. "You're my best friend...and I can't breathe around you."

I tense up. "What does that even mean?"

Her tear ducts well. "You're holding too tight. And I'm suffocating."

I grimace and lean against the tree. "I love you. You know I do. You can't tell me I don't."

"You're twisting my words, Benji."

I shake my head, pantomiming punching the ground.

"And...you need to learn to let go."

No. She didn't just go there. "I loved my father more than you can ever understand. And you won't let me grieve."

Michelle breaks. "Fifteen years. Fifteen. Years! I grieved John, too. But you're not grieving anymore, you're just...angry. Do you think you honor him with your hatred?"

"Hatred," I growl. "You think this is hatred. You want me to understand your feelings when you don't get mine?"

Michelle looks away.

"This is personal to me in a way it never will be for you."

Michelle swallows and looks at her feet.

"I mean, can you cut me..."

"You married an illegal immigrant, Ben..."

...

...I choke. "What?"

"On our wedding day," she sniffs, "I was out of status."

I shake my head. "No. No. That's bullshit."

"My lawyer lost my paperwork and I missed a deadline. Why do you think it took so long for me to get citizenship?"

I'm at a loss. "I...what do you...why didn't you tell me?"

Michelle pulls out a Kleenex and blows her nose.

"Shell – "

"A month ago you told my colleagues that you would have me deported. 'Just pack my bags and go.' And you ask why I never told you?"

She lingers as the tears stream down.

"The things you say...and think...are personal to me in a way that you will never understand."

Michelle stands and composes herself for a second, then her voice cracks.

"I'm sorry I couldn't give you another John..."

"Sweetheart, please don't go – "

"No!" She throws her hands at me and runs sobbing into the Cherokee.

She pulls out of the driveway...

...and out of my life forever.

A bluebird flies from the Sycamore.

Now I weep.

My last Angel has flown away...

...

02:10:36

It was Saturday, December 23rd.

Ira was wrong. Kennedy made it through the night, but he didn't look so hot. His scar looked infected, intermittently oozing black puss. Minty soaked her bandana in ambrosia and applied it to his skin, soaking it into every pore. The ambrosia and the warmth of the flag seemed to stave off the poison within.

The fruit sustained all of us. There was an infinite supply; it replenished itself every time we picked it. Armed with Liberty, I thought, we could outlast Morgan and Tyranny forever up here, sealed off by a wall of Guardian Angels. Ira carried fruit out to them as I held Pearl tight. As long as they remained in their place, as long as we all stayed in our place, we would be safe.

Because I had the sword.

I, alone.

Ira handed me two pieces of fruit. I gave one to Pearl and ate the other. Ira looked at me askance.

"Ben," he said, "why don't you let me hold her for awhile."

I stared up at him in disbelief.

"If that's alright with you."

"No, Ira, it's not alright with me," I said coldly. "*I'm* her Champion. No one wields Excalibur but *me*."

Ira's jaw dropped. He put his hands on his head and paced anxiously as Minty consoled him.

Pearl shifted uncomfortably. She watched Benjiro closely as he struggled in his mother's lap. I squeezed her closer.

Kennedy watched me intently. His skin barely held its color, and he labored under shallow breath.

"Ben," he said with difficulty. "Come over here."

"I can hear you," I said.

Kennedy's eyes traced me and Pearl.

"Have at it, Jack."

"The sword," he struggled. "It needs a whetstone."

"Well I have her."

Kennedy laughed, not of mirth or merriment, but dead man's desperation.

"Maybe…when it all falls…I'll find Jacqueline in the Ash Heap…under the rubble somewhere…"

"It won't fall, Jack. I have Excalibur, and I'm not letting her go."

Hanako ascended mournfully uphill holding Benjiro tight. I knew that helpless look in her eye. I'd seen it in the mirror. The helpless, hopeless, bottomless feeling of watching someone you love deeply taken from you by a ruthless agent of fate. Hanako now knew that sucking emptiness that wraps itself inside and around you, filling every wound and crevice of your being with a thick black darkness.

Minty knelt before me. "Ben...I don't know if you know this, but we're trapped. What are you gonna do?"

I held Pearl closer. "As long as Liberty is mine, no harm will come to us."

I nodded toward Morgan. He hadn't moved a muscle in twenty-four hours.

"He can cackle all he wants, but her Champion has her."

I looked the girl over.

"She is the sword in the stone. We can't lose, Mint. Trust me."

Minty's face turned sullen, and she turned away. Morgan whistled.

Kennedy coughed black blood.

"The sword needs a whetstone," he said.

I leaned back against the stone. As I drifted off, I felt the drip of hot tar against my skin...

...

...Mackenzie Masuda knocks on my open door.

"Yeah, Mac," I say, "Come on in."

She scans the paperwork on my desk. "You look busy."

"What? No." I snap out of my trance. "No. I just...was spacin' out a little."

Mac sits and folds her arms.

"What can I do for you?"

She shakes her head. "What can I do for you?"

I crack lightly. "Nothing. I don't think..."

My voice trails off. My eyes shift to and fro.

"Mac, have you ever spent nineteen years punching the same target, and all it does is break your knuckles?"

"I haven't, actually. I'm not even eighteen."

I snap and point at her. "That's right. April fourteenth."

She raises her brow.

"I was just looking at the D.C roster. I saw your birthdate."

"Oh," she nods.

An awkward pause.

"Maybe stop punching it?"

I cock my head.

"Do you know anything about aikido?"

"Vaguely. I think my dad learned it when we lived in Okinawa. It's like karate, right?"

"Mmm," she squints, "not so much."

Mac gathers her thoughts.

"In most martial arts, you attack and defend on a line. Punch. Block. Kick. Block. But in aikido, you fight in a circle."

"Interesting."

"The goal isn't to attack your opponent. It's to use his own force against him. He attacks straight on, you step aside and spin him to the ground."

I ponder that. "So I should throw a hook instead of a cross?"

Mac frowns. "I don't know what you're wrestling with, Mr. U. But whatever it is, let it come to you."

I shake my finger at her. "That's good advice, Mac. I'll think about it."

She smiles.

"What did you come here for?"

Mac pushes an envelope across my desk.

"D.C. deposit," she says. "For me and Tyson."

I'm taken aback. "Wow, Mac. Your family is so generous."

"We've known hard times, too."

Daniel Bannister pokes his head in. "Kenzie, I gotta get to the tux shop."

Mac gets up and gathers her things. "Your Angels might pierce your heart, Mr. U. But they never fly away."

As she walks out, I fiddle with the envelope and look at my monitor, lingering on the first name on the class roster:

ATWATER, TYSON I.   DOB: 09/11/2001

Twenty Six

Camlann

01:09:22

It was the morning of Christmas Eve.

My mind slowly crumbled, piece-by-piece, as the Tree turned black. The fruit no longer replenished, and the remnants began to rot. There wasn't enough to sustain the Guardian Angels who ringed the tree, even for the day. Many grew tired and cold, coughing in fits as the frost reached them. Ira and Minty wandered around the circle strengthening them with whispers, but their spirits were buoyed only for a time. Still, they never flagged, and they never faltered. They were determined to die before surrendering Liberty to her enemies.

Hanako had difficulty keeping Benjiro warm as the grass slowly withered and snow re-appeared in patches inside the circle. Pearl struggled to get out of my lap and hug Benjiro, who repeatedly reached for her. I snatched her back as Hanako brought Benjiro back to herself.

"Pearl. Stay here." I seethed. *"I need you."*

Pearl and Benjiro both cried.

Minty continued to treat Kennedy with our dwindling fruit supply. Pearl tried to lunge for him, and I pulled her in again.

"No," I said, shivering.

Ira, visibly angry, trekked up the hill with a cautious teenage boy, the older brother of the girl who first knelt two nights before. He was skin and bones, tired and poor and hungry.

"This is Matthew Takei," Ira said, words weighted with steel. "Seventeen. His sister is Samantha. They're from Hemet."

Ira placed his hand on Matthew's shoulder.

"Go on. Tell Mr. Upson here what you need to protect him."

Matthew hesitated. "I…we're pretty hungry. I don't…I don't know how much longer we can hold out. We need more fruit."

I laughed incredulously. "You're joking, right?"

"No, sir. We're all committed to her." He pointed at Pearl. "But we can't hold this demon off forever."

I stood up, still holding on to Pearl. *There's. No. More. Fruit.*

"Sir, there was plenty yesterday…"

"Get back in position, Matthew."

Matthew's eyes widened.

"Now!"

The kid's jaw dropped as he studied me up and down. He lowered his head and returned down the hill, broken.

Ira watched Matthew trudge back from his spot on the side of the hill. Enraged, he turned to face me.

"He's all that stands between you and Morgan!" Ira yelled. "You thankless bastard!"

I spat. "Corporal Hayes, I thought you don't do this for thanks?"

Ira clenched his fists, shivering, and pulled within an inch of me, Pearl squeezed between us.

"Ira – "

"I already died in the snow," he said, teeth clattering. "I'm not interested in watching *these people* do the same. Do you understand?"

I looked downhill, where the circle weakened.

"Like I told you. I do this for *her*. I don't do it for you. And neither do they."

I stood stoic. Ira searched me with his eyes.

"Unbelievable. The sword is right in front of you, and you can't see it."

"I have the sword in my *hands*, Ira. We're *safe here*. Do you see Morgan doing anything? No. Look at him. He's anxious. He can't get past our barricade – "

"Our *barricade?*"

"Yeah. That's right. Our perimeter. Our *wall*. Stay inside the circle. That's an order, Corporal."

Ira choked. "An order?!"

"I'm the Champion. She chose me. Not you. Not even them."

I waved at the prisoners.

"So I, alone make the decisions. We stay put, and we run out the clock."

Ira was moved to tears. "You're a Tyrant."

He tore the chevrons off his sleeve and tossed them at Hanako.

"Liberty is finished…at the hands of her own Champion."

Ira walked off the hill and vanished into thin air.

((…dead weight…we don't need him…))

"Life is for the living," I said.

Minty steamed. Something broke inside her. Her head shot back and forth between Morgan and me. The eye that found mine quivered; her tear ducts went blood red. She lowered herself into a seated position and closed her eyes. She wept uncontrollably.

Morgan howled with delight.

"I'm lovin' this back here, John," he hollered from the rock. "Keep at it."

I whispered to Pearl. *"You belong to me now. Do you understand?"*

The girl whimpered, "I don't belong to anyone."

"I pulled you from the stone. *You're mine forever.*"

Her skin turned colder.

Kennedy whispered in his gaunt state: *"The sword needs a whetstone…"*

~

00:21:37

By evenfall, coughing and shivering could be heard from everywhere around the tree. While the infantry rotated out for hot meals and warm showers, the Guardian Angels were locked in place on an involuntary hunger strike. They slept in shifts, huddling together for warmth. That they had any warmth to give was nothing short of a miracle. Some, in defiance of the frost, burned so hot within that they shed layers of clothing, wicking sweat from their skin. Matthew and Samantha Takei were among their number.

Theirs was a different fire.

The soldiers took note of the Angels' courage. Some had abandoned their positions and returned to camp, visibly disgusted at Morgan and Travers, whose motives for laying siege to a girl under a Tree defied reason. Governor Warren, however, still hadn't left Morgan's side.

"Hey John Brown!" Morgan shouted. "Let's get to know each other. You're prob'ly wond'rin' who I am. When I died!"

He spat and pointed at his face scar with his thumb.

"1836. Took a bayonet to the head at th'Alamo. But I ain't from San Antone. I'm a Marylander like you. Born and bred."

I pulled Pearl onto my lap to draw from her warmth. There was little to be had. She was on the wane.

"I was on th'lam, John Brown. A fugitive from Dorchester County for destruction of property."

He pointed at Minty.

"That."

Minty sat stoically, legs crossed, eyes closed, her mind carried away to another world. The Sheriff waved his hand at her dismissively.

"Worked on a plantation, and, wouldn' ya know it, when I tried to brain some runaway nigger with metal, this lil' Jane Brown steps in front of me and I smash *her* skull. Made her all droopy-eyed and dumb as she looks. She's possessed, John Brown. She talks to th'devil. Has fuckin' visions an' shit. I mean, look at all that voodoo trancin' she's doin'."

Minty's left eye fluttered. Morgan spat black tar and tobacco juice onto the white snow.

"She casts a mighty spell, that one. One-woman proof her sort ain't got our brain power. But hey!"

He traced his scar.

"Justice got me in the end…and now I *am* Justice."

Morgan leaned back and closed his eyes, humming an ancient tune:

Turkey in de hay, turkey in de straw!
Roll 'em up an' twist 'em up a high tuck-a-haw!

Minty twitched.

Governor Warren, who had spent the last forty-eight hours twiddling his thumbs, spoke up. "John Brown, is it?"

I eyed him coolly. "So you say."

"Just bring Pearl to me, please. General Travers has agreed to release all of you if you give her to me tonight. No charges will be filed."

I held Pearl tighter. "A devil's bargain! They mean to destroy her, Governor. You know who and what she is."

"Yes," Warren trembled. "I do, and I see that now. But in the last forty-eight hours, I've come to suspect…whether you mean to or not, you will destroy her, too."

An arrow to the heart.

"I know you mean well, sir, but right now, you serve who and what it is they serve."

Warren's words made me sick to my stomach…deep down, I knew he was right. I was alone with Liberty on a one-man island, a petty little hill to die upon. Pearl felt colder, weaker, dispirited in my arms. I had fed her what rotten ambrosia remained. I looked back at the Tree, where Kennedy looked pale as a ghost, coughing intermittently to signal that he hung tight with us:

"The sword needs a whetstone…the sword needs a whetstone…"

Under that same Tree Hanako held Benjiro even tighter than I held Pearl. They ate from the same rotten tree, and both had grown gravely ill. As Hanako wept, her tears fell black on the white snow.

But she's alive. How is that…

No.

I wiped the sweat from my brow.

Black. Like slick oil. Like hot tar…

…oozing from a dying tree…

…coating a cabin in the Waxhaws…

…and another at Manzanar….

…seeping through the walls of Erna Petri's cell…

…*and mine.*

I looked down on the Guardian Angels gathered around the skirt of the Tree on Christmas Eve. They had made themselves a shield against Tyranny, defending Liberty at great personal cost. They, more than I, were Liberty's warriors.

Her veterans.

Her *people.*

Now they starved, hermetically sealed from the nourishment they craved, even as they shielded it…

…

…*they are a caravan of Guatemalans, Ecuadorians and Salvadorians fleeing from cartels across the desert…*

...they are a sea of Syrians floating aimlessly on the Mediterranean, displaced by the cruel barbarism of Platov and his puppets in the Levant...

...they are the spirits aboard the St. Louis brushing past Liberty...

...broadcasting a scrambled symbol...

...of Tyranny in Liberty's robes...

...as she turns them away from Elysium...

...and sentences them to Hell on Earth...

...

"They're not the same."

((...they are no different...))

...

...they are a young Honduran boy...ten years old...alone in a dank cell...his name is Johnny, and Tyranny's black clad thugs took him from his father... their hearts are as cold as ice...today he clutches an otter in his hands...

...

...the one a sweet, sweet French girl gave him to hold his hand through the night...

...

...then I saw her there...where she had gone...where she had been all this time...

...and I cracked. I could do nothing else.

Clear tears streamed down my face. My heart of stone crumbled as love crept back in, tenderizing me from the inside out.

The fog dissipated from my mind...

...

...this is my island, my fortress of paranoia...

...

...it has happened here...I said it couldn't, but it has...right under my nose.

...

...what have I done?

...

...I have become Tyranny...

...

...by claiming Liberty for myself...

...and she whimpered in pain.

...I looked down. I gripped her right arm tight, so tight that my hand hurt.

I gasped and released. Tears streamed down the young girl's face as she cried silently. Her arm was raw...and pink...a fresh bruise forming at her elbow...

((...I bruise easily, Mr. Upson...))

...I was frozen, petrified in horror, carrying the deepest shame I had ever felt.

What have I done?

Pearl stared up at me, blinking blight green. They were pleading with me...*she* was pleading with me...

"Benji..."

...I gently lifted her up and placed her on the snow.

"Go," I whispered.

Her heart fluttered. Her skin turned golden yellow as the sun, her youthful vigor restored. Excitedly, she plopped down next to me, resting her head against my side and placed her tiny right hand into mine.

"We're gonna make it through the night," she said.

Minty shook in her meditative state. Her left eye fluttered.

Hanako, prompted by an unspeakable force, scooted up to sit next to her. She began to meditate.

"Misogi," she whispered. *"Ken ni wa nureta ishi ga hitsuyōdesu."*

Minty joined in...

"Ken ni wa nureta..."

The Guardian Angels followed...

"Ken ni wa nureta..."

Within minutes, the entirety of the Manzanar War Relocation Center was loud with the same echoing refrain. Morgan covered his mouth in derisive laughter.

"Ain't this some pagan-ass yellow shit?"

Minty approached and towered over me as maniac and menace.

"To pass through the Gates," she said coolly, "you must be purified by the cool, clear waters of the River."

I cocked my head.

"Every sword needs a stone. A *wet* stone."

Minty reared back and spat in my face...

...gasp!...

...I was dipped in a frozen lake, the ice cold penetrating every cell...

...

"Get up, Benji."

It's seven a.m. I'm not getting off this couch.

"Hey. I'm not gonna ask you again. Stop feeling sorry for yourself and get up."

Dad hovers over me in his white Navy uniform. He waves his hand over the coffee table, where a bottle of Jaegermeister and three empty beer bottles stand guard around a Sega Dreamcast controller.

"If you're going to stay with us while you recover, Benjamin, your mother and I simply ask that you observe a few courtesies."

I squint and sit up gingerly. My left knee went under the knife last month. I hate Vicodin. I numb the pain over the liquor store counter.

"For example: don't get piss drunk on our couch and fall asleep playing video games."

I hold my head in my hands. "I don't know if you've noticed, Dad, but my career is over. My life is over. So...maybe cut me a break?"

"What are you gonna do, Benji? You gonna stay mad because a pinch runner for the Salem flippin' Avalanche came at you with his nails up? Life isn't fair. Roll with it."

I scoff. "A year ago I was on the 40-man roster of the NL Central Champions. I was the heir apparent at first base to a guy who hit ten more dingers in a season than Babe Ruth ever did. Then all of a sudden I can't hit the ocean with an oar, and I get spiked covering home because our God damn catcher was out of position. That's not unfair, it's unjust."

The sunlight shining through the window is blinding. I scan Dad's uniform.

"I thought you were going into work in the afternoon."

"I was," *he says,* "but to be perfectly honest, Benjamin, I can't watch you wallow in self-pity another day."

"Just say 'I told you so.' Admit it, you're glad I got hurt. You never wanted this for me. You wanted me to take that USD scholarship and go to law school like you."

Dad grinds his teeth. "How dare you. Your mother and I supported you from day one."

He dons his white officer's hat and picks up his briefcase.

"I'll be at the Pentagon if you need a juice box."

"Captain Morgan makes juice boxes?"

He sighs. "You're driving me off a cliff, Benjamin."

Dad slams the door shut. I angrily pluck The Washington Post off the coffee table and scan the headlines for September 11, 2001.

Just another Tuesday morning in paradise...

...

...I was greeted on Christmas morning by a sacred cherub.

"Good morning, Benji." Pearl lay flat on the ground at my right shoulder, moving her arms up and down and her legs in and out in the snow, giggling like a fool.

I shook from head to toe.

That dream. Buried deep down in my depths, I had shoved it back down beneath the surface for nearly nineteen years. Now it was right in front of me, dancing before my eyes, even when shut. It took the gravelly growl of darkness to dissolve it...

"God damn, John Brown."

Morgan had been sitting on that rock for sixty straight hours. The evil undead have no need for rest in their perpetual state of restlessness.

"You've been there so long you done killed that tree," he mused.

The Tree was on its last breath. We were trapped with nothing to sustain us. Below, the ring's second wind had almost gone out. Most of the Guardian Angels were passed out, and the shield appeared to be down. Morgan tossed rocks onto the hill to demonstrate that he could shoot any of us whenever he wanted.

What is he waiting for?

I retrieved my phone.

00:10:42

((...wait him out, Nicholas...))

Morgan didn't have to do anything...*because I wasn't.* I had been sitting alone holding Liberty, taking of her fruit as it rotted from within.

Ira was right. He was running out the clock.

"Seems to me, John Brown," Morgan crowed, "that you'd be much better off on our side! In fact, I think you'd be a perfect fit for our new world. You have the right...*pallor* for it."

His laughter echoed through the camp.

I pulled the coin from my pocket. It was as heavy as lead.

The message echoed over and over in my mind...

((...our Greatest Love we give...our Greatest Love we give...our Greatest Love we give...))

...then my mind turned over the words of a carpenter from Nazareth...

((...no man hath greater love than this...))

...and another Gospel I first heard under the Virginia dogwood....

((...unless a seed falls to the ground...))

I studied the coin more closely. The sun whispered:

((...do you rise, Son of Liberty, or do you set?...))

...

I looked at Morgan, seated on the rock, clutching the handle...the *hilt*...of his Colt .45...

...the sword in the stone...

My heart swelled in my chest, pumping blood through me at a feverish clip. The floodgates opened. I held the coin and whispered:

"Set, Sun of Liberty. Set."

I turned to young Pearl, still gleefully making angels in the snow.

"Pearl, sweetheart, I'm gonna do something crazy. Then I won't see you for awhile. Can you do just one thing for me?"

Pearl slowed her flapping. I kissed her on the forehead.

"See Benji through the night."

Pearl winked. Then she stood and wailed as she ran uphill to the Tree, where a sickly Hanako sat with a sicklier Benjiro. She jumped into Hanako's lap and grabbed Benjiro by the hand. The Masudas cried on cue, mother and son.

I found Minty under the Tree playing with Kennedy's hair. I towered over her.

"Mint," I said. "I'm not fit to be a Champion."

She raised a skeptical eyebrow.

"I surrender."

I tossed her the coin. It changed color in mid-air. She caught it with both hands and examined it on all sides, then glanced up at me. I opened my arms wide and winked.

Minty nodded and leaned over Kennedy, hugging him tight and whispering in his ear as she cried. I grabbed Minty by the nape of her neck and threw her back. She tumbled down the side of the hill to Morgan's delight. I snarled. She removed her hat and pulled the chevrons from her sleeves.

"Pharaoh has my people again," she whispered through tears, then vanished.

I loomed over Kennedy and pressed my hand against his scar.

"Goodness, Jack," I said. "Who did this to you?"

I winked. Kennedy struggled to smile.

"Whoever it was," he coughed, "he did me a favor."

I grabbed him by the lapels and hissed. *"He won't miss this time."*

Kennedy giggled with delight. "Go to hell."

"You first."

I yanked the flag from Kennedy. He coughed and he quivered, and his eyes traveled a great distance. He whispered into the air:

"...never turn your cheek..."

Piece by piece, John F. Kennedy disintegrated to white ash, then floated away into the Manzanar sun.

I scowled and spat, and wrapped the flag around me.

Morgan stood to his feet and drew near as I descended the hill.

"John Brown," he said. "Son of a bitch. Ya came to your senses."

"I'm not a betting man," I said. "But I know how to play the odds."

We stood face to face. The burn marks on his neck were gruesome up close.

"Y'know, son," he said, putting his hand on my shoulder. "I still have to shoot ya, but I'll let you pick. In the head, where you can go meet your daddy...or in the heart, an' we'll giv' ya the pow'r to crush every one o' your enemies. *You can be one of us."*

I dropped to both knees and spread my arms wide, opening my chest to him.

"Life," I said, "belongs to the living."

Morgan chuckled. "Poetry, compadre."

He pulled the Colt from his holster and pointed it at my chest.

"Any other beautiful words, Mr. John Brown?"

I averted my eyes and mumbled….

"...war...miracle alone..."

"What's that?"

"I said,

> *In the heat of a cold, dark war*
> *No Champion can conquer alone..."*

He clicked the hammer…I showed him my eyes…

"…but a miracle appeared in Manzanar…"

Morgan's eyes widened in panic. He moved his arm up to my head as two ghosts materialized behind him. A United States Marine pushed down on his elbow and held it in place. A Union spy wrapped one arm around Morgan's head while the other pressed a coin of solid gold into my hand.

I opened wide the Gates of Hell…

…as Morgan pulled the trigger…

…burying the sword deep into my heart of stone.

Twenty Seven

Ashes

I straddled Morgan at the foot of the bed. He screamed in agony. I delivered a solid cross to his head to shut him up, then pulled him upright by the lapels, driving his nose to the hole in my chest.

"...the sword in the stone!"

I shoved the wide-eyed Morgan back onto the carpet. Minty and Ira panted from exhaustion as they held tight to the ageless mercenary. I nodded to both of them. I sincerely regretted my actions on the hill. They knew. I didn't have to say a word. The high-pitched whistle of the wind through the aperture in the window said it for me.

We had knocked down the Gates of Hell.

We had reached the Ash Heap.

It was my hotel room at The Quicksilver, Room 704, only here the walls were choked with weeds and slathered in tar. The sky outside was a shade of crimson darker than black; thunder and lightning flashed across a canopy of sulfur housing the snows of nuclear winter. Across the river of sludge stood the Washington Monument, charred and cracked, and beyond that the hollowed-out fiery shell of the Capitol.

Pearl.

The alarm clock read *11:08*. The exact time I left the Rotunda.

I knelt back down in front of Morgan.

"Welcome back to the Ash Heap," I bragged as he whimpered, his gray eyes wide open in terror.

I felt no fear, no pain, even as the lead bullet spun around in my heart. I watched the hole in my chest smoke as my skin stitched together over it. I flipped my coin of pure gold.

"I have to say, Nick. I think you're better suited for this world than ours. Want to know why?"

Morgan wheezed. I met him nose-to-nose.

"You have the right pallor for it."

I winked and rolled over. In one motion, Minty hoisted Morgan up over her shoulders, squatted, and thrust him wailing into the window, shattering it. His body disintegrated on contact with the cold air, and his blackened spirit streamed away, drawn by an invisible force to some netherworld of horrors beyond even this one.

Minty stared out the window, motionless. Expressionless. She brought her hand to her temple; lips curled upward in a satisfied smirk.

"Mint," Ira said, placing his hand on her shoulder. "You alright?"

She shook her head and laughed, then turned to me.

"Do you know where you are?"

I toed the black bird silhouette in the thin red carpet. "Yes."

"You know what you have to do?" Ira added.

I nodded again. "I have to get to the Capitol."

I looked at my phone:

00:10:33

"Plenty of time," Minty said. "After nineteen years."

I blinked. "What do – "

My breath caught…

…my stomach turned over…

… my body quaked from head to toe…

"…where is he?"

Ira nodded out the door. "Where you left him."

I nearly swallowed my tongue.

"Go. We'll make preparations."

I burst out the door and bounded down seven flights of stairs. I pushed through the hotel's rotating doors and saw the rising smoke.

My north star.

I flew like Gump through the empty streets of Crystal City. I had no difficulty breathing, even as nuclear ash fluttered from the Martian-red sky. I dashed toward the highway and through the underpass, until I arrived at my destination.

A five-sided behemoth, headquarters of the United States Armed Forces.

The Pentagon.

~

00:10:11
My heart beat into my hands and feet. The great and terrible image stood ominously before me: the canyon where that lemon farmer had driven the Boeing 757 looked smaller than it did in the photographs. I never came to see for myself. It was less threatening when it was larger than life. Now it was life-sized.

Real. Too real.

Surreal.

No more buried dreams. Into the crevasse.

I traversed the memorial grounds, rows upon rows of benches with the names of those departed souls. I braced myself, then entered the heart of the wound.

Scattered debris filled the darkened cavern. An airline seat. A desk with a crushed Compaq Presario monitor. A coffee maker. A file cabinet. A charred emergency exit door. An electric fan. Law books. A pair of Adidas. Cracked frames with photos of President George W. Bush and Defense Secretary Donald Rumsfeld.

I neared the smoke...I could see the fire, contained, brilliant.

I tripped and fell to one knee. A thick hardbound book lay before me, a cardstock ticket sticking out of its yellowed pages.

I carefully extracted it. The stub had been torn:

Roger Dean Stadium • Jupiter, Florida
Grapefruit League ~ Sat Mar 18 2000 ~ 1:15 p.m.
SAINT LOUIS CARDINALS
-vs.-
LOS ANGELES DODGERS
Sec 108 · Row 11 · Seat 4

"Get up, Benji."
I froze in place. I dared not look at him
Not in this place where I left him.
Where I drove him.

"It's okay, son," he said. "It's almost over."

Unconsciously, I snapped my head up. The fire illuminated his face.

He looked the same as he did that Tuesday morning, still wearing that white Navy uniform. His name plate read "UPSON."

I spat it out....

"...I'm so sorry, Dad..."

I lost control, and a father embraced his boy for the first time in nineteen years.

His name is John Eric Upson, Judge Advocate General for the United States Navy. He died at the Pentagon on the morning of September 11, 2001, at the hands of Tyranny himself.

Yet even the Gates of Hell couldn't keep us apart.

~

00:09:59

Pure water flowed endlessly from the canteen. I could have lapped at it for hours, and it never would have run dry. Dad stood upright against a crooked pillar of melted steel, arms folded, watching me intently.

"You look like Marie," he said. "Your mother."

I sat up against the wreckage. The fire rose steadily from this small clearing through the cracked roof several floors above. Where it touched the crimson sky, the red melted away in favor of a deep violet-blue night brightened by an infinity of stars.

"Most people say I look like you," I said.

Dad shuddered. "I would never wear anything as ugly as that Army green."

He read my nameplate.

"CAREW. As in Rod Carew?"

"Yeah. Cover for my last assignment."

"Where? When?"

"Manzanar. Christmas '44."

He whistled. "Tough place."

"The worst."

"Frank did a lot of penance over that."

"FDR?"

Dad walked over to sit next to me on the ground.

"The very same," he said. "Spry he is now, out of his wheelchair."

I felt my chest with my hand...the lead bullet still spun inside...

"I'm dead now, aren't I?"

"Not quite."

I gazed into the fire. "I've seen this place. The Ash Heap of History, where Tyranny reigns. This is where König and his comrades came when they died."

I looked at Dad.

"Why are you here?"

He raised his eyebrows. "This is where you left me, Benjamin."

My tongue dried in my throat. "Wh...what do you mean? You're real, aren't you?"

"Oh, yes, I'm real."

I scanned him up and down. "You're not dead either, are you?"

Dad shook his head.

"You're like Jack. In limbo." I couldn't hold back the tears. "For nineteen years?"

"For me, more like nineteen seconds," he explained. "I was headed to the courtyard just before the plane hit."

I was shattered, heavy-laden with guilt. "And the whole time...you've been a prisoner here?"

Dad brushed debris off his pants. "I'm no one's prisoner, Ben. At least...not the way you'd think."

I cocked my head. "I don't follow."

Dad twisted his lips, the way he always did whenever he was searching for a creative way of explaining something. I saw the light bulb go off.

"I'm guessing you entered here through your heart," he said. "Am I right?"

"Yeah. We did."

"If you entered your heart, where would you be?"

I shook my head and shrugged.

"Somewhere inside yourself."

I pondered. Then my heart sank. "So I'm imagining this. It isn't real."

"No. It's very real. Just as I am."

Dad pressed my hand against his body. It felt like Kennedy's.

"This place," he continued, "the Ash Heap as they call it…it's a breath away from all of us. It's where our Shadows lurk, just beneath the surface. You and your partners entered through your heart, the seat of your subconscious mind. So in this sense, Benji…I'm here because this is where you left me."

I felt it rising, the cresting wave, like it did that day at Huntington Beach Pier on April 14, 2002. This time, I didn't hold it back. Half a lifetime of guilt, anger and regret flooded from my heart, through my eyes and out onto the floor of this wretched world where I thought I had banished him. I collapsed my head onto my father's lap like a four-year-old. It never seemed to stop. He stroked my thick dark brown hair, same as his, and let me convulse for an eternity.

"It was my fault," I sobbed. "You wouldn't have come here…"

"No," he said. "No, no, no. It happened because it was going to happen. Let the Course have its shape. Forgive yourself, Benjamin."

The weight of infinity lifted from my shoulders.

My father and I spoke for what felt like years about everything and nothing.

"Nineteen years," I said, wiping my nose. "I can't believe it's been nineteen years."

I sighed.

"I've made a mess of my life, Dad. I don't even recognize myself. Bitter. Angry. Hostile. I'm forty-one, but I never grew any older than twenty-two. I even drove Michelle away. The most gentle, beautiful, intelligent soul in the world, and I walled myself off from her so I could stay angry at dead terrorists. They poisoned everything. They didn't just take *you* away from us. They took me, too."

Dad stared into the flames. "Tyranny took a lot more than three thousand that day."

I looked up at the patch of starlight beyond the red sky above. I reflected on the late Summer of 2001: the best of times, and then the worst of times, in the blink of an eye.

"Everything changed after that," Dad continued. "The Silent Echo of Tyranny reverberated across the country and around the world. Before that, at the dawn of the new millennium, we thought Liberty had him on his heels. The Soviet Union was gone. Democracy was on the ascent. But 9/11 gave Tyranny a second wind. It enabled him to wiggle through small things into the hearts and minds of the American people."

"Your murder was no small thing," I protested.

"No, you're right. It wasn't."

Dad folded his arms.

"Do you remember when we buried Rachel's cat in the backyard?"

"Scarface? Yeah, in the snow. It didn't go well."

"That's what happens when you give a Long Beach boy a shovel in Rocky Mountain permafrost."

"Didn't it bend the shovel?"

"It did, it did…"

"…we tried to burrow him in headfirst, like a drill…"

"…got him about halfway down…"

"…stiff tail sticking out of the ground like a flagpole…"

"… 'Dig, kitty! Dig!'…"

The Upson boys were in stitches.

"Oh, man," I said. "That was hilarious."

"It was, it was," Dad said. "For you and me…but not for my little girl."

Dad bit his lip.

"As much as I hated that mangy thing, Rachel loved it warts and all. Sardonic and irreverent my daughter may be, she is still my little girl. She has a tender, fragile heart made of flesh, not stone. You know she saw us digging from upstairs, right?"

"Yeah. She told me later."

"She never told me. She took it with her to my grave. Small thing," Dad pinched his fingers, "small crack. But weeds of resentment grew through it. Held it against me forever. It was traumatizing for an 11-year-old girl to watch her daddy mock a living thing she loved. I didn't mean it, but that didn't matter. Not to her. The large door of history swings on small hinges."

I braced myself.

"Same thing happened to you in the snow."

333

"Auraq."

"You think your deep animus toward the 'Other' started here at the Pentagon? That weed took root long before that. Then after 9/11, for you all of them were Auraq, whether you realized it or not. Deep in your heart, you believed they all hated America, they all hated me, and they all hated *you.*"

He stuck his finger in my chest to make his point.

"Bin Laden's henchmen took my body, but Tyranny aimed straight for that soft heart of yours and made it stone."

I looked away.

"Kiddo, don't take it personally. He did that to a lot of people that day. Turned my generation into a bunch of reactionaries addicted to legends peddled by that... 'President.'"

Dad made air quotes with his fingers.

"The Apprentice," I exhaled. "I sat out that election. Michelle was gone and I was just...numb. The past few years have been crazy, but until this journey I didn't really see what was happening, the things going on underneath the surface."

I shook my head.

"He has to be defeated."

Dad sighed. "Cut off one head of the dragon, and another will arise to take its place."

"So it's true. The Apprentice is the seventh head of Leviathan. The seventh head of Tyranny."

Dad shook his head. "A Tyrant can only arise if the people let him, Ben. And whether or not the Apprentice falls, his spirit will linger, just like Jackson's, just like Nixon's. You will contend with Tyranny for generation after generation until time draws to a close, and a winner is declared. Because Tyranny resides in only one place."

Dad leaned in and pointed his finger straight at my heart.

"The Republic belongs to the people, Benji. But only if we keep it, and after 9/11...we didn't. Because we forgot how to love our neighbors. Because we went *numb*."

I stuttered. "I-I was numb for months. Mom was a basket case. Rachel...she coped in her own way."

"An *entire nation* lacked the skills to cope with it. They say it was like Pearl Harbor, but I don't agree. Back in '41, they heard about it on the radio and read about it in the papers. In '01, we watched it on live television. And it was civilians, for the most part, not soldiers or sailors. Our neighbors, our co-workers, our husbands and fathers, mothers and daughters. It's natural to be enraged at an act of mass murder. It's what we did with that anger that would define us for generations to come."

I rubbed my eyes. "Dad, it was hard. It was so hard. You have no idea how much losing you ate me alive inside."

"Oh? I lost everyone."

Dad stuck his hands in his pockets.

"And Liberty lost another Champion."

Dad pulled out a coin, just like mine, only it wasn't made of gold. It was a precious metal like none I had ever seen, glinting with hues of gold and silver and bronze. Depending on the angle at which he held it against the fire, it refracted any and every color of the rainbow. Its brilliance was almost blinding.

I pulled mine out. The new inscription read:

UPON THE ALTAR OF GOD

"You were the Champion," I exhaled.

"For nine years. From the time we moved to Colorado until we came back to Virginia. I had to be ready to come to Pearl's aid at a moment's notice. Of course...that made me a target for König, just as Salaam was a target after me."

"It's no wonder I've had such a hard time with this. I've had such big shoes to fill."

Dad snickered. "Benji, I'm flattered. But I'm not the demigod you've spun so many legends about in that head of yours."

Dad searched the floor with his eyes.

"Liberty doesn't take perfect specimens into her crucible, son. She works her alchemy on any who seek her out. The tired, the poor, the huddled masses – we're all just *prima materia* she transforms by fire into the most precious metal. Boy did Pearl have her work cut out for her with a self-righteous son of a bitch like me."

"The hell you say, Dad."

"The apple doesn't fall far, son."

Dad sighed.

"You never knew your grandparents, Jim and Esther Upson."

I paused. "You mean Esther Atwater...don't you?"

"Yes. Those Atwaters were crazy folk, she told me."

Dad sighed.

"Anyway, your grandparents were wonderful people, but especially her. Losing both of them at fourteen gutted me. For the next ten years, I looked sideways at every Mexican or Spanish-speaking person I saw, because *one* drunk Mexican drove his car into them. It was irrational, but it gave me someone to blame other than God or chance. It wasn't until law school that Professor Gates threw me a life vest."

"Zora," I exhaled.

"She saw right through me. I went to law school to make a boatload of money to fill the void my parents left. I told her as much during office hours, told her about the accident. I even confessed to the roots of my bigotry, thinking she would sympathize with me and help me work through it. Boy, was I wrong."

"What did she say?"

"She told me about this time when she was twenty, on the Fourth of July. She was at some diner minding her own business when some racist punk verbally accosted her. Turns out that Pearl was the waitress and came to her aid; thats when they became friends. And do you know what Zora told me next?"

I leaned in, riveted.

"She said, *'I would be well within my rights to use that one white man's racism to hate all white people, and that was far from the only time it happened. It still happens. I could have turned my death by a thousand cuts into a rally cry for bloody revenge. But I didn't. And neither, for that matter, have most of my black brothers and sisters whose ancestors were dragged here across a sea of fire, or the millions of every color and creed who crawled to this city on a hill on broken glass...*

"Our last best hope for refuge from the reign of Tyranny may chew us up and spit us out, but we keep coming...and coming...and coming...because we see the lighthouse in the fog. We see her in her rapturous glory, and we keep our chins up and our eyes on Liberty, never forgetting our hard beginnings but never letting ourselves be defined by them. And you know something, John Upson? That is exactly why they come across the border, too.'"

Dad was getting riled up...at *himself.* I never saw this side of him in all of his years alive on this planet. He was always the cool voice of reason in rooms churning with fire.

"Professor Gates reached across the table and took my hands and said, *'John, there are many like you in this country who nurse your grievances against the stranger, the fatherless and the widow, who wrap it in the flag and call it patriotic. But to real patriots? It's just pathetic.'"*

I flinched.

"Then she threw a glass of tea in my face."

I laughed out loud. "She does that."

"It was my baptism," Dad laughed. "A way of sobering me up to see that my selfish little Tea Parties were nothing more than pity parties. It took years to transform into the man I was, to become husband to Marie and father to Ben and Rachel. It required an alchemy of the heart, mind and soul. Just like the one you've undertaken. The one initiated by Zora's grandson, the son of another Champion de-railed by injustice. The one you have followed through, until it brought you here to me."

Dad stood and lifted me with him.

"You found Excalibur," he said excitedly.

I nodded.

"Show me."

I moved the flag and unbuttoned my jacket.

"It's still in there, isn't it?" he marveled. "It's still spinning."

I nodded. "A sword in a heart of stone."

Dad shook. "Was it Morgan?"

I nodded. "I guess you could say the Sheriff shot *me.*"

Dad looked away. "He's a real son of a bitch, you know that?"

"Was," I corrected. "Nicholas Morgan *was* a son of a bitch."

Dad's eyes widened. "What do you mean 'was?' What happened?"

I shrugged.

"You tell me right now…"

"I dragged him here," I said. "Squirming and cowering. Then Minty put an end to him."

Dad chuckled deliriously. "You're kidding."

I shook my head. "No, sir."

"God bless you, Harriet. Morgan has been the quiet influence behind every act of lawful injustice since 1836. He targeted me for years. Used to call me John Brown."

"Me, too."

Dad covered his mouth, his eyes shifting ponderously.

"Tyranny will find a replacement. He always does. Still…my son has truly become greater than I."

He adjusted the flag on my shoulders.

"But let us not speak falsely. The hour is late. The battle is not yet won. To preserve Liberty on Earth, you must kindle her flame here in the Ash Heap."

"Pearl," I said. "She's in the Temple. In the Rotunda."

"König has captured the Innermost Chamber, and now he's running out the clock."

Clock. I checked the timer on my phone:

00:08:15

I was startled by the sound of a bugle blowing reveille in the distance. I heard the thunder of footsteps and the whinnying of horses. I grabbed Dad by the jacket.

He gently pushed my hand away. "Relax. You're in the Army now. Your generals approach."

Dad led me out of the crevasse. Through the ashen snow, four riders approached on the red horizon, a fifth horse running in tow. Each rider carried a shield.

"Four horsemen," I exhaled, "and me. I feel like the odds are stacked 10-to-1 against us."

Dad pondered. "Do you remember your first Angels game?"

"Of course. Against the Royals. Reggie Jackson hit his 500th home run."

"Do you remember the final score?"

I closed my eyes. "Royals 10, Angels 1."

"Ten to the those with the kingly power of Royals; one to those who dance with the better Angels of our nature."

"Ten percent," I laughed.

"With these four, I'd say I like your odds."

As the riders approached, I knew immediately what he meant.

~

The cherry blossoms bloom as Tyson and Sara gaze out over the Tidal Basin at the Jefferson Memorial.

"They would make such a cute couple," Anna Bannister giggles.

"Possibly," I say. "He has to get over himself, first."

Daniel calls Anna over. I sneak up within earshot of the Cute Couple...

"...he's intimidated," Tyson says. "T.J. talks a good game, but he knows he can't walk it."

"He's suuuuch a good writer, though," Sara responds. "That quote on the ceiling gave me chills."

Tyson grins. "Girl, all I gotta do is read you the Declaration of Independence?"

Sara laughs. She peers over her shoulder at a man emerging from a slab of white granite.

"He's pretty forgiving," she says. "I'll bet they're friends now."

Tyson snorts. "Doubt it."

"Why not? Isn't that his dream?"

Tyson grimaces.

"What?"

"My grandma used to say that just because something is self-evident doesn't mean it's self-executing."

Sara arches her eyebrows. "What's that mean?"

"It means," Tyson answers, "there's gotta be truth before reconciliation."

Sara ponders. "Huh. I never really thought of it that way."

Tyson thinks about taking Sara's hand...then backs off.

"You're right, though," he says. "He is a good writer..."

He looks back at the man in granite.

"...but he's no King."

~

He strode in on the back of a white Arabian. Martin Luther King Jr. was not as I imagined. His right cheek bore the faded remnant of an entry wound traveling through to his left shoulder. He was driven by temerity and tempered by severity, with fire in his eyes and belly. A man of peace teetering on the edge of war, his sole weapon was the silver horn on his back.

Beside Dr. King a tall ginger-headed man rode atop a golden palomino. Thomas Jefferson's face was solemn and penitent; he radiated humble certitude from his core. He had the air of a man who came to his convictions long before his courage, whose every action was soaked in redemptive purpose. His right arm was stiff from his wrist to his elbow; his horse carried a white feather the size of a Scottish claymore in its mouth.

Flanking King and Jefferson on either side were Ira, carrying a 48-starred flag like a lance atop a black destrier, and Minty on a red mustang. Behind her, Minty towed a fifth horse, a silver-coated Friesian mare with golden mane and a shield on her saddle.

"*Noxie,*" I whispered. *"The Night Horse."*

Dr. King dismounted and approached. "John, is this your boy?"

Dad nodded. "Dr. King, Benjamin John Upson. Ben, this is…"

"Martin Luther King," I exhaled.

"Junior," he said, extending his hand. *"'Honor thy father and thy mother, so that it may go well for you in the land the Lord thy God has given you.'"*

I grasped his hand nervously as Jefferson offered his.

"Benjamin," Jefferson said. "It will be an honor to ride with you Today."

Puzzled, I moved my finger back and forth. "You two are friends?"

Dr. King grinned. "Cain did not cease to be Abel's brother when his blood found the soil. Neither do I fear my brother's Shadow in the valley of death, nor he mine."

Jefferson brought his hand to his chin. "Upon the scales of judgment, I was weighed and found wanting. My sins earned me a place here in the Ash Heap. But through a journey through the dark night, often with Martin nearby, I found peace in penitence. Now I remember my oath. I will never crack the slaver's whip again. It has my hostility now and evermore."

Dr. King looked to Dad, sorrowfully. "It's a shame you won't be joining us, John."

I swiveled my head. "You're not coming?"

Dad bowed his head. "My sands run low. My nineteen seconds are nearly up."

My heart sank. "Understood."

He set his hand on my shoulder. "Let's get you in the saddle, shall we?"

Minty brought Noxie forward by the harness.

"Hey girl," I said, petting her dazzling coat. "It's been nearly a second."

Noxie neighed sweetly as I climbed into the saddle. Dad grabbed the harness.

John Eric Upson guided Noxie around to the north side of the Pentagon to the ruins of the Navy-Merchant Marine Memorial, by the banks of the oil-and-tar-slicked Potomac. I dismounted.

"This is where I leave you," Dad said. "Your generals will lead you across the river."

I looked north toward the Arlington Memorial Bridge, leading from Arlington National Cemetery to the Lincoln Memorial. The Potomac boiled over with hot sludge onto dead grass. Beyond, I heard the low din of millions of Shadows marching on the Mall.

"Pop," I said. "I can't do this without you."

Dad grabbed me tight. "You don't need me, Benjamin. The Shadows you fight Today are from *your* mind. Take heed of the wisdom of those who have gone before you, but in the end your own counsel you must keep."

Dad looked to the four horseback warriors.

"Today, will you ride with the Champion?"

They answered in unison. "Aye!"

Dad looked to me. "Where Tyranny confuses, consolidates and controls, Liberty enlightens, empowers and engages. You are the sword, Benjamin. Drive deep into König's heart, and put all of his Apprentices on notice, from now until the end of time, that we answer to Her alone."

I let the tears stream down.

"Am I ever going to see you again?" I asked.

Pop snapped his fingers. "In the blink of an eye."

He kissed me on the forehead and cradled my face.

"Hang together."

"Or we'll all hang separately."

I let him go and pulled back onto Noxie.

"Oh, one more thing," Dad said. "You left these on the coffee table."

He retrieved three empty beer bottles and tucked them into my saddlebag.

"In case you encounter any Rogues along the way."

Son of a bitch. I laughed and saluted. "I dig it."

I turned to my generals.

"Warriors! *Let's roll!*"

I kicked the Night Horse into gear, and my generals followed up Mount Vernon Trail. I turned to see my father saluting at full attention. Speck-by-speck, he faded to ash and floated away to the navy starlight above. At the Pentagon a fire went out, and for the first time since Tuesday morning, I was whole.

Good. I have a Tyrant to overthrow.

Twenty Eight

Field of Broken Dreams

From the foot of the Lincoln Memorial they hissed and howled, moaned and growled. Countless tar black Shadows, silhouettes of thought in base human form, peeled themselves raw from the sky and filled the four corners of the Ash Heap.

My Shadows...and Ours. Yours and Mine.

The seventh head of Tyranny.

The muddy Reflecting Pool teemed with oil black frogs, croaking and growling as they rose from the hidden depths of the abyss. They were restrained from attacking by some invisible barrier. Cecil Barton, Tyranny's Censor, stood in a suit and bowtie in the shallow waters on the near end of the Pool, madly shouting whispers at us. From the cracked Monument, an old anthem echoed like a scratchy phonograph...

"...O beautiful for spacious skies..."

...I picked up spare words from a layered track underneath...

((...justice...liberty...strength...your eyes...))

I sensed these Shadows were energized by the agitprop. As their angry energy grew, so did my irritation. A thick cloud of melancholy and confusion descended upon my mind and settled in.

Sound and fury. The first wave of resistance.

I checked the clock:

00:07:22

Dr. King approached. "Before we move an inch past these steps, we have to override that signal."

"Right," I replied. "Send the trolls back to the basement."

"What are your orders, Benjamin?"

"I... what...you don't *know*...?"

Dr. King put his hand up. "I know *exactly* what I would do. But you are the Champion, and we came here through *your* mind. Only *you* have authority to command."

"Right."

I relaxed and closed my eyes, settling into my own body. I tuned into the frequency carrying that subtle B track into my mind….

((…justice…liberty…strength…your eyes…))

((…your eyes…))

Pearl's face flashed in front of me. *Her eyes.* Those shimmering emeralds.

Emeralds…Oz…that's it.

"It's time we paid attention to the man behind the curtain."

I kicked Noxie into gear.

"Hya!"

The horsemen charged down the steps, stopping before Barton and dismounting at water's edge. I stepped to within an inch of Barton's breath. He was nervous and panicked, sweating oil and tar. A black raven sat on his shoulder, whistling airily into his ear. Barton repeated the raven's mad ravings word for feckless word:

"The haji killed your daddy he killed your daddy they all killed your daddy how can you trust them they don't love America they don't know America but you know America they're coming to take it away it's not racist to think that it's not racist to say that the globalists are saying that build a wall build a wall make them pay and build the wall around your country around your home around your family around your heart and mind and…"

I stepped back. "I'm tired of this channel."

Dr. King pulled the horn from his back. It was long and sleek with no valves, and made of the purest silver.

"Fill our ears with that pure sound, sir."

Dr. King brought the horn to his lips.

"Time to wake the sleeping giants," he proclaimed in his ministerial tone.

Dr. King pointed the bell directly into Barton's face. The raven twitched – as the Censor accelerated his delirium:

"...I don't see this I don't hear this I won't speak this 'cause it's fake fake FAKE FAKE FAKE you FAKER you LIAR you HYPOCRITE you SNOWFLAKE ESS-JAY-DOUBLE-YEW..."

Dr. King pressed his lips against the mouthpiece and blew...

...a deep vibration rumbled, and then...

...BOOOOOM!!!!!...

...the sonic blast knocked Barton one hundred yards into the Reflecting Pool; his raven squawked and turned to fire, flying east toward the monument. Barton screamed as he hit the sizzling waters and dissolved to black smoke, then streamed away. The Reflecting Pool boiled the frogs alive...

...they croaked and they choked...

...kekkk...

....kekkk...

...kekkk...

...with each empty croak and each empty choke, my mind grew sharper...

...and sharper...

...as if a cloud lifted...

...the frequency hum stopped...

...and I could see with absolute clarity.

As the pure sound swept through the Ash Heap, the Washington Monument convulsed with lightning and thunder...it cracked at the foundation, splitting up the side all the way to the apex before the stone crumbled, raining debris upon the Shadows as it fell to the Earth, crushing everything below. Where the Monument stood, a skinny copper tower shorted, sending sparks flying. The anthem ceased, and the tower played only the hidden track underneath:

Oppression is justice
Bondage is liberty
Your eyes tell you lies
Look upon the gaslight
For your eyes tell you lies

The sound was nauseating and sour now absent its sweet honey coating. I watched the fiery raven land on the opposite side of the Pool. It unfurled its wings and spun as it grew and grew into the fiery shape of a man. The fire abated, and a figure emerged in red-and-white robes, an elderly man...

...

...Father Carlo...

...

"The man behind the curtain," Jefferson said. "Cardinal Carlo di Lorenzo, Tyranny's Hierophant."

The old fraud, the wolf in sheep's clothing, screamed. Black fire rose from his mouth and nostrils, shouting into the void:

"I am the way! I am the truth! None shall come to Liberty but by me!"

His volume increased exponentially, nearly shattering my eardrums. Twelve Shadows emerged from behind the Monument to encircle it.

"The Censor keeps the lie under wraps," I panted. "The lie first told by the Hierophant, the False Prophet."

"Unquestioned orthodoxy," Jefferson seethed. "Tyranny over the mind. It has my eternal hostility."

"You've exposed it, Ben," Dr. King said. "Now you must extinguish it."

I examined the giant feather in the mouth of Jefferson's horse...

...from the horse's mouth...

"Tom," I charged, "has anyone told you that the pen is mightier than the sword?"

"Of course," Jefferson replied, looking to Dr. King. "But it's self-evident that a powerful voice can carry the message further."

Jefferson removed the feather. He knelt before the Reflecting Pool and dipped the tip into the black waters. It soaked the entire feather, turning it silvery gray. Jefferson pulled the feather from the water and presented before Dr. King.

"No Justice flows from unclean hands," Jefferson declared.

Dr. King pointed the horn at the feather and slowly blew. A higher-pitched sound flew out and scorched the feather with red and blue fire. The flames melted the feather into a pure pewter blade with a bronze hilt.

Jefferson held out the sword to examine in it. He flicked his wrist, and it fanned out into five blades, one for each rider. He tossed one to each of us.

"Mr. Jefferson," I commanded. "Strike down the False Prophet with extreme prejudice. Dr. King? Let's play something in a higher key. *Hya!*"

We rode hard east across the black waters of the Reflecting Pool, with Jefferson in the vanguard. The waters behind us turned to pure crystalline blue in our wake. The blackness seemed to retreat away from us, and each successive step grew harder and harder as the black water became thicker and thicker, as if it had turned to tar. As we bore down on Father Carlo, a gnawing sense of doubt and opposition arose from within.

((...no...you can't....not you...God said so...))

I shook it off...

((...reason and logic...the Devil's tools they are...))

"Ben!" Dr. King shouted. "Remember your oath!"

Jefferson raised his sword, prepared to strike.

((...he can't rebel...the LAW is the LAW...))

Father Carlo steadied himself to breathe fire and brimstone on us, his eyes red with hostile intent...

...hostility...

I shouted directly at Father Carlo. "I have sworn upon the altar of God..."

...Jefferson reached...

"...eternal hostility..."

...Jefferson swung...

"...over *every* form of Tyranny..."

...Jefferson connected...

"...over the mind of man!"

Noxie leapt from the water and landed ten feet past the edge. I circled her back in time to watch Father Carlo, cleaved in two, disintegrate to smoke and black ash.

The Tower went silent. The waters were pure...

...

00:07:01

Three heads down, three to go.

The eerie quiet on the Mall made me uneasy. It brought our daunting next task into sharper relief.

The Shadows before us were unlike any I'd encountered. They were just as shapeless and malignant and formless as the others, if not more so. But they were denser. Stronger. Each carried the form of a spear. I sensed that they could do real harm...even to my friends here.

"Deadcoats," Minty panted. "The General's troops."

She pointed two miles East toward the Capitol. Where General Grant once rode Cincinnati, General Maurice Travers sat atop a pale horse of death, holding a scythe in his hand. The General roared, and the Deadcoats echoed, banging their spears against the ground.

"How are we getting past them?" I asked.

"Concentrated power of will," Minty proclaimed. "The General rules by force, we must counter it."

As she spoke, line-by-line the Deadcoats marched toward the Monument.

"They're gonna try and disable it," Ira observed. "If we send up our signal, it'll weaken their defenses."

Shit. Think...

The Deadcoats pressed forward, methodically.

...this is a terrible dream...

...

"Dr. King! Do you remember all of your dreams?"

"I just might," he answered.

"You and Minty climb that tower. Move the beacon and find that signal."

I turned to Ira and Jefferson.

"We'll hold them off on the ground."

My generals agreed. "Yessir."

"Forward. *Hya!*"

We rode to the base of the tower. Minty and Dr. King leapt onto the side scaffolding and began their ascent. As they did, the Deadcoats broke into a run with a rebel yell.

The three of us below dug in and braced ourselves for slaughter…

…

00:02:49

The Deadcoats were winning, wearing us down by attrition as white ash swirled. We fought off every wave, dissolving each soldier with sharp pewter. Every time we did, the sound of silence from the tower grew more deafening. Scores of Deadcoats leapt onto the tower. Minty alone dispatched most of them as Dr. King struggled against their pull to inch up to the antenna. It was slow going.

Below, the howling Deadcoats focused their attacks on me. I deflected most with the shield, but occasional glances and blows would nick my person, sparking sharp pain, sadness and discouragement. These enemies were the storms of life itself, the lies and injustices we inflict upon one another. Every time we cleared a wave, joyful for a moment that sunlight had broken through, another would follow, stronger than the last. The General had taken it upon himself to ride forward, pacing back and forth on his pale horse and twirling his scythe like a baton. It was as if we fought the night itself…

…

00:01:55

…the rings of Saturn closed on us from all sides, strangling us.

Then they inflicted their first casualty.

Ira Hayes fell by the spear, his horse with him.

I wept vinegar for him, stinging my eyes, as his lifeless husk lay motionless on the ground beneath his destrier…

…

00:01:17

…above, Minty hadn't moved in minutes.

A Deadcoat neared the antenna.

Fifty feet below, an exhausted Dr. King aimed his sword at the Deadcoat and flung it through him, impaling him on the ground.

Now he had nothing to fight with…

…

00:00:57:56…55…54…

...Jefferson fell, and with him his memory.

Dr. King was near the top, knocking Deadcoats away with his shield. He was almost out of gas.

The General swung his scythe around, hungry to kill...

...

00:00:47:08...07...06...

...I gained my second wind and annihilated a host of Deadcoats, bellowing at the top of my lungs. For the first time, I saw that the Shadows were afraid.

They dropped their slings and arrows, in retreat, making a lane between me...

...and the General.

He mocked and cursed the Shadows and spat fire onto the ground. He held the scythe out toward me, ready for a joust.

I had nothing left.

Neither did Noxie. She collapsed to the ground, exhausted. I fell with her, and rested against Ira's destrier.

The Capitol rose before me. The Statue of Freedom was excised from its meridian. Tyranny was now the tallest thing in Washington, in spite of all my striving...my fires were nearly out...

...the General spun his scythe...I could hear him whisper...

((...I could kill you here or on Fifth Avenue, and still you would be mine...))

...I imagined what it would be like when his flag ascended every pole in the land. To the naked eye, it would look no different than the one draped around my shoulders. Underneath it would bleed red and gold...

...Travers circled as he lowered the scythe. White ash painted the red sky around him. In the blink of an eye I knew that I truly would never see my father again...

...

...five hundred feet above, a single finger flipped a switch.

...an antenna moved, ever so slightly...

...it picked up a signal from another Tower, whose torch swirled with copper and lead...

...the torch whirled to life...and a subtle hymn spun back...

((...I have a dream...))

I felt my strength return.

The General gave no indication that he heard it.

But someone behind me did:

"You picked a hell of a hill to die on."

I began to turn...

"Eyes front!"

The pale horse dug in to make its final charge.

"Let him come to you."

I tightened up. "Yessir."

I stared Travers down and held my arms out. The General sneered and kicked the pale horse into gear. Mud flew as the colt dashed forward...

"Steady..."

...my heart raced...

"...wait..."

...he was nearly upon me...

"...not yet..."

...I braced myself...

"...NOW!"

I ducked left as Travers swung the scythe.

"HOO-RAH!"

From the ground, Corporal Ira Hayes leapt onto the pale horse. He tackled the General and wrested the scythe from him in one fluid motion. Ira tucked and rolled up to his feet, took three steps forward and mercilessly slashed the General's throat. Travers choked as black tar gushed from his neck, evaporating into black smoke. In seconds, his body dissolved into thin air, joining his Brothers elsewhere.

The Deadcoats screamed and dissolved with him.

The Mall was clear. Jefferson rode up beside Ira, who turned to me and saluted.

"We await our next command, sir," he said.

Noxie crawled back to her feet and shook herself out. Shakily, I stood.

"Thank you, Ira," I said. "Truly. For everything. Thank you."

He nodded.

Dr. King and Minty descended. The volume on the Tower crescendoed to a roar. A righteous man spoke truth to power in the language of dreams; it echoed to the red mountains of Georgia and back.

I checked the clock.

00:00:26:21...20...19...

I climbed onto the back of Noxie and took the reins.

"We ride."

Jefferson eyed me close. "Something tells me you won't be needing your sword."

"Tom, I *am* the sword. *Hya!"*

We charged forward across the empty Mall. We rode unmolested up the embankment and leapt, crashing through the glass doors of the Speaker's Balcony into the Capitol.

We had breached the Temple Mount.

Twenty Nine

Den of Thieves

00:00:22:38...37...36...

The Capitol corridors were cold and uninviting, yet they drew us in. We encountered no Shadows. They had all been dispatched to the Mall, and disposed of in kind.

We found Gould hiding behind an ornate chair in the Speaker's Suite. With no Hierophant to shroud his greed in religiosity, no Censor to twist the minds of his subjects, no General to conquer worlds and markets on his behalf and no Sheriff to do his dirty work, the Oligarch had nothing and no one to protect him. One look at us, and the joker fled like a thief in the night.

So it is with Mammon: any earnest weapon raised against him shall prosper.

And he left us with another. Ira examined Gould's cane in his hand, pointing at the golden bundle of rods with the head of an axe.

"I've never known what this thing is."

"A *fasces,*" I said, turning it over in my hand. "Ancient Roman symbol for power."

He handed it to me. "You'll need all the power you can get."

Minty approached. "He has her in the Rotunda. We don't have much time. What are your orders?"

I looked around at my four horsemen. This was excellent company to keep.

"Haunt the castle," I said.

I pulled Dad's three glass bottles from my saddlebag, then slipped them onto my right thumb, index and pinky fingers.

Dr. King cocked his head. "And might I ask what you plan to do with those?"

I grinned from ear to ear. "Dr. King, when you've spent the last thirteen years of your life with teenagers, you learn the hard way the power of mockery and scorn."

~

00:11:53...52...51...
I watched from the shadows as König knelt in front of Pearl's near lifeless form, whispering sweet nothings into her ear. She looked frail and gaunt, broken by a malignant and selfish shell of a man who sought to make her his puppet. This was where we first met, when the roof tore apart and fire fell from the sky. Now a reddish-pink hue illuminated the center, a beam of light tapering like an hourglass as it rose from the floor up through the crimson heavens.
((...no time...unless you accept...Liberty will surely fall...))
I took a deep breath...and began...
...clink...clink...clink...
The clinking of the bottles was repetitive...cloying...*irritating...*

...like a horde of cicadas, it was low...subtle...*eternal...*

...the kind of sound that slips under one's skin...

...down to the final nerve...

König slowly panned the rotunda, sniffing as if the vicious idiot could smell sound. Subtly, just under his left temple, he...

...pulsed...pulsed...pulsed...

...and he...

...ticked...ticked...ticked...

...as I...

...clinked...clinked...clinked...

...oozing under his skin, rubbing him raw from the inside out...

...König spun around in place...the acoustics made it impossible to know where the sound was coming from...

...and then, starting with a whisper, then repeating over...and over...and over again...until it roared like a lion announcing itself to its prey...

"Koooooooöniiiiig...come out to plaaaay-ay..."

...over...and over...and over....

...and over...until...

"Shut up." he hissed. *"Ich bin der Herr dieses Reiches! Gehorche meinen Befehlen!"*

No. I didn't obey.

"Zeig dein Gesicht, du Feigling!"

"I'm here."

BANG! König fired his Walther into Minty's entryway...*1*...

"...no, here..." BANG! 2...

"...not there..." BANG! 3...

"...here..." BANG! 4...

"...listen..." BANG! 5...

"...warmer..."

BANG! 6...

"...hotter..." BANG! 7...

"...ice cold..." BANG! 8...

...two left.

"Can o' corn!" I yelled.

I chucked two bottles into the air with the loft of a Texas Leaguer. As König fired and shattered them both, I *zinged* the third square into his nose. Black blood flowed as he grasped his face, squinting and cursing.

Engage.

I ran full speed into the Rotunda and charged into König's body, knocking him into the Signing of the Declaration. He slumped against the wall; I pushed him to the ground. I reared back with the fasces and brought it down hard toward his face. He reached up and blocked it. I kept pushing, and he kept pushing, strength against strength, line against line, neither budging...

...then König released...driving his knee into my gut...

...*oomph!*...

...*gasp!*...

...knocking the wind out of me. Momentum wedged the *fasces* into the marble floor an inch from König's head. He thrust me off of him; I landed next to Pearl in stinging pain. König yanked the *fasces* from the floor. He stood and brushed his suit, noticing a small tear in his jacket on the left lapel.

"*Tsk-tsk-tsk.* This is a bespoke Brioni! You can't just buy this off the rack, Ben!"

He flung off the jacket and tore off his tie, unbuttoning the top collar of his shirt and loosening his cuffs. He looked me up and down and let out a mocking laugh.

"First, you are Stasi and try to kill me, now you are U.S. Army and try to kill me. Honestly, Benjamin, are you sure you know where your loyalties truly lie?"

He spied Betsy draped around my shoulders, keying in on Platov's burn mark in the middle of the circle of stars.

"I admire your commitment to your flag. But *thirteen* stars?"

He moved his hands back and forth.

"*Ehhhh*, that's some tacky nostalgia, don't you think? I mean, talk about clinging to the past! But I'll give you some credit, Ben. I look in your eyes, and I see you have resolved your daddy issues."

He golf clapped. Then wagged his finger.

"But I still have a toe-hold."

König rushed forward and kicked me *hard* in the groin and spat.

"Sterile cuck! *You...are...no...man!*"

I rolled over and groaned. Pearl lay next to me, eyes swirling gray and mouth moving mechanically, making inarticulate sounds. She was fading fast.

"But *she...she* is a real woman," König boasted as he loomed over her. "Absolutely beautiful."

I gazed up at him in surprise contempt.

"What? You think I don't love Liberty too? You think the strongest man in the world would *hate* its most beautiful woman?"

He knelt and stroked her silver-gray hair.

"I would *never* kill my own bride on our wedding day, which you so *rudely* interrupted."

König stood to look at his watch.

"In five minutes, she will be as alive as I am. Forever my bride of stone, an empress of beauty, *Liberty and Tyranny as one.*"

((...not kill...snuff out...))

König stood over me, feet planted on either side of my hips.

"What good is beauty if you can't have it to yourself?"

He squatted slowly, then crawled his hands out on all fours. Tyranny in all of his infinite horror weighed down upon my heart, mind, body and soul, as König crawled out and smothered me with his body and breath. Black tar oozed from every pore, dripping from his dark, empty essence onto my skin. It burned, and I bellowed in pain.

"You wish you could be me," he whispered. "You and I are a lot alike you know. I was restless, too. Angry. Bored. Yet there is a difference between you and me. *I have no use for love.*"

He kissed me on the forehead. It burned, and I screamed...

"Power is far greater than love, Benjamin. You choose love, and power will take it from you...*every...single...time.*"

König drove his fist into my solar plexus. I howled as he squeezed my cheeks together with one hand.

"Love never returns affection. Love is your enemy. It gives nothing, and *takes everything.*"

((...you came to take what isn't yours...))

((...you took it all away from me...))

...black smoke crawled from König's nostrils, into the shape of a frog, then that of a man, a beast, a Shadow of a man. *Turannos* was here, in my own image. I relaxed and surrendered as he descended upon me, letting the tar sink under my skin. As König cackled with delight, the oily black flowed through every vein and into the Innermost Chamber of my heart, sending me a world away...

...

...I awake with a jolt on cold cement.

The walls are bright and fluorescent. The clock reads 3:21. The darkness of pre-dawn suffocates the skylight fifty feet above, funneling down into the narrow confines of the stark white cell, where an oppressive black mold grows in the corner.

I roll to my side. There's a book under the bed, a paperback. I reach for it and slide it across the floor. I spin it around to see the title on the binding:

Mankind's Search for Meaning
by Viktor Frankl

Michelle...
I sit up and flip it open to the title page...there it is...in red marker....

For Benji,

The man whose heart beats forever, and mine with it.

<<Tes yeux sont comme les étoiles du ciel>>
Love forever,
Shell

My heart climbs up my neck.
"Benji? Is that you?"
There she sits...on the edge of the twin bed in a blue jumpsuit. She is thin and frail, her face gaunt, her eyes saddled with shadowy bags, her sandy blond hair stringy and tangled. Her right cheek bears the echoes of a bruise...she is broken, and she is radiant...

"Michelle," I tremble. "Sweetheart. Where...where are we? What happened? Where have you been?"

She looks away. "Texas. They got us, Benji..."

My pulse accelerates. "Who?"

"Homeland. ICE. Customs. Whoever they are."

Michelle looks me up and down. I could see the whites of her baby blues.

"Are you here? Or are you just another Shadow to torment me?"

I slowly put my hands on her bare arms, lightly tickling the skin. I haven't felt her touch in four years.

"It's like a lucid dream," I say. "It's really me, Puddin'."

She laughs, with no loft in her spirit. "More like a lucid nightmare."

Michelle lifts her arms. She is chained to the bed.

"I wear them for him now."

I swallow all of my pride. "To think you once wore them for me."

"Benji, no..."

"...yes, you did. I put them on you. I held you captive to my pain, and I burdened you with putting my broken dreams back together."

I looked away.

"I'm not the young man you met in Georgetown. I haven't been for a very long time."

"No. You aren't."

She lifts my chin and scans my eyes.

"You're something different altogether."

"I've had a hell of a year."

She trembles and bites her lip. "Me too."

"How did this happen?"

Michelle sniffs and nods at the bed on the opposite wall. He's only a boy, no more than eleven. Latino, dark brown skin. He's fast asleep, curled up with a stuffed otter in his shackled arms. He has a red wristband with a number and a name:

VILLALOBOS, JUAN

"I've been treating Johnny for two years. Goes by Johnny so the white kids at school don't tease him. The cartels killed his papa, and he and his mama escaped to Colorado. ICE raided his house in Arvada, then I followed him here and demanded access. When I saw what they did to him..."

Michelle's head drops.

"...he reminds me of you, Benji..."

Michelle bawls. I embrace her.

"They're torturing children, Benji. These pieces of shit are torturing children..."

I rock her. "I know."

She sniffles. "They flagged my file. They claimed I fraudulently obtained my citizenship, that I married you just to stay."

My breathing becomes heavy. "Nobody called me about this. Nobody knows you're gone?"

"It's been over a month. I couldn't talk to a lawyer. I haven't spoken to Papa or anyone. People in here are getting sick...very sick...something is happening here...and they don't care who lives or dies..."

Michelle shook her head.

"What am I going to do, Benji?"

I search desperately for words of comfort. I remember the book.

"There is hope," I say. "Even in the darkest hours, when the walls are caving in on you, there is always hope. Because you have purpose. Because you are alive. Because you have love."

I glance over at the little boy on the other bed. He coughs violently...my heart shatters for him...

"Do what you can for Johnny. I will find you. I promise you."

I caress the bruise on her cheek, my heart broken.

"Tell me who did this to you."

"Benji –"

"I need to know."

She cries and holds my hand against her cheek, and in a flash I see it. I see the man – the coward, shielded by the law – who struck my wife with a billy club. It drives me back to tears.

"I'm so sorry." I wipe my cheek. "I'm so sorry."

Michelle looked deep into my eyes. "I have vivid dreams every night. This is the first time it feels real. How do I know it is?"

I glance down at her left hand, to the third finger. The diamond glistens. It gives me a spark of hope.

I slowly remove the band from my finger and slide it onto hers. I hold her hands in mine.

"When you wake up, you'll have two rings on your finger. Then you'll know."

I can't stave off the flow.

"I don't know what happens next. But this I swear upon the altar of God. I will always love you unconditionally. I ache for you to be mine again, but more than anything I want you to be yours. Free to be the beauty you are, to shine your light upon the world. That is the Greatest Love I can give you."

I kiss her. Deeply. Passionately.

And then I let go.

I mouth, 'I love you.'

Michelle reciprocates. 'Je t'adore.'

She puts her hand on my face, caressing the scarring at my temple.

"I keep hearing this whisper, and I can't get it out of my head."

All around us, the walls catch fire. Michelle pulls me close and whispers into my ear.

((...the sword needs a wet stone...))

...

The dreamscape dissolved. König snapped his fingers.

"Ben. For fuck's sake, snap the fuck out of it."

The Shadow was gone.

I laughed...and laughed...and *laughed*...

König snorted. *"You've lost it, pal."*

Still laughing, I whispered softly.

"I surrender."

König furrowed his brow.

"What?"

"I surrender."

He grinned and pressed his nose close to me.

"Ben," he whispered, *"I need you to say th – "*

The waters gathered...

...I spat...

…straight into his left eye.

König screamed as the saliva burned scalding hot in his tear ducts. I looked to Pearl.

Hang on!

I rolled König over and kneed him in the groin, then stood him up and dragged him by the collar of his shirt, kicking and screaming. I pulled him fifteen feet past the exit and dropped him on the ground, giving him a right cross to the face.

"I hate to be the bearer of bad news," I seethed. "But your trophy wife just left you at the altar."

Ira, Minty, Jefferson and Dr. King surrounded us.

"Do you mind babysitting?" I asked.

Minty nodded. "Go."

I raced back into the Rotunda. Pearl pressed herself up unevenly, buoyed by a second wind. I retrieved the *fasces* cane and rushed to the edge. I wedged the axe-head into the corner of the floor and wall and dragged it in a wide circle around the Rotunda. It sparked and burst into multi-colored flame. The fires climbed the walls and up the underside of the dome.

Panting, I offered Pearl my hand and pulled her upright.

"Who taught you how to do that?" she asked, weakly.

"A little bird," I replied.

I wrapped the flag around us both. Pearl stared at the gaping hole above the Rotunda.

"She looks majestic, doesn't she?"

I looked up with her, where the fresco once was. A speck of yellow light broke through the crimson, pushing against it as it swirled outward. In the center sat the image of a woman, a daughter of Africa, enthroned on a rainbow in the golden sky. Her face shone like the dawn as she brought three goddesses into her bosom, bestowing life and liberty on the Earth below.

In an instant she vanished, and with it the golden light, displaced by that awful shade of crimson, deeper and darker than black. The fire that began at the outer ring of the Rotunda spiraled inward with centripetal force. *Now. Now is the time.*

Pearl whispered. *"Will you dance with me in the flames?"*

I nodded, and gently wrapped my arm around Pearl's waist. I extended our arms and twirled her around; we whirled about in Tyranny's fire, Liberty and I. We were both of us free.

Together, we danced.

Together, we burned.

And together, we died.

III

The End of History

Thirty

Her Excellency

So this is death...
  ...red. Cardinal red.
In every direction.
  There are no directions.
No up, no south, no east or left.
  There is only immersion.
Color permeating all.
  Dissolving all.
    The scarlet baptism...

       ...

((...drink...))
  ...the cleansing fire...
    ...everything is crisp...
      ...everything is clear...
        ...through the veil...
          ... I reach for her...

...as a passenger aboard this vessel...

...with a barefoot servant to see me through the night...

...on and on it rocked and rolled, a sea of humanity tossed about an ocean of grief. We were packed together like rancid salt fish. I shivered in the dark, a Girl without a name...

...

...I was seven when they took me, the daughter of a *griot*, a Storyteller for Our People. My father reclined under the *baobab* tree singing of Sundiata, Father of Our People, on his *kora* of twenty-one strings.

"Who is the Mother of our People?" I asked.

"I don't know, Little Bird. We remember Fathers here."

"In another place they must remember Mothers."

"Wouldn't that be a fine place to be, Little Bird?"

I fell asleep in Father's lap, and I dreamed of Her again... I felt her in my bones...

...

...I awoke in the arms of a Strong Man with cruel eyes. I couldn't feel Her, not even in my bones. Father and the *baobab* were gone...

...

...we slept in the belly of a beast called *Fil-liss*. Black pitch oozed through wood, suffocating us one and all. I cursed the name of *Fil-liss*...she swallowed me and cut me in two, until I was both a Girl and a Thing...

...the Four Tooth Man was only a Thing now, eyes rolled to the back of the bug-filled skull on my belly. I hoped the bugs would dig deep and hollow me out. I was too tired to be a Girl...

...I might as well be only a Thing...

((...curse her...))

"Curse you..."

...

...I dreamt of a Girl from a place called *Gaul*. She became a Woman, then her friends and enemies made her a Thing...

"Libertas," was her name, *"though I have many others."*

Sick I was, near the Devil's door.

I floated on an Angel's hope in an ocean of despair...

...

...*Fil-liss* lay still at water's edge. In *Boss-tunn*, a fat chalky ghost rambled in a strange tongue. I heard one word:

"Sold!"

He gave me to the *Weet-leez*: *Jawn*, a powdery man and *Suh-zah-nah*, his pretty wife.

They called me *Fil-liss*, too...

...

...between chores, I learned *ing-glish* one word at a time:

"House."

"Table."

"Scrub."

"Fold," which sounded like "sold…"

Within the year, a Girl was now Phillis Wheatley, and only spoke English; her Father's tongue escaped her lips and flew away to the *baobab*…

…

…I was a quicker study than Nathaniel or Mary. Soon, Susanna taught me the Gospel of John.

"'Gospel' means Good News."

I read all the News fit to print in that Book: the Good, the Bad, the Ugly. Jeremiah delivered the Best News, that God loved the stranger, the fatherless and the widow…

…

…at Old South Church I pestered Reverend Cummings about Jeremiah. He was delightful, but Miss Cotton got mad and scolded me to Mr. Wheatley.

"Put your pygmy on a leash, or we'll have an uprising!"

Whatever a pygmy was, I didn't want to be one…

…

…in Boston Common there was a Tree like the *baobab*, taller than the North Church. Mary called it an "elm."

Her spirit was there, at the foot of the Great and Mighty Elm.

…

…I read everything: Plato and Virgil, Milton and Pope. I adored Milton, and dreamed of a paradise lost, redeemed from a Beast by the Lady of the Silver Lake and Severn stream. She had many names, and knit hope from spools of despair…

…

…I dreamed of Her again. She called herself "Columbia," and she set her pretty feet upon our mountains to bring Good News…

…

…in Mr. Wheatley's study I opened a book by a man named Locke…

…

((…drink…))

All mankind, being equal and independent, no one ought to harm another in his life, health, liberty and possessions...

((...drink...))

Every man has a property in his own person. This nobody has a right to, but himself...

((...drink...))

To love our neighbors as ourselves is such a truth for regulating human society, that by that alone one might determine all the cases in social morality...

"*A weighty volume, Little Bird,*" said Mr. Wheatley, when he found me in the study. "*What did you lift from it?*"

((...pour...))
...
...and so she spoke through me:
"*Where there is dust, there is rust; where there are seeds there are weeds.*"
...
...late at night, I heard them whisper...
"*...she is an oracle, Susanna...eleven, and she speaks with authority...*"
"*...of what...did she speak?*"
"*...a Gospel of Independence...*"
"*...what do we do?*"
"*...fetch her parchment and quill, and let her set this world ablaze...*"
...
...one morning Susanna gave me a gift, a brown leather diary.
I wrote poetry by candlelight... the pages never stopped turning in this diary of infinity...
...

...I wrote often under the Elm, the Liberty Tree. My heart swelled watching Samuel Adams and the Sons of Liberty thrust their torches into the darkness of Tyranny...

...

...by eighteen, my pen was mightier than Excalibur. The Wheatleys promised to free me if I found a publisher to support me...

...

"New England has no appetite for the prattling of a slave girl. Not with Liberty at stake."

So Nathaniel and I set sail for England, after a printing press and an audience with a Tyrant named George...

...

...in England I found a publisher for my poems. My fame spread throughout England and back to the Colonies. Some thought I was a parlor trick...

" Such insight could never proceed from the dull mind of a Negress..."

...

...the Sons of Liberty were sweet and sour. The virtuous mixed with the violent, who fought only for their Rights as Englishmen. And I was no Englishman...

...

...denied their Rights as Englishmen, they dipped Englishmen in black tar and doused them with white feathers. The English responded in kind. Still, I was neither Englishman, nor American...

...

...I challenged the Sons gathering at Old South Church, dressed as Natives to dump tea in the Harbor. *"The tax is an affront,"* I said. *"Your Cause is just. So fight in your own dress and let the enemy see your face, lest any say you lack the courage of conviction."*

I drew a stern rebuke. *"What would a slave know of Liberty?"*

They threw a Tea Party that night; it was sweet as honey, yet sour as citrus...

...

...Susanna was sick. She kept her promise.

"Fly free, Little Bird."

Mr. Wheatley signed my freedom.

Four months later, Susanna was gone.

I was free at last, and terribly alone…

…

…I purchased a horse with a silver coat and golden mane. I called her Equinox, as she rode fastest on the edge of night…

…

…I met an Englishman under the Great and Mighty Elm, the poor son of a London cobbler, who sailed the Atlantic with wife and son. He heard me in Tottenham, then had dreams of Her.

"Libertas," I said.

"Columbia," he said.

His name was Jeremiah Tucker. His roots grew to the center of the earth…

…

…in Boston the Redcoats tightened their grip, and Revolution rode upon every tongue.

So Liberty stirred…

…

…at Lexington, a shot echoed silently 'round the world, sinking into the hearts of Champions…

…

…the Redcoats retreated and sealed Boston from the world. The Continentals laid siege under the firm hand of a giant among men, General George Washington. In Washington men placed their trust.

I purchased a silver dagger with golden hilt. War had come, for the Devil stirred its flames…

…

…the Redcoats felled the Great and Mighty Elm with axe and saw, to cut Her off and snuff Her out. They nearly succeeded…

…

…as the Sons of Liberty turned on their own…

…

"Spy!"

"Tory!"

"Traitor!"

Drunk on spirits, they tied Jeremiah naked to the stump and forced the Liberty cap on his head. They tarred and feathered him, then cut him loose. I watched as he held up his arms, retreating on all fours, as the drunkard charged with his blade. The drunk called his sword Excalibur, and he buried it deep in Jeremiah Tucker's heart.

All in the name of George.

"For Washington!" cried the errant Sons of Liberty as Jeremiah bled into the soil…

…

…I wept over Jeremiah, holding him in refulgent arms. I wept for the stranger, the fatherless and the widow. In the shadow of the phantom Elm Liberty stirred my quill to parchment. I sank into the soil poisoned by Redcoats and Sons of Liberty alike.

Bittersweet the nectar fell and stained the paper as I wielded Excalibur against the night:

"To His Excellency, George Washington…"

…

…a seed died and broke open…

…

…I sent the letter away, in the hopes of glad tidings in return…

…

…months later, the British fled Boston with tails tucked under. From an unexpected caller I received an invitation. I answered…

…

…I rode Equinox into Cambridge on the night of March 20, 1776, arriving at a two-story yellow house where two Continentals crossed muskets.

"Who goes there?" the Short Soldier barked.

I dismounted and retrieved the letter. The Tall Soldier read closely.

"You're Phillis Wheatley?" he asked, incredulous.

"I am," I replied.

"Surrender your arms."

I pulled the dagger from my ankle holster and handed it to him, gold hilt first.

"Goodness, Child," the Short Soldier said, "who gave that to you?"

"No one," I replied.

The Tall Soldier sneered. I followed him into the manse.

In the parlor, His Excellency read by a roaring fire. He was barrel-chested and brawny, his auburn locks receding at the temples.

"General?" said the Tall Soldier.

"Sergeant Atwater," Washington replied.

"The Wheatley girl."

Washington looked upon me in wonder. His heart raced as he set his book aside.

"My dear lady," he said. "Please. Come sit."

I sat uneasily, clutching my diary to my chest.

"It is an honor to meet you."

I blushed. "The honor is all mine, Your Excellency."

"I am no royal. Call me George."

Washington eyed my diary.

"Your pen is quite prolific. Is that a sample of what comes next?"

"After a fashion."

"Your most recent work captured the soul of a young nation."

Washington poked at the logs in the fire.

"Dare I say, your pen is mightier than any sword. More than once my men hailed Columbia as they charged into battle. So courageous they were that it seemed they weren't fighting the Redcoats, but rather…"

"…the night itself," I finished.

Washington drew back in amazement. "Yes."

His breathing grew heavy and labored.

"She is real. Isn't She?"

I nodded. Washington trembled.

"She speaks to you. Doesn't She?"

"Yes."

"She speaks *through* you."

Washington knelt to the floor.

"What does She say?"

Tears welled at the ducts. I wiped them away.

"Please, Miss Wheatley. This War is far from over, and we require Liberty's assistance. As her heaven-defended race, I implore you."

My mouth went dry. "You have it wrong, General. It is Liberty who requires *your* assistance."

"Of course," Washington pleaded. "Anything."

I closed my eyes, and beheld her celestial gaze.

"Miss Wheatley?"

"Let my people go."

Washington paused. "I don't understand."

I opened my eyes. "Let my people go, as an example to the nations. Let the House of Washington shine as a City Upon A Hill."

Washington raised himself slowly to his chair. He was dejected.

"I sympathize with your convictions, I really do," he began uneasily. "Especially given your prior station. But this is a complicated matter. It must be treated with the utmost delicacy."

I swallowed the air. "Of course."

"Many free Negroes serve in our ranks. I believe they would agree we cannot afford to disrupt commerce at this juncture, or risk losing the Southern Colonies. Our first aim is to win Independence."

"And after that?"

"That…is a matter entrusted to men more learned than I."

I clutched my diary tight.

"Susanna taught me well," I said. "I'm as versed as any in the philosophies of Independence. I drank them at the Wheatley table, just as you, and Dr. Franklin, and Mr. Adams, and Mr. Paine have. The righteous rhetoric of Independence is compelling. Yet it is only one side of the coin."

Washington shifted, uncomfortable.

"We decry the Tyranny imposed by a faraway king, and our Cause is just. I believe in it fervently. Yet I have never encountered Tyranny in a faraway land. Not in Africa. Not in England. I have only looked in the Devil's eye here on Columbia's soil, and that by the very men seeking relief from Tyranny's mortal strain. Tyranny knows no borders, respects no sovereignties. He resides not in London or in Rome, but here in Cambridge, in the hearts beating in this very parlor. Independence from Britain means nothing if Liberty and Justice for all do not swiftly follow. But there is Good News, if you have ears to hear it."

I opened the diary. Its infinite pages shone forth with blinding light. My mortal flesh could scarce withstand it. Washington fell to the floor as dust and ashes:

"Please, Miss Wheatley! Please close it! It is far too bright!"

And then she took hold, speaking through me words never written or spoken, before or after:

If Liberty you truly seek,
The Crown of the Humble, the Sword of the Meek
Search within and you will find
Who troubles your heart, enslaves your mind

Self-evident is th'Eternal Truth
The hope of the fount we drank in youth
Born free and equal, we rise from the Dust
Then shackle ourselves with chains of Rust

What rusts will corrode, what corrodes will perish
Still this Higher Law we cherish
'Tis only from death that springs forth life
'Tis only with struggle, 'tis only with strife

In fields fertile and futile Liberty plants her Seeds
Whilst Tyranny sows his ersatz Weeds
They grow together, the tares and the wheat
In winter's chill and summer's heat

Yet in the night that wanes the darkest
Liberty gathers her glorious harvest
She raises the restless, the tired and poor
And shepherds us all to Elysium's door

So let no man blaspheme, let no man defame
The sonorous harmony of Liberty's name
For so long as the Earth spins 'round the sun
There will be Liberty for all, or Liberty for none.

The light receded. Every ounce of my being convulsed in the afterglow of Liberty's glory. Washington was on his knees, prostrate, lips moving in ceaseless prayer. I rose and placed my hand on his back.

"She is coming, *Libertas* is coming, to save her heaven-defended race from the shackles of Tyranny. She is coming, *Columbia* is coming, here and now, to this continent, to turn lead into gold. She comes at daybreak to pierce the darkness and show the world a more excellent way."

Beads of sweat formed at Washington's brow.

"Free Negroes fight for one George...as they fight for another. Tell me, Your Excellency. Will you be Moses...or Pharaoh?"

Washington searched the room, struggling to regain his bearings. The vision had torn him in two; his heart swam in the turmoil.

"It's a beautiful vision, Miss Wheatley," Washington stammered. "Truly."

Nervous, Washington looked at the clock on the mantle.

"Alas, the hour is late. Let us escort you home."

...

...silently we rode side-by-side into Boston, the General stealing furtive glances as Sergeant Atwater and two Continentals took the rear...

...

...then I heard it...the cry...

... the terrible, lonesome cry of first breath...

... again...

...and again...

...and again...

...

"Hya!" Equinox burst forth like lightning.

"Miss Wheatley!" Washington cried.

Four horsemen rode in hot pursuit of the Night Horse, silvery harbinger of golden things to come...

...

...in the shadow of the Elm I knelt at the spot where Jeremiah Tucker died. A patriot had planted a pole there, crowning it with Liberty's red cap. As Washington and his accompaniment dismounted, the crying grew louder...and louder...

...then...

...a miracle...

...the soil...

...it rose...like leavened dough...

…from the elements she was knit together…

…her heart and lungs…

…nerves and spine…

…tissue and bone…

…her limbs and her very skin…

…then at last…

…her eyes…her deep brown eyes…the color of the earth…

…a swirl of golden hair sprang from the Angel's crown. A gust of wind whipped through the Commons, spilling the breath of life into her lungs…

…the child breathed her first as the sun conquered the horizon on the twenty-first of March, 1776…

… dried ink came to life, muted whispers roaring as a lioness:

> *"Celestial choir! enthron'd in realms of light!*
> *Columbia's scenes of glorious toils I write.*
> *While freedom's cause her anxious breast alarms,*
> *She flashes dreadful in refulgent arms.*
>
> *See mother earth her offspring's fate bemoan,*
> *And nations gaze at scenes before unknown!*
> *See the bright beams of heavens revolving light*
> *Involved in sorrows and the veils of night.*
>
> *The Goddess comes, she moves divinely fair*
> *Olive and laurel binds her golden hair:*
> *Wherever shines this native of the skies,*
> *Unnumber'd charms and recent graces rise…"*

The child shone like the dawn. Washington knelt beside her, removing his cap.

"I am not seeing this," he labored. "My eyes are not seeing this."

Swaddled in my shawl was the Child of Ages, who once walked the streets of Rome.

"Liberty," I said. "Columbia."

Two Continentals dropped to their knees. Sergeant Atwater reluctantly knelt with them.

"Her presence," Washington choked, "will ignite fire in the hearts of patriots. If only the world could see her, they would know her and pledge their allegiance to her."

A cold chill ran up my spine, and the air felt heavier. A great dread came upon me.

"She isn't safe here," I muttered.

I looked to Washington pleadingly.

"She escaped Tyranny, but he will come for her."

Washington pondered. "Perhaps she ought to walk among us under a different name."

Washington placed his tricorn hat on his head.

"I leave that to her Mother."

I cradled the newborn close. I doted upon her almond brown eyes and her hair of gold like the sun…so I named her after dawn's early light.

"Aurora…"

…through the cardinal red comes the echo, thrice over…

((…Aurora…))

((…Emmaleigh…))

((…Pearl…))

…and I called for her again, a fourth time…

…

…

…

...

...

...

...

Thirty One

At Water

...the rushing river splashed onto the smooth black granite. My eyes drank in the blue sky like a tonic; I searched the heavens in vain for the source of this light and warmth. It came from everywhere and nowhere. Here, there was no sun.

This world needed no sun.

I rolled over and dangled one arm over the edge, where the waters spilled into the abyss below. No word in any tongue can describe what sprang from my hidden depths. It was a fusion of excitement and terror, yet not both, nor either, nor neither. It was a third flavor, a light that expelled the darkness even as it embraced it. It was evening and it was morning, my first day.

It was good...

...it was *very* good...

...I laughed...

...and laughed...

...and laughed...

"If you plan on jumping, do it already."

I knew that voice. I had heard it from my own lips.

She sat cross-legged on a gray boulder at the edge of the river, slender and pristine, her deep, dark brown skin matching walnut eyes. She donned a pearl necklace and a dirty, raggedy white dress, long black hair falling in curls over her collarbones. She scrawled in a small brown journal with a white feather quill.

"Mother," I gasped.

Her pen moved as her lips remained still.

"What are you writing?"

"Words," she replied without looking up, "sometimes phrases. You know. As one does."

I marveled at the trees lining the riverbanks, a seamless blend of breeds all bearing one fruit of many colors. Beneath the waters a flurry of brightly colored marine life moved in every direction, unimpeded by the river's current.

"Decide. Jump or get off the rock."

She glowed from her very pores, and the stroke of her quill was so light and elegant it must have been magic.

"Who are you writing to?" I asked.

She uncrossed her legs and dangled bare feet over the water.

"Posterity," she answered, twirling the quill around her fingers. She cast no shadow, and the blue sky faded to white gold around her dark frame.

Phillis Wheatley was majestic.

"Welcome to Elysium, Benjamin. We have work to do."

~

I followed several paces behind Phillis on a highway of gold hugging the south bank of the river. I wish I could remember everything I saw. In seconds and centuries at once, the Elysian Fields passed in a blur. My feet never touched the ground.

I only remember that *feeling*.

Like when Dad returned safely from the Gulf. When Michelle said "yes." When I first put on a Cardinals uniform. Pure *happiness* captured in my core and sustaining me through the edge of endless nights.

That's what it was like to walk through Elysium.

We came to a dock and climbed into a small boat moored to the side. As we rowed upstream, a constellation of thirteen stars appeared overhead. Phillis' eyes lingered on them in ponderous silence.

We rounded the river bend. Upon a hill on the south bank stood an immaculate estate, the heavenly replica above of its counterpart below.

Mount Vernon.

A small sloop dropped anchor at a long pier, its white masts drawn up. *The Phillis*.

"We're here," Phillis announced as we pulled up to the dock.

I stepped out of the boat and panned around. Every flower, every rock, every movement of life was crisp and clear, radiant and pristine. It took my breath away.

"It truly is beautiful here," Phillis began, "now that its Master has been liberated from bondage."

"Washington," I exhaled. "Father of our Country."

I turned back to Phillis.

"And Wheatley. Mother of Liberty."

"Only in the figurative sense," she declared.

I grew excited. "I'd love to meet Washington."

"Another time. His Excellency rides to and fro across the Earth. And as I said…"

Phillis waved at the ship bearing her name.

"…we have work to do."

~

Even in Elysium's air, the hull of *The Phillis* was dark and dank, as despondent as she had been on Earth, when I first set foot on her decks. The floor was covered in broken metal cuffs and chains; it still stank of blood, sweat and vomit. I lived fifteen years of Phillis' life in the blink of an eye, yet I still could only fathom what it was like to live through such hell.

Phillis stood motionless over a spot near starboard, where Liberty first came to her.

"After we captured this vessel, I instructed Captain Reyes to keep her in her original condition. To remember…"

Phillis paused.

"…to remember our hard beginnings, and the cruel world into which my Daughters were born."

Phillis laughed and cried at once.

"How can so great a blessing come from such evil and suffering?"

She looked to me, with boundless affection in her eyes.

"You gave your life for Hers. What do you want to know?"

"I want to know what happened to you, after Aurora was born."

Phillis swallowed hard. "It's not a joyful tale."

I took a seat on a barrel.

"Very well. I returned to Mr. Wheatley's home, where I boarded, with Aurora and three armed guards. I nursed her for seven nights before he took her."

"König?"

She shook her head. "Sergeant Lionel Atwater."

I felt my first real sorrow in Elysium. "My ancestor."

Phillis nodded. "He was one of the guards. He was angry that I, a black woman brought to America in chains, curried favor with Washington, his hero. So he killed the other two guards and blamed me."

"You?"

"He told Washington I was a Tory, because my works were published in England. He took Aurora from her crib; I confronted him with my dagger and he subdued me. He took my dagger and my journal as a prize and rode off. Sergeant Atwater told Washington that I went insane and attacked him, that I wasn't fit to raise a fair-skinned goddess."

I scanned the hull and reflected upon my fleeting experience under Phillis' skin. Her young self never could have imagined the bittersweet taunt of freedom awaiting her in America.

"Everything fell apart after that. My writing floundered, so I married a free Negro named John Peters. I tried to fill Aurora's void with my own children; two died before John was imprisoned for his debts while I was pregnant with his third. I had to go to work as a scullery maid and lived in squalor. I died of a broken heart on December 5, 1784, at thirty-one years old."

Phillis sensed my unease.

"Are you uncomfortable?"

"No," I said. "I do feel sadness. Thoroughly."

"Whoever said there is no sadness in paradise was mistaken. It's here, but we're free of its control. The citizen of Elysium is healed of his wounds, but he still feels the scars of Earth."

"Pain without suffering."

Phillis nodded. "Wholeness."

"Purpose." It was a sensation I couldn't possibly describe.

A sly grin crept across Phillis' face. "Purpose, yes. And even in losing Aurora, there was purpose."

I wiped a tear away from my eye. "How?"

"After my emancipation I became friends with a young black orphan named Natalie. I introduced her to General Washington, who agreed to take her into his employ as a free woman after they moved on from Boston. When Sergeant Atwater presented Aurora to His Excellency, he called upon her to be the girl's wet nurse. She followed Aurora wherever she went for the rest of her life, even accompanying her on her mission to Creek Territory. Natalie was part of Aurora's Resistance, until she was captured by the Tennessee regulars."

My heart sank. "Aurora...when she surrendered to Jackson..."

"...she offered herself into captivity to try to free Natalie."

((...I will never free her...))

I felt a lingering chest pain, like my heart was aflame. "Jackson refused."

Phillis nodded. "And gave her over to his favored Commander."

I swallowed hard. "Titus Atwater."

"And while enslaved, she gave birth to a son named Israel, whose wife bore him a daughter named..."

"...*Mariah,*" I whispered, astounded.

A tear formed at the corner of Phillis' eye. "On my deathbed, I wrote Natalie a letter, addressed to her at the Servants' Hall at Mount Vernon. Along with the letter I enclosed one item."

I exhaled. "Your diary."

"With the instructions that it be handed down to Natalie's descendants in perpetuity."

I was amazed. The pieces slowly came together in my mind.

"If I might ask," I pressed, "what exactly is in that diary?"

Phillis stood and motioned toward the ladder in the aft of the hull. We ascended up the ladder through a trap door into the captain's quarters. As it had been in the Gulf, the quarters were simple, brown and austere. On the center table sat a living map of the Course of Human Events, covered with surveyor's instruments. Above the map stood an hourglass whose final sand had fallen, serving as a paperweight for a familiar etching of a winding snake, divided into several lengths with the names of the original colonies upon each one. At the bottom in bold capital letters was the phrase...

"*...join or die,*" I whispered.

I grabbed the living map and set it upon the etching. The snake lined up perfectly with the Course of Human Events. Each of the waterfalls matched up with one of the divisions between the etching segments. Each of the map segments still read:

Vita

Libertatem

Beatitudinem

"This is incredible," I exclaimed. "Ben Franklin made this etching in 1753, at the beginning of the Seven Years' War. How..."

Phillis smiled. "Dr. Franklin divined the shape of this leg of the Course of Human Events and buried it in that etching."

I traced my finger along the length of the Course, from the Revolutionary watershed to the Civil War to World War II all the way through to...

"Wait a minute," I said. "Before there were only three waterfalls. Now there's a fourth..."

...I pointed...

"...at the End of History."

"Of Course," Phillis replied.

"That's the waterfall I awoke on...when I got here..."

"Correct."

"...Today."

Phillis nodded. I measured out the roughly equal lengths between the waterfalls…

"…these are the days that Liberty was reborn. Aurora on March 21, 1776. Emmaleigh on January 1, 1863. Pearl on December 7, 1941 and…"

…I looked up…

"…March 10, 2020. Today."

Phillis set her journal on the table. "What do you know of the legend of the Phoenix, Ben Upson?"

My pulse accelerated. "It's…a bird…a legendary bird…at the end of its life it burns up, and then…"

"…it rises from the ashes."

My heart pounded. Phillis opened the journal. Its pages were luminous and intense.

"Aurora grew up as Washington's daughter," she said, "but she was closer with her Uncle Benjamin. After Mr. Atwater brought her to General Washington, he sent her along under guard to Philadelphia, where she was present with Dr. Franklin, Mr. Jefferson and the Committee of Five as they drafted the Declaration. These were learned and devoted men, but it was the presence of Liberty herself who brought the Revolution to life."

"The Gospel," I said.

"Yes. The Gospel. Aurora's very presence was contagious and brought many Colonials who knew her to their knees. But it drove others mad. They coveted her power but not her love. Like Caesar, they wanted it for conquest and greed. Some made attempts on her life, just as König had. None succeeded. Dr. Franklin knew why. The Gospel had come to him as well…"

Phillis flipped through the journal and it went on and on and on, casting a spectrum of color against the walls of the cabin.

"Benjamin Franklin knew that the greatest danger young Aurora faced was not from the hand of death, but from the unnatural extension of her life. For dust she is, and to dust she must return."

"Ashes to ashes," I said.

"Dust to dust."

"The seed must die…"

"…and yield a tenfold harvest."

I panned the cabin. "That's why Tyranny comes after her with lead. To kill her is to see her reborn, stronger. But to preserve her in stone…"

"...is to render her a lifeless, useless idol."

"To prevent her from growing..."

"...and seeding new life even stronger than the life that came before it."

I looked down at the map. "The Course of Human Events flows in one direction...and when it reaches these points in history, it must either fall..."

"...or be eternally...dammed."

My breath caught. "Rendering the water stagnant. Nothing moves forward."

Phillis nodded. "Each of the Sisters was born into one Crisis, and died in another. Each walked the Earth as Liberty in a different era, each expanding and improving on the works of her Sister before..."

Phillis leaned over the map and pointed to the first waterfall...

"Aurora," she began, "the innocent visionary born to Revolution in Boston at dawn's early light, who breathed *life* into the fledgling young Republic..."

((...vita...))

"...Emmaleigh, the resilient advocate born into Civil War at Gettysburg, who labored to keep alive the spark of *liberty* for all when Tyranny clawed to reclaim it from her..."

((...libertatem...))

"...Pearl, the brilliant optimist born into World War under a palm at the Harbor that bears her name, whose *pursuit of happiness* bubbled over into the world..."

((...beatitudinem...))

...

Phillis closed the diary and set her finger on the fourth waterfall. "None of this happens of its own accord. Human Events arise from human hearts, just as Liberty was reborn in mine."

She pointed directly at my heart.

"That is the battlefield where Liberty and Tyranny fight their perennial war."

"Of all hearts," I asked, "why did the fate of the entire world come down to mine?"

Phillis wandered around the cabin, hands behind her.

"Seven billion theaters," she said. "One war. In each theater, her Champion has a decision to make in the heat of battle. Either he will steal Liberty's light for his own glory, or he will fight Tyranny in the shadowy muck of his own heart, offering himself as a sacrifice on the altar of Nature's God, so he can give life to those he loves."

She paced closer and closer.

"In every season, there is a turning, and in every heart a decision. If Liberty rises in one, it rises in all. If it sets in one, it sets in all. It is said that if a man dies, so dies an entire universe."

Phillis stared deep into my eyes.

"If not you, then who?"

She picked a thread from my shirt.

"The Champion rides the Night Horse through the ashes..."

Phillis blew on the thread, and it burst to flames. She grinned from ear to ear.

"...so the Phoenix might rise for all."

I took a deep breath. Phillis grew excited.

"Come. Watch the Elysian sunrise with me."

Phillis brought me to the bow of the ship. Slowly, this world illuminated itself in a dazzling array of colors. I could see cities and forests and mountains and lakes near and far...

((...I go to prepare a place for you...))

...this place was pure, but not perfect, an unfinished project. Heaven's foundations rested on Earth.

((...life belongs to the living...))

I realized then that I hadn't thought of him since I arrived.

"Is my father here now?"

"Yes," Phillis replied. "Of Course."

I smiled. "Good."

"Would you like to see him?"

"Of Course. But not Today."

Phillis seemed surprised.

"I'll see him Tomorrow. For now, I'll let him rest."

Phillis folded her arms and pressed her tongue into her cheek.

"Is there anyone else you'd like to see?" she asked.

My mouth twisted at the corner. "Does a ghost crave a cheeseburger?"

~

Down river, beyond a field of dreams, there is a place near a spectacle of twisting trees and weeping willows overlooking a crystal blue pond. A trail of gold leads to the pond from the river, lined with every hue and shade of rose. If you travel far enough, you may come upon the lush grove garden of a Great White Manse, a place the alabaster statues once called home.

Today a man walked down that road, his feet bare and trousers rolled above his ankles. He hung his coat over his shoulder and tried to whistle, but his tears wouldn't let him. His nerves shot through with the unbeatable wholeness of being, he entered a lush garden ringed by trimmed green hedges and stopped cold at the white gazebo.

She swung gently and blissfully from the bench. Whole. Content. Needing nothing more but desiring it nonetheless. She was ravishing in that orchid summer dress.

His French girl.

"Jacqueline?"

She flipped her dark brown bob and rest her finger against her cheek. Her smile reached across the garden, inviting her beloved to drop his burden and come Home.

"Dance with me, Jack," she laughed.

Jack welled with joy. "As long as you never turn your cheek again."

Jack ran to her; they embraced for a thousand eternities. Then he took her in his arms, and they danced cheek-to-cheek in the fire of an Elysian twilight. As he looked over his beloved's shoulder, he thought he saw a Man in the Looking Glass. The Man said "thank you," and he did as well. Then the lovers spun and danced free.

If ever you travel down that road, you'll still find them dancing Today.

~

We stood at the watery precipice on the smooth granite rock, where the river of time drops like the sands of an hourglass to the uncharted worlds below.

"So we come to the End of History, Benjamin," Phillis said. "Here. Now."

I gazed over my shoulder at the Course of Human Events, the river that waters Elysium, paradise beyond any I could have ever imagined, life as I always wanted it to be.

"If you wish to stay," Phillis said, reading my mind, "I can't deny you that choice. Today a child is born anew from the ashes. Life belongs to the living, and She lives because you died."

I peered over the precipice. Through the mist rising from the waters far, far below, I could perceive nothing but impenetrable vapor. Faintly, I heard the sound of bitterness rise back to me, like that of children weeping and gnashing their teeth. It was unbearable to listen to.

I inclined my ear. Softly at first, I heard another sound. It was bitter like the others, but sweet, though not bittersweet. It was as pure and whole as the song of the siren. One cry brought hope to despair, blending together as one sound that reached to the furthest corner of my soul.

"It's not finished," I said. *"I'm not finished."*

Mother looked gently upon me. "What lies behind us and what lies before us are tiny matters compared to what lies within us."

...I made my choice. I captured Elysium in my heart...

...I looked...

...and I leapt...

...

...

...

...

...

((...Isabella...))

Thirty Two

The Altar

The Florida sun beat down on Roger Dean Stadium as the Barenaked Ladies played over the loudspeaker. I creased the brim of my new Phoenix Firebirds cap, just how I like it. I pulled the cap down over my head enough to be perfectly inconspicuous.

I looked at the date on my ticket stub:

SATURDAY, MARCH 18, 2000

This has all been done before.

It was the bottom of the third, and the Dodgers led my Cardinals 4-0. One level below, behind the first base dugout, I watched as Mom, Dad, Uncle Craig, Rachel and Michelle in her damn Expos hat sat at the edges of their seats. Their eyes were glued to the on-deck circle and the lanky 21-year-old, lefty-hitting first baseman who, unbeknownst to them, was currently pissing himself.

Pearl popped an obnoxiously large bubble. Her eyes were glued to the scorecard she marked with a golf pencil. She hadn't said a word since the first pitch, her ears covered with an obnoxiously large pair of headphones.

There was one out. The Dodgers' pitcher today was a legend; they called him "Bulldog," Little did I know he would be the only Major League pitcher I'd ever face. He retired the first seven batters he faced and now stared down the eighth, our speedy second baseman. I was pinch hitting for our wild starter, who had walked home four runs in the top of the third.

THUMP!

The ball slowly rolled down the third base line. The batter caught the defense on their heels and zipped to first for a bunt single.

I watched myself freeze in the on deck circle. I remembered the exact word that ran through my young mind:

((...SHHHHHHIIIIIIIITTTTTT...))

My family cheered. They shouldn't have. I would pay for that bush league move.

Pearl took off her headphones. "Hoot's fucking with you, Rook."

I covered the sides of my eyes. Pearl cackled villainously and shoved her headphones back on.

The P.A. announcer came on over the speakers.

"Pinch hitting for the Cardinals, first baseman number seventy-nine, Ben Upson!"

The crowd...uh...*acknowledged.* Young Ben took a few practice swings and dug into the batter's box. He stared up at Bulldog, sixty feet six inches away. From the stretch...

((...shit...shit...shit...))

...he delivered...

...a *sizzling* fastball right at Young Ben's head.

He dropped to the dirt in sheer panic. The crowd booed. Rachel held Dad back from climbing the dugout as she unleashed her own profanity-laced tirade.

Our muscular left fielder barked from the on-deck circle.

"Bulldog! Why don't you throw at me, huh?! You don't think this Sweet Baby could take it?"

Young Ben pulled himself up off the dirt as Blue warned each dugout. The Dodger catcher mock-held Young Ben back, though he wasn't going anywhere. A jaw session ensued. Pearl tapped me.

"What did you say to him?"

I smirked. "I said, *'Fuck off, Todd.'*"

Pearl howled with laughter.

"You're the most immature goddess I know."

Todd called time and went to chat with Bulldog. Mom screamed things I can't repeat in respectable company.

Young Ben dug in, angry. Bulldog threw to first base six times in a row.

Then he threw a cutter that buckled Ben's knees. He tried to knock it out of the yard; he spun himself into the ground instead.

"*I'm already cool, Rook!*" shouted some jackass Dodger fan below. "*Thanks for the breeze!*"

Pearl couldn't contain herself. I sank deeper into my chair.

1-1 count. Bulldog threw four more times to first. The crowd booed. Now Michelle joined Mom and Rachel, heckling in French like a trapeze artist from Cirque du Soleil.

Circle change. Ben was way ahead of it. "*HEEERIKE!*"

Now the count was 1-2. Ben was getting flustered and impatient.

Come on, Benji. He's wasting energy trying to rattle you, throwing to first. Let him come to you.

Ben stopped and took a deep breath. He seemed to relax.

((...work the count...work the count...let him come to you...))

I sat up in my seat.

Ben waited on the next pitch. Curve ball. Out of the zone. 2-2.

((...wait...wait...))

Two more throws to first.

Fastball. Just off the outside corner. Full count.

((...you have him...))

"Now you have him," I said. "He's embarrassed he can't get the rookie out with his best stuff. He's gonna throw his..."

((...slider...))

"That's right."

((...he only started throwing it last year...))

Ben said something to Todd. Todd pounded his mitt and changed the signal.

"Feigned confidence. Perfect. Piss him off."

Bulldog set and delivered.

A slider.

((...like Bud Black to Reggie Jackson...))

Swing.

CRACK!

((...didn't even feel it...))

The ball carried...I closed my eyes and tuned into the Cardinal broadcast...

((...Upson hits a high fly ball to left-center...White is on his horse...back...at the track...at the wall...it is GONE! In his first at bat against Major League pitching, Ben Upson hits a two-run opposite field home run in a five minute, six-pitch at bat. Viña crosses and here comes Upson. Lankford and Edmonds are there to greet him, and Upson has cut the Dodger lead in half. Upson was patient and waited for a gift on the altar, and he crushed it...))

I watched Young Ben blow a kiss to Michelle behind the dugout.

"Nice dinger," Pearl said. "Without the sacrifice ahead of you, it never would have happened."

In Section 108, my real Number Eight Hitter hugged his wife, eternally proud of his boy.

"I think I know what you mean."

~

Pearl drove south to West Palm Beach in a red-orange BMW. When I had jumped from the waterfall in Elysium, I had expected to awaken in the Rotunda. Instead, I found myself on a couch in Pearl's oceanfront apartment, next door to an ostentatious seaside resort.

"You have one more assignment," she announced, tossing me my Firebirds hat. *"But first, a ball game."*

After watching myself in the only Major League game I'd ever appear in, I sat in the passenger seat with the window down, feeling the soft breeze with my hand.

"So this dinner party," I asked, "what's the occasion?"

"It's an engagement party," Pearl replied.

"Anyone I know?"

~

I gripped the door handle as we inched to the curb. I surveyed the house. Other than a fresh coat of orange paint, it looked worn and comfortable, like an old pair of shoes. The palm tree at the entryway was taller. A Ford Focus and Saturn Ion sat in the driveway. In the street, a Latina girl flew past on a Razor scooter.

Clementine Lane was a different place altogether.

"Back to where we started," I sighed.

I stared into the dashboard.

"It doesn't feel the same without Jack here."

"Nothing does," Pearl said, freshening up in the mirror.

I carried a bowl of fruit salad to the door. I spied a copy of *The Palm Beach Post* wedged in the flower bed.

Pearl rang the bell. The door opened and I flinched.

"Pearl!" exclaimed the young woman with black hair and turquoise eyes. "I'm so happy you could make it tonight!"

"I wouldn't miss it for the world, dear," said Pearl, handing over a bottle of white wine.

Young Marissa Barrios hugged her warmly as I stood slack-jawed and dumb.

"Ahem," Pearl said as they disengaged. "This is my plus one for the evening, from Colorado."

I stammered. "Uh…I'm…John…no…um…Upson."

Marissa laughed. "Good to meet you, John." She hugged me and pecked my cheek. "I'm Marissa…uh…Barrios? Atwater?"

Marissa was happier, lighter than the broken woman I knew in another lifetime.

"Come in, you're the first ones here."

Inside everything was different, and everything was the same. The furniture was newer and whiter. A 42" RCA tube TV with cable box displaced the Magnavox. The coffee table sported an issue of *Time* with Amadou Diallo on the cover, with insets of John McCain and Christina Aguilera. Under dimmed lights the *Notting Hill* soundtrack played on a six-disc CD changer.

A raspy voice came from the kitchen.

"Riss, is that Pearl?"

"Yes, Mama," Marissa replied.

Marissa's mother sniffled. It sounded like she was crying.

We rounded the corner into the kitchen. Marissa's mother turned from the sink, and I nearly made her wear the fruit salad.

"OH MY GOD!" she shouted…

...she was sixteen the last time I saw her in this kitchen, when her mother viciously slapped her for the crime of being a teenage girl. She was fifty-three, and now as then she wore a lime green dress. Her eyes watered from the chopped garlic and onions on the cutting board.

"Mama!" Marissa chastised her. "You look like you've seen a ghost!"

Mama's bottom lip quivered. *If only she knew.*

The sliding glass door opened. A Spanish man in an apron entered from the patio.

"Tiffy, baby, I heard you scream....HEY! It's Pearly Pearl! The matchmaker!"

He jogged over and hugged Pearl.

"Sebastian!" Pearl said. "This is John."

He shook my hand. "Sebastian Barrios," he said, "and this...petrified woman...here is...my wife...Tiffany..."

I stuck out my hand. "Tiffany, we've never met before, I'm – "

Tiffany knocked my hand away and wrapped her arms around my neck.

"Pearl has told me so much about you, John!" she shouted.

She lowered her head and whispered into my ear.

"She's coming tonight, Jack. I'm so glad you're here."

Tiffany let go. I caught Pearl's devious eyes as they danced around the bonfire of implications.

Holy shit.

~

Tiffany gave us a tour of the house. We came to Jimmy's old room, now the guest room, and Tiffany locked the door. Photos on the wall opposite the day bed told the story of the last forty years.

Tiffany trembled as she touched a photograph of her, her father and her stepmother, a police dispatcher named Cindy, on a sailboat in the Florida Keys. It was taken sometime in the late sixties.

"You changed his life, Jack," she said, tearing up. "And mine."

I was taken aback. "I...I...don't know what to say."

Tiffany blew her nose into a tissue.

"I was sitting in the car at the jail that night. I watched you two hug. I don't know what passed between you, but in the blink of an eye he changed. You were his firework on the Fourth of July. He stopped drinking. He left my awful mother and quit his job at that awful factory. He became a teacher and a civil rights activist. Wayne Carmichael, jaded veteran, took me with him to Selma to march with Dr. King."

Tiffany trembled as she looked at Pearl.

"You were with us. So was Zora."

She turned back to me.

"That night on the Fourth of July, he first called me his diamond."

Tiffany trembled as she motioned at Pearl.

"I have some idea who she is. I feel it whenever I'm around her. I get the same sense from you, only… you haven't aged a day. Are you…some sort of angel?"

"I'm just a man," I answered.

"Whoever you are, I've been waiting a lifetime to meet you again. So I could say thank you."

Tiffany wrapped herself around me, sobbing into my shoulder. I tentatively hugged her back.

Downstairs, the doorbell rang. Tiffany jumped.

"Hey baby girl," came the low-timbre voice.

Marissa squeaked. Tiffany exhaled, then changed the subject. She touched a color photo of a young man in uniform, his arm around a curly-haired teenager in plain clothes.

"You remember Jimmy and Wam-Bam, don't you?"

I studied it closely and laughed. *That son of a bitch.*

"I do. Wow, that's Jimmy…and Wam-Bam….I *definitely* recognize him. When was this taken?"

"1971. Just before Jimmy left for Vietnam."

Tiffany choked up. I understood immediately.

"I'm so sorry," I offered.

"Mother didn't want him to go, but he got drafted…"

Tiffany shook it off.

"Oh!" Tiffany sprang open the closet and knelt to the floor to retrieve a cherry red box. She pulled out the black-and-white photograph of Wayne and Hank Finkelson…and Hank's dog tags.

"Um…so…this was Dad and his best friend in the 285th, Hank Finkelson. Dad told me this story that same night, on the Fourth of July…"

Tiffany re-told the tale I once lived through her father's eyes. She got some of the details wrong, but her telling sounded like how I would have described it to her. She glistened at the recall of a third person memory.

"One year before I was born, Hank Finkelson gave my father life."

Tiffany started to shake.

"And as long as he was alive, he protected me from *her*."

She folded her arms.

"I don't know why Marissa invited her grandmother. She is…vile…and *racist*. You saw it, John, on that ball field. This is the same woman who walked out of my wedding when the priest asked for objections. She hated Sebastian, and now Marissa thinks she's going to approve of *Keith*?"

Tiffany exhaled.

"This dinner is going to be a disaster."

Pearl touched Tiffany lightly on the arm. She melted and relaxed.

"Dear," Pearl said. "This is South Florida. We know how to weather storms."

Pearl turned to me.

"We nest in the eye."

Laughter drifted from downstairs. Zora and Sebastian, in particular, pumped it out in fountains.

I cleared my throat.

"I'd like to meet your future son-in-law."

~

"Dude, I'm telling you, it's a bonanza right now. A feeding frenzy."

Keith Atwater sucked down his SoCo and lime on the poolside patio while I cradled my lemonade. Sebastian manned the grill on the other side of the patio.

"Our company is going to be a gazelle. Have VCs and angel investors all over it. You think Microsoft is big now, in ten years it'll be a dinosaur. Little guys like us are moving too fast for 'em."

Keith Atwater and Abdul Haq Salaam were two different people, yet exactly the same. I only saw Salaam during his trial for a crime he didn't commit. But Keith was alive. Vibrant. Optimistic. A post-racial Generation Xer who, at the dawn of a new millennium, saw nothing but bright blue skies ahead. He reminded me, in many ways, of his great grandfather Ray.

"A gazelle, you say?" I asked.

"Yep. Gazelle. Ever read *The Roaring 2000s*? Harry Dent? Says in the new economy, companies have to be small and agile to outmaneuver the competition. We can tailor our services to customer needs, put tech in the hands of the people. No need for big tech."

"This anti-trust suit against Microsoft has to be encouraging."

Keith chewed on an ice cube and grimaced. "Oh hell no! My mom's the lawyer, I'm a libertarian. Get the regulators out of it!"

"So what are you selling?"

Keith smiled. "You have a cellular phone?"

I nodded.

"Desktop? Laptop?"

"Both. And a tab...uh, a tabbed...tabbed filing system."

"Alright, so, all of those are big, heavy and clunky, right? But if the twenty-first century is gonna be about gazelles, then everybody has to be able to move around, not stay in one spot, you follow?"

"I do."

"So Ubicon manufactures chips that combine all of that into one handheld device, on one network you could access from anywhere, like pulling rain out of a cloud. Phone. Web browser, *real* web browser like, *full Netscape*. PDA, like a PalmPilot. Listen to satellite radio. Anything you can do electronically, you can do that on a device using a Ubicon chip."

Keith took a sip of his SoCo.

"Hell, man. I could even imagine somebody writing an entire novel on a handheld device."

I laughed, nervously for some reason. "I imagine that'd be tedious."

"Maybe not a novel, but you get it. Soon this entire country is going to cross the Rubicon. There's a new world taking over. When it does, we're not going back."

I was at turns excited and pained for him. I found myself praying for God to ease the burden awaiting him.

In an instant, the air felt thick and heavy.

The sliding door opened, and there she stood.

Sebastian banged out the Star Wars Imperial march with his tongs.

At seventy-eight she looked a hundred and twenty, smoking her cigarette, body shaking from head to toe in vicious wrath.

Her eyes never left mine. Nor mine hers.

The eyes of Dorothy Jane Carmichael, née Tucker.

Great grandmother to Tyson Immanuel Atwater.

Thirty Three

Seeds

CLINK-CLINK-CLINK!

"I want to thank y'all for being here," Keith began as he stood up. "Especially Marissa's grandmother, whom I just met."

The table giggled uncomfortably. Dorothy wasn't even looking at him. Like a bulldog, she locked in on me, never blinking. Keith's toast was a bit long-winded, but the Cal Tech alum had a lot to say.

After he finished, we got down to the cedar plank grilled salmon. Small talk ruled the table. Pearl, Marissa and her maid-of-honor Amanda talked fashion. Tiffany and Zora, who volunteered as Palm Beach election monitors, griped about the county's confusing "butterfly ballots." Sebastian and Marcus debated whether the Heat could take Kobe and Shaq's Lakers in a seven-game series. Keith insisted to me that the business cycle was finally broken, and that the next twenty years would bring about an unprecedented period of peace and prosperity. He claimed that the fall of the Soviet Union marked the "end of history," as if the world stopped spinning…

…

…Dorothy cleared her throat…everyone at the table stopped…

…

"Do I have to be the only one here with any sense? Do I have to be the one to point out the 800-pound gorilla on the patio, here?"

Zora clenched her napkin. Keith grabbed her wrist.

"Ms. Tucker," Keith began, "if my engagement to your granddaughter in any way – "

"Oh, shut up and stop prattling you egotist! I'm talking about him!"

She pointed her crooked finger at me. I calmly swallowed my salmon.

"Don't think I don't recognize you, Jack! You're not fooling anyone, this is Florida! I've seen better age reduction surgery on a pelican!" She spat out the "p" in pelican.

Marissa, paragon of patience, grabbed Dorothy's hand softly

"No, Grandma, that's John."

Dorothy slapped Marissa's hand away, stunning her.

"Grandma!"

"Like hell you're John! Your name is Jack!"

"Dorothy," Sebastian interjected, "lots of people named John go by Jack. John F. Kennedy did."

"Oh, yes, that philandering Catholic. Hero of yours?"

Dorothy laid into me.

"You attacked me with a baseball bat on July 4th, 1962, after I caught you spying on Tiffany at the park. She remembers. Tiffany!"

To my left, Tiffany clutched her butter knife, usually the first clue in a murder mystery.

"Tell them! Tell them what I said when I got to the park! Tiffany!"

I realized at that moment how deeply Dorothy had kept her daughter in psychological bondage. Even after Wayne liberated her to be her own woman, her mother maintained an emotional foothold.

Tiffany fumed. *"'Get your dirty hands off my daughter...'"*

Dorothy sat back, smug and satisfied. "See? Even this little c–"

"'...you mongrel bastard.'"

The table had been silent, and it got quieter.

"You weren't shouting at John, Mother, you were shouting at Diego! You..."

She stopped herself, then relented again.

"...you walked out of my wedding, *your own daughter's wedding*, because I married a Cuban!"

"Oh, here we go," Dorothy bitched. "Don't change the subject, missy. I want this man out of my house, now!"

"THIS IS NOT YOUR HOUSE!" Tiffany exploded in tears. "Sebastian bought it from Daddy! He was *better! Smarter! Kinder!*"

"Oh, so kind. Wayne Carmichael. You know he slandered me to Norm Kettlebeck and that taco partner of his? The same 'man' who abandoned his battalion when the Nazis ambushed them in Belgium? Hid in the forest with some kike? The Army thought the coward was dead, and Merry Christmas 1944! Here comes the War Department with a telegram to my diner! Boy, was that a wonderful four months of grief for *nothing*. I was so grateful he was alive I let him put you in me the damn second he got home! Took me years to realize that the coward that came back wasn't the same man who itched to kill every kraut he saw. By then, I was stuck with him."

Dorothy snarled.

"I was stuck with *you*."

Keith was already consoling a bawling Marissa. Dorothy plunged the knife in further.

"Couldn't even come back with his own dog tags, the pussy."

Tiffany seethed. *"He was captured – "*

Dorothy cupped her hands. *"Newsflash, Tiffy, the good ones don't get captured."*

Tiffany stood up and threw her wine glass against the patio, shattering it. She stormed off into the house sniffling. Sebastian gave Dorothy a dirty look and followed after.

Double play. Two down.

"Drag her off, bring on another!" Dorothy cried.

"Grandma," Marissa cried. "This is my *engagement dinner*. What are you doing? Please. Just. Learn to be nice. We're here to celebrate."

"Celebrate? Why would I celebrate something I don't know? I'm here to investigate."

She pointed.

"Keith, is it?"

Keith grit his teeth.

"You might be one of the good ones, but color me skeptical. Pardon the pun. Or not. I don't care."

Dorothy pointed at Zora.

"You this boy's mother? Tell me. What's your story?"

Zora chuckled. "Lady, you couldn't handle my story."

It was clear that Zora had neither the tolerance nor the patience for Dorothy's antics.

"In any event, you have no love in you, and you are lost."

Zora got up, pecked her son on the head and squeezed her future daughter-in-law, then walked inside. Marcus followed.

Strike 'em out, throw 'em out.

"There was a time," Dorothy said to Marissa, cutting asparagus, "when people weren't so damn sensitive. Your generation is so absorbed in your own feelings you can't see straight. Grow a thicker hide for God's sake! Your great grandmother gave me grief for marrying a Scotch-Irishman, so if you want to breed with a black, you have my blessing. See? I don't see color. Progress!"

Dorothy raised her glass and drank from it like Henry VIII.

Marissa wrestled her way out of Keith's arms and ran to the door. Amanda chased after. Keith slammed his fist on the table and followed them both.

Quick work. Seven batters down.

That left Dorothy, Pearl and I on the patio, each of us calmly eating our salmon.

I leaned into Pearl. *"Seabass has* got *to share this recipe."*

Pearl nodded. *"As soon as I lay down this bunt. She's gonna throw at you."*

"I can duck."

Dorothy barged in. "So. Pearl. I hear you're Keith's fairy god– "

Pearl wrapped Dorothy in a warm embrace and kissed her hot on the lips.

For the briefest moment, Dorothy's eyes turned gray.

Bunt perfectly executed. Pearl caught her off guard and got to first base.

Dorothy snarled as Pearl skipped inside.

"Your hooker is a lesbian, Jack."

"Is she?" I said, sipping my lemonade. "Neat."

Irritated that I didn't take the bait, Dorothy threw her napkin down and walked inside. In the living room, I watched the family part like the Red Sea.

Liberty rattled her. She'll be back.

The gas lamp flickered, and then it went out.

Throw me your slider, Bulldog.

.

~

Dorothy returned to the darkened patio. She seemed comfortable in the dark. I imagined she sat alone eating a lot of meals that way.

She didn't waste time.

"You're still here?" Dorothy charged, lighting another cigarette. "That figures."

I sipped my lemonade patiently as Dorothy berated me.

"You should be an old curmudgeon like me, but you're the same age now as you were then. What are you, some kinda demon?"

"No, Ms. Tucker," I replied "I'm just a man."

"Ha! Like hell you are! I saw you pop out of nowhere on that baseball field, you conjurer of tricks!"

She drew another long puff.

"Whatever the hell you are, you're a nuisance, and I swear on the Good Book there's a place in hell with all of your names on it."

Slider. A pitch she doesn't know how to throw. I uncrossed my leg and set the water down.

"You know, Dorothy," I began, "I actually grew up Lutheran. I know the Bible, and I know the Gospel."

She blew smoke.

"I take it you've read the Ten Commandments?"

She scoffed. "Yes."

"My father was in the Navy, so we moved around a lot. Every base had a chapel, and every chapel had the Ten Commandments listed somewhere inside. As a child they always filled me with fright that, if I didn't obey them perfectly, I would go to hell when I die. So I memorized them."

I took a drink.

"They're common sense, mostly. But the tenth one always confused me. You know the one I'm talking about?"

Dorothy just stared at me, lifeless.

"'Thou shalt not covet.' Confusing. I mean, how is it a sin to desire something? It says we shouldn't covet our neighbor's things, but what if I want to buy my neighbor's house? Is it a sin to make him an offer? That didn't make sense. So I ignored it. Then one Sunday, the chaplain gave a sermon on the Tenth Commandment, and everything made sense. He said that coveting isn't about wanting the things we want. You want to know what he said coveting was?"

Dorothy shrugged lightly, her face placid.

"'To covet is to issue an ultimatum to God.'"

Dorothy put out her cigarette in the ashtray.

"Did you ever want anything so badly, Dorothy, that you would steal it? Have you ever owned anything you so strongly feared would be taken from you, that you would kill anyone who even looked sideways at it?"

Dorothy's breathing increased ever so slightly. I leaned forward.

"Have you ever learned that it had been taken from you, and because the thief was gone you took it out on the messenger?"

Dorothy swallowed. "What in the name of God are you talking about?"

I eased off. *Gently.* "You can see how it might happen, right?"

"No."

"No?"

"I'm not stupid enough to do that. What do you take me for?"

"By no means, and I didn't say that. But, if I might ask, why did you think I was talking about you?"

Dorothy stonewalled and looked away. *Pivot.*

"Do you like baseball?"

"Excuse me?"

"You and I met at a baseball field about two blocks from here. You want to know why I was there?"

Dorothy shrugged.

"I was a scout."

Dorothy scoffed. "Then how did you know my name? How did you know Tiffany''s name?"

"Your husband was shouting at you both before I intervened."

Dorothy became uncomfortable in her seat. *Circle around. Keep her steady. She wants to hurt you, don't return the favor.*

"One of the best players I've ever seen was a kid from Carolina. His name was Bobby Clemens."

Dorothy flinched, ever so subtly.

"Your house is on Clementine..."

Flinch.

"...so that's what reminded me. Funny how our minds associate things like that."

Small eye twitch. She gripped the chair.

"Bobby was a legend in his day. 'Sweetness,' they called him. Smooth right-handed swing, ran like a gazelle. Fifteen-time All-Star, he won two World Series' and, get this, while he was on the Pittsburgh Pirates he was also in the Marine Corps reserve. A man of faith, family, flag…a real patriot, a real son of the American Revolution. Speaking of which – "

I cut her off before she could cut me off.

" – speaking of which…your last name is Tucker?"

She swallowed hard. "Yes."

"Are you by chance a descendant of Jeremiah Tucker?"

She gasped in the dark.

"Ms. Tucker, hold on."

I stood up to the gas lamp. I spat into my hand, put my fingers next to the switch and snapped. Instantly, what was once an artificial gaslight was now powered by the light of Liberty.

Tears streamed quietly down Dorothy's face, caking it in mascara. Her body was still clenched tight. Consciously, she resisted me, but subconsciously she was rocked. *Triggered.*

"Anyway," I said as I sat down. "I love history, and a friend of mine who is a high school teacher told me a story about Jeremiah Tucker. Do you know how he died?"

She cleared her throat. "Bayonet at Bunker Hill."

I shook my head. "He was killed by fellow patriots at the Liberty Tree in Boston Common. The night he died, the story goes, a woman came to his aid. Her name was Phillis Wheatley. Do you know her?"

Dorothy shook her head.

"Ms. Wheatley was a poet, and that night she wrote a poem to George Washington, about a goddess she called 'Columbia.' There is a line in that poem that I think truly encapsulates what it means to be an American:

> *One century scarce perform'd its destined round,*
> *When Gallic powers Columbia's fury found*
> *And so may you whoever dares disgrace*
> *The land of freedom's heaven-defended race…"*

Dorothy sat up. "Believe it or not, Jack, I am the least bigoted person you'll ever meet. I believe that God gave this continent to good Christians of Europe to steward for others. Who is this Phillis Wheatley? Tell me more about her."

"Oh, quite a woman. Like your grandfather's great grandfather, she lived in Boston under British occupation. She, too, had come from across the Atlantic, though to be fair she had beaten Jeremiah to the colonies by fourteen years. Anyway, we got sidetracked. Bobby Clemens."

She tightened again.

"He was a Hall of Fame player, *and* a humanitarian….and in the process of providing relief to his native Carolina after a storm hit, he died in a plane crash. On December…"

Tighten. Flinch.

"…31st, 1972. It was absolutely devastating. All of his dreams for his family…"

I snapped.

"…taken in an instant. I can't even imagine…"

Shuffle. Flinch. Tighten…engage.

Dorothy spoke: "Mr. Clemens sounds like he was a wonderful man."

"He was," I said. "But, please. Tell me about Dorothy Tucker."

She inhaled. "Not much to tell. Born outside Fresno, grew up in a small town in California. Worked in a bakery. Worked in a diner. Got pregnant and married in that order."

"Tell me about your dreams."

She grew bitter. "I've never had the luxury of dreams."

"You must have had some…what about friends? Who was your best friend growing up?"

She looked away. "I haven't spoken to Rita in decades."

"Rita? Who's Rita?"

Dorothy swallowed. "Rita Alfaro."

"Alfaro. Spanish?"

"Mexican. She," Dorothy seemed ashamed to admit it, "she was Mexican."

"Was?"

"Don't ask me if she's still alive."

"What happened? Was there a…falling out?"

Dorothy smirked. "Why do you care?"

"Our lifetimes are intertwined, Dorothy."

Dorothy looked up to the sky. "Rita refused to come to my wedding. To Wayne."

"Why?"

"Because I was pregnant. Rita was a good Catholic girl, and told me she couldn't 'in good conscience' condone the parents of a bastard."

"Tiffany. You don't consider her a bastard…do you?"

"Of course not. But when all of your closest friends are Mexican Catholics and they all condemn you, it's…"

"…hard not to internalize the things they say about you, right? It's like you know that you're one thing, but everyone tells you you're another, like you're…two people at the same time?"

Dorothy shuffled uncomfortably in her chair.

"You said you worked at a diner," I said. "In California? In the '40s?"

"Rita worked there, too."

Behind Dorothy's head, in the living room, I watched as the rest of the dinner party sat enraptured by the proceedings.

"Your diner," I continued. "Was it segregated?"

"I never enforced it," she said, defensively. "Believe me."

"I do. It wasn't uncommon in those days for younger wait staff to buck the discriminatory instructions of their managers." I didn't know if that was true in general; but I knew in her case it was, and I needed to establish rapport.

"All I wanted was to be an American girl who married her American boy and lived happily ever after. That's it."

"And then you thought it was taken from you. When the War Department brought you that telegram."

Dorothy's eyebrows knit together. She pulled another cigarette from her box and lit it.

"Do you remember the man who delivered the telegram?"

She shut her eyes. "Clemente. José Clemente."

"Sounds similar to Bobby Clemens."

She put out part of her cigarette. "I can assure you they're nothing alike."

"I wouldn't be so sure about that. Because, see, Clemens' real name was Roberto Clemente. From Car-oh-lee-na, Puerto Rico."

Conflict. Deep, dark conflict.

"As a Puerto Rican," I said, "Mr. Clemente, just like the white Mr. Clemens you envisioned in your head, is a member of 'freedom's heaven-defended race,' just as everyone in this house is."

Dorothy furrowed her brow and squinted. The wheels of cognitive dissonance were churning upstairs.

"The reason this is difficult for you to grasp right now is not uncommon. In fact, it's just what I said at the beginning."

She looked up.

"Once upon a time, you issued an ultimatum to God."

I sat up in my chair.

"You just told me you were nothing but an American girl who wanted to marry an American boy. You told me that first José and then Rita took that away from you."

"I didn't say that."

"Not in so many words, but you said it. Your Spanish-speaking Catholic friends, judging you. You had dreamed that Rita would be your maid-of-honor, hadn't you? Then she took it away. And you remembered that another Hispanic person took it away, too. I assume Rita was there at the diner with you?"

Dorothy trembled as she looked me up and down. *Now she recognizes me.*

"Soon you believed that everyone who looked like José and Rita was an invader out to take your American life away. Even still," I cleared my throat, "even still, the fact remains that nothing had been taken from you. You had Wayne. You had your wedding. You had your daughter and then your son, your own flesh and blood. You had them – "

I paused for effect.

" – and *still* you coveted them. And because you coveted them, you lost them."

War raged inside her. I could feel her heart palpitating from where I sat.

"You were so intensely afraid they would be taken from you that you whispered in your heart, 'I will keep this life that God has given me on my terms, and my terms alone. The blessings of Liberty belong to me, and should God send anyone to take it from me, I will kill, steal and destroy them, and anyone made in their image.'"

Dorothy labored to breathe, and to keep from strangling a new messenger.

"Why did you lose it? Because one summer day in 1962, you decided to take it from someone else."

A fire raged. *Stoke it a little...*

"The kid I was scouting that day was named Diego Reyes. The same boy you raised a Louisville Slugger to on that field. When I saw him play, I thought to myself, 'John, this kid is the next Roberto Clemente...'"

Dorothy sat at the edge of her seat to protest. *Douse the fire.*

"Did you know that exactly a year before that, Diego was the only one of ten Cuban boys to survive a firing squad?"

Doused. Dorothy sat back down, stunned.

"I can only imagine the terror he felt, blindfolded, as a Tyrant *far worse* than King George III threatened to take his life at sixteen. He would have been well within his rights to grow angry and bitter. Yet I watched him play the great game with gratitude and...*joy. Pure joy.* Like he was in heaven. Until..."

Dorothy squirmed.

"...he offered a pretty blonde girl a flower, and her mother threatened to take everything away from him with one swing of the bat."

A bead of sweat formed at her brow. *Conscience pricked...now transfer it.*

"I heard that your grandfather's great grandfather crawled backwards on all fours when the Sons of Liberty killed him. He was no soldier. He was the immigrant son of a shoemaker. He didn't want to fight; he just wanted to live. If he could have articulated that, he might have said something like..."

Bated breath. Pause to let it hang...

"*No quiero pelear.*"

...linger...linger...let it ring inside her.

"Jeremiah Tucker. Diego Reyes. They both share one thing in common with you and I and all ten people in this house. We are *all* members of freedom's heaven-defended race. Not the white race, or any other. Nothing less than the entire human race. You want to know how I know that?"

Dorothy held back. *She knows.*

"Because Phillis Wheatley is black."

Pop! goes the legend.

"Your grandfather's great grandfather didn't die for a legend. He died for a dream."

I took a drink of lemonade and set the glass down.

"*Her* dream."

Dorothy labored to breathe.

"You haven't forfeited that dream, Dorothy. You have a beautiful granddaughter about to marry a wonderful young man. It's clear to me that she loves you unconditionally. One day, she and Keith may have a child, and that child will need all the unconditional love in the world. Because there will be many who won't see that child as a member of Liberty's heavenly defended race, and they will make his life hell. And the only thing in heaven or earth that can defeat that hatred is the Greatest Love…"

Dorothy stared back through me with fire in her eyes.

"…to lay down your own life upon the altar of God."

Dorothy leaned in. She rubbed her cigarette out in the ashtray and let it fall as the embers quickly burned out.

"What a wonderful little speech," she spat.

I sighed. "Dorothy…"

"Fuck. You."

Dorothy stood up, grabbed her purse and walked back toward the house. The rest of the party cleared out as she opened the sliding glass door.

I sat alone by the pool for a minute, sipping my lemonade and second-guessing myself. I had waited for the right pitch and swung, and it felt as if I had just struck out.

The sliding glass door opened. Marissa stepped out, folding her arms and slowly pacing toward me. Her mascara had dripped down her face, smearing her cheeks. Dorothy had ripped her in two tonight, and there were fragments of her all over the ground.

She took Dorothy's seat and sat quietly. An awkward pause lingered. It was almost certainly more awkward for me; this was a woman whose older self I'd briefly dated, sitting before me in her youth. I knew her future, and that of her husband and yet unborn child, a future that would betray the bright optimism of the day. I couldn't share any of that with her. I didn't know what to say to her at all. She relieved me of that burden.

"I'm sorry you had to witness all that," Marissa sniffled. "I don't know why I thought she would be any different tonight than she always is. I should've listened to my mother."

Marissa sighed.

"She's a monster."

I set my lemonade back on the table, leaned back and scratched my chin.

"So am I," I admitted.

Marissa cocked her head. "You seem perfectly nice to me."

I slowly shook my head. "Everybody presents well. Or...most of us do, at least. But we all carry wounds that haven't healed. We all have live skeletons in our closets."

"I guess so. Apparently, Grandma has a lot more than I ever thought."

I nodded slowly in agreement. "She thinks she's damaged goods. So she damages others."

Marissa folded her hands onto her lap, clutching them tight. "I saw your lips moving a lot more than hers. What did you say?"

"The truth. In a spirit of love."

"And even after all that, she still walked out."

Marissa shook her head and bit her lip.

"There's just no love in her," she whimpered, on the verge of tears. "She's lost."

No. I won't leave her like this.

"Listen, Marissa," I began. "I teach U.S. history and civics to high school kids, juniors and seniors mostly. I love my job. Even with all the crap I have to wade through with parents and the school district and state standards and terrible pay...it's all worth it if I can reach one kid."

I leaned in to meet her.

"I'm not just talking about grades or test scores. I mean the whole person. If I can encourage that one kid to pursue his dreams or to overcome her insecurities or to see life itself in a way that they'd never considered...that's a success. Because the one thing I've learned about difficult people, obstinate people, even those we'd consider bad people, is that they are still people. They're dust, just like you and me."

Marissa nodded slowly, her eyes glued to mine.

"You're under no obligation to indulge your grandmother's dark side. She's clearly toxic and abusive, and I think you're right. There is no love in her. It would probably be for the best if you cut her off completely. But..."

I paused and shook my finger for emphasis.

"...that doesn't mean you let people like her steal your hope, or your faith in humanity and the better angels of our nature, or your belief that a better future for you and yours is possible, even attainable. Because if there's anything I know about hope..."

I exhaled.

"...it's that it's worth keeping."

Marissa studied me for a few moments, then she burst into a cathartic laugh.

"Thank you, John," she said, brushing back her hair. "That's a really good way of looking at it."

The sliding glass door opened. Keith paced toward us with his hands in his pockets.

"Everything okay, baby?" he asked.

Marissa nodded. "Tell everyone else it's safe to come out here."

She looked to me and smiled.

"Before dinner gets too cold."

~

The clock on the dashboard read 11:08. We stood on the beach next to that ostentatious seaside country club. The moon waxed gibbous, only a sliver away from full, shining bright on the otherwise pitch-black Atlantic.

"It turned out to be a nice night," Pearl offered. "All things considered."

"Yeah," I admitted. "I couldn't get through to Dorothy."

Pearl smiled. "The seed is planted."

((...unless a seed falls to the ground and dies...))

A deep sadness gripped me. My eyes turned moist; I wiped it away.

"Is this the last time I see you?" I asked.

Pearl gazed at the ceiling of night, at the brightness of a thousand stars that went out long ago.

"Tyranny has many Faces," she said. "So do I."

"Cryptic to the end," I replied.

"Always."

A wave of emotion rose within, a boundless affection for the meddling Capitol docent who saved my life by destroying it. Pearl tiptoed barefoot over the sands of time and wrapped her arms around me.

"I'll see you soon," I whispered. "Isabella."

She released me and picked a thread off my chest.

"Go on, Ben Upson. Tell them her story…"

Thirty Four

Today

He looked majestic, His Excellency, seated high in the clouds. He always had. Only now I saw the shadows break across his face. They scattered his golden light around the Rotunda, where it rebounded as sound, a soft whisper fading into faintly visible form...

...relax your eyes...

...there she is.

Her shape, her outline, her...*no, not a shadow*. There is no turning in her. A silhouette, maybe, or an echo. Whatever you call it, it's definitely her.

"Mother."

"And here I thought my son had mommy issues."

Anna Bannister laughed and elbowed me in the ribs.

I laughed...and laughed...she laughed back harder...and so did I...and so did she...and soon we were engaged in a machine gun volley of laughter...then it tapered off.

Anna sighed and panned the Rotunda. "Speaking of mommies, where's that old lady you were talking to a second ago?"

I scanned around, only then re-gaining my bearings. Everything was as it was before I closed my eyes one year earlier, a swarm of tourists and spring breakers. But no Pearl.

"I guess I need to get my eyes checked. I could have sworn she picked something off your shirt, then *poof!* She's gone!"

Anna tittered nervously

"Riveting conversation, was she?"

"Yeah," I replied. "She was..."

"Criminy, Ben, were you in a knife fight?"

Colonel, boundaries be damned, aggressively pressed his thumb against my temple. Reid gawked ten feet behind him.

I felt my head. *It's still there.* I looked Colonel up and down with fresh eyes. There was an ironic twinkle in his.

"I haven't been in a fight since I was eleven, Sam."

Colonel grinned. "You and I both know that's not true."

I cracked, then looked down at Colonel's watch: *11:09*

"Hey, where's Kathy?"

"Right here."

I turned to see Ms. Waylon, eyes strained and exhausted behind her cat-eye glasses. I caught the eye of the young man behind her. Tyson still had his kill switch engaged; it had been less than twenty minutes since we butt heads downstairs.

I reached into my satchel and handed Ms. Waylon my clipboard.

"Take the reins," I said. "It's been a long day already."

Ms. Waylon guffawed, incredulous. *"I've been running things all day."*

"I know," I admitted. "And I promise you, it's for the best."

Ms. Waylon glowered at me, then spun back around and called the students to take roll.

Tyson and I stayed locked on each other. He blinked, and in that moment something passed between us. A subtle tear formed in the veil. *I'm sure he didn't feel it.*

His eye fluttered. He turned away cautiously and found Sara's hand. I noticed the small chain hanging out of her jeans pocket.

Ms. Waylon shouted: *"Alright, Warriors, let's roll!"*

Outside, the clouds had melted away, save one; it hung over the District like an albatross. I rubbed my ears and listened…the static, the buzzing, was gone. Everything was crystal clear. I exhaled in relief and climbed aboard the bus. I told Ms. Waylon I'd need shuteye on the way to Philadelphia. She received it well:

"You're an absolute lunatic right now."

I propped my legs up in the far back corner next to the lavatory. I sat unevenly…

…*my phone.*

I fetched it out and turned it on. I had two text messages from the blocked number:

Truth first. Then reconciliation.

The other was a CSV contact file:

A Servant's Hall
320 Arch Street
Philadelphia, PA 19106
(215) 555-1787
Ask for Lucy

I saved it and popped in my earbuds. George Harrison sent me off to sleep safe in the assurance that the sun had risen anew.

~

The light signaled to cross North Third Street.
"Where are we going, Mr. U?" Reid whined.
"Little side field trip, just for us, Mr. Collins."
I heard Reid tap Tyson on the arm.
"Dude, is he gonna kill us?"
"Keep your hands to yourself," Tyson snapped.
While the rest of the group traveled from the National Constitution Center to the Liberty Bell, Tyson and Reid had a date at the house of a few Friends. The Arch Street Friends Meeting House has stood since 1805, a simple red brick building with minimal ornamentation. As we entered, a plain-clothes docent motioned, and we took a hard right into the sanctuary. The interior was almost entirely wood, fashioned by a carpenter named Owen Biddle. The vaulted rectangular sanctuary was expansive, with rows upon rows of long pews facing straight ahead to an altar with a back bench. A second level of benches overhung the floor. The walls were solid white, reflecting simplicity and equality.

We made our way to the front, near the lectern. The boys sat apart in the front pew.

Reid scanned the room. "What are doing in a church on a school field trip, Mr. U?"

"Truth and reconciliation, Mr. Collins."

A thirty-five-year-old woman with dark brown hair and rosy red cheeks, white floral blouse and blue jeans approached from the back of the sanctuary.

"Lucy?" I asked.

"That's me. Benjamin Upson?"

"Indeed."

She eyed the two teenage boys, and shook each one's hand in turn.

"Tyson Immanuel Atwater…and Reid Abner Collins."

The boys were taken aback by her familiarity.

Lucy sat in front of us and clasped her hands together.

"My name is Lucretia Coffin, but please call me Lucy. I'm a member of the Arch Street Friends Meeting House, and this place," she motioned, "has a very important role in the rich history of this country. We're usually open to the public, but today we are closed. Mr. Upson and I have arranged for you to have this sanctuary to yourselves."

Lucy clapped and looked to me.

"*Tabula rasa*, Benjamin. They're all yours."

"Thank you, Lucy."

Lucy took a seat at the back of the sanctuary. She was joined presently by a Marine and a railroad conductor turned spymaster.

I straddled a wooden chair between Tyson and Reid on my left. I looked at both of them and tapped my fingers.

"Have either of you been to Philadelphia before?"

They both shook their heads.

"I used to come here a lot when I lived in D.C. It's…unique, a city beset by contradictions. They call it the City of Brotherly Love, but to an outsider it doesn't always feel like it. The mood here, most days, is gritty. The people here have a thick outer layer of skin between them and the rest of the world. They say New York is prettier and Washington is smarter, and Philadelphia is the tomboy with dirt under her nails who drinks and swears and fights, and nothing more."

I looked to the ceiling.

"They're wrong, though. This is a great city, worthy of its name. Behind all these tough exteriors beat the softest hearts in the most loyal people. So many people are so inauthentic, but Philadelphians are nothing if not raw…and real…"

I panned the sanctuary.

"I'd like to think it's the lingering Quaker spirit. These are a people who truly take life as a gift, who live to be simple and free. The Spirit of Liberty herself flows through them; it's no wonder they took up the abolitionist cause. And *here* they gather together not out of fear or coercion or adherence to tradition, but because of the bonds of mutual affection they hold for one another. They are brought here by Love."

I pointed at the two of them.

"Brotherly Love."

They both shifted uncomfortably.

"Brotherly Love lies at the heart of all reconciliation."

I bit down.

"*Truth*...and reconciliation. Truth is essential to Love. Without Truth, reconciliation between brothers is impossible."

Both of them braced for tongue-lashings.

"The Truth is that I've failed you. Both of you."

Both of them stared at me in bewilderment.

I was stoic, but not cold. I'd shed many tears on my journey to Elysium and back. Now I was balanced. Now, I was at peace.

"You'll be the first students I've ever told this. My father..."

I paused to gather myself.

"...my father was a Judge Advocate General in the Navy. Brilliant man."

"A badass," Reid offered.

"Yes. He was and...still is..."

I exhaled.

"...but what you don't know...is that my father, John Eric Upson, died in the terrorist attack on the Pentagon on September 11, 2001."

All signs of bravado and subtle resistance faded.

"Until recently, I never had a healthy outlet for the rage I felt inside. I never allowed myself to feel it all the way through. So I buried it, chose to forget it, tried to stuff those feelings down and get back to the charmed life I lived before. But it built and it built like a tempest in a teapot, until one day I just...popped."

I rubbed my temple, feeling at my scar.

"My Dad was everything to me. A real patriot. He's the one who taught me to love my country unconditionally."

Reid smirked and cocked his head at Tyson. "Did you hear that? Mr. Ups–"

"On what planet, Reid, would you believe that this story is meant to vindicate you and what you've done?"

Reid stopped, jaw open.

"You need to listen good. Because I have some harsh Truths to tell you today."

Reid sat back and folded his arms, as though I betrayed him. Tyson studied me closely, wondering who had invaded Mr. Upson's body.

"See, like you, Reid, I used my patriotism and my family history as an emotional crutch. I used it as a way to camouflage my fear and my pain...and my burning hatred for a Saudi lemon farmer named Hani Hanjour, who overstayed his visa and flew that jet that killed my father."

I paused to let it all sink in. Reid shifted uncomfortably, while Tyson leaned in.

"He took everything from me. I can still say that. I hate him and probably always will. But I allowed that hatred to fester and bubble over until it poisoned me and the way I saw my country, the world...my friends and neighbors. I didn't recognize it, but I became someone I never thought I'd become. I became a bigot."

For the next half hour I spilled my guts, about my irrational obsession with illegal immigration, my receptivity to junk information that played on my fears, my Islamophobia, my hypocrisy with respect to my French wife, and how I ended up driving her away.

"I had the American dream, and I lost it. Not because someone came and took it away from me. I gave it away. I see a lot of my fellow Americans doing the same, and from what I've seen and heard, we are selling our Liberty down the river and walking right into the arms of Tyranny."

I looked at Reid, who chewed on his thumbnail.

"You're walking down that path, Reid, and I've enabled you. For that, I am truly, deeply sorry."

Reid threw up his arms. "That's bullshit, Mr. U!"

I leaned back and let him have the floor.

"You're telling me that you all of a sudden buy into his race-baiting? It's slander!"

"Raising the alarm against racism isn't 'race-baiting,'" I said. "It's *testimony*. It's *accountability*. And I have no qualms telling you that what you did to Tyson two nights ago…"

Indignantly, Reid pointed at his black eye. I waved him off.

"Tyson's not off the hook for that, Reid. But right now you need to take account of your own attitude and actions, and the impact they have on the people around you."

The kid scoffed.

"Let's work backwards from what prompted this."

I pointed in a circle at his eye.

"You bought Tyson a ticket to Kenya. You spent, I assume, your parents' money on a prank to tell the one black kid in class that he ought to literally 'crawl back to his shithole' in Nairobi, Kenya. Tyson, do any of your ancestors come from Kenya?"

Tyson shrugged. "They didn't keep track of that on slave ships."

"So Reid, I ask you: where did you get the notion that Tyson comes from Kenya?"

"We just," Reid squirmed, "picked a country at random."

We? "Okay, let's assume that I believe you. Let's assume that you *really* picked an African country at random. Why?"

"I…well…just…"

"You could have picked Spain. Or England. Or Ireland. Or Poland. His mother is Cuban, so why not send him to Havana?"

Reid looked away. "It wasn't my idea. It was Skylar's."

On the bus…when she whispered to him.

"It was her dad's American Express card. He said it was okay. He thought it was funny."

My heart jumped. "Nelson Lund approved this?! Why?!"

I looked to Tyson. He didn't look remotely surprised.

"What kind of father…"

Reid sat up, indignant. "What kind of father blows up a church?"

My stomach dropped. Tyson slumped in his pew.

Reid turned giddy. "Yeah. My dad looked it up. Tyson's dad is a Muslim terrorist. Just like the ones who knocked down the towers and the Pentagon. Trash."

Tyson cracked his knuckles. *Reid's trying to provoke him. Again.*

"So why do you keep taking Tyson's side? Aren't you always saying there's two sides of the coin?"

In the back, Ira stood, prepared to intervene. Minty pulled him back down.

"Yes," I replied. "That was my father's favorite phrase. And it means that there are always multiple ways to see an issue. It doesn't mean that some of them aren't completely worthless."

"Wow, Mr. U," Reid countered. "You're a bigger snowflake than I thought."

Tyson sat up. "You ever have a cop point his gun at your head and pull the trigger?"

Reid froze. Tyson convulsed, straining hard not to explode.

"They arrested my dad with me in the truck, and they found the detonator in the cab. Do you know any terrorists who drive around with their own detonator in the cab of their trucks?"

Somewhere in that thick skull of his, Reid's wheels started to turn.

"We used to be friends, Reid. Before you started drinking your daddy's Kool-Aid. Then you stopped seeing me as a person. Before you started seeing me as a Thing."

I could hear it...the cracking...sturdy walls inside Reid's heart and mind started to sway at their foundations. They were strong, though. Resilient. Nothing would be decided Today.

Today, Reid would fight: "My dad is a great man, and you'll never measure up to him. Don't ever speak of him again."

Tyson looked away. "Then I have nothing left to say to you. There's no love in you; you're lost."

Reid flinched.

"Go to the Liberty Bell, Reid," I said. "Check in with Ms. Waylon, and let Skylar know I'll be speaking with you, her, and both of your fathers."

Reid's shoulders heaved. "About what?"

"To offer them an apology ..."

Tyson sat up.

"...for enabling their children to swing their privilege around in my classroom. I'm instituting a zero tolerance policy for grown men using their children as pawns to antagonize a young man who deserves far better. I can see in your eyes that you're conflicted, but you have a choice to make."

Reid's shoulders heaved. He tried to re-assert control, but I intuited that he knew he was on defense.

"You," he said, "you don't have the right. I'm…I'm not the criminal here…I…"

Reid retrieved his phone and dialed.

"Don't bother," I countered. "If your father wants to talk to me and threaten my job, give him my number. Tell him to call me in an hour. I'll tell him *exactly* what I just told you."

Shocked and embarrassed, Reid hung up. He shoved his phone in his pockets and whistled on his way out the door.

When it closed, Tyson lost all control. I rushed in to embrace him, and he wrapped his arms around my neck.

"I miss my Dad…I miss 'im…"

Tyson wailed from every corner of himself.

Through blubbering tears he whispered in my ear all the things I knew about his father's wrongful conviction, his life sentence, the white nationalists who targeted Salaam and Tyson both. Soon, Tyson's tear reserves were tapped, and he slowed down. Gently I rocked him and pecked him on the head.

"Sometimes I just wanna die," he moaned. "They split me in two, and they're never gonna stop coming for me."

I pulled Tyson's face in. "Look at me, Tyson."

He sniffed, his eyes shifting to and fro.

"Four years ago, I swore an oath to your mother to look after you as if you were my own. And I failed you."

Tyson nodded, rubbing his runny nose.

"I've talked at you, preached at you, and I've never listened to you. I've never tried to understand before making myself understood. I am sorry. It stops now. It will never happen again."

Tyson inhaled sharply…then relaxed. I sensed a great weight lift from his shoulders, as if the world had climbed down from off his back. I reached into my satchel and pulled out his diary.

"You dropped this," I said.

Tyson grasped the diary and brought it in. He studied it quietly, shaking his head.

"I'm sorry I threw this," he offered.

"Forgiven," I replied. "But you just need to tell me one thing."

Tyson raised his eyebrows.

"What does it say?"

Tyson smirked and handed the diary back to me. I opened it.

I flipped through the pages for what seemed like an eternity, endless poems and songs and tales of hope in the face of adversity, from one generation to the next, until I finally came to the page I was looking for. Faintly, yet visibly, a quote rose up to the surface of the paper...just as soon as it did, it faded from view, leaving the page blank.

"It's a story, Mr. Upson," Tyson offered.

"An endless story," I replied, "of hard beginnings."

"Hard beginnings," Tyson laughed. "That's what it means to be an Atwater."

No kidding. "I think that's what it means to be an American."

Tyson nodded. "Yeah. It feels like we're in the middle of another hard beginning."

I put my hand on Tyson's shoulder. "How do you want yours to end?"

"I just want to be whole, Mr. Upson. Like I was before they took my dad away from me."

I swallowed hard.

"He taught me to love Liberty. Just like your dad taught you. He taught me to believe that the world was mine for the taking, that nothing could stop me. Then..."

Tyson looked away.

I had to say something. "He's innocent, you know."

Tyson jerked up, searching me with his eyes. "How do you know?"

"I was at his trial."

Tyson looked me up and down. "How? Why?"

I opened my mouth...and shut it. I didn't know how to explain.

"You're one of them, huh?"

"Who?"

"The Sons of Liberty."

I nodded. "A *very* recent state of affairs."

Tyson shook his head.

"What are we gonna do about Reid?" I asked.

Tyson shrugged. "He is what he is, man. He'll never change."

"Maybe, maybe not," I said. "I have to admit I had higher hopes."

"Me too. That's why I bothered trying to explain things to him on the bus."

Tyson turned to me.

"I don't hate him. I don't hate anybody. But like you said you can't have Love without Truth."

"Truth, and only then reconciliation."

I tapped my fingers on the bench.

"This country is a mess. Our lives are messes. My wife is locked away, like your father. I know both of them are innocent, and yet I don't have the damnedest clue what I can do to change things."

Tyson sat back and pondered. "My Grandma Zora used to say that you don't need to change everybody's mind to change the world. You just need one out of ten."

((...10-1...))

"We can only plant seeds and pull weeds in the soil we stand on."

I nodded. "Yeah. You've been planting alone for too long. From here on out, we sow those seeds together. I'll follow your lead."

"Don't make promises you can't keep, Mr. U."

"Okay," I said. "What if I swear an oath?"

I knelt in front of Tyson and put my left hand on his knee as I raised my right.

"I, Benjamin John Upson, do hereby swear upon the altar of God eternal hostility against every form of Tyranny over the mind and body of every person who walks this Earth. I swear this oath to my brother, with whom my Liberty is intertwined, that I will watch over and defend him in constant vigilance against every act of Tyranny in every facet of life. This I swear, and upon the altar of God do I now swear it."

Tyson sniffled and knelt. He closed his eyes and gave the same oath, word-for-word.

"Mr. Upson," he said, a tear streaming down his face, "this is the first time in five years that I feel like someone really listened to what I'm saying. Like I have someone in my corner."

"Don't congratulate me," I replied, "for doing what a decent man should."

Tyson looked over his shoulder at Minty. She beamed.

"It's good to have friends in your corner," Tyson added.

"Indeed," I said, nodding at Ira. "Someone to fight for...and with."

I tapped on his bandaged hand.

"Not always with our fists, like Ol' Jack Johnson. But still. We fight."

The two of us stood and exited the sanctuary. I wrapped my arm around Tyson's shoulder as we made our way toward Independence Hall.

"You know, Mr. U," Tyson said, "I take back all the things I said about you to my mom."

I stopped cold in my tracks. "What do you mean?"

Tyson laughed. "I said you'd be a terrible dad."

My giggle crescendoed to a roar.

"I think you'd be an above-average dad."

"Boy," I said. "Can you imagine a broken-ass wreck like me raising the next generation?"

Bzzzzzzt.

It was Tyson's phone. He pulled it from his hoodie pocket:

I love you, Tyson. Stay safe on your trip.
~ XO, Great Grandma

Tyson smiled. "Stranger things have happened, Mr. U. Stranger things."

Epilogue

Dreams of Elysium

The Signers' Room at Independence Hall was nearly empty, the perfect place to sit alone and reflect.

"A lot of ghosts in here."

Colonel set his hand on my shoulder as he saddled up next to me on the bench.

I smiled. "If only you knew, Wam-Bam."

Colonel chuckled. "I take it you deciphered that omen."

"I did. It was the longest second of my life."

I adjusted the hood on his West Point sweatshirt.

"You were a shy and scrawny little boy, Colonel. What happened?"

Colonel grinned. "One day, on the Fourth of July, I watched a man jump out of nowhere to defend the stranger, the fatherless and the widow from a vicious act of Tyranny. I saw that this man wasn't a hero. He wasn't perfect. He was flawed and weak and scared, like me. He received no reward for his actions, and was willing without hesitation to risk his own hide to save a kid he didn't even know."

Colonel pulled a coin from his pocket. It looked like Dad's, a rare metal reflecting every color of the rainbow.

"He dropped a coin, like this, only it was pure lead. I was only eleven, but it spoke to me. In the few seconds I held it, it gave me both conviction and courage to match it. It gave me the strength to rise from the ashes of my broken home to be the man I am today."

I laughed heartily. *Life is truly stranger than fiction.*

Colonel sighed. "Did you get the text Principal Pearson sent?"

"Yeah," I said. "It's a shame we have to cut this trip short."

"Better safe than sorry. This virus looks pretty nasty."

I exhaled. "It's true now more than ever."

Colonel cocked his head. "What is?"

"That I am my brother's keeper."

Colonel smiled and reached into his hoodie pocket.

"Speaking of which," he said, handing me a white scroll with a red ribbon. "Lucy told me to give you this."

"What is it?"

Colonel grimaced. "Liberty is born anew. But you know he'll come after her."

I nodded in agreement. "He came for Aurora. He came for Emmaleigh. He came for Pearl. He'll come for her next."

Colonel looked away. "He will. I don't know what comes next, but Tyranny will come with all of his ferocity, like Herod in Bethlehem, to steal Liberty from her cradle. But we'll be ready."

He stood.

"And we'll fight him until our dying breath."

Colonel saluted and started out. He doubled back.

"You know, Ben…it only took one selfless act by a broken, washed-up ballplayer to give Liberty a fighting chance. Imagine what might be possible if an entire generation did the same?"

I smiled. Colonel saw himself out.

I inspected the seal: a red sun, peering over the horizon.

"You have set, Sun of Liberty," I told it. "How will you rise?"

I broke open the seal, and unfurled the scroll. It was in red ink, in Pearl's handwriting:

March 9, 2020

Dear Benjamin,

I write to you on the eve of our first meeting. Should you receive it when I expect you receive it, you will have completed your journey. You have undergone the alchemy of the heart to become Champion of Liberty.

And I am gone from this world, joining my Sisters before me.

But from the ashes rises the Phoenix, and Today Liberty dawns anew. At the moment of my death, another warrior was born.

My Sister. Isabella, born into a time of crisis and conflict. Like the Suns of Liberty who rose before her, the spirit of Revolution courses through her veins…

…and like her Sisters before her, Isabella Upson will require watchful guidance to shepherd us into the next era of Liberty…

"…Isabella…Upson…?"
My hands shook…
…that was the end of the letter…
"…where's the rest of it…?"
…
…I looked up…
…
…everyone was gone…
…
"…hello…?"
…
…the trees outside were autumn shades of red, brown and gold…
…
…the ink dried on the parchment on the dais…
…and a little golden-haired girl cried as she rocked in her Uncle's lap.

"Shh, shh, shh," Dr. Franklin gently whispered. "Perhaps we may abolish the evil when the new Congress assembles. I promise to fight for nothing less. You have my word, Little Miss Wheatley."

Aurora shook her head.

Dr. Franklin sighed. "I admit that this Constitution is a bundle of compromises. But it has promise."

Aurora stared into Dr. Franklin's bifocals. "Either we have a monarchy or a republic. Which is it?"

Dr. Franklin sighed and pondered. "On the balance…a republic. If you can keep it, Little Bird."

Aurora jumped from Dr. Franklin's lap and paced, her eyes searching the ceiling.

"A house divided cannot stand," she protested. "No nation can long survive half slave and half free. If Tyranny comes for my Mother or brother, he will doubtless come for me."

Dr. Franklin lifted his black cane to reveal a golden Liberty cap at the end.

"I know that you know this symbol," he said, "and I know where you know it from. It is a sigil from another time when you walked the Earth. It is the sigil of the captive set free."

Aurora stepped forward to inspect the cane.

"I remember," she said. "I wore it in Rome, before I was rendered unto Caesar."

Dr. Franklin pointed the cap end of the cane at the chair in front of him. It bore the insignia of a sun peaking just above the horizon.

"Throughout this Convention," he said, "through all of the wrangling and hand-wringing, I have been forced to stare at this sun. Every day I asked myself, 'Is this Sun of Liberty rising, or setting?' It nearly drove me mad. Today I have decided. But you, my lady, who lives to set the captives free, what do you think?"

Aurora closed her eyes and planted her feet firmly in the ground. She grimaced.

"Tyranny brings darkness," she said. "Eleven years after we declared in this house in my name that all men are created equal, we have rebuked it. The slaver's whip will lash us all. There will be war between brothers...we will advance, and we will retreat...many hearts will turn to stone. And yet..."

Aurora breathed deeply.

"...the stone the builders rejected has become the cornerstone. There comes a generation who will remember first light, and fight to preserve the blessings of Liberty. They will face the enemy at home and abroad. They will fight for hearts and minds, and if they have the courage of conviction, they will triumph. The Suns of Liberty..."

Aurora opened her eyes.

"...the Suns of Liberty will rise."

Dr. Franklin smiled. "I agree."

He stuck the end of his cane into the back of the chair. The cap end sparked and blazed and spun into liquid fire, a disk of rare metal forming, an inch-and-a-half in diameter and thick. The coin glinted with gold and silver and bronze and refracted every shade and hue. Dr. Franklin tossed it to Aurora; she caught it clean with her right hand. At will, she raised her arm and turned the coin into a fiery torch, then retracted the fire back into the coin.

"Can you make another one?"

Dr. Franklin obliged. He tossed the new coin to her.

"Dear child," he said as he hobbled up on his cane. "Let us not speak falsely, for the hour is late. My old bag of bones requires a hot meal and a cold pillow. Your Father will be back shortly."

He kissed her on the forehead.

"And your Mother would be proud of you."

"She is," Aurora replied.

At that, Dr. Franklin limped his way toward the door.

"Uncle Benjamin."

Dr. Franklin turned around. "Yes, my dear?"

"No. Not you."

She turned and flipped me the coin. I caught it on the fly.

I read the inscription:

WE SWORE AN OATH

"Didn't I tell you to keep it?"

The girl stared back at me with two penetrating aquamarine eyes, brown skin and jet-black hair. I flipped the coin over to the other side:

AND WE WILL KEEP IT

Slowly, Isabella faded away.

"Who is she, Mr. Upson?"

I turned. Mackenzie Masuda, Sara Finkelson and Tyson Atwater stood resolute, shoulder-to-shoulder, each fueled by the fire of uncommon valor. Sara and Tyson wore the dog tags of each other's great grandfathers; Mac carried the Army chevrons of a former Marine. Each held a coin in their hand reflecting every color of the rainbow.

"She's a warrior," Mac declared. "She looks fierce."
I heard a child cry in the West.
It was the battle cry of a new birth of freedom.

THE END OF HISTORY...

Songs

Apollo's Creed

Now in the Course of Human Events
We remember first light
As we sail into night

We hang together
In constant vigilance
We pledge allegiance
To Liberty and Justice for all

In defiance of Tyranny
Our Greatest Love we give
Upon the Altar of God

We swore an oath
And we will keep it

The Labor Song of Libertas

If Liberty you truly seek,
The Crown of the Humble, the Sword of the Meek
Search within and you will find
Who troubles your heart, enslaves your mind

Self-evident is th'Eternal Truth
The hope of the fount we drank in youth
Born free and equal, we rise from the Dust
Then shackle ourselves with chains of Rust

What rusts will corrode, what corrodes will perish
Still this Higher Law we cherish
'Tis only from death that springs forth life
'Tis only with struggle, 'tis only with strife

In fields fertile and futile Liberty plants her Seeds
Whilst Tyranny sows his ersatz Weeds
They grow together, the tares and the wheat
In winter's chill and summer's heat

Yet in the night that wanes the darkest
Liberty gathers her glorious harvest
She raises the restless, the tired and poor
And shepherds us all to Elysium's door

So let no man blaspheme, let no man defame
The sonorous harmony of Liberty's name
For as long as the Earth spins 'round the sun
There will be Liberty for all, or Liberty for none

Afterword &
Acknowledgements

Like Tyson Atwater and the rest of us who call ourselves Americans, this book arose from hard beginnings. I began writing *American Phoenix* in July 2017, six months after the man I call "the Apprentice" first occupied the White House. It was a perilous and uncertain time, particularly for those of varying political stripes who foresaw the impending damage to our country, its people, and the fabric of democracy itself.

Many, myself included, grappled with how best to explain that historical moment to an American public ill-equipped to understand the nature of Tyranny and the imminent threat it poses to the Liberty we hold dear. As a lawyer and civic educator, I soon found that traditional tools and strategies for imparting knowledge were inadequate. What America needed was a renewal of its own story, a story rooted in truth, justice and equality to displace the self-serving and destructive legends we've imbibed, legends that imperil the lives of the most vulnerable among us.

In short, America needed to be re-acquainted with Liberty. Like Phillis Wheatley, we had to feel her in our bones.

Bringing Liberty to life in these pages was not a solo venture; no book is. Every author needs a mirror – a Looking Glass – to reflect the work back, to make it crisp and clear. In my case, the support and feedback I received over the last three years was especially critical. After my own trauma and neurological issues de-railed my young legal career, I set out on this project blind. I had never written fiction before, and I'd never undertaken anything so daunting. It was only with the help of the ones I trust that I was able to make it to the finish line...

...to my father, Michael Daniel, whose sacrifices and steadfast support of my dreams above his own made everything I've achieved possible; and to my mother, Eileen Daniel, whose encouragement, eternal optimism and early commitment to this project helped buoy me through all of my self-doubt and uncertainty...

…to Amy Daniel, who helped see me through my darkest of nights; and to James Denmark, whose pushed me to open the doors of my own creativity…

…to my grandmothers, Oma Carlisi and Cynthia Asplund, for their unconditional love…

…to my uncle, Brian Daniel, the inspiration behind Uncle Craig…

…to Heather Azcarate and Ryan Azcarate, my Sun Devil siblings whose inherent goodness inspires me…

…to my best friend, Joshua Seidel, and Allison Laskin, who own one of only two copies of the "Cranberry Edition" of *American Phoenix*…

…to my audiobook narrator, Jack Nolan, for his enthusiasm in tackling this project; and to Auby Meletio, a fellow traveler in creative fiction…

…to Sean Martorana for his exquisite artwork in designing the cover of *American Phoenix*…

…to Carmen Stewart, whose binge read of my first draft and notes in response assured me I was on the right path…

…to Jacklyn DeMar, whose insight into the mind of an avid reader helped me craft a better story…

…to Layla Weide, whose honest feedback helped me see my blind spots and kept my own worst writing impulses in check…

…to Melissa Swanson, whose empathy and intuition opened my heart and mind to possibilities beyond my wildest imagination…

…to Wendy Westergard, whose insight into the human condition helped me to see how trauma shapes us all…

…to Echo Running Wolf and Erika Vanecek, whose keen eyes both spotted potential issues in my earliest drafts…

…to Allison Counsil, whose friendship and devotion to magical realism helped push me through the last steps of this project…

…to Julia Lopez, who encouraged me to step into my passion…

…to Samantha Clements, who helped me break through writer's block with one simple trick…

…to my colleagues in civic education: Richard Clark, Brien Karlin, Sam Macaluso, Matt Ochs, Denny Martindale, Scott Maryott, Barry Peterson, Linda Akers, Justin Champagne, Zelalem Bogale, Will Hull, Katie Boland, Kim Stanhouse, Erin Lewis, Liza Prendergast, Katie Brown, Mark Molli, Trey Delap, Shane Piccinini, Dan Wong, Judy Simpson, Kit McCormick, Kathleen Dickinson, Mark Towell and Milton Hyams…

...to the students whose journeys into citizenship have intertwined with mine, in particular those who have been present on this journey, especially my kids from Unit 5: Maggie Arden, Maggie Boucher, Tommy Brooksbank, Karla Burcham, Kate Butler, Maddy Bydalek, Ethan Champagne, Ana Cisneros, Samantha Clements, Marissa Comcowich, Kailey Conrad, Sarah De Gues, McKayla Dolder, Ashlee Dreher, Gigi Etem, Sophia Gholdoian, Jake Hoberg, Rami Itani, Hannah Jackson, Kyra Johannensen, Donner Kahl, Lauren Kinder, Ben Lerude, Kat Lynch, John Mendelsohn, Ben Murphy, Ben Nebesky, Alex Osborne, Lauren Pagni, Makayla Shoults, Carmen Stewart, Eric Urban, Jacob Wait, Atley Weems, and Kelsey West...

...to the professors who shaped my understanding of American law, history, and politics, and the importance of fighting for equality and justice: Scott Casper, Angela J. Davis, Bill Eubank, Paul Figley, Matias Hernandez, Liz Keyes, Andrew Nolan, Michele Pistone, Jayesh Rathod, Tony Varona, Steve Vladeck, Steve Wermeil and Rick Wilson...

...to the Arch Street Friends Meeting House, for welcoming me into their sanctuary in the earliest days of writing *American Phoenix*...

...to the countless others whose contributions to my life and this work would fill volumes...

...to those who have gone before us in the spirit of Phillis Wheatley, Mother of Liberty...

...and to Nature's God, the ineffable Source of All Things, who endowed us with certain inalienable rights, among them Life, Liberty and the Pursuit of Happiness, and in whom we live and move and have our being.

Further Resources

Between the World and Me, by Ta-Nehisi Coates (2015)

Common Sense, by Thomas Paine (1776)

The Federalist Papers, Alexander Hamilton et. al. (1787-1788)

Flags of Our Fathers, by James Bradley & Ron Powers (2000)

Harriet, the Moses of Her People, by Sarah H. Bradford (1869)

Hiding in Plain Sight, by Sarah Kendzior (2020)

John F. Kennedy and the Second Reconstruction, by Carl Brauer (1977)

Letter from the Birmingham City Jail, by Martin Luther King Jr. (1963)

Mankind's Search for Meaning, by Dr. Viktor Frankl (1946)

Nineteen Eighty-Four, by George Orwell (1949)

The Origins of Totalitarianism, by Hannah Arendt (1951)

Poems on Various Subjects, by Phillis Wheatley (1773)

Policing the Black Man, by Angela J. Davis (2017)

Scenes in the Life of Harriet Tubman, by Sarah H. Bradford (1886)

Second Treatise of Government, by John Locke (1689)

Separated, by Jacob Soboroff (2020)

Stamped from the Beginning, by Ibram X. Kendi (2016)

The Souls of Black Folk, by W.E.B. Du Bois (1903)

The Trials of Phillis Wheatley, by Henry Louis Gates Jr. (2003)

Unforgiveable Blackness, by Geoffrey C. Ward (2004)

About the Author

Scott Daniel (B.A., University of Nevada; J.D., American University) is an author, civic educator and former attorney. Along with his closest friends, he teaches the Constitution to seniors at Reno High School through the *We the People* program. He previously moonlighted as a part-time sportswriter for *Silver and Blue Sports* and *The Cauldron. American Phoenix* is his debut novel. He lives in Reno, Nevada.

Made in the USA
Coppell, TX
11 July 2020

30763698R00260